ARTEM: VENGEANCE

>>>BOOK TWO<<<

JEZ CAJIAO

Table of Contents

THANKS

Hi everyone! Well, this is another fine mess you've got me into Stanley… How to write more thanks?

KISS principle, I guess? (Keep It Simple Stupid, for those that don't know!) SO! I need to thank a few people, and I think this time around? It needs to be the Legion!

First and foremost it'll always be Chrissy, my wife and partner in oh so many crimes. I love you.

Second? Geneva. She's both wonderfully mad, and constantly working at a hundred miles an hour. Far too frequently I throw things at her and basically say 'fix that', and to date she's not even stabbed me once! How cool is that? Not sure how much longer I'll survive, but hey.

Kristen is next, dealing with dozens of our jobs and trying to keep the wobbly wheels of madness on the straight and narrow, bless you!

Emily, our wonderful formatter, reminding me of soooo many details, massively appreciated believe me! Thank you for keeping us more or less on the right path!

May is our Typographer extraordinaire and fixes the covers and makes them pop, and Marko, of course is our wonderful artist!

Now, these next people hardly ever get mentioned, honest, but they're insanely important, and they do a wonderful, and massively needed job. My Beta team!

You buggers are fantastic, and I couldn't do it without you all, Scott, Richard, Spencer, Neil, Shawn, Chris, Kat and Keith, Dantas and Ben! Seriously, you're wonderful!

Next, and fairly important?

Our three new members of the family! Brian J. Nordon, Michael Head and Rachel Ni Chuirc (Pronounced 'Knee Kirk').

Lastly and most important? Our Legionnaires! Those of you that have joined the LitRPG Legion be that on FB or discord or elsewhere, all of you lunatics that follow, read and support us, THANK YOU!

Welcome to you all, we as Legion are damn proud to be here with you.

-Jez 24/07/2023

CHAPTER ONE

I arched my back and groaned. I was aching from head to toe, and unlike the way I'd like to be, this had absolutely nothing to do with a great sex session.

First of all, my sort-of girlfriend, Reign—we still weren't exactly sure what was happening between us yet—was unable to have sex, or even orgasm currently.

That wasn't down to my shitty abilities either, but that wasn't the point.

The point was, that I'd been on my hands and knees for ten minutes trying to get this job done, and still I had more work ahead of me.

"You gonna give up and admit you can't do it?" Luna called through to me from where she relaxed, leaning against the doorframe.

"Fuck," I said clearly. "Right. Off."

"There's no shame, you know." She laughed. "Most people can't do it."

"I can and I goddamn will!" I turned back to the object of my ire. Three more attempts were made, several minutes of it as I struggled back and forth, before scowling as I bundled the fitted sheet up, rolling it into a tight ball and shoving it into the drawer under the bed. "Fine! Fuck it!"

"I'm telling you, the ability to fold a fitted sheet is proof of witchcraft." Luna pointed a frozen treat at me, fresh from the freezer.

"Oh fuck off with that. I used to be able to do it, must be the wrong sheet or something…"

"Sure, sure…he still complaining about the sheets?" Reign asked, walking in from outside and dumping her bag on the table with a clank of metal and a groan of relief as she shook her arm out. "Fuck that's heavy."

"Yeah. Keeps going back and trying again every few minutes. So, what's that?" Luna stood and crossed the short distance from the seat she'd been lounging in to the fridge freezer, pulling the bottom half open and ripping free two more treats.

She tossed one to me, and the other to Reign, who snatched it out of the air, grinning as she read the label.

"Oh man, Strigoberry?" she crowed. "I've not had these since I was a kid!"

"Melun?" I grunted, reading mine before tearing the label off and balling it up. I tossed the rubbish back to Luna who caught it and Reign's, before dropping them in the bin and returning to her seat.

I tasted the iced treat and sighed, tugging the door to my bedroom shut behind me as I walked out, taking a seat at the table and sighing as I sat back, sucking grimly as I tried to ignore the lure of the sheet.

"So what's in there?" Luna asked again.

Reign shrugged. "Bit of all sorts. Some of my gear, a couple of gun kits I had laying around in my locker at the guild, and a set of step-up chargers for the grazer, expensive, but worth it."

"How expensive?" I asked, curious.

"Twenty thousand." She winced. "They came in from a job last night, and Julius knocked me. Said they'd be going on sale to the general guild later today, and then the net if they didn't sell, but considering they're almost a hundred grand for these normally? I had to get them."

"Had to?" I asked with a sad smile.

"Had to," she insisted. "I've got a third of a battery left on the grazer, one, out of three."

"Mine's dead," Gessh said, sitting up from where she'd been laid flat, relaxing on some packing crates, stretching her back out. "Will it work on mine as well?"

"Should do." Reign smiled. "That's why Julius suggested them to me, twenty thou is a hell of a price, I know, but…"

"But considering a recharge for mine is five hundred?" Gessh shook her head. "I've one goddamn battery and its five *hundred* a recharge, with that?"

"We can plug it in, and it'll recharge the power cells as part of our rental here." Reign nodded. "Mine are three hundred a go to recharge, and three of them? That's nine hundred a mission if I use them a lot, or twenty grand and it's done."

"I'll pay half," Gessh offered. "As long as I can use it too, obviously?"

Reign grinned. "That's why I bought it."

"Transferring." Gessh transferred the money over, and Reign winced again as the credit transfer came in, and the 'wellness clinic' took their forty percent from her.

She was up to seventy odd grand saved when we spoke about things this morning, and she'd sworn she was saving to get the implant out as her first priority.

It was her choice, I mean, they were taking forty percent of everything she earned until that money was paid off, and she owed just under two hundred grand, meaning that she needed to earn at least three hundred grand more, by my admittedly rough and ready calculations, to be free.

I liked Reign, and yeah, we'd fooled around a bit, and she was important to me both as my right hand—heh—in the squad, and as my friend, not to mention that she was a fucking terror with a sniper rifle.

We'd not gone further in our relationship yet, not just meaning the physical side, which she at least had intimate knowledge of *me* from, but also emotionally.

We liked each other, genuinely, I thought.

What had happened though, had been right after a fuck load of fighting, daft flirting and the pair of us nearly dying. That meant that for now, I was taking things slow.

It also meant that while I'd agreed I'd help her pay off her debt, I wasn't cleaning out my credit account to do it. We had to be sensible, and if it took a week, or a month, we'd get her paid off.

Normally earning that kind of money in such a short timescale *was* insane, most merc contracts paid far, far less after all.

We had a few advantages though.

First and foremost, we were a team, one that already had each other's back and that had been forged in some serious fights together. That meant we could take on contracts that others couldn't or shouldn't.

Secondly, we were registered as Specter hunters, and business was good. The various companies paid a small fortune to have their premises secured against the specters, and each kill got us paid.

Lucky might be dead, but THE orc as everyone called his boss—Oshbob—wasn't, and he was more than willing to use ex specter parts in his chop-shops.

That meant that we could be paid for killing the specters, loot their weapons and mods, sell them as well, and get more experience working and fighting together as a unit.

Luna and Gessh were sisters, half-orc women who were happy with rifles and as trained soldiers, holding the line, but when it got close in and dirty?

That's when they excelled. They had a pair of vibro-swords, the metal honed to a ridiculous edge, and set to vibrate at a high frequency, enabling them to cut through steel with only a little effort.

Between them as ranged and then close in fighters, and Reign as ranged and sniping, we had a good set up. I was an experienced Sergeant from the APS squads, used to commanding a team of armored suits that were rightly feared on the battlefield.

We'd been betrayed and backstabbed on the last mission we went on before I was kicked out of the army, with all but two of the team lost, and those two were currently hidden in cryosleep in the Fingers.

The massive and yet horrifically mauled mountains had been the site of some of the worst wars of the old world, the mountains shredded and gouged by some form of weaponry that nobody could identify, but what was known was that it was orbital, and that the armies that had been battling it out there were all lost.

The mountains themselves were reduced to 'fingers' curled and gnarled, with massive holes bored through in all directions.

The end result was a place of terrible beauty, where boulders floated, carried by electromagnetic charges, and storms were the norm. Scanners were useless, as the insane levels of electromagnetism and the left-over scrap and fragments of the armies that died made all but the best equipment useless.

Pilots, both of fixed wing fighters, drones and helos, being the arrogant shit stains that they were, liked to fly through them, rather than over or around, and so when our transport had done that, we'd crashed there. We'd suspected we were being hunted; Richie and Sync from my old team, the only other survivors besides myself, had buried themselves in a cave and gone into cryosleep.

Now, I was finally making inroads into the *real* mission, which was to get my suit up and running, to get to them using the locational data they locked into my suit, and then to get them back here and living life again.

I'd added in that I wanted that bastard Major Marcial's head on a pike as well, as it'd come out that he was responsible for fucking us over on the last mission, not my actual captain, Tyrannus, as I'd thought.

I'd started torturing Tyrannus, and it'd all come out.

Not that I objected to torturing Tyrannus. The little bastard had tried to steal my suit, and now it was in the warehouse below us, in goddamn pieces.

Half the fucker was missing, and it was going to take weeks if not months to earn enough to have it repaired.

The only consolation?

I'd looted something that might just turn it all around.

A specter incursion had been started by goblins on my first trial mission with the guild, hundreds, literally, or specters hunting goblins, which was weird in itself. Yes, the specters typically wanted to slaughter anything, and yes, goblins were fucking annoying, but specters were usually only after mods.

The goblins typically didn't have any of them, or active nanites beyond the low-level background number everything on the planet had these days, and so the specters tended to kill goblins if they found them, but had no interest in actually hunting them.

The device the goblins had been hiding though?

It was a crude, but massively scaled down version of a bit of classified kit that the APS carried on special missions. It was known officially by some stupid acronym, but we all referred to it as the stripper.

It literally stripped the 'pure' nanites from the bodies of those you used it on, and pure nanites were the basis of *everything*.

Any mod you chipped, you needed pure nanites to run and integrate, or you'd end up a specter. You wanted to stay young and healthy? Nanites. You've been stabbed, shot, burnt? Nanites. Hell, there were classes of weapon that required nanites to form the projectile, because only pure nanites could form the perfect fractal patterns that would do the job.

Nanites could make anything from anything, and the only reason we weren't all living in the lap of luxury, was because there were never enough of the little fuckers.

Every hospital, every chop-shop and every high-tech bit of kit required them, and the gulf between the amount of nanites that were produced, and the number needed only grew every day.

Most nanites were produced by the government in a specialist site, beyond that, small numbers of pure nanites could be culled from monsters, but the tech needed?

It was insanely classified, and they didn't lease our time out for cheap.

I'd heard that there were a few APS specialist monster hunters out there that had been licensed to carry the equipment, but that was almost certainly bullshit.

Or not, the way my week was going.

Regardless, if I could get the kit up and working—and I thought I could, I just needed some parts and a few extra bits—then we had a serious secondary income source.

I dismissed the thoughts about our current situation and focused in on the conversation with the others again, catching the end of Gessh's words.

"…save a fortune."

"What?" I asked, sitting up. "Sorry I was miles away, thinking of shit."

"Thinking of her elf-ass you mean," Luna joked, sitting down at the table next to me and shoving me with one heavily muscled shoulder.

I almost fell out of my seat, the sisters were much stronger than a plain old 'vanilla' human like me, but caught myself and bumped her back.

"I was thinking about ways to make money," I corrected her, and she nodded.

"So you can get in her ass sooner. See, I told you all he was obsessed when we first shared that shower."

"Fuck's sake!" I groaned, playing it up a little. "We did NOT share a shower! If we did I'd have either a much bigger smile on my face, or I'd be a lot more depressed than I am. Now, can we move on? How are we saving a fortune?"

"The grazer charger." Gessh smiled, taking pity on me before Luna could say anything else. "I was saying if we all switched to grazer or laser weapons we'd save a fortune on ammo costs."

"No chance," I said. "Seriously, it's been tried again and again. They invented slug throwers what, a thousand years ago? Sure there's been a few rises and falls of tech and society since then, but we're still using them now for a reason.

"Reflective coatings, specter tissue, solid armor and shields? They're far less useful against solid projectiles than they are energy weapons. Hell, plasma weaponry is massively more powerful, as well as not giving a shit about reflective surfaces or more, it just doesn't work. They're great as secondary weapons, no chance we can rely on them as primary, not long term."

"Well, I love mine." Reign shrugged, drawing her fingers down the length of the large grazer sniper rifle. "Sure, I'll still carry 'Old Faithful', but when I can? Well worth using it." She tapped her fingers on the barrel and smiled, and I found myself smiling back at her automatically.

"Okay then, so what's the plan for the rest of the day?" Gessh asked. "Please tell me no more cleaning…"

We'd spent yesterday and most of today so far cleaning the warehouse to within an inch of its life, scrubbing out the main shared areas like the kitchen and storerooms, then spending more damn hours cleaning out our personal rooms.

I'd gone all out with mine, and as such I'd needed to replace the damn bed.

I'd stripped the sealed top sheet off and taken a single look at the mattress underneath, then I'd dragged it outside and put an incendiary grenade to work.

Whatever had used the room before me? I had to assume there was an incontinent tiger or something involved because the masses of hair, the strong smell of piss, and the sheer number of dried turds in the corners of the room?

It'd been a disgusting nightmare when I'd opened the door, coughing in the acrid stench that had washed out and over us all. Gessh, who'd been arguing as she was a half-hair taller than her sister, and therefore the 'biggest' of us all, and so needed the biggest room, had coughed, retched, and then walked away from it.

Reign had shaken her head and refused, the smell no great issue thanks to the patch we both had for our brain mods, but the little nuggets that were left everywhere? Too much.

It'd taken me six hours.

Six fucking hours to make that room almost clean, and burning the mattress had been the final straw.

I'd ordered a replacement—four hour delivery slot, thank the gods of chrome and blood—and I'd decided turnabout was fair play. Reign had teased the shit outta me enough times, so I had a shower and climbed into her bed with her.

I'd put pants on, and she had her underwear on, but it'd been a long ass night despite us both being exhausted. She'd cuddled in to me, said quite plainly that the blowjob she'd given me earlier was all I was getting and that I'd better not wake her up by prodding her with it in the hopes of a rerun, then we'd both tried to sleep.

"More cleaning," I said sadly. "The communal areas are ready, here at least, and our rooms are livable now, if not great…"

"I got more cleaning supplies as well," Reign said, and I smiled my thanks at her.

"Good! So, as I was saying our living areas are all good now, but next? We need to sort the damn warehouse, and get it ready for the next job."

"Which is?" Luna groaned.

"Oh you're going to love it," I assured her, grinning.

CHAPTER TWO

"You lied to me." Luna growled, staring up at the massive transport crate that had taken five orcs to manhandle into position yesterday. "You said I'd love it. This is about as far from what I'd love to be doing right now, as fucking possible."

"True, but it's for a good cause." I panted, stepping back. "Fuck's sake I wish we had a crane…"

"We'll need one," Reign said. "I'm not doing that ever again!"

"Yeah, well." I shrugged, collapsing atop an abandoned section of packing crate and looking up at the protective housing for my armor, and smiling despite everything.

As an APS operative, I was fanatical about my armor, about making goddamn sure it was just right, loaded and polished, maintained and fucking ready at any minute to unleash hell and damnation.

As it was right now? It was stripped down to the skeleton, missing the majority of the parts that it needed for just about anything—including the goddamn power supply—and it hung suspended from the frame with loads of space around it.

It was *mine* though.

It no longer belonged to the army, and because of the way I'd gotten it back? It wasn't even registered. No tracker, no hardwired explosives ready to turn me to paste if I misbehaved, none of it. It, and I, were both free.

"Why would we need a crane?" Gessh asked, staring up at it, reaching out to touch the fingers of one robotic hand, shaking her head at it. "Damn, they're beautiful."

"It's a work of art," I agreed. "Honestly though? The transport container is designed to house all the parts needed, and when the suit is in the field and can't be returned to base for work? It doubles as a repair and work housing.

"That means that we have a repair and upgrade cradle that can hold the suit at least, and while it's not great, it'll work for any APS unit."

"You thinking of stealing the recovered parts from the ones we fought?" Luna asked. "Because no offence, boss, but they're gonna be under serious security…they weren't supposed to be possible to steal in the first place, remember?"

"No, we leave those," I agreed. "What we do, is repair my *suit*. Then once it's up and running and we've got the system in place? That's when we get my suit registered, but with Bowdoin's help. We make damn sure I can use the suit in public, and we start clearing out specter nests the easy way. The four of us, taking down two or three nests a day? I see us getting real money, real fast."

"I'll not say no," Reign said. "But isn't that asshole major going to come after us?"

"We can only hope," I said. "The suits he sent were from his own black squad, or ghost squad or whatever he's calling it. He's gonna have to hide them if they come after us again."

"So hit us when we're underground?" Reign asked. "Doing a specter nest or…"

"Or here." I nodded. "We'll need to sort this place out, get some serious defensive shit in place, both for APS and for normal scavenging scumbags. The advantage is? They come after us underground? We win and we can take a fucking suit hopefully…steal it away and hide it, then we retrieve it later for one of you."

"Would it work?" Gessh asked. "I thought nobody could use them besides the original operator?"

"That's true, mainly." I grinned. "The advantage though, is that it's nanites that make that happen. As well as the physical joining of man and machine through the spinal tap? There's also a fuck load of nanites that are needed throughout the armor. Believe me, first time you join with it? It's like you're bathing in a vat of them. They're needed to literally bind the armor to you. I could probably move it, even now, without my spinal tap, but it'd be hard and slow.

"With enough nanites though? I could reconfigure a suit to accept you. Get a spinal mod, train you up, do the full nanite rebonding? We could do it. The reason the suits are scrapped is that it's actually cheaper, the sheer fucking number of systems that'll need to be replaced, and the number of nanites that we'll need to do this? They're insane.

"We'll need more nanites, per suit, than a chop-shop goes through in probably a *year*, hence why it's ridiculous normally. If we can get that system up and running though?" I nodded over to the Stripper parts spread out on a table nearby. "That's something we could do, like really do. We might have to swap out specter hunting for monsters, I've no idea what specters are like for pure nanites, but we can try."

"Okay." Gessh sighed. "So we've got this housing into place, and hooked up, its drawing power, now what?"

"Now we clean this room to within an inch of its life. We can't use it, not filthy as it is."

"Why not?" Luna growled. "Fuck's sake, Kabutt, yeah you're the boss and all, but seriously? We left the army to get away from all that 'polishing the shitter with your toothbrush' crap. The room is fine, sure it's a bit…"

She broke off looking around the room and we all did the same.

It was a rectangular room, longer than it was wide, with half the upper floor taken out for living quarters, and the other half left as part of the warehouse, presumably for particularly tall units or whatever.

The state the room was in though?

One wall was all old shelving units, most of which were either collapsed or broken, or covered in piled crap. Whatever the previous owners had used it for officially, it'd clearly been a chop-shop of the non-organic kind at one point, with a winch system and pulleys—in totally the wrong area for us to have used them, sod's law—and a drop down section to allow mechanics to work under a vehicle if need be.

There were containers that held used motor oils, chemicals that were marked for 'disposal by official means only' which presumably meant that they were regulated, hence why they'd been left here.

Bins held collections of screws, nuts, rubber bungs and fuck knew what else, all of them coated in a thick layer of grease and grime, then finally topped off with a wonderful collection of spider webs and vermin droppings.

All in all the room was fucking filthy, and that didn't even include the broken boxes, the damaged tires stacked in the corner, nor the vast collection of papers, packing crates and so on that Oshbob had left.

There was at least a good day's work in it for a professional cleaning company, if we'd been able to get one to come to such a godforsaken shithole part of the city.

I wasn't looking forward to what was coming.

"Okay, so maybe it's a bit dirty," Luna finished lamely, clearly knowing damn well that her 'it's fine' attempt was falling on deaf ears. "But seriously? Beyond this section of the building for *your* suit, what more do we need to clean?"

"All of it," I said. "Not even looking at the suit and how much anything like all the floating crap in here would fuck with the internals, but that?" I nodded to the collection of cables and insanely high tech on the other table.

"You think you can get it to work?" Gessh asked and I nodded.

"I've used them before, the design? Its fucking brilliant, shrunken down to a fraction of the size the kit normally is, and the way its laid out? It should work, but, and I'm being clear here, it *should* work. I was trained, all the APS operators are, to repair our gear. This looks like I can make it work, but we'll need some very good gear to fix it."

"What's wrong with it?" Luna asked, stepping over and lifting one end of the mass of connective wires, plates and projectors.

"It's broken," I said simply. "It was torn free of whoever, or whatever, was using it, and I do mean torn, there's multiple places that look like stress fractures and breaks. There's a missing section that looks to be the holding area for the nanites, that's fine, I've got some ideas for that, and frankly that's the least technical part of the system. The main issue, is that a fucking goblin was hiding it in a potty on its head."

The others all winced at that.

"Exactly. The entire thing is covered in grease, sweat and filth, and before I can even consider fixing it up and testing it? It needs to be clean. I'm not spending days working on the fucker, to dump it on the table there and have some rat piss on it or chew the wires. We need to clean this place, seal it from anything getting in, and then we need to damn well set up an area we can work on sensitive electronics in."

"A clean room?" Reign asked. "I've seen them in vids, and if that's what we need...?"

"No, we don't need to go to that level, and if we did, hell it'd break as soon as we took it into the undercity. We just need to get it working and sealed up again. Some of the sections I need to work on can be sealed inside rubberized or plastic containment, and we can get kit to do that, it's cheap enough. What we need though?"

I looked around, making sure they were all on board.

"We need this place fucking spotless, as clean as we can make it, and a decent electronics station to work at, then we need to make it as secure as possible. For now, nobody knows we've got anything, beyond Oshbob, and he wants us to fix it all up, that gives us some time to get things sorted. Then if he, or anyone else tries to rob us once we've got it all working? They get fucked up."

"Tell me we can hire someone…" Luna whispered, and Gessh hit her across the back of the head good naturedly.

"You always want to avoid the work for a few credits." She sighed. "Seriously, sis, for what it'd cost, not to mention the risk we'd run? It's not worth it. A day, maybe two of hard work and we're laughing. It'll cost hundreds of creds to pay someone else to do it, and how often did we wish we could get a job that paid that in a day? Better to save the money and just work."

"I know…" Luna growled, shaking her head. "I just fucking hate cleaning."

"Me too," I said, then snorted at the incredulous look on Luna's face. "Seriously? You think I want to clean it? I want to ignore all of this until my suit is ready, then slaughter some fucks and move us all into a pleasure garden to chill. If I could not do this? Believe me I would, but we need to fix our gear, so come on."

"Quicker it's done, quicker we can relax," Reign grumbled, picking up some rubbish from one of the benches and looking around aimlessly. "Fuck's sake, where do we start?"

"At one corner," Gessh said, pointing. "Those roller doors open out into the fenced-in area, we get them open, and we drag anything and everything we don't want out there. Fuck it all, there're companies that take crap away, even if they don't clean, they'll send someone to pick through it and see if they can smelt shit down."

"What about the tires and so on?" I asked.

"Get it all outside and believe me, there'll be a company somewhere that makes money from it all, even if we have to pay them to take it, it'd be worth it."

"Can you sort it?" I asked and she frowned then nodded.

"I think Oshbob said something about a company that did that kinda shit, I'll ask Dondo about it. He's one of the guys there."

"A guy?" Reign grinned, "We were there for like half an hour, and we spent all of it talking to Oshbob, how'd you find the time to…?"

"Oh believe me, she has her ways." Luna snorted. "Half our conquests were me going to the loo or the bar and coming back to find her dragging some guy around by his dick."

"As long as everyone's having fun I don't see the issue!" Gessh laughed. "Right, you fuckers, start cleaning, I'll go find Dondo."

"No fucking him while we work!" Luna growled. "Seriously, you pull something like that and I'll…"

"Sorry, can't hear you!" her sister called back, already running for the door, laughing.

"I mean it!" Luna bellowed, starting off after her.

"Fuck's sake, I feel like we're child-minding at times," I growled at Reign.

"You love it really, now come on, the sooner we get this clean, the sooner we're back out and earning. The sooner we earn more creds? The sooner we both get laid." Reign snorted and balled up a filthy rag, before throwing it at me, before bending over at the waist to pick something up from the floor.

She paused, and grinned, seeing me admiring her ass. "Unless of course, you don't want to get laid any more…?"

I was moving before she finished speaking.

CHAPTER THREE

The rest of the day was a blur of crappy jobs, of cursing when something ran out from under equipment we were moving—sometimes spiders, sometimes rats, sometimes who knew—and finally of me cursing the name Oshbob to the fucking high heavens.

Dondo apparently did know a company that would collect all the crap and get rid of it, for a fee. When Gessh had told me how much later on—three hundred fucking creds—I'd almost told her to fuck right off.

All this shit could be smelted or recycled, so whoever took it all to the relevant places would be getting paid for the privilege.

Hell, we could leave it all out in the open and the street rats—the various millions of feral kids and gobbos that lived on the streets and in gangs—would nick it all, given a bit of time.

The issue was that we didn't want those fuckers hanging around and seeing if we were doing anything interesting, or possibly valuable that they could steal and sell. Also, we needed it done now, because we were all impatient fucks, and really?

Three hundred creds wasn't that much, not when you had the creds anyway. It was only a week ago that I had less than two hundred creds to my name after all.

In the end we'd agreed, and he'd taken the creds, agreeing he'd get the company to clear it all away by dawn.

He was as good as his word in one respect, by dawn the entire lot was indeed gone.

The issue was that he'd apparently gone straight to Oshbob, who'd pocketed the creds, and had sent a load of 'his' goblins straight over to collect it all.

That fucking orc had managed to make us pay to rent his place, pay to have his people 'smuggle' my armor *across the fucking street* and he'd insisted that we had to clean the place up as part of the deal. Now we'd done that, and he'd charged us to take away the crap *he'd* fucking left in the warehouse!

I didn't know if I hated the sneaky conniving bastard, or if I was starting to get impressed.

Either way though, we'd ended up working our fucking asses off all day, and Dondo apparently worked Gessh—and possibly Luna—hard for half the night as well.

By the time an unexpected alert went off I was sandy eyed, exhausted from almost no sleep, and I was grimly determined that sound deadening insulation was going to be one of the first major purchases I made for my room.

I was also seriously ready to fucking shoot someone, so the alert was almost welcome, even coming as it was before 0400.

I dragged my clothes on, and then my armor, before striding out into our 'kitchen' and grabbing guns from the locker we'd had installed there.

Fuck food, we could order pizza and whatever else in we needed, but a damn good gun safe was a necessity.

"What is it?" Luna asked, stumbling out of Gessh's room, yawning and struggling into her pants, as Dondo continued to snore on the bed behind her.

"Fucking timing!" Gessh growled. Following her out, bleary eyed and pulling her clothes on as well. "I literally just got to sleep!"

"We know," Reign said. "Believe me, we fucking know." She grabbed a box of ammo and started reloading her sub machineguns as quickly as possible. "Fucking should have done this earlier…"

"Get dressed," I ordered the girls. "Boot him out, and get your gear, it's an all-hands alert, something just went shit for the guild and we're on standby."

"Standby for what?" Luna asked, yawning hugely.

"Weekly rotation," Reign explained, sighing. "Fuck's sake, didn't you read the contract? Every team has a week, we're team seventeen out of thirty-nine, so we won't get called on again for a while, but as long as we're in the guild, we have to respond to a call for aid."

"How often does this shit happen?" Gessh called to us, hurrying into her room and grabbing some more clothes, before kicking her sleeping 'friend' in the foot. "Up and at 'em, sunshine. Time to fuck off."

"Already?" he mumbled.

"Yeah, we've got a job and you can't stay here."

"Okay…" he groused, starting to search for clothes as Reign replied to Gessh, and I saw far more of the big fucker than I wanted to.

"Not very often, and we get double pay when it does, bonuses are well worth it, but…holy fucking shit, is that real?" Reign continued.

"His nickname's Tripod." Luna grinned. "Now you know why."

"Should be fucking horse, damn!"

"I'll be walking funny for a while," Luna admitted.

"LALALLALALLA!" I called as I covered my ears, much to their laughter, as Reign patted me on the shoulder.

"There, there, Kabutt," she said making a fake sad face. "It's okay, you're only human…"

"Fuck right off all of you," I said grimly. "Reign, sort the transport. I'll get details."

"Yes boss," she said nodding, the joking atmosphere dropping as I issued orders. "Gessh, check the charger once you're dressed. Luna, grab your gear and two boxes of ammo, we can cross load on the way…"

I pulled up the job details as I was speaking, reading quickly and wincing at the distance, it was across the fucking city, right up against the eastern wall, and I knew what that meant. Even as I started to read the details.

JOB: ALERT! EMERGENCY RESPONSE!

Team-17 as the emergency responders for week 35 are required to assist Team-22 at location [location included].

Beware! This location has been identified as a probable outbreak area—

Team-22 have activated emergency beacons and are awaiting rescue due to overwhelming Specter influxes driven by unknown third party.

Bounties confirmed:
- 3x [GHOUL] have been tracked on site, not verified as Terminated
- 1x [Unknown variant] not verified as Terminated
- 100x [Standard Specter] not verified as Terminated

Supplemental:
'We're fucking low on ammo so bring any rifle and pistol you've got and fucking hurry!'
—Badger, Team Lead, Team-22

Accept Job?

I accepted it, getting a green light from Julius as well, a 'I see you're going, so thanks' type of thing.

It took a few minutes, that was all, but this time, in addition to my rifle, my revolver, two medikits—one small, one medium—and grenades—one flashbang, one EMP and two incendiaries—I also had my looted plasma sword.

It was recharged, good for about an hour of solid use, and as I attached it to my back, Gessh called up from below.

"Grazer's charged!" she shouted joyfully, and I sighed.

"I told you it was worth buying." Reign leant in close, her lips almost touching my ear as she whispered in it.

The shiver that ran down my back at the closeness of her lips reminded me just how goddamn badly I needed to help her pay off that debt.

A minute later and Dondo was walking sleepily out of the front gate, as a high speed cab touched down inside the now cleared area at the front.

We piled in, two boxes of rifle and pistol ammo dumped on the floor between us as we loaded any and every empty magazine we had.

Fifteen minutes later—and eight goddamn hundred credits for the emergency flight, eight fucking *hundred* for a cab—and we were touching down by the eastern wall, the doors of the cab lifting smoothly as we dragged ourselves out as fast as we could.

It was time to get our game faces on.

The area we'd landed in was a shithole normally. Hell, in general rules, if the center of the city was where ninety-nine percent of the creds were spent and generated, and the further out from that point you went, the less of each?

We were literally up against the edge of the outer wall.

The only reason this area wouldn't be called a slum, was that slum dwellers would be fucking furious at the comparison.

The wall that surrounded Artem was massive, insanely thick and over engineered, with everything from gamma cannons to spikes dotted here there and everywhere on the outside of it to discourage visitors.

Despite all of that, and the fucking size of the thing—it towered over us, blocking out the light—somehow monsters, scavs, nomads, slavers and who the fuck knew what else, made it inside on an almost daily basis.

It didn't help that the wall was over seven hundred years old.

It also didn't help that it was constantly being rebuilt, repaired and fucking reworked by the lowest bidder, and that the absolute minimum was spent that could be spent.

That meant that while the wall might not be breached in your area today, if you lived or worked next to the wall, it would be breached eventually, and when it was? Sometimes it took days for anyone outside the local area to notice, or even fucking care.

Because of that while people complained about living literally cheek by jowl in the arcologies, they'd rather live there than anywhere near the wall.

Entire sections of the poorest and most fucked up people in society lived there, pushed out as far as they could be by lack of money, by growing degradation of their implants, or a million other things.

When we scrambled free of the cab and looked around, I couldn't help but curse.

The wall that towered over us here was riddled with rust, and I could see fresh blood and bullet casings strewn about in the mud of the abandoned parking lot. That there were no bodies, and the distant, echoing gunfire from somewhere below was sporadic and panicked?

This was not going to be a good one.

"Team-22!" I sent to the lead of the other group. "Team-17 here, just landed and incoming with ammo and reinforcements…status?"

Silence was the only response, and I knew this was going to be bad.

CHAPTER FOUR

"Find a way down to them," I barked to the others, already starting forwards, searching the lot for an entrance or access hatch.

The cab took off in a blast of downdraft, the gentle early morning drizzle blasted out in all directions as the high speed transport rocketed upwards into the night, curving away from the wall and back towards the center of the city.

"I've got drag marks!" Gessh called, and I cursed, diverting from the building I'd been headed for, and hurrying back to catch up with the others.

Gessh was in the lead, shotgun at the ready as she approached a building on the other side of the lot.

This was an old squat building, three stories, wider at the base than the top, and angled slightly inwards. The walls had clearly been designed to draw attention, and in some long forgotten past they might have actually looked imposing.

Now they were covered in graffiti, most of the windows were smashed, and the inside looked like an entrance to the underworld, never mind the undercity.

As I passed through the ruined doorway, the door itself long since ripped from its hinges, I couldn't help but shiver. I wasn't a religious man, but fuck.

I really could see this kind of place as an entrance to a hell of lost souls.

"Looks like some old tech worshipping sect," Reign guessed, and I frowned, looking at her, before moving in closer.

"The rogue AI?" I asked, glancing around at the inside of the building, stripped down to the goddamn framework as we moved in deeper.

"The Keeper?" Reign snorted. "Dammit, Kabutt, I know you were army through and through, but seriously? It's embarrassing how little you know at times. The Keeper is supposed to be one of the very first Tier Fives, it went rogue and escaped into Aug-World. Now it helps or hinders as it decides, right?"

"Yeah?"

"This looks more like one of those old upload centers, where the pure chrome believers used to jack in and try and upload themselves into the next world…"

"Fucking religious nutters," I growled.

"Found it!" Gessh called back. "Hatch in the floor, recently covered over again, but there's blood stains leading to it, or I'd have missed it."

"Who the hell covered it over?" Luna groused. "Specters don't think like that?"

"You think there's someone else?" I asked, heading over, and wincing as distant gunfire echoed from somewhere below.

"Not sure, just specters don't usually think like that, or at all. Could be a ghoul-led incursion?"

"Maybe." I shrugged. "Maybe not, maybe it's slavers using specters as cover, doesn't matter. What matters is we've got a team stuck down there. Find a way to open that." I ordered, before sending a call request to Julius.

"Kabutt," he greeted, yawning. "How're we looking? You found '22?"

"We've got gunfire below, and signs of a firefight, no bodies, looks like they were dragged down and the entrance sealed…"

"Found it!" Luna called, triggering a release, as the hatch clunked, the locks disengaging.

"We're heading in." I shrugged. "We'll be back in touch as soon as we save them all."

"And if you don't?"

"Then I guess we won't be back in touch." I snorted. "Fucks' sake Julius, try and keep up, man."

"If you get in the shit, pull out," he ordered after a long few seconds. "We'll always try and come after our teams, but sometimes, you need to be realistic. I'm gathering reinforcements now, but we're at least an hour away, so if you get in the shit and can't get out, get your backs to a wall and hunker down. We'll come for you."

"Appreciate that." I cut the connection, looking to Reign who was standing by the hatch, hand on the lever on the top, and watching to make sure I was ready.

"He give you the 'we'll come for you, we're all family' speech?" she asked.

"Said we were to be realistic, and if we couldn't get to them, to hunker down and they'd be with us in an hour."

"Sounds like he's getting pessimistic in his old age." She sighed. "Used to be he promised he'd always come for us, then we'd all rib him about that later."

"Dirty bastard." Luna grunted, then nodded at the hatch. "Ready."

"Ready," Gessh said.

"Ready," I agreed, rifle at my shoulder and zeroed in.

"Opening." Reign grunted, hauling back, then staggering when the hatch opened easily.

The three of us stepped up, guns pointing down, the blood all over the hatch and on the rungs in the tunnel leading down making it clear someone had dumped the bodies in…then they'd followed them, judging from the smear patterns in the drying blood.

There was nobody in sight now, and we followed them in.

At the bottom of the ladder, I took point, with Luna behind me, then Reign, and last of all Gessh, as we passed bodies piled to the side of the corridor, slowly leaking blood.

"This doesn't look good," Luna muttered, and I had to agree, moving quickly, but as quietly as I could in the lead.

The bodies we passed were mixed, some specters, clearly old and long 'dead' even if they'd been moving around under their own steam.

The others?

A mix of city dwellers of all ages and sizes were laid here and there, arms flopping to the floor and blood seeping from them, pooling under…

"Shit!" Reign snarled. "Bet you it's fucking chromers!"

"What?" I froze and looked ahead down the corridor, totally confused as she started swearing and Luna and Gessh joined her. "What the hell?" I hissed, still staring down my rifle, watching my zone.

"Chromers…you know, those nutters who believe in joining with the machine?"

"The full metal ones?" I asked, confused. "What the hell has this to do with…"

"There's some that follow specters!" Reign clarified.

"Why?" I asked, moving off again, hurrying down the corridor, checking connecting passages and keeping going, following the blood trail that ran down the middle, as the last of the bodies fell away behind us.

"You know those rumors about the sentient specters?" she said in a voice pitched to only carry to us.

"Yeah?"

"There's rumors that some of the chromers took to doing deals with them."

"Why?" I asked, shaking my head. "First off, *specters*, they'll kill you if you have mods, and all chromers *have* is fucking mods, certainly no brains!"

"Yeah, and if you meet a sentient specter it's never going to end well for you. They're supposed to be like that thing that chased us after the bio-farms, fucking mental and heavily armed," Gessh added.

"All rebuilt and shit," Luna agreed succinctly.

"Yeah, well, some of the chromers have splintered off from the main sects…they decided that maybe the baseline specters are those who weren't pure enough, and the sentient ones? They're prophets or some shit…" Reign said with disgust. "Seriously, don't ask me why, because I don't fucking know, I just remember Julius saying a bunch of them had to be run out of the guild a couple of weeks ago. He tried to figure out why they were doing what they were doing, probably hoping to sell our services or something. They were trying to find out where the biggest concentrations of specters were, to go and do…something? Fuck knows what, but Julius kicked them out after listening to their mad shit, and a few of them went mental at him for 'defiling' their beliefs or something."

"Okay, so religious nutters, what's that got to do with—"

"Those bodies back there had their mods still. If it was specters? They'd have stripped them, and left the bodies out in the open…"

"You're thinking it's chromers? Why not scavs?" Luna asked.

"This place," Reign said. "It's set up and hidden. If it was scavs using it, they'd be raiding the local area for gear then fucking off back out into the wastes."

"Could be smugglers," Gessh suggested, when gunfire rang out suddenly from a corridor to the right, one we'd just passed.

"Team-22!" I barked, sending the call to any of the seven man team that we'd been given the contact details for, and hating that I was reliant on keystone calls rather than a proper military grade tac-net. "Sound off for fuck's sake, this is Team-17!"

This time when there was no response. I shook my head and barked an order to the others. "Fuck it, follow the gunfire."

Luna was the closest to the corridor and took the lead, shotgun raised as I fell in behind her, the whole team picking up speed as we ran towards the sound of rapid fire. We made it maybe ten meters before a T-junction gave us a choice of right and left, and the gunfire led us down the left passage, passing through a cunningly concealed fake wall that we'd have totally missed, if not for the fact it was left wide open.

This time, when we reached the end of the corridor, it led down another flight of stairs, and then opened out into a large room. There were dozens of long tables running side by side with what looked like a failed hydroponics or drug lab setup, but about a quarter of the tables had bodies laid on them in various stages of being carved up, and the back wall was entirely taken up with refrigeration and storage lockers.

I paused, staring at the literal chop-shop before us, in horror. We all joked about them. Hell, carvers' premises were so heavily joked about and been called chop-shops for so long that it was practically the official name for them now. I couldn't remember the 'real' name for them off the top of my head, but this?

This was a true 'chop-shop'. A black site where people were being rendered down to body parts for sale.

A bin sat to the right hand side of the room as we moved slowly through it, eyes wide, and a single glance in revealed masses of damaged organs, ones that had presumably been ruined in the removal, or infected or diseased or whatever.

"I…I'm changing my guess," Reign whispered. "Chromers wouldn't do this…"

"Who would?" Luna asked, equally horrified.

"It doesn't matter!" I snapped. "Focus!"

I took the lead again, running now, splashing through puddles of blood and piss, heading for the far end of the room, and a door propped slightly ajar by a foot.

I reached the door and pushed it open with the barrel of my rifle, seeing the figure in full 'medical' scrubs on the floor before me. A shotgun blast in their lower back had ended their interest in carving people up permanently.

I stepped over them, the room beyond a mess of splatted blood. A wall panel, presumably once an integrated screen, flashed and fizzed sparks, cracks leading out from a central impact point, one that judging from the strands of hair matted in the blood there, had come from the body slumped on the ground below it.

"Shit, that's Christos." Reign cursed, hurrying past me, and kneeling next to the body, checking the neck for a pulse, then shaking her head as she looked back at me. "Dead."

"How much ammo has he got?" I asked, and she frowned, then checked.

"Plenty, two full mags for the rifle, one for the pistol and…"

"Grab them," I ordered. "The message we got was from the team lead for '22, Badger, and he was low on ammo, and surrounded by specters. If this is one of the team, up here, and dead with plenty of ammo? What the fuck happened?"

"No clue, let's move on though," she agreed, falling in as we took the exit at the back of the room. The next two rooms were empty pretty much, then a kitchen—little used—and finally a pair of small living quarters…

…then a wall. We'd reached the end of the road.

"What the hell?" I snapped, confused to all fuck. "Where the hell are they?"

"Christos was cold," Reign said. "There's no way that gunfire was from him."

"Fuck's sake, we miss a room or something?" I asked, as we started heading back, only for Luna to stop us, sniffing the air in the second of the empty rooms.

"You smell that?" she asked, and I shook my head.

"Smells like…old boots?" Reign asked.

"And sweat and blood," Gessh agreed, nodding. "I thought it was the other room when we came in, that it was those fuckers, but it's not."

"I can't smell anything besides Christos and whoever that doc was," I said, shaking my head.

"Yeah, well, you're only human." Reign smiled, taking the edge off the comment, as I glared at her.

"You're all half human," I pointed out.

"And that's why we're having difficulty pinpointing it, rather than seeing it instantly, so shut the fuck up alright, boss?" Gessh snapped, sniffing as she and Luna moved around the room. "Here…"

The area she pointed to was in a clear section of the room, sure, but it was literally just that, there was fuck all special about it, two light switches, and a long overhead recessed strip light that bathed the room in a dull yellowish tinged light.

The wall was tiled from floor to ceiling, and lines of cracks ran between the tiles, making the wall look weird but…

Two light switches.

I saw it at the same time that Reign did, reaching out and flicking the one on the left, getting nothing whatsoever, and the then the one on the right, again to no response.

I frowned, having been sure we'd found it, until Luna sighed and pushed Reign aside, then flicked both switches in time with her sister, who'd stepped up without being told.

There was an audible clunk and whirr, and the entire section of the wall started moving, sliding back hinged at the top and lifting at the bottom, to reveal a new staircase, one that was entirely metal and roughly maintained, as the stench hit us full force from whatever was ahead.

CHAPTER FIVE

We hurried down the stairs, weapons ready, but the sight when we reached the bottom and moved out onto a metal gantry?

It was nothing like what we'd been expecting.

Below us was what looked to be one of the old reservoir tanks, massive things designed to hold millions and even billions of units of water for the city in times of drought and so on. It'd been long since abandoned, and then repurposed.

We stood on a metal gantry that ran across the middle of the basin, and below us? Easily several hundred specters milled, with the basin vanishing into the distance beyond the range of our enhanced optics.

The clicks and whirrs of old mods, the occasional cry as something triggered a vocal processor and the clinks and clangs of bodies bouncing off each other in the darkness below us impressed the need for silence in ways that an order never could, and we slowed, staring with wide eyes.

"There's hundreds," Reign whispered.

I nodded, looking to the right and left, before speaking softly.

"Luna, take the left. Gessh, the right. Reign, stay here. Let's check out the size of this place, don't fire unless you really fucking need to, swords and knives only."

The gantry crossed over the middle of the basin below, but it also ran left and right vanishing into the darkness, attached to the walls. As the sisters split and headed along those paths, I moved out over the center, as Reign used the scope on her grazer to check the basin below.

I moved slowly, the metal underfoot creaking occasionally as I searched, the cross hatch pattern that the entire system was made of making it easy to see through it to the ground far below.

Here and there I could see evidence of recent firefights, bodies laid still in true death, stripped of their mods. I saw pipes and old machinery that covered the inner walls of the basin, and some of them were damaged, the edges looking sharp and recent, as the smell of recent gunfire and blood hung in the air.

Worst of all though were the bodies. Some of the specters were covered in wet blood, and I saw the remains of a body against one wall, broken and forgotten.

The left arm was gone entirely, as was the right foot, and the head had been cracked like an egg. Blood dripped from nearby mechanisms where it'd presumably sprayed at some point recently.

Their rifle was laid on the floor nearby, and I winced, seeing a hatchet like mine, snapped off at the handle, the rifle's butt glowing with a single red LED that proclaimed to those that knew what to look for, that it was unloaded.

I paused, staring down at the body slumped in death, and the slowly spreading crowd of specters, and I gritted my teeth, shaking my head in anger.

Not only were we too late to the fight? We'd arrived just in time to see the specters winding down. It didn't make sense as to why the door above had been closed off, but fuck it, you never really got to know all the ins and outs of another's life, never mind their death.

I moved on, scouring the ground, looking from the gantry way ahead, to the sides where Luna and Gessh had vanished into the distance, when I saw it.

A tiny light, a laser pointer or something similar, flashing at me.

It was a single burst of light, a rangefinder or something, then it vanished, then it was back, three sharp pulses, then vanished again.

I moved forwards quickly. It'd come from somewhere just beyond the range of my optics, and I frowned as I made it far enough along that I thought I should be able to see something and instead saw…nothing.

The basin below me was circular, and had clearly been intended as a series of circular units. Presumably they'd once had a top to them, and the gantry passed over that. Internal walls ran under me now, sealing sections away from each other, with doorways between them, so that if the owner wanted they could be used individually or as a whole.

The internal walls had sections that were covered in mechanisms, and others where they were blank, and yet…

Luna and Gessh were roaming around the outside of the setup. Reign was somewhere behind me, and with her better scope on her rifle I had to hope she could see me and was watching.

I started to wave my left hand up and down slowly, then made a 'move up' hand signal, before starting again.

All the time, as I did it, I was staring at the area I thought the light had flashed from, seeing a shadowed mass of complex rusting machinery, and fuck all else.

The walls of the tank were about forty meters high, and several hundred across, making the specters below me pretty much the limit for my current upgrades, and I cursed over the thought that there could be anything down there, and I'd have no fucking clue.

Sections lifted up higher, like they had where we'd entered, the specters being maybe fifteen meters below us, but here it was steadily sloping further and further down.

I'd gotten pretty turned around as we'd gone lower and lower, but I was guessing that somewhere nearby was the wall, the outer city one, where it sloped down into the ground.

It couldn't have been that though, and I was sure I'd seen light flashing…maybe it'd been a reflection off a bit of metal?

I was still frowning, trying to work it out, when Reign almost gave me a heart attack, appearing by my side and grabbing my hand to stop me waving.

"What's up?" she whispered.

"*Fuckin…*" I took a deep breath, shaking my head as I looked at her. "Fucking hell, Reign…warn a guy, alright?"

"What did you want?" she asked in a low hiss. "I think they can sense us…"

I looked back down. More and more faces were starting to lift up, casting about and trying to pick up the source for the nanites they could presumably sense nearby, not to mention whatever else the fuckers had for senses.

"Dammit…look there," I said, pointing to where I thought the light had come from. "I saw a…"

Light shone at us from a section of piping about halfway up the wall, and this time it was steady, making damn sure we saw them, before it winked off again.

"It's a survivor," Reign said. "Using the rangefinder on their gun maybe?"

"I'm thinking stealthed."

"The specters are close to them…" She winced. "Don't suppose you've got a rope?"

"Nope. You?"

"Would I be asking you if I had one?" she countered, looking from side to side, then lifting her rifle and sighting in, scanning things outside of my range. "Okay, there's a section where the wall is close enough that we can probably catch them if they jump, but that section is close to a staircase down as well."

"Right?"

"So, we basically need to get them the fuck away from that section, and whoever it is can either climb up, or down and run across."

"So get the specters away from there you mean?"

She nodded again, waving a hand as if to say 'get on with it, that's fuckin' obvious'.

"Is there another way down?" I asked and she shrugged.

"Not that I can see…but I can only see so far. Gessh and Luna should have reached the far side by now."

"Okay, we need to rig something, just in case, a couple of grenades where the path leads down maybe, then if we get swamped it'll take the path up out—"

"If we do that and there's any more survivors down there, we're pretty much giving up on them," she pointed out and I swore.

"Okay, fuck it," I growled. "Let's get Gessh and Luna back here, and get ready. We make sure there's no more ways up here, we don't want to get swamped if we can avoid it."

"What's the plan?" Reign asked and I shrugged.

"I'm thinking we go with overwhelming firepower. We get him across to the nearest point to climb up, and I drop down with my plasma blade. I cut a way through to the bottom of the stairs while you three cover the sides and rear as we run for it."

"And the rest of the team?" Reign asked. "Remember, we still don't know who that is, they're in stealth suits, so they might be one of the team, or…"

"Or they might be one of the fuckheads who lived and worked here." I groaned. "Yeah good point."

"So…" We both looked over the side, then Reign signaled down to the person in stealth. Using hand signals she conveyed 'stay there' and 'be back in 5'.

Then we moved back quickly, more growls and clatters rising from below as a few more of the stumbling specters saw us and tried to figure out how to get up.

"So?" I asked in a low voice.

"So I wanted to get back from where he might be able to hear me," she said. "Look, he might be a member of either our team, or the local fuckheads that are chopping people up for parts. Either way, we need to get them and find out what the fuck happened here. If they're from our team? They'll know what happened to the others, or at least have a clue. If they're the local fuckers, same, except they'll probably know who and what the hell was going on, and…" She shot me a downright evil smile.

"They'll also know who financed this and where the fucking money is. There's nothing we can do for the dead, not here, but we can find it out, and either leak it to the corpos and the press—they'd have a field day using it to distract us from whatever shit they need to hide—or we use it to blackmail the fuck outta them, clean their accounts out, and *then* we do all of that."

"That's…" I broke off.

"Look, Kabutt, I know it's not nice, but that's the way the world is, I'm just saying we could get something for us out of this."

"I was going to say evil, but magnificent," I said. "I think we should leave it to Julius though, he'll be here with the rest of the guild soon, and as our 'boss', it's both his problem, and his privilege."

"Damn, fine," she grumbled.

"Besides, do you really want to try and sell the story to the press? They'd fucking dig your past up and shit on it just for fun, you know those vultures."

"Fair point," she groused, then waved ahead, nodding. "There's Luna."

Less than a minute later we'd met up again and were backing up into the stairwell, moving back from the edge where the few specters at this end of the basin below could see or sense us.

"Where's Gessh?" I asked Luna, who hesitated.

"No clue, my gantry went around the outside and then stopped, there's a fuck load of specters, but no way up or down, so I came back. I expected her to be here. What did you find?"

We filled her in quickly as we could, waiting quietly…until the sound of crashing metal, followed by sudden and heavy gunfire rang out.

"Gessh!" Luna swore, spinning on her heel and starting to run, and we followed after.

CHAPTER SIX

We took the right hand side of the gantry, all three of us running with Luna in the lead, each footfall making the old metal bounce and clatter.

It didn't take long to find Gessh, but when we did? Fuck.

The gantry was old and made of steel, presumably, anchored into what appeared to be a stone bracing with some form of steel used to anchor it.

I guessed that much because as soon as we took the branch that appeared to the right, opening into a second basin area, the twisted and here, badly rusted metal that had once been the gantry way that had looped it, now led down at a sharp angle into the middle of a virtual mosh pit of specters.

Gessh was hanging desperately from a stanchion with one hand, her shotgun dangling empty, her sword in its sheath but out of reach as she tried to drag herself up.

She'd clearly emptied the shotgun first, then ripped her handgun free, and was firing almost at random as arms reached up for her, boney claws tearing at one leg.

She heaved, muscles standing proud in her left arm as she tried to lift her whole body with one arm, her body armor, her guns, her gear, all of it weighing her down, and yet she was dragging herself up and free…

…until a waving hand snapped over her foot and closed with a crack.

She screamed, the cybernetic hand clearly more powerful than her boot could protect against, whirring and closing tighter and tighter as she was dragged downwards, her handgun barking out one more round that ricocheted off something metal below her.

Then the mag was empty and her second scream rang out, as Luna roared and opened fire. The shotgun was a semi-auto, and fuck the echoing booms as she emptied the magazine were painful.

The chamber was thrown into almost daylight brightness as she fired shot after shot into the figures below, throwing them back, before the magazine clicked empty.

I hesitated as Luna dropped prone, grabbing her sister's arm and hauling her upwards. The far side of the gantry *looked* stable, more or less, but as Luna heaved, Gessh cried out again.

The specter that had her by the foot originally was dead, its hand still gripping the foot, but the arm severed halfway down it's length.

That dangling section though was more than enough for another to grab, and then another grabbed onto them. Gessh was being dragged inexorably downwards, and I knew what I had to do, as I dropped my rifle, its restraining sling dragging it back against my chest as I drew my own shotgun.

I fired half the mag at the specters that were pulling themselves up the angled gantry, then leapt, kicking out as I dropped.

I hit an upturned face with both feet, the neck snapping as she was hurled from her feet, and I landed on the bottom of the basin with a squelch of old mud, watered liberally with blood and fuck knew what else.

My training was to land with a roll in these circumstances, to absorb the impact and spread it out, then come to my feet, but to do so here, surrounded by hundreds of specters would be suicide.

Instead I twisted and staggered, pain shooting up my left leg from the awkward landing, even as I locked my shotgun onto the bodies that were gathered around Gessh's dangling form.

I opened fire, emptying the remainder of the magazine, all solid slugs, most punching through body after body as I blasted them away from her.

Luna roared with the effort as she dragged her sister upwards, rolling to pull Gessh over her own body, and onto the gantry that creaked and groaned under them.

As soon as my magazine clacked on empty, I slammed the shotgun back into the sheath as I ripped the handgun free and opened fire three times, two headshots, one upper chest.

The bodies fell back from me, and I swapped my handgun to my left hand, dragging the plasma blade free with my right and triggering it.

The darkness of the abandoned basin was banished in an instant as the light of a constrained sun flared to life. The greys and greens, the washed out 'wrong' colors of the bodies all around me were banished as they sprang to full 'life', only to have that last semblance of life ripped from them by the passage of my blade.

I spun, blade extended at waist height as I sliced it through the bodies around me, metallic screeches, buzzing, and explosions of freed gasses and liquids erupting into the air.

As soon as there was enough room that I was no longer trying desperately to just hold my own, I was moving, heading to the fallen section of gantry.

I glanced up at it as I closed the distance, seeing the weakened connectors, the rusted through sections, and I cursed.

We'd been damn lucky that section hadn't come down already, and judging from the shaking underneath Reign and the others, the one they stood on wouldn't last much longer either.

"Get back!" I called out, before spinning and lopping a head off as another closed on me. "Get around the other side, be ready and I'll fight my way around!"

"We could get down…!" Luna shouted, even as Reign fired, over and over.

I saw suddenly what I'd missed before. While I'd been frantically dicing and slicing, burning the bodies and hacking them apart as they closed, Reign had been keeping the next wave from overwhelming me.

Another body dropped, a single headshot punching through from just above the left eyebrow, back into the brain, sending the body to the ground.

"Go!" I ordered, holstering the handgun and taking the blade in both hands, as I ran in the other direction, right at the thickest concentration of the enemy.

I figured they were bunched up for a reason, maybe a narrow passage from the basin, like the one I'd seen from above.

Whatever it was though, there were at least a hundred more ahead of me, and probably another hundred in the basin spread out behind. That meant either I pushed through in a single go, and ran…as well as got insanely lucky, or?

Or I had to cut the numbers down.

I was operating on a mixture of APS training, of army tactics, and a healthy dose of fucking madness and desperation.

The biggest advantage I had was the plasma sword, far and away it was the best weapon for this environment, and definitely for these fuckers.

It did damage to the mods, yeah, that sucked, especially as I might be costing us hundreds, possibly thousands of credits worth of loot, but if I didn't live to claim it? Fuck it.

Against flesh and blood enemies—which these were, even dead and resurrected as mad puppets of technology—the plasma sword barely registered the impact.

That wasn't to say it didn't cost me power, the blade was draining its battery at a horrific rate, but rather than the hundreds upon hundreds of rounds I'd need if I was trying to do this with a rifle? Hell yes.

I raced into the thickest press of the specters, and I slashed right and left, carving a path inwards, bodies collapsing, arms flying free, flashes as metal reflected or partially deflected my blows.

Then I spun and raced back the way I came, sword flowing in a figure of eight, lopping off arms, legs and heads. I shifted to the right, taking two more out, then darted to the left, taking another down.

I spun and kicked out, planting my foot solidly against a chest, sending the staggering figure tumbling from its feet, then spun as I dropped low, the blade tugging slightly as I carved through legs that drew near.

Then I was off again, sprinting at a narrow gap in the closing encircling force, and through.

Seconds later I was out, the light of the blade casting shadows of madness on the walls as I heard distant gunfire raging, and I saw the wall appear before me.

Twisting, I planted one foot against it, and turned back to face those I knew were following, panting for breath as I counted, more and more stumbling and squelching out of the darkness. Dozens came, and then more, the gaps between the filthy, bedraggled figures filling with more of their kind.

I kicked off the wall, running to the right, sword flashing and flaring as I swung, dragging it through the outstretched arms, necks and heads.

I let them tumble to the floor as I raced back across the closing arc, hacking them from their feet one after another. They kept coming, not one of them so much as fucking hesitating as I cut their companions down, but unlike them, I couldn't keep this frantic pace up, one trip, one slip, and I'd be mobbed before I could recover.

Skidding in the muck, I twisted, hacking out, the blade rising over my shoulder and cutting down into the chest of the figure before me, its cybernetic arms reaching for me, before collapsing, but as I looked left and right I saw more and more closing on me.

As much as I'd cut down literally dozens already, there were more coming. I'd ran from one spot to another, hoping to thin the herd, planning to try and cut most of those already in the basin down. I'd thought that if I could do that, if I could clear the area behind me, I could cut their numbers down, force them back to the entrance to the basin, and there manage them…somehow…

I was clearly fucking wrong though, as the enemy seemed endless!

I swung again and again, forced to give up a step, then another, being driven slowly back. The next in line that attacked I swung at his head…only to have him duck, the blade clipping the very top of his head, and throwing me off balance as I staggered, swearing as a second leapt at me from behind.

No longer were they the slowly staggering or moving, mindless specters, I realized, stepping to the right and spinning on my heel, chopping through the leaping one at waist level, sending him to the floor in two halves.

The eyes around me, the sensors and optical processors, the cameras and desiccated, fleshy orbs all seemed to flare to life as they closed, and I swore loudly, knowing what that meant.

"Ghoul!" I bellowed into the flaring darkness and shadows. "Fucking ghouls!" I repeated the warning, unsure if the others could hear me, but damn well determined that when, not if, I got out of this?

I was investing in some much better goddamn armor.

Hacking right and left I widened my stance automatically, years of training in the dojos, repeating the katas that we were taught as a unit, came back to me like never before.

In my ears I heard Scott, our melee specialist, and far and away the most naturally gifted of us all with in-close fighting, as he swore and cursed, good naturedly bullying us all back to our feet as we laid around exhausted.

We'd done it, grumbling all the time, as we'd forced ourselves through one more kata, one more training session, one more blur of blades as we trained until it was muscle memory, and the mind truly seemed to disengage.

Now, as then, it came to me.

That sense of disconnect as the body reacted, the jerky movements that were created as the brain attempted to inflict control upon it, vanished.

The mindless state, the Zen, or as Scott had called it, the *Mushin* came to the fore, and I seemed to retreat from my body, hovering behind me, watching both as if through my eyes, and yet set aside, an emotionless observer.

My body moved, almost dancing, as the blade existed apart from me no longer. Bodies collapsed, flames spreading and flaring as old cloth and flesh caught light.

I watched as my body flowed from stance to stance, dipping to one knee in 'The Kingfisher Rises', then launching forwards, the blade beating left and right in great arcs that flowed from one side to the other in 'Beating the Reeds'.

I pirouetted with a grace I would have sworn I was incapable of, even in the dojo, with solid ground beneath me, and yet I managed it here, the blade reaching out in a spiraling arc that gave 'Fireflies dance' its name, and all around me bodies fell, many diced and sliced over and over.

I lunged forwards, suddenly back in primacy as the gunfire rang out, a solid slug hitting my left shoulder and ricocheting off, then another hitting me solidly in the upper right of my chest.

Staggering, I almost fell, but pushed on, the pain radiating out from the chest, letting me know that the bullet had been stopped by the armor, but not fully.

That fucker was going to leave a bruise.

I saw him before me, both eyes replaced by a single band across his face, six glowing optics staring at me, a pattern of reds, blues and purple that glowed malevolently in the darkness as he fired again.

This time, one of his mindless drones caught the bullet for me, taking it in the back of the head and dropping bonelessly out of the way as I lunged to the left, stabbing out straight, the blade sinking into a torso, then ripping out to the right, eviscerating the specter.

It collapsed, hacked almost in two, and a bullet flashed past my ear, close enough I could feel its passage, as more and more gunfire rang out distantly.

I took two quick steps to the right, keeping bodies between the ghoul and I, stopping the fucker having a clean shot at me, as I cut and sliced.

Another from behind leapt at me, the body hitting me square in the back and sending me staggering forward three steps, the head dipping, aiming for my throat…

…then meeting the hissing, spitting coronal flare of the plasma sword as I dragged it back.

I felt the heat, as close as the blade was to my flesh, and yet still it was distant. Mushin cradled my mind as I cut and lunged, twisted and kicked.

A figure to my left took my foot in the stomach, doubling over as the blade hacked a body apart to my right, and I distantly noted that at some point I'd drawn the vibro-blade, holding it in my left hand.

I ripped the blade across the throat of the figure as it folded around my boot, severing the head, then stuck it downwards into the meat and bone of its shoulder and flipped the body aside.

I'd never felt so 'at one' with my surroundings as I did then, and I moved entirely on instinct, a step to the right as I straightened up, the plasma sword extended forwards, taking a figure in the head, driving through her face and out the back of the skull, before I rolled my wrist, the blade flashing right to lop off an outstretched arm, and then a second hand.

As the body before me collapsed, my left hand came up and back then flicked forwards, the vibro-blade flashing end over end to sink tip first into the Ghoul's skull with a meaty 'thwack' as its last bullet flashed back along the path.

This one connected.

I'd not had the chance to buy a new helmet yet, not a decent one, and I'd been wearing one of those we'd looted, a half helmet, covering the top of my head and the sides, low at the back of the neck, but exposing my face, and the bullet hit the padding on the right hand side, where it ran along the temple.

The metal there—a single arc that was clearly designed for just this—sent the bullet off again into the darkness, but not before the damage was done.

The world spun around me, light and noise like someone had set a fucking flashbang off against the side of my head deafened and blinded me, sending me to the floor.

I landed on all fours, the plasma blade—automatically—cut off as soon as the grip was released, and that was probably all that saved me from cutting myself in two.

The specters staggered and slumped as the ghoul's death brought a loss of control and guidance, but on the floor, reeling, stunned and with what had to be the beginnings of a concussion, I missed the chance to take advantage of it.

The next thing I felt were hands.

Arms wrapping around me, fingernails dragging and ripping free of rotting hands as the specters fell on me. Teeth chewed on my armored shoulder, frantic fingers ripping at my armor, trying to find a way inside. I curled into a ball on instinct, as more and more of them fell on me, and I shook, trying to reboot my brain, trying to make sense of it all.

Then my fingers found it. unconsciously I'd reached up, and yeah. Here it was.

I ripped the incendiaries free, dragging the pins out, snarling in my hidden cocoon under the pile of specters, refusing to go out on anyone's terms but my own.

CHAPTER SEVEN

I counted down, the standard five count for an incendiary grenade.

Five, as the pins fell free.

Four, as I shifted, getting my knees under me, bracing.

Three, as fingers grabbed at the edge of my helmet from behind, scrabbling across the padding, then shifting and gripping.

Two, as I threw my arms out and flipped the grenades into the mass all around me, before hunching down as low and small as I could go.

One, as the fingers tore into my face, and my left hand tore the medium medikit free of the pouch, my right dragging my revolver free.

Zero, as night was once again banished from the depths of this place. I roared in animalistic rage and pain, as the grenades went off, searing into life.

The world around me erupted into fire, horrific heat flaring out from the phosphorus, the compressed gas that would normally have fucked the entire basin up, caught and prevented from spreading in the normal pattern by the sheer press of bodies.

One side of the basin was filled with fire still, the explosion rocking the building, while the other had been compressed down, the gas expanding, but trapped by a literal mass of bodies.

The second grenade was forced into more of a rocket engine release, rather than a dispersal point, and specters were sent flying in all directions, flaming.

I rose in the middle of it, as flames literally passed over me, I forced myself to my feet, biting down on the medikit's rubber bungs, spitting them out and stabbing it into the only flesh I could reach, my own fucking face.

As I did it, teeth bared in a rictus of pain, a specter set alight and clinging to my back, the basin exploded in flames and flying body parts, and my revolver barked over and over.

A screeching figure appeared before me, flames wreathing it, arms outstretched as my revolver bucked, the slug taking them in the face, sending them catapulting backwards.

I flicked the gun around, pressing against the forehead of the flaming fucker on my back as it tried to chew on my armored throat, before bucking again, and releasing me of my unwanted passenger.

I turned and held my breath, the flames channeled outwards and away by all the bodies around me even as I fired twice more. Running, stumbling flame-wreathed figures tumbled to the ground. Puppets with their strings cut.

The medikit dumped its full load into my face, a writhing seething mass of nanites that tore forth, repairing even as the flames and horrific heat damaged me, and I ripped the empty container free, tossing it aside.

I released the magazine, losing it in the madness as I slammed a fresh one home, the gun accepting it, clicking as it slid the first round into place, and a half second later it was sent rocketing from the barrel.

Reaching down into the muck, I felt the hilt of the plasma sword, lifting it and triggering it to life again, as I stepped up and onto the literal mound of smoldering, burning bodies that surrounded me.

I turned, revolver tracking the next target, bucking and sending a figure tumbling, then another, then I missed. My lips curled in anger, drying from the heat, feeling like I was standing in a crematorium, as I stepped down and strode forwards.

I stepped over the ghoul, seeing only a handful more specters between me and a blackness that spoke of the next basin, and I fired twice, bodies seeming to flip from sight with the force of the impacts.

The last three ran at me, and I spun, pirouetting on one heel and I beheaded them both, then lined the revolver up on the last, pulling the trigger again.

His feet came up as his head went back, looking like he'd been clotheslined as he flipped, crashing to the floor. With that the basin before me, was suddenly empty.

I strode forwards, heart hammering as the world around me slid slowly back into primacy. The distant sound of gunfire grew closer all at once, and I snarled, flicking the release on the plasma blade. The containment arc crackled and released as I rolled my wrist away from myself, the flare of fire billowing forwards and dissipating. I clamped it onto the bottom of my back, the mag-plate catching it and holding the hilt and projector, as I slid another magazine free, releasing it from the revolver, catching it and sliding a new one in.

I listened to the comfortingly familiar sound of the hurricane revolver as it reloaded, the 'clack, clack' of the revolving cylinder as the magazine pushed bullets up into it, each locking into place before it moved on.

The final 'clunk' as the last chamber clicked closed reverberated through the gun, and I holstered it, drawing the rifle up and to my shoulder, stepping forward, drawing in a long breath as the temperature finally dropped to a level that was similar to the depths of the fucking desert.

My lungs felt burnt by the heat, my skin peeling in places from the equivalent of sunburn, while other areas, notably my face, was suffering from serious blistering, not to mention the damage done to my eyes.

The only reason I wasn't crippled was that heat damage, as minor as its changes were physically, compared to flesh being pierced, torn and stripped away, was far easier for the nanites to repair and replace.

As I strode into the next basin, I saw the reason for the gunfire, even as my brain stepped up a gear in its processing of the world around, reaching almost normal levels of competence.

At the opposite end of the basin, standing side by side, almost shoulder to shoulder, were *two entire squads* of the guild.

Julius had made it, and they were fucking slaughtering the specters with sustained gunfire.

I sagged slightly, the relief bubbling inside me, making me feel almost weak at the knees…until I saw movement behind the squads.

Julius and the two new squads stood at the head of the basin, where the slope increased sharply down to the piles of dead and dying specters, and they fired steadily, shifting from one to another, making sure of each target as they went.

Behind them though, where the steps lead down from the gantry way, movement was clear, and it damn well wasn't friendly.

"Julius!" I sent, and again cursed the lack of a proper tac-net. I was forced to send it through the keystone, like I was making any other call, and his fucking RI or keystone settings refused the connection, returning a bland 'please try again later'.

I recognized the fucking message, it was like one the army had set up for me to give to fucking officers that were wasting my goddamn time!

"Reign! Luna, Gessh!" I barked into the keystone instead, and due to their being acknowledged as part of my team normally, the connection was accepted.

"Kabutt!" Reign responded, clear relief in her voice. "You fucking lunatic, where the hell are you?"

"I'm in the basin, Julius and the others, do you know where they are?"

"They're here?" she responded. "Oh thank fuck, we're low on ammo, and that's with the fucking reloads, okay we rescued that guy, and—"

"They're about to get jumped!"

"What?"

"Julius and the others, they won't accept my comms, there's movement behind them, I can fucking see it in the light of their gunfire, they're being set up!"

"What the hell are you going to do about it?" Reign asked, and for a second I paused, wanting to shout something like 'why the fuck is this down to me?'

It was though, and I damn well didn't have long. Whoever was lining up behind them was in a mixture of stealth suits and active-camo, that they were triggered now spoke to their intentions.

You did NOT sneak up on people in a firefight without unfriendly intentions. You certainly didn't run down batteries and move in that level of gear without a damn good reason.

The very best case scenario was that they were likely to be shot by their friends should they need to retreat. No this was clearly an ambush, and I cursed, wishing I had a better fucking rifle for this, a sniper setup at least, but no use whining.

I pulled the EMP grenade out, thumbed the activation and threw it as far to my right as I could.

The basin sloped up towards the others and the fuckheads behind them, and with the wall of the basin on my left, I was left with few places to be.

I crouched, sending one last message to Reign and the others, fairly sure they'd be safe from the effects, the propagation on them was shit after all, but still.

"EMP out!" I barked, before cutting off the comm, and setting all my electronic systems, including my goddamn eyes and more, on a three second shutdown and reboot.

I braced myself, rifle aimed as best I could, and as my eyes blinked offline, then a shout and echoing crackle and boom rang out, I opened fire.

Three shots, one after another careful to keep the angle the same, and making only slight shifts to the left with each one as I pulled the trigger.

More screams rang out, and as my eyes booted up, I heard the gunfire shifting, hammering into the ground nearby.

I hunched down, pressing myself as flat as I could, waiting as my systems rebooted, and gritting my teeth as sudden shouts and gunfire rang out.

There were a few seconds more of pitch darkness, where I didn't dare fire, knowing that the chances were that I'd hit Julius and his people more than anyone else, before my eyes flickered back online.

Blinking, I ignored the 'reboot' and similar messages, sighting down the rifle as its less advanced sight flickered and whirred, adjusting and zooming in.

There!

Julius and his people were fighting, the ambushers not in position, and caught as out in the open as he was, their stealth suits powered down by the EMP.

Both sides were firing at each other, their armor taking hits, some shrugging off, others penetrating. I opened fire as well, aiming carefully, picking off the figures still on the stairs, as someone started firing into their backs from behind the group.

That did it, the short, brutal fight breaking down as the ambushers, were in turn ambushed.

I managed to get off two more shots, mentally marking down another kill, before the last shot rang out, and the fight was over.

What would have been a one-sided slaughter had ended very differently, and I sagged with relief as I saw the figures slowly standing again, heard the shouts for medikits, and recognized Julius' voice bellowing at the squads to 'sound off'.

I lay there for longer than I meant to. I realized later, my body, pushed far past its limits in the dancing kata, had practically shutdown, and I'd gone borderline catatonic until hands reached down and gently turned me over.

CHAPTER EIGHT

The noise of the others had become a buzz in my ears long since, and despite the stress I'd almost fallen asleep in the adrenaline crash.

Now, as the lights bathed me, I reached up, accepting a hand from a battered Luna, who half dragged me to my feet.

"Fucks' sake, boss," she said, shaking her head. "I know you're lazy, but having a nap in the middle of a firefight?"

"Hey…," I croaked, before licking my lips and trying again. "I made…sure the fight was done…first."

"Yeah, yeah," she said, shaking her head.

Gessh pushed in, grabbing me roughly in a bear hug and pulling me in tight. "You stupid fucker," she whispered into the side of my helmet, barely loud enough for me to hear. "You saved me you stupid fuck, now what am I gonna do with you?"

"You're gonna hand him over unless you ask me real nice to share." Reign pushed her aside and took her place, staring into my eyes and shaking her head, before pulling me close. "You mad bastard," she whispered, before pushing me back long enough to kiss me.

I grinned, then sagged as my knees buckled, others grabbed me and I was lowered into a sitting position as Reign checked me over, looking for wounds.

"You're actually okay?" she asked a few seconds later, shaking her head as if she didn't believe it herself. "How the hell do you keep doing this crap to yourself?"

"I just do what comes naturally." I shrugged and got a disbelieving smile from her as I reached up and pulled the helmet off. "I swear I'm investing in a better fucking helmet though. I'm sick of them always breaking."

"Kabutt." The voice came from my left and I looked up wearily, seeing Julius limp over. "How you doing you crazy bastard?"

"I'm alright," I said. "Tired, but that's it, you?"

"I feel like I was hit by a transport." He twisted slightly and winced as something twinged. "That was you then?" He jerked his head back behind him, taking in the fight presumably, and I shrugged.

"The EMP and the gunfire?" I asked. "Yeah, best I could come up with on short notice."

"It nearly wasn't enough," he said, his voice low and tired. "They got a few good people."

"Who were they?"

"The fuckheads who lived and worked here," he said. "Shift-change apparently, they came in behind us and closed the place up, armed up, and came expecting to ambush us."

"Nearly worked as well," I agreed.

"Damn right." He sighed, pulling his helmet off and scratching at sweat matted hair underneath. "That's the problem with fighting specters, you get in the mindset of slaughtering them, they feel no fear, no remorse, and so the only way to take them down is with overwhelming firepower. The best way to kill them in a situation like this? It would be the worst against thinking opponents."

"Why the hell didn't they just fire from above?"

"Not enough room," Reign replied, cutting in. "When we came up from behind them, the way the gantry twists, only two of us could get around, so they moved down, thinking they could spread out and kill the entire squad in one go. It was risky, but if not for you being a lucky fuck it'd have worked."

"Luck-schmuck," I muttered. "Tell me I'm getting better guild rates and a bonus after this." I directed that to Julius, who snorted, then nodded.

"Maybe a bonus, but you'll damn well pay your way like the rest of us," he said, but I saw the quirk of a smile.

"Worth a try. So, what now?"

"We finish the sweep, make sure that there's nobody else down here, and no more specters, then we report this, too many non-specter dead to avoid ACE being involved…and there's the door."

"Door?"

"A door," Reign repeated. "Literally, a big fuck off door in the wall."

"That's where they normally are, right?" I said, too tired to give a damn about the details.

"True, but they're not normally buried below the Artem City Wall, and they don't normally offer passage through it," Julius added dryly. "That's one that ACE is going to go apeshit about."

"I thought that was how all the portals built into the underside of the walls were? Like hidden ways in and out for the wall teams?"

"Yeah, they are, but they're usually maintained and managed by the Wall. They're under the city's control. This one isn't. This is a fucking secret exit and entrance. A smugglers route, or in this case? A flesh stripper team."

"I'm calling in that bonus then," I said. "Fuck this shit, we'll help with the sweep, but any chance of us being out of here before those corrupt fucks turn up?"

"I think we can probably…" He trailed off as another of his guild member jogged over.

"Guild master, there's another basin behind this wall," the guild member said, nodding to the wall behind me.

"Fuck, gear up!" Julius ordered.

I waved at him wearily. "Don't bother, I already cleared it, or most of it anyway."

"You did that?" the guild member asked, frowning. "Who with?"

"Just him," Luna said shaking her head. "Mad bastard jumped in and started fucking them all up, while we pulled back to rescue Todds."

"Who?" I muttered blearily, only to have another figure step up and salute me, standing at parade rest.

"Corporal Severin Todds sir, scout," he said as I stared up at him, grudgingly noting the perfect salute.

"Fuck's sake, Todds, we're not the army," Julius said.

"No sir, but I need a new team, and this one rescued me."

"Subtle." Reign sighed, before nodding to Todds. "He's a father of two, single parent, so he needs the income, sarge, he's a damn good stealth assassin and scout, as well as not a complete asshole…"

"Thanks, Reign." Todds grinned and relaxed as I stood, returning the salute.

"I mean, sure he's an asshole…" She grinned. "Just not a complete one."

"And there's the Reign we all know and loathe," came another voice as a full blooded elf stepped up, joining the group. "Blunt and graceless in everything, but that's the human side for you." The elf glanced from Reign to me, and then clearly dismissed us both as he turned to Julius. "We've completed our guild obligation, and we're leaving. Have our cut sent to us by breakfast."

With that he turned and strode off, and I looked over at Julius, waiting for him to go apeshit, and was stunned as he just glared off after the departing team.

"What the fuck?" I said. "He's a dick to you, and you just fucking take it?"

"Leave it, Kabutt," Julius snapped, turning his back and walking away.

"The fuck I will." My adrenaline-ravaged body straightened, as I turned to the retreating elf. "OI!" I bellowed. "You, ya pointy eared cock-holster, get your arse back here and help clear the site, the jobs not done!"

My voice echoed around the basin for long seconds as he froze, before turning back and glaring at me.

"You *dare* to speak to me like that?"

"Yeah I fucking do," I growled, feeling new strength running through my body, driven by the surge of anger as I picked my way across the piled bodies towards him. "Considering I just saved your fucking life, and you don't even have the good manners to fucking help clean up? Yeah, I'll speak to you however I want, dickhead."

"You forget yourself!" he hissed. "You're nothing but a failure, kicked out of the army and without the good grace to slink away and die. Instead your surround yourself with mongrels and think that our forbearance is approval. Learn. Your. Place. Or I'll personally see you thrown from the guild, and stripped for parts!"

I stared at him, stunned by the vitriol, the sheer hatred I'd seen in his eyes, then I reached behind my back, and dragged the plasma hilt free, gripping it tightly.

"You fucking want to try that right now?" I asked him in a low, rough voice. "You ready to back your fucking words up?"

"Kabutt!" Julius barked at me from behind. "I told you to leave it, Sergeant!"

"Sir." I looked back at him, then to the elf, seeing the fucker was already walking off with his team.

"Leave it." Reign was there by my side. "Trust me, I'll explain later, just…leave it for now."

"He…"

"I know. Please," she said, and I glared at her for long seconds, before slapping the plasma blade back against the mag-plate.

"This better be good." I stomped back off and followed the others through to join Julius, who'd set off ahead of us.

"It's not good," Julius admitted when he saw I wasn't going to let it go. "It's not good, and I hate the situation, but that's life, we all have to put up with things now and then, and Trees is one of those."

"Trees?"

"It's the name he goes by, he's old school, thinks all humans are an affront against nature, Orcs should be enslaved with obedience chips and dwarves? Best not to even go there," Reign said grimly. "As to 'half breed bastards'? We should have been drowned at birth and our parents executed for the shame they brought on their houses."

"I thought the elven corpos were all about breeding the rest of us out of existence?" Luna asked, looking unimpressed, but unconcerned as well.

"They are, and yeah, they've been driving the whole 'spread the blessings' mindset for a while." Reign shrugged. "Some just refuse it. He's one of those that got kicked out for mouthing off too much. So now he and his team have to live with us filthy 'lesser races' and get real jobs. The majority of the guilds won't let their kind in, they cause too many problems..."

"But we needed money." Julius sighed. "I shouldn't have taken it, but we damn well needed to hire more to cover the contracts we have, and since I took it, well. He pushes more and more each day."

"The jobs not done 'til we've confirmed the site is clear though, right?" I asked, and he shook his head.

"The job for a reserve team, one pulled in when the shit hits the fan, is only to help rescue the survivors. His contractual obligation was done as soon as the fight was over, and Todds here was rescued. Now, if we're going by the contract, the job falls back to the original team..." He shrugged. "It was intended so that if someone was a dick about things, then the original team could get some help, but not have to share the overall completion bonus—if there was one—if someone arrived right at the end and hadn't really helped."

"That sounds..."

"Look, the contract is letter and intent, alright? The letter of the contract means they're done. The intent is clear that they *should* stay and help, but they don't *have* to."

"And threatening to have me booted?" I asked.

"One of the conditions they slipped into the contract when I took their money was that he can demand a review of any team and its actions, including any loot you might have recovered and not handed in. If that was the case, then yeah, he could enforce that we booted or censured you," Julius admitted.

"Fuck's sake, man, seriously? You mean that fucknut's got his boot on my neck?"

"Only if you break the rules," Julius said. "The first job? I told you it was fine as a welcome bonus, after that? He could, yeah."

"So if we loot the mods, we could be booted."

"Yeah...and you know he's going to demand an accounting of your actions soon."

"I'll give him an accounting alright." I lifted my plasma sword again.

"No, you'll damn well stay out of his way, sarge." Julius straightened, speaking with authority. "For now, I don't want you anywhere near him, and I'll be taking the recording of your actions today now, please."

"What?"

"The recording," Reign said quickly. "Yes, Guildmaster, our apologies." She sounded properly humble, which left me even more confused as I cut the recording, then sent it to Julius.

"All of you…" he said, then nodded. "Got them all, thank you. Recording off?"

"Yeah." I grunted, finally understanding as the hints were dropped.

"Great, so again, watch yourself. I'll have the guild AI scrub the majority of that conversation from the recording, but in future, remember anything you or we say, he might get his hands on."

"I don't give a shit," I said tiredly, sitting on a mound of corpses as the others looked around.

"Kabutt," Reign said after a few seconds. "How many of these did you kill?"

"I don't know…All of them?"

"ALL of them?" Julius repeated after a few seconds, as the others with him, the remnants of the other squad and Todds, one of the apparent survivors of Team-22 looked at me in shock.

"Yeah?" I said, shrugging. "It took a while, but apart from a handful of them that Gessh got earlier, I got most of them?"

"Okay people, lets reactivate recording please." Julius grinned. "I want this entire section scanned visually from one side to the other, I need a fucking record of this please."

"Of what?" I asked, forcing myself to my feet and looking around.

"Just do as you're told, Kabutt. Accept that as someone that rose to lead a fucking guild, I have the occasional reason for what I do."

"Yes, sir." I sighed, starting to look around, searching for the ghoul from before. Resolving that I might as well loot that fucker and get my damn knife back. It took a minute or two to find him, and most of that was spent fielding stupid questions, like; 'why are these all burned?'

"Because I set a pair of incendiary grenades off on either side of me," I replied grimly.

"On either side?" the idiot asked. "Why?"

"Because I was surrounded, obviously."

"But they're incendiary grenades!"

"Yeah?"

"They could have killed you!"

"And if I hadn't, they fucking would have."

"But the air temperature, even if you didn't get cooked to death straight away…"

"And that's why I stabbed myself in the face with a medikit." I sighed. "Seriously, if it didn't work? I was dead anyway, if it did? Well, here I am."

"I think the Sergeant has had enough of your questions, Filbert," Julius said, and I nodded him my thanks. "So, I think I'll need the AI to confirm this, but we're looking at over three hundred specters." He nodded to the room at large.

"Yeah?" I asked.

"In this basin," he clarified.

"Right?" I replied not getting what he was saying through the brain fog that had returned with a vengeance.

"You, Kabutt, personally killed more than most teams manage in a week," he said clearly. "We'll talk later about your bonus, but yeah, you earned the right to fuck off and avoid this part of the job."

"No." I sighed.

"No?"

"No," I repeated. "You're down a squad, and as much as I want to, we've already had a team of dickheads sneak up on us. We'll stay, but…"

"Yes?"

"The assholes who tried to ambush us?"

"Yeah?"

"We need some new gear…" I hinted.

"You killed at least four of them between you," he agreed. "Grab what you want, on my authority, and the guild will cover the cost of repairs of it."

"Fuck yeah." I grinned. "Stealth suits all round."

"Grab what you want, as I said, but sweep the area first, as near as we can tell the place is clear, but there were hidden rooms, so let's be sure," Julius clarified, and we did.

The cleanup and search took another hour, just making sure, and through all of it, Gessh hobbled, determined not to admit to the pain she was in, and leaving bloody footprints here and there.

We'd given her our medikits, and we'd found several more scattered about. We'd also—quietly—once we were sure the recording devices were off, and there was nobody nearby, looted one of the storage crates of mods.

The majority we left, they were needed to help to identify next of kin after all, but the ones that were in sets, and removed from single donors?

We looted something from each, and when we left, sitting back in the air-cab—enjoying a massage—we had a trunk full of parts. The massage was compliments of Johnny-cab and paid for by the 'discretionary fund' that was going to be fucking increased if I had anything to do with it.

CHAPTER NINE

By the time we got back to our new home, we were all filthy from the day's work, all knackered, and even Gessh had had enough of complaining that she 'was fine really'.

She was settled in the main living area, with her foot elevated and a shot of 'knock-out' in hand for if the pain got too bad, while Reign and Luna went to see Oshbob.

I hit the shower, covered in shit as I was, and scrubbed away what seemed like a damn months' worth of filth. Getting cleaned up and into almost clean clothes again afterwards, I returned to the main room, sitting down across from Gessh and shaking my head at the fucker's stubbornness.

"You can use that you know," I pointed out.

"I know." She nodded, forcing a smile. "I'll be…"

"Your fucking foot is wrecked," I said flatly. "You should have gone straight to Lion, but you insisted on waiting until the job was done. Well, it's done, alright? Take the knock-out, we'll wake you when we get to Lion, you can still pick your shit, so don't be so bloody stupid."

"I'm fine!" she snapped, her sudden surge of anger surprising me as she started to sit up, only to jerk and let a groan out between clenched teeth.

She'd been adamant that it was a replacement job, but she'd refused to let anyone look at it, but now? Blood was seeping out of the torn sections of her boot and I stood, moving round to kneel by her side.

Reaching out, I put a hand on her shoulder and she jerked, making it clear she didn't want to be touched. I accepted that, but I didn't move away beside lifting my hand, and I waited until she looked at me.

"What?" she growled, before shaking her head and trying again. "Sorry, Kabutt, look I'm…"

"If you say you're 'fine' one more time I will stab you with that knock-out," I said in a low, friendly voice. "You're not fine, unless 'fine' stands for Freaking Insane Neurotic and Excitable. Those are all things that are fine, in any family. They just make it more fun, but the state you're in?" I shook my head.

"Gessh, you've had five small medikits. That's the same as at least two full medium kits. You've been popping stims constantly, and you're dripping blood on the fucking table I spent two hours cleaning…STOP!" I snapped as she started to move her leg. "Fuck's sake Gessh, I told you to keep it elevated." I straightened the soaked rag that was under her foot, even as I straightened her leg out again.

"You were complaining…"

"I was pointing out that despite all those fucking nannites, enough to attach *two new fucking legs* no less, you're still bleeding!" I glared at her. "Do I need to make it an order to take it off and show me?"

"Fuck's sake, Kabutt, we weren't even gone half an hour, and already you're trying to order my sister to take her clothes off and show you?" Luna sighed, strolling in through the open door with Reign right behind her.

"You…oh bugger off." I snorted. "You were quicker than I thought you'd be."

"So you don't deny you were trying to get Gessh to take her pants off then?"

"Her boot actually," I corrected. "And you damn well know if I was going to tell her to show me anything for a twitch it'd be her tits, so now that's out of the way, how about we find out why Gessh's foot is so fucked up?"

"Damn, tired of me already." Reign sighed, moving around and standing next to me.

I straightened, putting my arm around her waist subtly and giving her a squeeze, before letting go, as we both looked down at the seeping blood.

"You can see it once we get to Lion," Gessh growled, lifting her foot down. "Did you sell those parts?"

"Yeah." Luna nodded. "Here."

I felt the knock on my ident, the same as I assumed the others did, and I accepted, nodding in approval as the creds were added to my current balance. Just over twenty thousand, adding those to the credits I'd already had, and the bonuses and various payouts I'd had so far, and even with paying for the repairs I'd needed from Lion after the major's betrayal, I was doing pretty good.

I had nearly a hundred and fifty thousand credits now, buying some things like the new mattress wasn't a frivolous expense after all, it was a fucking *necessity*.

We'd have more once the emergency job was paid out as well, but regardless, we weren't exactly hurting for money right now.

"Keep mine," Reign said, and I looked at her in question.

"What?" I asked.

"Look, we need a slush fund alright?" Reign said to us all. "If that hits my account, forty percent of it is gone straight away, and we damn well need to pay for some shit in here, like a decent work area, food, hell, some clean sheets please! Seriously, we need to set up an account for that, and rather than those assholes taking the creds from me, just call that my contribution for a while, okay?"

"Okay…you guys want me to hold this, or someone else?" Luna asked, glancing around, the slight twitch by the corner of her eye showing she was nervous about how we'd all react to her keeping the discretionary fund.

"You keep it," I agreed, twisting and popping my back with a grunt, then a sigh of relief. "Right, those stealth suits are getting fixed up for us by Julius, but we'll need to wait until they're repaired and the batteries are charged before we can do much with them, and I think we all need some gear. First stop, Lion's, and get Gessh fixed up, then we're off shopping. Any objections?"

"Fuck," Luna grumbled. "I hate shopping."

"Even for grenades?" Gessh asked, forcing a smile, and Luna shrugged.

"Taxi is inbound, three minutes," Reign announced, heading out of the room. "I'll hit the loo and catch up."

I nodded, then grinned. "Then we're off to Lucky's place," I announced, having just remembered it. "I've no fucking doubt they looted my quarters, but we'll check it out, then we're off after Lucky's room, loot that fucker down to the ground."

"Sounds good to me," Luna agreed, as she helped her sister to her feet, the two of them moving to the door. "You decided what you're going to do about Todds?"

"Who?" I asked, frowning, then nodding as my memory caught up. "The guy that survived this morning?"

"That's the one. Two survived, but that Todds, stealth specialist, right?"

"Yeah," I muttered, following the pair along as they took the stairs down slowly, the old metal creaking under our weight and steps as we went. "We'll see."

"We could do with a few extra people boss," Luna said, not taking the hint as we went. "A stealth specialist could be just what we need, Reign is lethal with her sniper rifle, and yeah, give her one of those suits and she's gonna dominate when she's got range, but a real stealth? If they're a specialist then they probably do hacking and shit as well, and we could really do with that, not having to hire Bowdoin for the jobs anymore?"

"Yeah." I sighed. I'd been ready to tell her to fuck off and we'd all talk about it tonight over pizza, but that was a fair point, and knowing how hard a real specialist was to come across? If I left it, they'd soon be snapped up by another team.

"You want him to join us?" I asked her, and she nodded.

"I think we could do with it," she said. "If he's as good as he seemed—he'd been clinging to the wall surrounded by fucking specters for twenty minutes and they had no clue he was there—then we'd be mad to pass him up."

"True, and for the stealth suit to hide all the emissions the way that one had, it had to be an expensive one…hell, twenty minutes and the fucker was still running? He's got some heavy duty batteries in the suit at least, most only last a few minutes at most. He's invested in his gear at least," I muttered, looking around the warehouse as we reached the bottom, and again considering the gear we needed to bring this place up to speed to work for us all.

It wasn't long before I heard the creaking and clanging of Reign hurrying down the stairs behind us, and then quickly after that, the warehouse was falling away behind us as we took off, heading sedately across the city to Lion's place.

Aircars were an absolute luxury, they really were, the trip by ground taxi would have been at least two hours, here instead we were landing after fifteen minutes, even the busy air-lanes far more convenient than the ground based ones.

The cab was a luxury in time only though, as despite the damn cost, the inside of this one was bare-bones when it came to extras.

It still cost us over a hundred creds, and I winced as Reign paid it. For some reason she'd taken to arranging these things and more for us. She'd unofficially become our quartermaster, which meant that realistically, when we all transferred our share of the cost to her, it cost us another forty percent on top. That needed dealing with asap.

The simple and fastest method was for one of us to take it over, but the time honored second in command slot in a squad came with certain duties, and honestly, she was too good at them for us to consider anyone else.

She was marking her position in the squad, and we'd all accepted it. As part of that, and by the end of the flight, she was mid call to Julius at the guild, accepting Severin Todds as a new squad member, on a trial basis.

He'd already been contacted and was apparently relieved over our decision. He'd agreed to meet us at my old apartment block, and as we half helped, half dragged Gessh out of the cab, Reign finished the call and nodded to me.

"You were right, Julius wants us to take on the other survivor as well," she warned me.

"What was his name?" I asked absently, checking the area, noting the gangbangers sat off to one side on a set of stone benches, watching us in turn.

"Ocracoke."

"Fucking mouthful there…" I muttered shaking my head. "What's he do?"

"No specialization, he's offered to train, but wants his team to cover the costs, so…"

"So nobodies paying for that for him, because he could just leave and we're all out of pocket." I shook my head. "Fuck's sake, I don't like it."

"Neither do I," Reign admitted moving in to walk alongside me, as we followed Luna who was half supporting Gessh.

"Tell him no," I said after a few seconds.

"Honestly?" Reign said, turning around and walking backwards, checking the gangers weren't following us. "I'd say give it a day or so. See what Todds says. Might be that he's good, just broke as fuck."

"Fine," I grumbled, uncaring either way. "Luna, you sure you don't want a hand?" I called forwards.

"I'm f—" Gessh called back, only to be cut off by Luna.

"We're alright boss. She's been carrying my drunk ass for years, about time I repaid the favor, and we all know you'd just try and get her naked."

"How the hell did I end up with a rep already?" I asked Reign with a sigh.

"It was when you tried to choke me with your dick." She grinned at me. "You really weren't subtle you know!"

"Fuck's sake!" I groaned. "I never should have—"

"So you don't want to do it again to me later?" Reign interrupted and I broke off. "Yeah, thought so!" She grinned.

"You…are you alright?" I asked, changing what I was going to say.

"I feel like I'm going to vomit at any minute." She sighed, seeing what I was getting at. "That's why I hit the loo, quick upchuck, then I was good to go again. Seriously, even that bit of fun, and how much I enjoyed it—which believe me, I know was a lot less than *you* did, but still—that was enough to leave me feeling like I'd basically eaten from one of those all night shitty meat bars outside of the clubs. Like I've got a few minutes to get to the loo before I lose all control?"

"Yeah?" I winced, feeling terrible I'd let her do it at all.

"Well, it's like that, and will be for a few more days."

"I'm sorry," I apologized unthinkingly. "I shouldn't have let you…"

"I did what I wanted to do," she corrected me cutting me off. "And I'd like to do it again, and a lot more. But yeah, me offering it again later today? That was a joke, sorry. You'll have to make do with your hand."

"I served ten years in the APS, I'm used to that," I joked, bumping her with my shoulder. "Come on, let's get Gessh sorted and get to work."

"Yes boss," she agreed with a grin.

Lion was half sprawled on one of the operation chairs as we entered, his left forearm open down to the metal core as he worked, sparks and more flying as he apparently fixed or upgraded one of his integrated tools.

"Be right with you…" he called over cheerfully, before seeing Gessh and the way she was limping. "Ah hell, girl, what did they do to you now?" He shook his head. "Seriously, give me two minutes, I'm nearly done."

"I can wait." She grinned at him, despite the pale skin that was starting to really worry me.

"Can we at least get the boot off now?" I asked as we lifted her into the other chair, and she nodded, letting out a long breath.

"I'm going to take this really soon, just…Lion?" she said, holding up the knock-out up where he could see it and nodding.

"Yeah?" he asked, glancing at the seeping blood from the boot.

"I need something stealthy and sexy, you get me?" she asked, and he nodded.

"Sabaton Industries," he replied. "You want awesome feet or legs? They're specialists, it's all they make. Well that and subdermal armoring, but that's for the really paranoid market. Here, check out this one."

We stood there silently as he apparently sent her a file, followed by a grunt from her, and then a quick non-verbal sibling discussion between Gessh and Luna.

Reign bumped me with her shoulder and nodded in their direction, as if to ask if I knew what was going on, and I shook my head.

"Tell me there's a discount for the pair?" Luna said to Lion.

"Not a chance," he replied with a shake of his head that set his wild hair bouncing. "I'd need to order them in, rush delivery by the Zon drone? It'd be here in an hour, and that'd be added to the bill if you're sure you want the pair."

"The pair?" I asked, frowning, before grunting as both Lion and Gessh sent me the same file.

Leg Mod	Tier: Three
The Sabaton 'Black Knight' package is for those who can lose a limb, and yet keep their good mood—and the fight—going.	
The Black Knight Full Limb replacement comes with a significant boost over any organic system, from a considerable improvement in speed, jump range and even including optional stealth enhancing cushioning plates on all surfaces, the Black Knight is an experience your enemies won't live long enough to regret!	
Black Knight legs come in three optional levels, Foot, Lower Leg, Upper Leg, but for the full effect? We recommend a full limb replacement.	
Note: *Sabaton Industries is not responsible for any injuries sustained using only one of the Knight class limbs without its assigned pairing.*	
Dexterity: 12	
Durability: 100/100	**Slot Cost:** 8 [4 per unit]
Availability: Orderable	**Credit Cost:** 59,999 Per Unit

I winced, looking at them, and asked Gessh bluntly; "Can you afford this slot cost?"

"I can," she assured me. "Leaves me with three points clear."

"You'll need to keep those points, if you want to wear a suit," I pointed out to her. "And even then, I'm not sure if you'll be able to get a suit that works with only three."

"The spinal mod?" Lion asked me, and I nodded. "Here."

The file he sent me was short and to the point, but damn, it was exactly what I needed, and I almost ordered it on the spot.

Spinal Tap	**Tier**: Two
The Okakanji Spinal Tap Mod is truly a game changer for those that require external linkages for racing, drone maintenance or even heavy construction. This model integrates with and enhances the myelinated neurons it connects to, creating a symbiotic linkage between the nanites and the user. This linkage enhances saltatory conduction from the spinal cord up to and including the entire neural pathway. **Note**: *Unconfirmed reports of up to 67mps have been claimed by this mod, although only for short bursts.* **Note:** *Claims on improved reflexes and improvements over other, competing systems, are valid only where the Okakanji system has been integrated with sufficient nanites. Due to the vast differences in biology this system cannot be guaranteed without sufficient nanites, and Okakanji systems recommend each individual have sufficient nanites on hand before integration.* *As always, as well as providing ground breaking technology, the spinal tap also offers additional attachment points for internal bracing, armoring or organ replacements* **Warranty**: [12 months] **Toughness**: 15	
Durability: 100/100	**Slot Cost**: 6
Availability: Orderable	**Credit Cost**: 149,999

"Can…can you get this?" I asked Lion, disbelievingly. I'd seen these fuckers claims, and spoken with one APS operator that had been testing one. Literally one guy. He'd vanished soon after completing training, KIA in the field.

Now though? I remembered the speed of that fucker, how for admittedly short busts, he'd been a blur across the battlefield, his normal speed was slightly faster than the rest of us, that was it. Literally 'slightly'.

It'd been enough that we'd ALL been fighting to get our mods redone with these, and we'd been told as one that the tests were inconclusive, and the army wasn't damn well spending that on us grunts.

Now though, knowing that the Major had his own black ops squad? I was betting this was why certain operators had just vanished, seemingly off the edge of the planet. None of his own team had seen Franklin die, they'd just gotten the flat-line signal, and a big explosion that left nothing identifiable.

We'd all thought something had gone wrong with the onboard reactor, and had spent days pouring over the details, searching for an issue that might cause ours to go next.

If it'd been a setup though, one that the major had done to get Franklin out to work on his team? Damn.

"I can, but I'd need paying upfront for it and it'd take a few days to get," Lion said, before holding his hands up as I glared at him. "It's not that I don't trust you to pay for it, and yeah, you'd have to trust me on that one, but frankly, I don't run any line of credit with these things. That's not 'don't like to', by the way, its 'can't'. So with this? I'd need to buy the fucker first, so yeah, you want it? I can get it, but seriously it's the only way I'm getting that in."

"Fuck."

"Is it good?" Reign asked, and I shared it with the group.

"Can you get four?" I asked, and Lion blinked in surprise.

"Shit Kabutt, that's six hundred thousand credits…you pull in that kind of scratch? Fuck yeah I can order them, but…"

"But?"

"But, if I order those, all at once, expect me to get hit damn soon after they arrive. There's some dodgy fuckers that try to do over the higher end chop-shops, alright? It's one of the reasons so many of us are under the 'protection' of the Orc or others like him. If you're not? Expect to get hit."

"And even with being under Oshbob, you think you'll get hit for those?"

"Hell yes. Four units that total over half a million credits? Fuck, man, that's worth more than my shop. I'd bet anyone that sees that order spreads the word, and that it's going to here? A shithole on the outside of the city? Fuck yeah. that's if they didn't just not bother to deliver."

"You think that's likely?" I asked, frowning.

"That they'd hit us? With that kind of disposable and easily moved gear, yeah."

"With the supplier not delivering it."

"Honestly, no, if we ordered them one at a time. It's if there's a single load of them in transit…"

"Lion?" Gessh interrupted.

"Yeah?" he asked, looking over.

"Fix my fucking legs, will you? Leave that bullshit for later?"

"Fuck, am so sorry, yeah! Okay, just the damaged—"

"The full set, both legs," Luna said, before looking down at her sister and grinning. "Looks like we need to save up for mine next then, or people will be able to tell the difference too easy."

"Don't worry," Gessh said, clutching her sister's hand in thanks. "We'll pay for it together."

"Ah, sisterly love, doesn't it make you want to vomit?" Reign said to me, smiling and winking at the sisters as they fixed her with a mirror-like glare.

"So, an hour for the legs to get here, and a few hours for the attachment?" I asked Lion and he nodded, already cutting the boot away from the Gessh's foot as the girls presumably transferred the credits over.

"It's on order now, thank you," he said to them, then nodded to me. "Yeah, four hours or so, maybe five, depending on complications. It'll clean me out of 'nites as well, so if you need any for medikits, you'll need to get them elsewhere."

"Damn." I grunted.

"Okay, well, Todds is waiting for us at the arcology, so…" Reign said and I nodded.

"We'll get a taxi there, I can sort it," I offered. "Luna, Gessh, you alright here?"

"We'll be fine," Luna assured me, even as Lion pulled the boot apart, a sludge of congealed blood and flesh sliding free, along with what looked like minced bones.

"Fuck!" I gagged, even as Gessh raised the knockout canister, and unspeaking, stabbed herself in the leg with it.

She was out in seconds, as Lion, utterly unphased, poked and prodded at the mess that was her foot.

"Impressive," he muttered. "You can see where the nanites tried to reconstruct the foot, but without a medical guidance program, there was just too much wrong."

"Explain?" I requested, only half listening as I ordered a cab for Reign and I.

"Basically, medikits work because there's a clear bit of damage. A bullet hole for example, the mass is preprogrammed into us and into the 'nites, they orient as to location, and rebuild. With her foot? It's too much, whatever hit her pulped the bones and surrounding tissue, the 'nites were trying to rebuild but the mass was just mush, so they couldn't form a cohesive framework to build on. Looking here?" He pointed to a section that just looked wrong and I nodded, gritting my teeth.

"Looks like some thought they were working on a ribcage injury, sections of bone were being rebuilt into a rib, and this looks a little like lung tissue…then the rest were tearing that apart and trying to reconstitute her foot. That's the problem."

"Fuck that can happen?" I asked, shaking my head.

"Why the hell you think you don't just pop a medikit and close all the hospitals then?" Lion snorted. "Kabutt, seriously, medics are more important these days than they ever were in the past, just now most of them in addition to their medical skills are programmers and hackers as well. You know this, surely?"

"Yeah, I just never saw a lung in a foot before," I admitted.

"You're lucky, I've seen a lot worse," Reign said sadly. "Come on, let's leave Lion to work, and Luna to drool over him."

"I'm not drooling," Luna growled.

"Maybe not, but you bit fast there." Reign grinned, heading for the door.

"You did," I agreed, winking, then heading for the door as well. "Shout if you need us."

"We won't," Luna growled. "I'll see you lovebirds back at the house."

"Play nice now!" Reign called over her shoulder as I hurried to catch up to her.

"You really think Luna and Lion…?" I asked her, climbing the stairs behind her, and admiring her ass as I did so.

"Na, I was just sick of the pair of them making comments about us that's all, and it'll make it really awkward for her, because Lion likes her."

"But she doesn't like him?"

"More like she really likes Dondo," Reign admitted. "Gessh and Luna come as a pair, and that puts a lot of men off, despite the posturing and the shit that most guys spout."

"I bet." I shook my head, then couldn't help but wince. "And as Dondo works for Oshbob…that fucking Orc really is everywhere isn't he?"

"Like a rash," she agreed, the pair of us coming to a stop outside and looking about, noticing the gangbangers that looked from us to the door we'd come out of, and the lack of the sisters. "You think we need to do something about them?" she asked, and I checked them over quickly.

"Fuck it, we've got a minute or two before the taxi," I agreed.

"What you want?" one of the gangers asked as we walked towards them, handguns being readied visibly.

"Just a friendly chat," I said, moving closer, my right hand holding my rifle grip at the ready, finger laid across the trigger guard, ready.

"Yeah?" he grunted. "You can fuck off with your friendly…"

"Listen, fucknut," Reign said with a wide friendly smile. "We work directly with Oshbob, if you know who that is, then you know to fuck off and leave our friends inside alone. If you don't, then you're too dumb to be left alive, so how about you pick real quick?"

"Huh?"

"She means fuck off right now, or we kill you all," I clarified. "Seriously, we're armored, your piddly little handguns aren't going to do much more than piss us off, her grazer though? That'll reduce you to a pile of disassociated atoms. Just fuck off alright, we're not in the mood."

"You better…" the ostensible leader—or loudmouth—started, only to be grabbed by one of his friends who apparently knew Oshbob. Thirty seconds later and they were slouching away, attempting to appear as if leaving was their decision all along.

"I don't actually know if I'm pissed they know him and we didn't have to fight, or glad," I said as we wandered over to the air-cab as it pulled up.

"I'm glad." Reign sighed, laying her rifle in the trunk and unburdening herself of most of her gear, before climbing in. "And you know that street trash like that don't know what an atom is right? Never mind what 'disassociating' means."

"Yeah I know," I grumbled, dumping most of my gear in with hers and climbing inside, sitting on the seat with a groan.

"So…" Reign said as we lifted into the air. "You ever have sex in one of these?"

"Uh…no?" I said eyes widening slightly.

She grinned. "Just curious."

"That's cruel, you know that, right?"

"Maybe I'm taking notes for when the mod is out." She shrugged, and I glared at her, mind racing.

Glancing about in the cab, I gritted my teeth. There was plenty of room, or there would be in a Johnny-Cab, as we'd want both the guarantee of no recording while we fucked and the soft furnishings.

I'd just never really considered it before.

Well, I *had*. But that had been more along the lines of the fantasies I had now and then of being rich and having a private aircar, and a bevy of young filthy elven women to fuck senseless every night.

Those kind of daydreams might as well include some of those that modified themselves as pretend 'kitsune' as well for how fucking likely they were to ever come true, but hey.

"So, you've been quiet a while…" Reign grinned, and I realized at the same time as she did, that yeah, I was fucking blushing and sporting a hard-on that I could have used as an offensive weapon. "Oh…is that a gun in your pocket, or are you just pleased to see me?" she asked, with an evil grin, as the air-cab beeped to signify the landing was imminent.

"Fuck's sake!" I growled, trying to think calming thoughts and staring out of the window as the cab sank lower and lower, the nearby walls soaring up past us as windows flashed by.

Just before we settled down, I felt a hand unexpectedly squeeze my crotch, and breathy whisper in my ear, promising that we'd share that cab ride alone 'soon'.

That undid all my hard work in an instant, and then the doors were opening, as Reign stepped out of the left doors, and I struggled to straighten, stepping out of the right, and coming face to face with Todds.

CHAPTER TEN

"Sir," he saluted, and I growled, trying to hide that fact that I was back to swinging a solid damn fire extinguisher in my pants.

"Quit that," I growled. "You served?"

"Yessir."

"Call me Kabutt, Boss or Sarge," I ordered, before glancing over at the grin on Reign's face and shaking my head at her games.

"You ready for some fun?" Reign asked him, and he nodded.

"Always."

"Glad to hear it. Okay, we're here on a quick raid, we'll be hitting an apartment that Sarge was assigned upon leaving the army first…" she said, before going on and explaining the mission from there.

I nodded my thanks to her for not saying anything else, as I moved around them both, gathering my gear and repacking it as I liked, making sure all the straps and magazines were clear.

The next few minutes were filled with small talk as we crossed the plaza outside the arcology, entering by my old entrance, and exchanging a knowing nod with Stinger, as she squatted in one of the corners of the foyer, apparently pissing.

Knowing who and what she actually was, I genuinely wasn't sure if she was or not, but either way I saw it as it was now, an act that made everyone dismiss her entirely. Even Todds turned away in disgust, while myself and Reign nodded a greeting to her.

The wink she shot us could have meant anything, but the message that arrived a few seconds later was very clear.

Anthos Black still lives…

I nodded again, sending her a message back.

Not for fucking long.

That was it, one of the most feared and respected assassins in the history of Artem was pissing in the corner of my old arcology, and wanted us to kill someone for her, and damn soon.

Weird the way life turned out.

"Someone should do something about people like that," Todd growled as the doors shut on the lift. "Fuck's sake, it smells like she's been in here as well."

"Yeah, but that's city living for you." Reign grinned at him. "Admit it, where else would you get to see such varied characters?"

"The local nuthouse?"

"Sometimes I wonder if that's what the city is." I shrugged and looked out of the window at the buildings flowing past as the lift rose higher. "The entire fucking city feels like a damn nuthouse."

"There're crazy people and then there're people that piss in the corners..." Todds said softly shaking his head. "You guys know her or something?"

"Why'd you ask that?" I wondered frowning.

"Neither of you seemed surprised by her, just nodded." He grinned. "Sorry, it's the scout in me, I was trained to spot details."

"Yeah, we had a few interactions with her, she's a bit..." Reign started and I snorted, cutting her off.

"She's a bit savage that's all, best to keep on her good side, unless you want her pissing on you?"

"I'd shoot her," Todds said, then shrugged. "But if she's got issues, I guess maybe just nod and smile? Fuck knows, but I'm betting someone that fucked up doesn't last long unless she's a pet or something, best not to fuck with her."

"Smart man," I said. "Okay, we've got another minute or so before we get there, time for a quick breakdown mate. Who are you, what can you do for the team and why should I care?"

"Okay, sorry boss, head was all over there. Right, I'm Severin Todds, father of two, single parent which means that my kids are in day school right now, and when they get out I either need to run to collect them, or arrange for a sitter. Happy to do that, but it costs, so you know, I need to be earning all the time. If possible? If you could factor that into missions, like if we're going to be gone all day and night, just let me know, ya know?"

"Makes sense, don't worry, if I can I'll let you know."

"Great, well, I'm ex-army, Stealth Recon, and ex scout, they sound like the same thing, but they're fucking not. Stealth Recon is get in, get out with the info, nobody knows you're there, scout? That's get in and out with the info, but getting back with the info is what matters, not the stealthy part. It's a constant worry when you're told to scout as opposed to stealth, because they're basically saying 'we want the data more than we want you back'." He shook his head and smiled sadly.

"Lost a lot of friends to those missions. Stealth Recon though? That's where we hit the target, get what we need and get the fuck out, nobody ever knows we were there."

"I like that," I said. "I'd rather have you around after the mission than lose you on the first one. Tell me about your skills."

"Breaking and entering." He snorted. "Sorry, that was what got me into the army in the first place. I was a sneak thief and burglar, got caught by some seriously good tech and was given the option of six years in service or six years in jail. I took service."

"And?" Reign asked, as the doors whisked open, the strangled fart in place of a chime letting us know we'd reached my old floor.

"Interesting noise," he said diplomatically, shaking his head as we stepped out into the dimly lit nexus of corridors. "So, this is welcoming..."

"We killed the guy that was the local floor gang lord a few days ago, and most of his gang," I explained. "So if we see gangers, be ready for fun."

"Joy…you don't mind if I…?" he asked, lifting the hood of his suit in question.

"Hell yes, go for it," I said. "In fact, you scout ahead. We're headed to this apartment first…" I sent him the details for my old apartment.

He nodded, pulling the stealth suit hood up and pinching it closed, and I admired the quality of the suit as it cycled through chromatic swirls before fading from sight.

In five seconds he was literally invisible beyond a slight distortion as he moved and the cameras failed to keep up with the projectors. Either way though, in the darkness it was a hell of a thing to see. Or not, as it was.

"We need a decent tac-net," I growled for about the hundredth time, and Reign nodded.

"After we've done this, take whatever loot we've got, and trade it in for whatever grade of armor and tac-net we can," she suggested.

"Definitely," I agreed, as the pair of us, rifles held ready but not to the shoulder, moved quickly along the corridor after Todds.

Five minutes later I was staring into the small, shitty apartment, and I resisted the urge to curse. I'd expected no less, genuinely I had, I mean, why the hell would Lucky have left it alone, but still.

He'd broken in, or had his men do it, the gun safe had been raided as had everything else. My few personal possessions had been broken and thrown around, and I shook my head at the sight of a kid running away wearing that goddamn awful shit that Fergie had talked me into buying oh-so long ago.

They'd broken in and left what they didn't want strewn about. Then the local kids had been playing in the apartment and had clearly nicked anything they wanted.

My personal possessions were long gone, and I could see that from the door.

"Anyone got an incendiary?" I asked after a few seconds, not really serious, but smiling sadly when Reign pressed one into my hand silently. "Thanks," I whispered. "That door able to close?"

"I can force it closed," Todds offered, and I nodded.

"Good enough."

"Give me a second."

He went to work, kicking and twisting the door until it clicked back into the runners, then slid almost closed, He stopped it there, and paused as he looked back at me.

"One thing boss, if the fire suppression doesn't work…that's a hell of a risk for the rest of this floor. You really think that's a good idea?"

I hesitated, before cursing and passing it back to Reign.

"Fine, fuck it," I growled, knowing he was right. I waited as he let the door close, and I turned my back on the last of my old life, beyond Richie and Sync of course.

"Lead the way to here," I ordered him, shooting him Lucky's old address, noting the lack of any comment as he led us right back to the lift, then past it three doors on the right.

This time when we reached the door, it was intact and sod's law, the code Lucky gave us didn't work. Typical.

"Well, time for me to earn my keep I guess," Todds whispered, blurring back into visibility, and moving in close to the door, pulling out a few small tools and a scanner.

"So, you were going to tell us about your skills?" I reminded him.

"Might as well show you," he said, the smile clear in his voice. "So as I say, I was a scout, started out that way, and after I survived long enough? They promoted me, saw I had a gift for it, and make me Stealth Recon. Spent a year in serious training, hacking I was always shit at, the programming side just…" He shrugged.

"It's not for me, you know?" he admitted. "Mechanisms though?" He gestured to the door frame where he'd already pulled a section that looked like all the others apart. Inside I could see the cogs and magnets that formed the actual mechanism for the door. He made a few little taps here and there and then set off a brief electrical flash in the dimness of the corridor, and suddenly the door was sliding back, smooth and easy.

"So yeah, hacking the lock for that might have taken me all day as a programmer or a hacker, but as a mechanist? Ignore the governing systems and apply a charge to the rollers once the lock is disengaged. The system doesn't even know the door is open, and if anyone looks at the system logs later on? It's not been tampered with at all. Anyone comes looking for how this happened? They'll spend forever looking at that, convinced that a master hacker did it and cleared away any trace. In reality? Machines make sense, computers don't. People forget that we had mechanisms long before computers, and all the coding in the world doesn't affect the real world without a mechanism."

As he spoke, he quickly reassembled the covering to the wall, and Reign and I exchanged a look, before starting into the room.

We moved slowly, rifles up and sweeping, checking the corners, the walls, the floor, anything that might hide a turret or a target, we checked and thoroughly.

Moving through from the entrance, with its nice seats, the desk that was set up with a single chair behind it—presumably for Lucky to try and look important, because I was betting the books on the shelf behind him were fake—and into the next room?

I was stunned.

The greedy fucking bastard had literally smashed through the walls of three, maybe four apartments! They'd all been redone, bracing put in place, and a massive bed was set in the second to last room, with sights out across the fucking city!

I'd been surviving in my shitty fucking apartment, and this gangbanger was fucking living in a the lap of luxury in comparison!

There were stacks of data decks, a handful of scattered bullets, some jewelry, a small stack of credit chips—all fucking useless without Lucky's goddamn thumb—and a bunch of random shit.

I moved into the bedroom and started tossing the place as Todds worked on the door into the last section, hopefully an armory, but we'd see soon enough.

Reign and I searched the room quickly, finding more random stuff, a collection of plastic dolls from a popular daytime tv show, a couple of glass ornaments, a projector that when Reign tapped it started playing a projection of Lucky fucking two women, and apparently doing a terrible job of it, despite their porn-star cries.

Reign turned it off, then for good measure smashed the chip that held the data, before pausing and looking around.

"Those data decks..." she said, grinning.

"Yeah?" I asked.

"Let's face it, he was smarter than the average ganger, but not that smart, why would he need more than one?" she asked rhetorically as she moved over, triggering them and grinning to herself. "Jackpot."

"What?" I asked.

"It's the controller for the drug labs," she explained. "He's set them up to pay into a single account on here, he needs to keep it away from himself after all, if ACE or anyone comes looking, a half-orc living in here? He's gonna get fucked. Instead he was playing the game, that's why he was always outside in the corridor, sitting on a shitty couch and acting like an idiot. It was to keep people clear of here."

"So what do we do with the controller?" I asked slowly.

"Up to you, but it's got control of the obedience collars as well."

"The fucking *what?*" I hissed.

"The obedience collars, you know what they are right?"

"Pain projectors, used to enforce control over slaves. They can be set to stay near a set point, like a slaver who travels around, or a fixed point, like a central room or whatever. I've had experience of them," I growled.

"Well, looks like as soon as we left the chemists, he had them fitted with obedience collars, and he's been making them work round the clock in that lab upstairs."

"Can you deactivate them?"

"We can." She nodded. "We can also send them a direct message. I suggest doing that first, if they're waiting for a chance they might just break for it, instead tell them that they're free and to, I don't know, find a real job or something after this. Then we deactivate the collars."

"I've got the door," Todds interrupted, and we both turned to him, rifles lifting...only to drop as we saw the room before us.

"Motherfucker!" I cursed, shaking my head in disbelief.

CHAPTER ELEVEN

Where these two rooms had been luxurious—for an arcology dweller at least—the last one was anything but. Four women and two men were chained up naked, arms raised above their heads, staring at us in terrified desperation.

It'd been a few days since we'd killed lucky, and the stench that rolled out of the room made it clear that nobody had been in to clean up, or feed and water the prisoners.

"Motherfucker!" I repeated, seriously wishing that I could bring Lucky back from the dead just to kill him again.

"Stop," Reign barked as I stepped forwards.

"What"?

"Don't move." She swore, shaking her head. "As soon as the door opened, the datadeck went active."

"And?" I asked exasperated, glancing over at her and seeing it was still held in her hand.

"I was still linked to it or I'd have missed it. As soon as the door opened the explosive armed. That's a trap."

"So what do we do?"

"Try and disarm it, or we're all fucked," she said, lowering her rifle and starting to work on the datadeck.

"Shit, the room is locked out," I growled, having just tried to contact Bowdoin. "I'm getting an error when I try and send out."

"I…" Todds winced as he turned back to us, being careful not to move his feet, rotating at the hip instead. "Sorry guys, I didn't consider the door might be trapped, not after the front door wasn't."

"It's fine." Reign waved the apology away, making me stare at her in confusion.

"What's fine?"

"It's a simple trigger." She sighed, straightening. "I turned it off, try sending a message now?"

I tried, getting a connection no problem, and I sighed in relief. "What the fuck was that?" I asked, looking at her. "It's literally that simple?"

"It was an on-off switch." She snorted. "There's a trigger if the door opens without it being disarmed, the explosives go live, and then if you enter the room? They go boom. If you flick the switch though?"

She shrugged. "Sounds stupid, being so simple, but…"

"But someone else put this in for a half orc gang banger." I groaned. "Okay, look. We know someone with the skill to make sure this is safe, right?" I asked and she nodded, pointing down with one finger in question. "Exactly, I'll make a call, see if they're interested in this, see if they'll check the place out and do…I don't know. Find out what this shit is."

"You can ask, but they were pretty adamant about not helping us until…?" She nodded towards Todds, who sighed.

"Look guys, I know I'm new, but seriously, either trust me or don't, but can we get a move on here, this smell, and these people? We need to do something, and quick. I don't think they've had so much as a drink in days."

"Standby." I sighed, putting the call through to Stinger.

There was a long delay, then an image of the crazy woman appeared in my connection, now well dressed and clean, her projection nothing like her public image.

"You called?" she asked laconically.

"We need a little help," I said, getting a swift shake of the head as soon as the words left my virtual lips.

"You know the deal—"

"I do, and I'm not asking for us," I clarified. "We just broke into Lucky's place, and we found some shit we weren't prepared for." I linked my eyes into the feed, and heard the hiss of disgust at the sight of the prisoners.

"That is unfortunate, but—"

"There's a shitload of high explosives around the room apparently, and we armed the trigger when we opened the door. We think we've switched it all off, but while I could call a hacker to check the controller…" I shrugged and looked at her appealingly.

"You'd rather have an explosives specialist make sure the room is clear?" She sighed. "There'd be a cost."

"There always is."

"Not what you're expecting." She smiled. "Anthos Black is gathering more of his 'product' ready for a trip out into the wastes I hear. Apparently someone disrupted one of his labs earlier today, and he lost a lot of credits. He's stepped up his timescale, so you can either hit him before he leaves the city tomorrow, or wait a month or more for another chance."

"He's taking them out of the city?" I asked and she nodded, sending me an updated file. "I'll check it out."

"Until then, One of us will come and examine the situation for you, what are your intentions regarding the group?"

"Uh, I don't know?" I admitted. "I was going to get them a drink and let them use the shower, then tell them to fuck off basically."

"You might want to reconsider that." Stinger sighed theatrically. "Two I can see are missing persons with a reward for their return…"

"A reward?" I asked hopefully.

"Not much, but you might as well claim it, Search the bounty system, you'll find the subsystem of missing persons. ID each and you've got an easy win. One of us is on their way now."

"One last thing…"

"Yes?"

"The chemists that Lucky was 'employing', he used obedience collars. We were going to set them free, so I just wanted to warn you, alright?"

"We'll keep an eye on the local supply and demand, make sure nothing strange happens," she assured me, before cutting the link and leaving me wondering what the hell that meant.

I relayed the information, as much as I could, then raised my voice so the terrified group inside could hear us.

"We've got a team coming, can you use your Keystones?" I asked, getting a shake of a few heads and that was it. "Fuck, well, I know some of you at least are on the missing persons roster, and there's rewards for you. We'll be claiming those, and you'll all be going home to your families as soon as we've got the explosives sorted I guess."

"Did you tell her about the chemists?" Reign asked, and I nodded.

"I did, she said something about monitoring the local supply and demand?"

"Probably in case it fluctuates, see who's moving in to fill the void," Reign suggested.

"Makes sense I guess." I shook my head. "So, you want to claim the bounties on these people?" I asked her and she nodded as I turned to Todds. "Reign will register the people as found, send an image to them and their location to a next of kin I guess?"

"Yeah, then the bounty pays out on confirmation that this is that person," Reign clarified. "I marked us all as involved, all five," she said, making it obvious that even though the sisters weren't with us, they still got a cut. "The payout will be released over the next few days."

I nodded, looking back in at the people hanging there, then quickly away again.

My initial instinct was to cut them down, or hell, at least remove the gags and see if I could give the poor fuckers a drink, and cover their nakedness, but knowing so little about how the explosives were set? There could be a secondary trigger or anything in there. It wasn't worth killing them and us, to cover them or save them another half an hour of being naked and thirsty.

Twenty minutes later, and the explosives were being stripped out, and blankets, drinks and a line formed for the shower, while the traumatized people begged for news about their loved ones. The six had been fitted with restraint collars, forcing them to stay in the apartment, even if they got free of their chains and unable to access their keystones.

Fortunately, there were groups that literally all they did was help with this, charities that dealt with trafficked people, and a swift call to one of them by Todds, and we were inundated with a group of tree hugging holier-than-thou types who glared at us, as though we were responsible for the things these people had gone through.

All in all, the only relief we got out of the whole thing, thanks to the glares and more, was that the controller for the chemists—who Reign had messaged, explained the realities of life to, and then set free—had also been used to store a lot of the credits the gang had been earning.

All five of us were just under sixteen thousand credits better off within an hour, and that gave us something to make up for the lack of any real loot.

We hit Gunther's, sold the spare gear that we didn't want to move through the guild, and I bought what felt like the most important purchase I'd made in forever.

Tac-Net	Tier: Two
This entry level Tactical Network is designed to pair up to ten units into a single highly encrypted communications grid. With the patented recycling encryption that only Lynyrd Corp can provide, you'll know your innermost communiques are secure!	
Note: *Guarantees are valid only so long as supplied by an approved Lynyrd retailer with this month's code!*	
Note: *Guarantee is valid only so long as original Lynyrd comms gear is used.*	
Durability: 76/100	**Credit Cost**: 8,999

The kit came with ten links as standard, three of which didn't work, but considering we realistically only needed five for now, and possibly one more in the near future? That was fine.

The fact that like most of the suppliers Gunther stocked, Lynyrd went out of business years ago, wasn't overlooked, but hey. I managed to get the price down to only nine thousand in the end using that detail to my advantage.

I also got a new full face helm, several upgrades to my body armor—new tactical vest and trousers, thank you very much Gunther and the ART Collective, whoever they were—and lastly six boxes of ammo and a handful more grenades.

That left us time to make a little detour to order an electronics bench and a clean room prep drone—basically it was a small, dumb as fuck drone that would keep a designated area free of dust, dirt and debris, but it needed the room to be clean before it could be deployed the first time—then we were done.

Todds went home, happy that the day had gone easily, and ready to get a few hours downtime with the family, when the call came in, twenty minutes after we'd all started heading in different directions of course.

"Kabutt?"

"Yeah, Julius?" I sighed. If he was calling it was unlikely to be for good news.

"Join us in virtual," he said, sending me a code then disconnecting.

"Fuck's sake," I grumbled, shifting to get more comfortable in the back of the cab and speaking to Reign quickly. "Julius wants me to meet him in virtual, nudge me when we get there if I'm not out before…"

"Will do," she promised. "If it's a virtual meeting then it might be good news, you think?"

"Is it ever?" I countered, shaking my head. "Just nudge me, and check on the girls will you?"

"Will do," she repeated.

With that, I sighed, and triggered the code, watching as the world around me vanished.

CHAPTER TWELVE

The room I found myself in a few seconds later was clearly a construct program, walls of polished wood with screens dotted around them here and there, showing details of the guild.

The floor was covered in a thick carpet, and when I appeared I stood with four other figures, two of which were phasing into existence as I blinked.

Julius stood across from me, waiting patiently with a circular table between us all, the four of us arrayed around the outside. I glanced from him to the table, seeing a large scale multi-level map that looked to be in a vaguely familiar shape for some reason, but that's all I had time to notice, before the other figure spoke.

"I demand an apology!"

I glanced at him, curious, only to find the fucker staring at me, and I froze, totally confused, before the credit chip dropped.

This was that elf wanker from the rescue op this morning. He was clearly expecting me to break down and beg for forgiveness for calling his mouth a cock-holster this morning.

"No," I said, then I looked back at the map, before glancing up at Julius. "What's up?" I asked as the other two finished appearing to my left and right.

They were, in no particular order, a tall half goblin and a short as fuck human. The half goblin with his long ears, pointed nose and a generally shifty expression made me want to check my credit balance, but that was instinctual.

I felt the same whenever I was aware I was near a lawyer.

The short human was broad enough he could have some dwarvish blood, but the clean shaven chin and shaggy mop of hair suggested otherwise. The pair of them kept silent as dickhead spoke over Julius.

"Thanks for—"

"You'll damn well apologize or I'll have you striped of your rank!" the elf snapped.

"Fuck's sake, Trees!" Julius snapped, turning to him. "No, you fucking won't, alright? If Kabutt breaks the rules, then yes, you can *request* a review of his status, and yeah, if he's done something wrong, you can *request* I take action, that's it though! You think that investing a loan of credits in my guild gives you power? Believe me, you keep this up and I'll damn well pay it back early, and boot you! Learn to goddamn behave!"

I grinned at the outraged expression on the elf's face, only to have Julius round on me next. "And you, Kabutt, you fucking idiot, you need to damn well learn to shut your mouth and keep your head down!"

"I didn't say anything," I pointed out entirely reasonably.

"You know what you did," he snapped, shaking his head. "The pair of you leave it, alright? We've got a confirmed Specter nest, and it's building to outbreak levels. I need to contain it, then cleanse the building and—"

"I refuse," Trees snapped. "I will not work with this creature, nor his half-breed pets. Remove him or my team and I are out."

"Trees…" Julius growled warningly.

"I mean it, *guildmaster*." Trees drew the title out with a sneer. "If they are in, we, are out."

"Fine," Julius said, straightening, and smiling, though it clearly pained him. "You sure about that?"

"Very." Trees smiled, turning to me and looking down his nose as if I was a bug that was crawling on his picnic.

"Fine, well, consider this your notice. Here's your money back, along with the interest agreed, and you're back to being a regular member of the guild, you're also missing out on the bonuses for this mission."

"Wait, what! No, I don't accept…" Trees said before he dissolved in a pixelated blur and vanished.

"Now that's sorted out, The mission is down to your three teams, I think you can still do it without any losses, but still, you'll need to be damn careful, as you're all I have to hand, and I'd rather have had that happen at the end of the mission than before it," Julius said with a pained expression. "Kabutt, stay back at the end of the briefing alright?"

"Yes, Guildmaster," I said formally, with none of the mockery that Trees had injected the title with earlier.

"Thank you." He nodded. "Okay, so this nest was reported by the Owlson Corporation, and for those that have noticed the layout of the floors? Yes, its inside one of the old fusion cooling towers."

The map switched to a live view, showing a section of the eastern wall of the city, and the great cooling towers that used to be used in the old fusion power plants over there.

They'd been converted from the massive towers that had each covered a city block, into businesses, production facilities, and more long ago.

Most had then failed, their location and shapes making them unsuitable for heavy manufacturing, and the spaces too large for anything else, with some insane zoning law preventing them being knocked down, or repurposed into badly needed accommodation.

They'd been moved into by gangs and bums, one had—for a short while—been used as a semi-official fight club, the top floor of the tower, circular as it was, being surrounded on all sides by cameras and massive cages.

The center had been converted into a maze of sorts, and the fight club had run once a week, releasing various monsters into the maze from the cages, along with those desperate enough to take the risk and the money to try and reach the center.

Only one had even managed it, as I remembered, and she'd died a few minutes after, a leg ripped off before the victory auto-cannons could take the beasts down.

Once people had realized finally that nobody really 'won'? That was the end of the show, and the various bastards that supported it drifted away to other blood sports.

Now, it'd become a nest of specters somehow, and we were being tasked to sort it out.

"I'd recommend you take some newbies to form the outer perimeter, and I'll set one of the less experienced teams to watch over them, keep the tower from being reinforced from below once you start to climb, but be warned!" Julius said. "I can't send less experienced teams into something like this, they'd be chewed up and spit out. You'll need a fuck load of ammo, and you'll need to secure floor by floor. The newbies will be able to hold a line, but you'll need to clear the area first, then we can seal the entrances from below while they do that. Once they're sealed?

"Take it damn slow, climb a level at a time, clear it, seal it, take the next one. Do not, under any circumstances, let yourselves get pushed into a corner where they can get at you. Remember these are specters, yes, but they're forming a nest and they're almost at outbreak level.

"For you, Kabutt—Liolet and Timur have been with me a while and already know—that means that there's at least one Ghoul, probably several, and if there's nowhere for them to flee to, we might get a chance at a higher level specter as well, a banshee or something else.

"That they're here means that you'll be facing the worst possible mixture, specters that know no fear nor pain, and are controlled and more or less experienced. This is where it's easiest to lose people, and that cannot happen. I'd rather we failed the mission and I lost my bid, than I lost your teams, alright?" He looked from one of us to the others, and I shrugged.

"Bid?" I asked.

"Damn, that's your question?" the half goblin asked, shaking his head. "The guilds bid for contracts, like a formal bribe, whoever makes the best offer gets the mission, as the government department that arranges these things are greedy fucks."

"Basically," Julius agreed. "It's a closed system though, so you might bid too low or too high and you never know it, so you literally gamble every day. If nobody else bid and we put up a single credit? We'd get it, if ten other guilds all bid in the thousands? We'd be marked as timewasters by the government and blacklisted from future missions of this size. They've got it stitched up tight."

"The newbies I can understand," said the human gruffly. "And as much as he had a decent kill ratio, Trees was an asshole, but I've never met this one before. Can we trust him to stand firm?" He looked at me, and I bristled slightly, before Julius gestured to one of the screens on the wall and spoke briefly.

"Watch the second screen, that's his recording from this morning, the third screen is showing an AI generated overview of his actions seen from above, along with a direct kill count."

I glanced over, watching as I raced back and forth, the flare of the plasma blade lighting the darkness, seeing it reflected in the dead eyes and optical pickups of the specters that were trying to mob me.

It went on and on, until Julius gestured again, and the feed sped up to a blur of flashing fire, teeth and glinting metal.

"Four hundred and eleven confirmed personal kills over an hour and seventeen minutes," Julius said eventually into the silence, the same figures flashing over and over on the third screen, watching as I pulled the rifle out and tossed both an EMP and started firing at the ambushers. "He's why myself AND

Trees, not to mention the rest of the teams this morning actually survived, so yeah. I'd say he earned a promotion to the more serious teams."

"I stand corrected." The human grunted, then grinned. "So, what did you say to the prick then?"

"Now, now, no need for that," Julius said sternly, while gesturing unsubtly to the second screen, as the sound started to play as Trees refused to help with the cleanup and walked away.

"…You, ya pointy eared cock-holster, get your arse back here and help clear the site, the jobs…" My voice echoed around the room for a brief minute before Julius waved again. "Whoops, apologies everyone, no idea how that happened. *Anyway*…any other questions?"

"EMPs?" the half goblin asked.

"Nope, the owner of the site is utterly adamant, any use of EMP and we forfeit the entire payment, including the bid."

"Fuck."

"Quite," Julius agreed. "Beyond that, minimal collateral site damage is requested, but obviously that's down to interpretation. I'd stress that you're climbing the stairs there to the higher levels, so damaging the stairs and structure you then need to climb? Not a good idea."

"Fair enough. Any restrictions on caliber?" the human asked and Julius shook his head.

"No, use whatever you feel is needed, again within reason. If you try to use a directional demolition charge, there damn well better be a reason for it."

"I like big explosions?"

"That's NOT a good enough reason," Julius said with a faint smile. "Remember, minimum collateral damage."

"You said there was a bonus when you kicked the pointy eared prick out?" I asked.

"I was lying." He shrugged. "Sorry, but it was a cheap shot. If you can beat your kill record though? Yeah, I'm sure we can come up with a reward, a little gold cup for your shelf or something that says 'I'm the best'," Julius said that last bit in a high pitched joking voice and I shot him the finger, as the other two laughed.

"Seriously though. Be careful out there, mission starts in an hour, that's the soonest the client could clear their people out, and they want us on site ready to go."

"I've got Gessh down for an op right now," I groaned. "Seriously, she's not going to be ready."

"Fuck!" Julius snapped. "Seriously, Kabutt, now of all times you tell me that?"

"Her foot was utterly fucked this morning, so she needed it replacing, her decision was to upgrade to new legs." I shrugged not overly concerned. "If we're late to the party, well, Reign and I can hold the line and we just don't go in until they can join us."

"They?"

"You think Luna is going to leave her sister unconscious in a carvers?"

"Fine. I'll tell the client two hours, but seriously, Kabutt, if its more than that, we'll lose the mission."

"Do we have to clear it in a set time?" I asked.

"No, but we have to start it in a minimum time period, and seal the outbreak before it can get worse."

"Every minute it's open and operating as a nest, specters will flock to it, nobody knows exactly why, but as soon as one passes a certain level? It's like someone sets a giant magnet there, all the local specters are dragged in, and the effect only grows the longer its active," the goblin groused. "Seriously you're a killer, great, but I *hate* dealing with newbies."

"You both got team tac-nets?" I asked and they nodded. "Can you open a code to me?" They both nodded, seemingly reassured a little at that suggestion.

"Okay, you can exchange numbers and promise to plait each other's hair when you get there," Julius said with a quirk of the lips. "For now though, any last questions before I call the client and confirm times?"

"No."

"Not from me."

"No?" I said last, and he nodded, waving the others away.

As they dissolved he turned to me, and we stared at each other for a long few seconds.

"So, you gonna kiss me or kill me?" I joked, getting a shake of his head.

"Fuck's sake, Kabutt," he groused. "Okay look, just so we're clear on this, the plan hadn't been to get rid of Trees, not yet, and certainly not in favor of you, you're efficient but fuck you're a pain in the ass. I wanted to make it clear that you don't hold any special power over things because I chose to keep you and boot him, the fucker was pushing too hard. If I didn't slap him down now? I'd never have gotten his boot off my neck."

"I understand. So what's the problem?"

"Two things." He sighed. "First of all, we're fucked for disposable cash, you fail this mission? The guild goes belly up. I cleaned out everything to get that fucker paid off."

"Shit!" I growled. "What the hell is the second thing then?"

"Even if we survive?" he said after a few seconds. "We need an edge to clear the field, we need to be able to clear places like this much faster. You know any of your old APS buddies that retired with their suits and that might be open for a few missions? I know of four upcoming nests that we could hit. I'd split the entire fee for them with them."

"The fee?"

"The guild takes a cut, and we make money on every specter killed," he clarified. "I'd split that, and if we could clear out all four nests? Or better yet, let them reach outbreak level, THEN clear them? We'd get serious credits, AND we'd have essentially depleted the surrounding areas of all specters. We could go back to culling the herds and making a decent wedge doing it, but without the desperation we're currently under, and we'd be able to get the guild back on its feet as well."

"Honestly?" I asked, and he nodded. "No."

"What...?"

"I don't know any other operators that got out with their suits. We were in six man teams, and most of mine died on the last mission..." I paused, wondering if I could trust him.

"But?" he asked. "Come on, Kabutt, there's something there, I can smell the burning hair as you concentrate."

"There MIGHT be a way to get a single small team. One that might even hang around a few weeks to months."

"How?" he asked quickly, desperation clear on his face.

"It'd not be cheap."

"Kabutt, a nest can run from three hundred to several thousand specters, each is worth a hundred and fifty credits to the guild, the city pays the hundred, the local business or corp pays the fifty. You get your share, the hundred, we get fifty more per kill, that sounds like a lot, but honestly, take the bids off and the operating costs of the guild house and more? I make less than you I bet."

"So let's say four nests, a few thousand in each, maybe a bit less..." I mused. "Let's say four thousand total, four thousand specters, me and my team...let's say ten of us. We make ten credits each per kill, plus half of that fifty, so say twelve credits, for ease of working here."

"Uh-huh," he agreed, nodding.

"That's only forty-eight thousand credits each," I pointed out. "Seriously, that's not gonna cut it."

"No, it wouldn't," he agreed, before grinning. "And that's where your friend comes in. How much do you think your share of four thousand specters worth of mods would run to?"

"Between ten of us? Four hundred mods?" I shrugged. "A lot."

"A hell of a lot," he agreed. "I make the recovery team hand in EVERYTHING."

"Everything?" I asked, a definite plan raising its ugly head at that. "You make them hand it *all* in, all guns, mods, loot, everything?"

"If that's what it takes, then hell yes. Look, I know the recover team make a killing on their loot, I turned a blind eye when I thought it was from smelting the mods down, and frankly, I don't need the shit that would come if I forced them to do this all the time, as I'm betting the majority of the mods they strip need a shitload of work doing to them to get them even clean enough to identify or weigh in as scrap. For this though? For a one off? Yeah. I'd do that, and you'd damn well make a killing, out of four hundred mods if you get even two hundred and fifty credits per mod—and I'm betting you get a lot more than that, you're looking at a hundred grand."

"Sure, but a corpo bodyguard makes that in what? A few weeks?" I pointed out. "They get none of the stress, none of the crawling through the fucking sewers, none of the ammo expenditure..."

"No, but you'd need to deal with corpos all day," he pointed out. "Here you'd have a home, as well as a guild around you should you get into trouble, and you'd be free to take or refuse jobs."

"So..." I paused, considering how best to say it. "...let's say that maybe, *maybe*...there's a way to get three APS in motion, there'd be some costs, you understand."

"What kind of costs?" he asked.

"I've got my armor," I said with a little smile.

"You've...you've got it NOW?" he asked, a desperate smile lighting his face.

"Yes and no." I held up a hand. "It's repaired but it wasn't finished, it was harvested for parts by an asshole in the APS Corps. I'm buying and fitting replacement parts now. The sooner I have those parts? The sooner I'm up and running."

"How much?" he asked, rubbing his chin.

"About a million."

"A MILLION?"

"I've got the skeleton," I said. "It's not even powered. At this stage its ready for slotting the parts, but..."

"Fuck's sake, Kabutt!" Julius snarled, "I swear you're like my ex-wife! Everything you promise is a fucking lie!"

"No." I resisted the urge to smile. "It's just not what you want to hear. Seriously, I can get my suit up and running, I'm not looking for you to help, and I'm sure as shit not being beholden to you for it. What I need? When the time comes, I need you to charter a guild official mission out of the city, and you'll need to accept some new members, as if they'd always been in the guild, without asking *any* questions. Alright?"

"Are they black ops?" he asked, and I glared at him.

"Which part of 'don't ask any questions' suggested 'hey ask any questions you want'?"

"Kabutt, I'm willing to skirt close to the fucking edge alright? To help keep my guild running, sure I might even turn a blind eye here and there, but if you're asking me to betray Artem..."

"Betray?" I asked confused. "Fuck no, they're APS, they're just unlicensed. Suits that I can recover, and operators that can use them you idiot. They're good people."

"So not operators from other cities?"

"Julius, if I could get another cities suits intact, I'd sell them in a heartbeat, just like if they could get our suits they'd not be working on specter clearance for a shitty guild alright? Sorry mate but it's true. We're in need of more or less honest work that's all, establish a history, then if this isn't working out, we'll fuck off and go corpo bodyguard. If it is? Well, we'll see then."

"So you just need a sanctioned flight out to collect and then no questions asked?"

"I'll sort the rest," I agreed, and after a long minute, he sighed and nodded, offering a fist to bump.

"Then it's a deal, and if this mission goes well? Maybe we can do something with the mods."

"Deal." I grinned, then disconnecting from the virtual as Reign shook me by the shoulder.

CHAPTER THIRTEEN

"Home again." Reign sighed, shaking her head as she looked past me to the building as we cruised to a landing. "Seems wild to say that. So, what'd Julius want?"

"We've got a mission," I said. "Big specter nest in one of the old fusion plant cooling towers. Two hours before the gig starts, that's all the time we've got, so we need to get things sorted now."

"Uh…" Reign drew out the sound.

"I know, But that dickhead elf pushed Julius, and he paid him off rather than put up with it. Now the guild has fuck all credits left, and they lose the bid for this? The guild is done."

"Shit, fuck's sake Julius, you had to do it now!" She snarled, clambering out, and I joined her.

"To be fair to him, Gessh was hiding how badly her foot was fucked, and even if she was replacing it normally, he had no way to know she was going for two full limbs."

"Crap," Reign growled, shaking her head. "We need a team, and we've got fucking you and me."

"And Todds."

"Point, if he can get a fucking baby-sitter," she groused, making an 'I'll call him' gesture with her thumb and pinkie, as I grabbed my gear out of the trunk.

While she was calling him, I reached out to Luna, getting a clearly bored half orc grinning back at me.

"How's she doing?" I asked.

"He's just about done, she's still out for the count, but these legs? Damn!"

"They nice?"

"Beautiful," she said, nodding, then patching in her optics, hastily covering her unconscious sisters private area with a hand across that section of her vision. "Whoops, sorry, shouldn't show you that until we're all drinking and playing cards." She grinned, before focusing in one the gleaming black metal legs. "Just look at *those*."

I did and I couldn't help but feel a slight surge of jealously.

They were, as she'd said, *beautiful*. All black polished metal and plastic, they were molded to look like a well-muscled natural pair of legs, but the build, the gleam, and the rest? They just looked amazing.

"I've been studying the specs," Luna said quickly. "They're jump-jet capable, short range, but seriously? We could get that upgrade to the calf's and literally leap over *buildings*."

"Well, you'll get the chance to earn a down payment on them if she wakes up soon," I interrupted. "We've got a job, big specter nest, and it's a three team one, that's how big, anywhere from hundreds to possibly thousands of the fuckers."

"Sounds great, when…?"

"Two hours."

"Uh…"

"I know." I cut her off. "Not my idea, the guild had to bid, or bribe, for the job, and it has to begin in two hours or they lose it. We're getting a bunch of newbies to secure the perimeter, but we need to be moving in, in two hours. Apparently the client is specific and an asshole."

I added that last bit in on my own, but fuck it, it fit the data as I had it.

"Two hours…Give me a minute," she said, shaking her head, then disconnecting the call to speak to Lion. I carried the boxes of ammo into the warehouse with Reign, the pair of us wincing at the down blast as the air-cab took off, rocketing upwards.

"Todds sorting cover," Reign called, shielding her face as best she could with arms full of boxes. "Says he'll be there in about an hour, and will wait on us."

"Good man," I shouted, before dropping my voice as the jet-like blast receded and we could hear ourselves think again. "Goddamn old model air-cars!"

"Yeah, the repulsors are much better, but hey, you pay for the privilege," Reign agreed. "So, how's Gessh?"

"Still out cold," I muttered, before perking up. "Here's Luna though, give me a minute." I keyed the accept, and nodded to Luna as she appeared. "Give me good news."

"Lion says she'll be finished in time, *but* she's going to need extra nanites to seal her up and get her on her feet. He doesn't have any, so…"

"I'll sort it," I promised, getting a nod from her.

"Then we'll be there, but we won't be much before the two hours…the old fusion plants you said, right?"

"Yeah, this is it," I said, sending over the locational data while trying to figure where I could get medikits from right now.

"The Pit?" Luna asked, and I shrugged.

"One of them used to be a live deathmatch place, long since closed down though. Specters live their now."

"That's all we need, fucking ghosts as well." Luna sighed. "Right, I'll get her on her feet, and see you there, bring ammo alright? I've got enough for today, but…"

"But you weren't expecting a nest." I nodded. "That's fine, I bought plenty, I'll bring it with us."

"Thanks, boss. Okay, see you there."

I cut the line, shouldering the door open as the locks disengaged, and we hurried inside, dumping ammo on the nearest counter and spreading gear out quickly.

"She can do it," I called to Reign who was dumping more gear on the other side of a table. "Luna says they'll be there, but we need to take their gear."

"Oh thank fuck!" She groaned. "Okay, give me a minute to set the drone on the clean and sterilize cycle—it might as well be working while we're gone—and then I'll start loading mags."

"I'll grab the gear, and order some food…"

"And drinks and stims!" she called as I hurried up the stairs, using the facilities, then grabbing drinks, and a bag for the various gear we needed.

Ten minutes later, I'd loaded up the bag, and a second, and the pair of us were busily munching on pizza and sodas, while loading magazines, the next hour leaving us both with aching thumbs and fingers as we loaded mag after mag, putting them aside, adding to the pile.

By the time the air-cab turned up, blasting random shit everywhere, we were knackered, which was a terrible way to start a mission, but we'd gotten everything we needed together.

The last minute delivery from a Zon drone of ten small and ten medium medikits was enough that it seriously fucked with my liquidity, but we needed them, and like the theory of a condom, I'd rather have and not need, then need and not have.

By the time we touched down on a stretch of scrubland outside the old cooling towers? The sun was down again, and a cold breeze was sweeping in, the promise of yet another downpour clear in the air.

"Hey, boss!" Luna called from the gaggle of people standing nearby—they'd backed off from the down blast and turned away, but were starting to look over now—and I waved to her as we set off to join them.

There were nearly forty people standing around already, with another cab— a ground one this time—heading across the wasteland to join us.

"Luna..." I greeted her, then shook my head as Gessh strolled up, a new bounce evident in her step. "...how's the legs?"

We all looked at her legs instinctively, despite them being concealed by her trousers and she grinned.

"Seriously, I need to buy a whole new wardrobe to show these fuckers off. Just wait till we get back to the warehouse tonight, you better not get too handsy, boss, because I'll be walking round with no trousers on any chance I get!"

"I get a hell of a reputation for absolutely fuck all," I grumbled, but inside I was smiling, seeing the look on Gessh's face, and the grin on Luna's as well.

"So, boss, this job, are we likely to make decent bank?" Luna asked, nodding at Gessh. "We've got some saving to do so I can get mine."

"Yeah about that..." I grinned, waving to the other squad leaders that I'd be with them in a minute. "Julius is basically up shit creek here, he's going to help us set up to do a recovery, no questions asked. I wanted to discuss it with you all first, but frankly when there's an opportunity like that, you don't let it pass. Tonight when we're all back and we're sure we're clear, I'll bring you up to date. Things just got a whole lot easier."

"Sounds intriguing," Reign said, passing one of the long bags to Luna. "Come on, everyone load up, while the boss goes and sorts the details with the other teams."

I nodded at the non-too-subtle dismissal and I left them to it, nodding to Todds as he hurried over to join the girls. I wove my way through the cluster of people, joining the human and half goblin as they made room for me around an upturned barrel that they had a map spread out on.

I shrugged, figuring it'd be easier to do this in virtual, but I guessed they wanted to keep an eye on people.

The half goblin was the first to offer a fist, and I smacked it in greeting, offering the same to the human a second later, who grunted and knocked it harder than need be.

"I'm Liolet," the half goblin said in greeting, "As I know that bugger Julius is crap at introducing us, you're Kabutt, and he's Timur, yes I'm a half gobbo, no he's not a half dwarf, he's just unfortunate looking. Any other obvious questions to get out of the way?"

I shrugged. "No, I'm good…actually, yeah, sorry, team specialties. Are you all-rounders or specialists?"

"Teams or us?" Timur grunted.

"Both?"

"We're hit and run," Liolet admitted. "Most of my team are half gobbos, you got a problem with that?"

I shook my head.

"Good, well, we're naturally good at hit and run tactics, there's fifteen of us, so yeah, sucks when it comes to dividing the loot, but works great when a couple of runners bring a mass of them into an ambush. That's how we prefer to work to be honest. We set up, create a choke-point, a few fall back positions, then we generally bleed them dry."

"We tend to move slow and steady, elimination and sweep," Timur said. "My team are fifty-fifty, standard assault load-out and heavy weapons, slow and steady keeps us all alive, we usually wait for Liolet to draw aggro, then we move in on the far side and crush them between the hammer and the anvil, but in a setup like this, we'd need more people for that to work."

"How many in your team?" I asked.

"Eight. Four assault, four heavy, loaded out with chain guns and assault shotguns, battery magazines." He jerked a thumb towards the massive backpack that sat on the floor next to him, and I nodded my admiration of the setup.

The backpack was similar to the out back mounted loudout I used in my APS, battery powered gravity feed that kept the ammo moving along a belt to the assault shotgun, able to hold literally hundreds, if not thousands of shells ready.

"Before we get started…"

"No I don't have one spare." He grinned at me.

"Ha!" I grinned back. "I wish! No I need a supplier for Dragons Asshole rounds…nowhere seems to stock them. You know anyone?"

"Nope," he said. "If I did I sure as shit wouldn't share that with anyone, they're rare, specialty rounds, and dangerous as hell. I don't want fuckers using them near me when I've not fought with them before."

He gave me a look at that point, then a gesture of his head to encompass some of those hanging around nearby and listening and I took the hint.

He knew someone, and if this went well he'd possibly share their details, just not out loud where the newbies hanging around could hear.

"Ah well, I can respect that," I said, then I patted the grip of my shotgun and grinned. "I'll warn you now though, I'm loaded with solid shot and bolo mainly, with a single dragon at the very end."

"So if I hear one go off you're in the shit?"

"Basically, yeah!"

"Sounds clear enough to me."

"And me," Liolet agreed.

"So, what's the plan?" I asked.

"There's four entrances," Liolet pointed out, touching four separate points equidistant around the map. "Too many for us to cover them all unfortunately. I'm suggesting we seal two of them, weld them shut, then we march in, clear as we go, and follow these corridors…"

He gestured to a series of interlinking rooms and areas.

"…there's stairs that lead down here…" A stairwell, clearly marked.

"…so we clear to there as a group. Seal up as much as we can, then my team set up choke points and fall back positions," Liolet finished.

"That's where we take over," Timur grumbled. "We split, one up one down, the up is literally just to hold the path, don't push deeper into the building, just hold the ground for now. If possible? We seal a door or two, more even, and just hold the area until the other team returns."

"The team that goes deep? If you're alright with taking that role;" Liolet spoke up. "You'd be looking for the access point. Find it, seal it, cut off any reinforcements. Once that's done you return to us, we load up and move out, if all is going well."

"And if it's not?" I asked, knowing what life was like.

"Then you get back to us. Timur will have sealed off most of the path to us, and I'll have a choke point and fall back locations set up. We bleed them dry, if need be we fall back and back until we're out of here and the newbies can earn some kills as well."

"And if there's too many for us to contain?" I asked.

"Then we fight until Julius gets here with reinforcements and we lose a portion of the pay, but we all live. That's the outcome here, no matter what, the teams survive, because if we don't? The guild is fucked. Too few teams means we can't meet our obligations, we start losing those jobs, the guild will fall. Then we're all back to slobbing around the shitty guilds looking for work," Liolet growled.

"You're not long out of the army right?" Timur asked me, before shaking his head sadly. "Believe me, you don't want to go from guild to guild. Some are good, like this one, but some? They'll stab you in the back as quick as the enemy…"

"Oh, I've heard." I thought back to those fuckers that'd dumped me in the undercity. "So, we're taking the basement, you're taking the upstairs, and you're building fortifications and a fallback?" I asked, getting nods. "Then good luck to us all, I need to activate the new tac-net, no time to do it yet, so give me a few minutes and I'll have my team working, and then patch to you both."

"Sounds good, ten minutes to the red line," Liolet reminded me, referring to the two hour deadline, and passing me a small welding kit to seal the doors if I found the entrance the specters were using. "Can you use this?" he asked, and I nodded, having seen and used them before when fixing armor and army gear.

"Yeah I've used them, we'll be ready," I assured him, before heading back to the others.

CHAPTER FOURTEEN

We were ready on time, which was a bit of a relief. I hated being late. It was the years of army training, where there was no such thing as 'on time'. You were damn well early, or you were late.

Sliding in on the deadline was an anathema to me.

Still, the five of us were now linked with the new tac-net, and as the individual units were decent ones, they offered a choice of sub-vocalization, full speech, or linkage to your keystone, which meant that we could focus and 'speak' without saying anything aloud with ease.

At last we could talk privately, and for the first time in probably my entire life, I wasn't concerned about a superior officer pulling the recording and punishing me for what they found.

All three teams jogged across the scrub wasteland, splashing through the rapidly forming puddles as the neon lights flared distantly, and I saw the first of the newbies—they'd all been clearly ordered to stay outside the tower, but a handful had been detailed for this job—standing by the door with a crowbar and a welding set.

Once we were inside the door would be kept ready, until one of the three team leaders sent a code word to them. Then the doors would be sealed. Not all of them, obviously, but two to prevent outbreaks.

The welding kit could be used to cut doors if we needed to, or to seal the door again behind us if we had to fall back, but it was best to have shit ready.

I keyed the command line, and spoke quickly as we neared the bottom of the building, curious as a thought came to me.

"So…just checking here people, but are we sure they know we're here?"

"They do," Timur grunted. "There's forty of us, all modded to fuck, the specters know we're here."

"So why haven't they come out?" I asked. "I mean if they know…why wait for us to dig our way in?"

"Who knows why or how they think, they just do," Liolet replied.

"Okay, let me and mine take point then," I suggested as we reached the door. "If for any reason they don't know we're here, then we can stealth kill some before they find out, right?"

"Kabutt." Timur snorted. "You're a good fighter, I'm sure, but they're specters. They don't think like that. You take one down? Even if they don't see you? Whatever is in control of it knows. It's a machine, they're not exactly contemplating their innermost existence you know."

"Yeah, trust us. We do this a lot," Liolet said. "Let Timur lead, it's his role."

"Fine." I sighed and shrugged, backing out of the conversation and switching to the team net. "Be ready here, people, the others seem to think the specters know we're coming, but they're happy to run blindly in…"

"Meat to the grinder?" Luna asked, and I tried not to curse as my thoughts clearly matched hers.

"Let's stay optimistic, but hey. So we're going down first…"

"Sounds fun," Reign said.

"…and the others are securing the floors then waiting for us," I finished, ignoring her. "We're to find the way the fuckers are getting in and seal it, I've got a small arc welding kit in my bag, we seal it, then we're moving back up, clearing as we go."

"Good old bug hunt eh?" Luna quipped. "Room by room, slaughter and move on."

"Basically, yeah," I agreed. "Where possible use melee weapons, save as much ammo as we can until we need it."

We had a veritable buttload of it, I had literally ten mags for the assault rifle, each holding thirty-five shots, five for the handgun, each holding eighteen, or three reloads of the revolving cylinder per mag. Then I had the three mags for the shotgun. Two were solid slug, one was a mixture of 'fun' rounds, bolo and solid alternating until I get to the final round which was the Dragon's Asshole.

Beyond that I had a single box of two hundred rounds for the assault rifle in my bag, four frags, two flashbangs, and unfortunately only the one EMP. We'd been told under no circumstances to use one, but fuck it, if it came down to that or our lives? I'd walk with our lives.

I'd given up on the hatchet, I'd carried it into three fights and never used the fucker yet, but I had both the vibro-blade knife and the plasma sword.

Then I had two small and two medium medikits.

I was loaded for fucking bear, and the others were the same, although the sisters were focused on the combination of the shotguns and swords as their primary choices, where mine was the assault rifle, meaning they carried a lot more mags for the shotguns than anything else.

Gessh had her grazer assault rifle for emergencies, and Luna her standard slug firing one.

Reign was already complaining about the weight of the batteries she had to carry for the grazer sniper rifle, but none of us were fooled. We'd tried to convince her to leave it behind and focus on the solid slug sniper rifle and she'd acted like we were trying to get her to sacrifice her first-born.

She'd given up on her assault rifle entirely, possibly due to the sheer size of the sniper rifle duo she was struggling with, and its ammo, but had kept a handgun as her last line of defense.

"Start recording!" Liolet sent to everyone. "Backup to the offsite guild repository, just accept the link people." I did as usual, not liking it but that was life.

Now as the newbie jerked the door open, stepping behind it and bracing herself ready, the teams raced into the ground floor of the cooling tower without a pause.

The darkness as we went inside caused the line to slow a little, even the best mods took a second to adjust from the flaring neon lights and falling rain outside, to the darkness inside, and we were all the same on that.

As soon as I was in though, I felt the hackles on the back of my neck rise.

The outside looked dilapidated, the concrete and steel construction leaving great long scars of rusted runoff marring the funnel tower shape, but inside?

The walls and ceiling were close in, seriously so.

Where I'd expected the entire place to look fucked, the floor and walls were solid, and the ceiling covered in a solid metal mesh. Here and there as we ran, I thought I spotted the tell-tale reflection of lenses, and I gritted my teeth, sending a comm directly to Julius.

"What's up, Kabutt?" he asked, appearing in the corner of my vision.

"The cameras," I said. "Are they active?"

"Not as far as I know," he replied a second later. "Sorry, sarge, give me a minute, just getting reports from another site run, it's not going well." He sighed, before looking back at something else. "Camera, cameras…yeah, got it here. They're full 3D projection types, sealed away apparently, too expensive to remove them, so we're to leave them be. The owner of the building says they're worth plenty and they've got plans for them, so you're to not damage them."

"Julius…" I said slowly. "I've got a really bad feeling about this place. You said it was used as a site for death matches, and had a maze?"

"Yeah, they shut it down a year or two ago I think. The fans drifted off when they realized that nobody could win."

"And it's the same owners?" I asked, going cold as I passed another offshoot doorway, each and every one welded shut so far.

"Unknown. It's a corpo deal, the old one shut down, but it might be…yeah, two of the 'new' corporation's bosses are registered as the old one's as well. Why?"

"Because I think they're filming us, and I think they're going to sell the footage of us clearing the specters out and use it for something."

"And that's why the want the cameras left alone." Julius groaned. "Well, they were weirdly specific about getting all the rights to the recordings you make. Fucker. I should have asked for more."

"Asked for more?" I growled, and he sighed.

"It's not that unusual, Kabutt. All client sites have cameras and so on, and they all get a copy of your sweep, it's so they can verify how many are killed etc. They have the right to share that recording if they need to, usually its insurance companies and so on. In this case, yeah, they're probably going to charge people to watch you fight the specters, dammit. It is what it is though, do the job, keep your people alive, and view it as if you're doing an advertising reel for the guild. Now, I need to go, shout if there's an issue."

With that he disconnected and I was left swearing, before calling the others, and then adding in both Liolet and Timur.

"Okay people, be aware, those cameras hidden about the place? They're probably live, recording all we do, this place was a broadcast point for death matches and shit like that, you better believe they'll happily share reels of us fighting the specters. Be careful, and for fuck's sake if you need to break for a shit? Check that you're not being filmed first."

I got a series of 'acknowledged' and 'motherfuckers' from the others, and the team leads dropped out of the net quickly, clearly spreading the word.

"Good catch there," Luna said in our tac-net as we continued along the hall, and I nodded my thanks absently.

"I'm hoping I'm wrong, but Julius doesn't think so," I said.

"Okay…I'm accessing…" Reign muttered into the feed, then started swearing.

"What?" I asked, before a new image was sent to me.

It was a broadcast studio, with a pair of talking heads sat in the middle around a desk, with images of specters playing on screens behind them…and yeah.

A line of us running through a corridor right in the center.

"Motherfuckers," I growled, before sending the link to both Julius, and the other two team leads, as well as talking to my own team. "Looks like we're vid-stars, people!"

"Great, I always thought you'd be the one to embarrass us publicly," Gessh shot to Luna, who started chuckling.

"Remember, nothing changed," I said, feeling anything but that it was right, but hey. "We're still being paid for this, and we'll still be risking our lives, so just act professional, rely on the team, and we'll get through this." I repeated into the tac-net.

Another round of acknowledgement and the first gun shots were ringing out somewhere ahead.

I resisted the urge to watch as I had no doubt the talking fucking idiots would be showing the world it, but that was a fight for a different day. As I'd cut the feed to the studio, the last thing I'd seen was the viewer counter.

It'd been in the low thousands when Reign sent it to us, it was in the high *hundred* thousand range when I disconnected.

We passed two more doors, both sealed, before we finally found some that could be opened, and by then the front line were encountering serious resistance.

"Taking the left," I sent on the command line, leading my team through the room to the left, the map telling me that we should be able to pick up a second corridor on the other side of this next room, then take the force that Timur was fighting from a second angle.

The room I led my team into was absolutely bare, almost surgically so in fact, even the floor was bare of anything beyond dirt, and I felt my stomach cramping as I moved through it, the door on the far side sliding into the wall recess to let me out into the next corridor.

That was where the problems started.

CHAPTER FIFTEEN

According to the map, there should have been a corridor that ran left to right past the room wed just exited, then at the end of the right hand side corridor, there should be the area that Timur was pushing into.

Nice and simple.

That wasn't the case though, the right hand side was entirely blocked by thick steel plating, leaving only the left, and that led away in the wrong fucking direction.

I paused, checking the map, thinking quickly.

If we went back, we would be sitting in a narrow corridor while Timur and his people fought against what seemed to be a heavy concentration of the specters. This route had to lead somewhere, and the floor plan wasn't exactly complicated, so we should be able to pick up the next crossing corridor easily enough and get around to help them.

Should.

I didn't like it, but I reported in.

"Timur, Liolet, the cross corridor has been sealed, working to find a way around the blockage, be aware the maps are inaccurate."

"Whatever," Timur snapped, clearly firing. "Just get your arse in gear!"

"On it," I agreed, moving out again, rifle up and leading the way.

The corridor we headed down ran for a dozen meters, before it hit a dead end, again, totally different to the map, and we were forced to take a left into one of the rooms that had been sealed off from the other corridor.

This one, like the last was square, old power distribution points and torn out light fixtures the only break in the four walls…beyond the two cameras in the top far corners of the room.

"This is feeling more and more like a setup." Luna was the one to say what we were all thinking, and I nodded, rather than responding, as we exited the room via another door, into a new corridor, still leading away from the others.

The concrete floor and roof changed into a metal gantry way, as rather than walls, we excited into the middle of the building, slowing as we saw the mess before us.

"Oh FUCK," I gasped, and the others echoed the thought, right before jammers came online, and we were reduced to point to point transmission, and a hidden door slid down behind us, cutting us off from the fucking corridor.

The door was massive, at least six inches of solid steel, and it'd nearly cut Todds in half, the fucker jumping through at the last minute, before it slammed down, and locking mechanisms engaged, as floodlights flared, bathing the area in brilliant clarity.

"Boss, I forgot something at the warehouse, mind if I go home?" Luna whispered as we stared in dumbfounded amazement.

"Me too," Reign said.

"Me fucking three," I agreed, before shaking my head. "Fuck this shit, Todds, get that fucking door open…"

"No chance," he replied, having already looked at it. "We'd need to climb around the outside of the gantry, you think that's going to work out well?"

I looked where he pointed, and I cursed.

The gantry we were in was a cage, that was clear, reinforced steel mesh that formed the corridor, but let you see though, and as evidenced by the rising clicks and buzzes, be seen as well.

The section we were in was nothing like the maps we'd been given, instead of level after level that had been built inside the old cooling tower, it'd been stripped back.

There were a dozen levels up and down around a solid concrete and steel block that jutted out into the middle of the tower. That block was clearly where we'd just come from, and I was guessing that was designed to make us think that the tower was as it'd been sold to us.

Now that we were in too deep to do anything about it?

It was clear the entire building was a trap.

Level after level up and down, of crossing gantry ways sealed all around, braced and built carefully to hold us, while cameras were set to record every detail.

This was a new deathmatch, one that was being streamed live, and the opponents were fucking *specters*.

They were everywhere, as the gate at the end of this section unlocked with a flash of lights and a whoop of alarms, designed to make sure that every fucker in here knew where we were.

The gantries we could see above and below were filled with specters, some small some large, several collapsed and being crushed by the mass around them, but easily hundreds in just the first level up and down from us.

I took it all in a fast glance, and then the floodgates were opened, and the first of them poured in.

"Fuck!" I snarled. "Advance!" I shifted to the right of the corridor, it was just wide enough for two to stand side by side, and one of the sisters stepped up to my left.

We took four fast steps, getting some room to move from the sealed door, some room to retreat if we needed it, and I felt someone pulling at my bag behind me.

"I'll try and cut us out of the cage," Todds said, and I nodded, shifting my aim and firing, single shot, round after round, aiming for the head.

Bodies fell, Gessh taking down at least as many as I did, her shotgun firing solid slugs that hammered through rotting corpses one after another.

The tide was solid at first though, dozens and then hundreds falling, the first relief we got in the fight was that there were so many bodies piling up that they had to literally struggle through them. We made it to the halfway point, and slowed, Gessh and I taking a knee and reloading as Reign and Luna fired over our heads, keeping the wave back.

The new full head helm made me smile grimly as the steady hammering of their weapons was reduced to a more manageable clatter, rather than deafening me as such weapons once could have done.

After thirty seconds though, Reign spoke.

"I'm gonna sweep the stairs with the grazer, full power sustained beam, see if I can get us some space."

"Do it," I agreed, and a second or three later the subtly wrong beam charged through the air, the hum deep enough that I felt it, balls to bones, but the effect on the specters was more pronounced.

Dozens of them simply collapsed, their metal and robotic components suffered little effect, but the flesh, living or dead, fell apart like overcooked meat, shredding into component parts.

Cybernetic limbs collapsed onto the floor, shreds of flesh holding onto them and torn, filthy clothing. While the limbs spasmed, following the last routing ordered into them; legs walking, arms reaching, hands grasping…they didn't take long to fail fully.

That the mass of specters, driven supposedly entirely by the need for nanites and mods, totally ignored the piled mods by their feet, clambering over them and fighting to get at us?

It proved beyond any doubt that they were being guided.

"How much did that cost you?" I called to Reign over the clatter and chatter of gunfire.

"Fifteen percent," she replied and I cursed.

"When I tell you, give me another one, higher up, aim for the floor above and drag it sideways fast, I want as many on the floor as possible, don't worry if you don't kill them, their friends trampling over them will do it for us. Use twenty percent, then hold at that, don't waste any more."

"Ready," she replied.

"Gessh, switch to shotgun, I want you and Luna to clear me a fucking path," I ordered, waiting as Gessh stepped forwards, and Luna stepped around me. I ceased fire, reloading quickly as the pair started hammering out solid metal slugs that punched through several at a time.

"Todds, what's happening with that barrier?" I barked.

"Fuck all, boss," he replied, sounding frustrated. "The mechanism is out of reach, and it's taking longer to cut through the gantry than I like, I might run out of charge before I've gotten all the way out, and then we're fucked."

"Stow it," I ordered after a second's thought. "Fuck this shit, this place was set up as a trap, clearly they set the place up for this, and expected us to march in, then spend all our effort on escaping, while they bring in specter after specter. Those numbers can't be unlimited, but if we can close off the area, we can cut them down."

"We're going with the original plan?" Reign asked, surprised.

"Nothing's changed," I pointed out. "If we can cut off the supply of specters, then we can finish the job. Artem City itself pays the bounty on the fuckers, so that way we save our teams, we save the guild AND we get paid. The owners pay a portion of that fee, but most of the fee comes from Artem's government."

"So?" Luna said, before cursing. "Reloading!"

"Me too!" Gessh snapped, dropping her magazine as I stepped up to their shoulders, the pair shifting to make room for me as I started firing quickly, my headshots really dialing in thanks to the dumb fuckers moving steadily, and the good rifle.

"So…" I said, lining up another shot and seeing the specter, a young woman with bright blue cybernetic eyes, drop as if her puppets strings were cut as the hole bloomed in her forehead. "We still get paid for this. Then we go to the fuckers that set this up to profit from our deaths…"

"Ah."

"And we profit from theirs instead," Reign finished for me, all of us having the same thought."

"Hell, yeah," Gessh growled. "So how the hell do we get from here, surrounded by goddamn specters, to there, curb-stomping some corpo fuckhead's skull in?"

"We clear the stairs up and down, and we go down," I said, "We cut our way where we can—we're definitely going to need to conserve ammo—and then we seal the lower levels. At that point we know we're dealing with limited numbers, and we cut our way back up. Every room, every level, we kill anything that's not us, and we keep going."

"Hell, the way these are moving? Something's gotta be controlling them, maybe one that's in charge? Something that we've not seen yet. Maybe if we could capture that…" She left unsaid that capturing any kind of specter was a pain in the ass, let alone something that could control all the others around it.

"We'll see what we can do. Even dead it'll be worth a lot of creds, and hopefully we can link up with the others soon," I said. "For now, on three Reign you wipe the next level, drag that beam nice and slow, make sure there's a good pile of bodies they need to climb over.

"Gessh and Luna, be ready to hammer those fucks back, while Todds and I get the fun job."

"What's that boss?" he asked.

"Well, the Specters are having issues getting over their dead friends, but we need to get past as well," I pointed out. "So we're piling those fuckers up at the bottom of the stairwell going up."

"Damn."

"Let's go!" I called out, and the sisters did. They'd been firing slowly but steadily, taking the specters down now that the initial press had waned, and that the majority were being held up as they clambered over bodies.

Instead now they moved with a will, charging forwards as I counted down, and Reign opened fire at the next level above. Todds and I set to with a will at the pile of bodies, dragging them aside and clearing a path as Luna led, turning left at the end of the T-junction, killing anything between her and the stairwell down, while Gessh paused for us to pass her, before she started to walk slowly backwards.

With the two shotguns firing over and over, and a good thirty or so specters above us reduced to collapsed, half shredded bodies, we had the chance to move and we damn well took it.

As soon as Luna was out of ammo, I stepped around her and drew the plasma sword, striding to meet the monsters of a thousand tales.

CHAPTER SIXTEEN

The fight wasn't short, clearing the way to the stairs wasn't overly hard, although that the gantry cage had been treated with something to prevent us cutting our way out was damn clear when I tested the plasma blade against it.

It *would* cut, the plasma sword was far more powerful than the piddly little welding torch's cutter after all, but even though I'd charged the battery in the plasma sword, and its containment chamber was at half strength, it clearly wouldn't last long. I could have probably used it to carve my way through the door behind us.

We'd not be able to close it though, and if they'd closed the next door, and the next? Eventually we'd run out of power and have to stop, and we'd have nowhere to run to.

No it was better to finish the mission, then ram the sword up the asshole of the people that thought they could profit from my team's death. Maybe use it like a combination blender and toaster for their internals.

I cut the first bodies down with a simple flowing figure of eight turned sideways, the old infinity symbol I'd once been told. Well, what it was, was great for a flowing movement that required just the snap of the wrists, and the blade could carve through outstretched hands, arms and then take heads with ease.

The stairwell down at the end of the gantry was a little harder.

Stepping over the bodies of those I'd just killed, and kicking limbs aside, I stabbed down and down, thrusting over and over, the blade sizzling through foreheads, into open mouths and through eye sockets.

As the brain, and frequently the head, was destroyed each time, the body collapsed, creating a larger and larger barrier as I kicked my way down, until finally, I had to stop, power down and switch to my handgun.

The advantage here was that I was standing over them as they tried to climb a mound of bodies, teeth chattering and arms reaching.

I lined up the shot, fired, moved to the next. Rinse and repeat, shots ringing out steadily behind me, until there was enough of a lull before me that I clambered onto the pile, and practically body-surfed my way to the bottom as they shifted under my weight.

Reaching more or less solid ground, I fired three more times, taking another kill after kill, before lining up on the fourth, firing and as he dropped the figure behind came into view…

And shot me in the chest with a tactical shotgun.

I was thrown back, the armor enough that I was winded and hurt, rather than killed, but still, one of my grenades on my chest started making a buzzing noise, and Todds tore it free, throwing it hard away, seconds before it exploded.

Fragments flew in all directions, Reign calling out in pain as one presumably winged her, then the sound was lost as Luna opened fire on full auto, returning the surprise for the ghoul that had just tagged me.

"Up and at them, boss…" Todds grunted, hauling me back up.

I coughed and forced air back into my spasming diaphragm, gasping in relief as the sweet filtered and cooled air provided by my helm flooded my lungs, and I reached down, pulling a small medikit out, then putting it back as I winced over the pain.

It hurt, fuck me it hurt, being kicked by a shotgun *always* hurt, especially when you're at the business end of it, but that fucker was firing a single action shotgun, and the slug had literally hit a grenade full on.

I was insanely lucky, I realized as I looked down at my chest and saw the dented plate that had been behind the grenade.

That shot should have taken me out, or at least the exploding grenade should have. That it hadn't, and that I was left with at worse a cracked rib, and probably not even that, just bruising?

The medikit could be saved for now.

I glanced back up and down the corridor.

To my left, as I stood, catching my breath against the side of the caged gantry, the stairwell down was being filed by falling specters as they tried and failed to climb over their dead brethren.

As they fell, they were stabbed over and over in the head by Gessh, who then stepped back and waited for the next, her handgun in her other hand, just in case.

Reign was in the middle, grazer at the ready, but waiting for the order to 'clear the path'. Todds was with me, and Luna was standing with her shotgun ready, waiting for whatever was fucking stupid enough to poke its head up now out of the lower levels.

I squeezed Todds' shoulder in thanks then moved up behind Luna, reloading my handgun as I went.

"How…we doing?" I asked Luna, wincing as my chest twinged in pain.

"Half a mag left, and a foul attitude," she said, making me smile.

"Glad to hear it, soldier." I grunted, forcing the next breath out, then straightening and wincing as the pain flared again. "Okay, take the lead, clear the next section. We need to keep moving," I ordered her, as more gunfire rang out from above.

I looked up, seeing the flashes of fire, hearing the thunder that had to be the assault shotguns on full 'rock and roll' and seeing dimly through the overlapping mess of gantries, the press of bodies high overhead being blown apart.

"Cavalry's here!" Reign called out, grinning. "Sounds like Timur just joined the party!"

I tried to connect to him, the tac-net should have been able to reach the other team leads despite the jamming field after all, but nada.

"We'll get this section cleared, seal the bottom, and move up," I ordered. "Come on, there'll be less control down here now the ghoul has gone."

"Let's hope," Reign agreed from behind.

We moved on, the corridor we were in was a short one, which explained how the ghoul had managed to get me by surprise, when I'd killed the one in front of it, it'd been half way up out of the next stairwell, and half out of sight.

When Luna had gone full auto? Even though she was using a much less powerful shotgun than the assault models that Timur's team used, it was still enough to shred that fucker.

As we reached the top of those stairs, and stared down them, the press of specters was much weaker, fortunately.

The stairwell looped around in a descending spiral, limiting range, but Luna didn't hesitate, and seconds later we were at the bottom, with her blasting twelve shades of shit out of everything nearby.

It was a massive relief as we reached the bottom, now several levels underground, although that only lasted until we came up against a single, open door into a large hexagonal, solid walled room, just as two more specters came staggering out.

They were cut down, but the way that the path led to here and no further?

"Now I'm not the brightest, alright, boss…" Luna started.

"But that screams 'trap' to me too," I agreed with a snarl, sticking my head in, then jerking it back.

Gunfire hammered into the doorway where my head had been a split second before, and the wall on our side deformed outwards under the sudden barrage.

"Fuck's sake!" I snarled, grabbing a grenade and pulling the pin, then tossing it into the room. "Fire in the hole!" I ground out.

"What's in there?" Todds asked, wincing as the explosion, magnified by the walls rang out.

"Ghouls I think," I growled. "Four of them that I saw, but I could only see a little, and an open door to the sewers."

"A door?" Todds asked, before moving up close to the edge of the doorway, and poking a little cable around the edge.

I assumed it was a camera of some sort, one of those fiber optics or a drone or something that he could see around, but before he could say anything, a robotic hand, all shining black and red bones, reached out and clamped over his wrist, dragging him inside with a scream.

"Fuck!" I snarled, darting into the room, handgun raised…only to be back handed across the face and thrown across the room as the door slammed shut, locking the others out.

I hit the wall, bounced off it and hit the floor, my helmet having taken the blow that should have killed me, and kept me alive. It still stunned me though, and before I could make sense of the world around me, another hand, this time snow white and highly polished, with gleaming red fingernails like drops of blood—it's weird the details that the mind latches onto with a blow to the head— clamped around my right wrist.

I was hauled up, dangling from my right arm, as I instinctively went for the vibro-blade in its chest rig with my left. Another hand gripped that wrist as my arms were yanked out to their full extension, as a half skull appeared. It was matte black, with an old national flag painted over the top sloppily and missing the lower jaw, then suddenly it was inches from my helmet, examining me intently.

There was a clicking, buzzing noise from it as I screamed, the arms holding me tugging taut and then twisting them against their natural range of motion.

It held me there for a long second, and I thought it was going to rip my arms free, my cybernetic one no match for its strength as my shoulder socket popped and cracked...

Then it relented, and let me sag in its grip.

The first thing I saw was Todds, held the same way to the side in two more hands, the same fucking specter holding us with multiple arms.

I knew instinctively this was a banshee, and now that I could see, I saw the ghouls behind it, encased in cages and locked into the wall, guns mounted on heavy duty welded frames and pointed at the door I'd entered through, while all around the room the camera's had been smashed with blatant fury.

Below us, hovering as we were, the light of the banshee's repulsors illuminated the torn hole that led through into the undercity below...

And dozens of faces stared up at us with slack, vacant expressions, devoid of everything bar hunger.

The specter, no, the *banshee*, was badly damaged, and seriously pissed! I could see sections hanging from the walls and ceiling behind it where the damn thing had ripped its way free of the undercity and into this room, leaving an arm or three behind, as well as a small section of armored carapace that's seemed to have had restraining bolts drilled into it.

Now it was free to move around the room, but that was it, the door that we'd entered by was too small for this behemoth, and the entire structure was designed to be a trap for us to have to fight the ghouls in, layers of solid steel making it up.

The banshee was at least two meters across, the skull extending on a cantilevered post, the arms hanging in rows and partially obscured from view by handing sheets of material.

Material that I identified as fucking body armor! They were arranged in overlapping sections, like a normal man might wear clothing, a long coat or something, this wore layer upon layer of body armor, mainly suspended from an armored, welded together carapace that looked weirdly familiar.

It took my addled brain a second to place it, and then my asshole clenched even tighter.

Before the APS suits were made viable, there was a single unit that filled the space between giant assault mecha piloted by people, and actual people fighting in more normal body armor.

They were an experimental tech, one that I thought, and that the army *swore*, had all been eliminated after they went rogue.

They were people, dead fucking soldiers, that were put into mechanized bodies, restarted into a sick parody of life, and sealed into crab-like armored shells. Then they were fitted with repulsors, heavily fucking armed, and sent to patrol the battlefield.

As weapons of terror? Fucking yeah, 'a'-game all the way, the effect that seeing something like that flowing towards you had on an enemy? Multiple weapons systems all firing in all directions?

A single Archaeon had been recorded eliminating entire battalions. They were a fucking unholy terror, and they were exactly what the army wanted to use...right up until they tried to stop them.

The Archaeon turned on their controllers, and fucking slaughtered anything that came nearby. The ten test units they produced had been patrolling the section of battlefield they'd been given for a year before they were pulled back—it was supposed to be a week, as a temporary measure, but fuck all is as eternal as a government 'temporary measure'—and when they were?

Their nanites had been increased somehow, by tens of thousands, if not millions.

Later rumors would say that they'd taken to harvesting the battlefield for nanites, the dead on both sides being torn apart, and then they'd fed on them. Those nanites had bullied the cerebral systems that the Archaeon used to operate, back into some semblance of life.

A life without memories of anything but that this was 'their land' and that they were at war with everything else. Directives were discarded, rules of engagement? Hell the various cities armies had basically given up on most of those long ago, but even the few rules that were left were utterly discarded.

It'd taken a full military deployment of assault mecha to take the fuckers down. That one of them was here? No.

My panicked brain rebooted at that stage and locked in on the figure that stared at me.

This wasn't an Archaeon, it *couldn't* be, not unless they'd *seriously* evolved. This was a specter, yeah, a fucking banshee, and that was enough to repaint my pants in all sorts of colors that stank to high heaven, but it wasn't an Archaeon.

This was a specter that had found an Archaeon shell.

It stared into my electrical pickups, as another arm lifted forwards, long elegant fingers and a hand that looked like it was designed to model gloves or something, all perfect angles and grace…welded onto the end of three full length arms, attached end to end to give it range.

That hand grasped me by the chin, tilting my head this way and that inside my helmet, before flicking the latch and removing it, tossing the helmet aside like garbage.

I hissed in pain as it twisted my arms one way then the other, clearly checking for something, as the others shouted and banged on the door from the outside, calling, asking what had happened and if I could hear them.

The thing clearly wasn't interested in Todds, beyond keeping him out of the way and under control, but the skull was shifting, examining me from various angles…before starting to search through my gear.

After a few seconds of my mind racing as I tried to come up with an escape plan, and it basically checking me over for anything interesting, I was suddenly slammed back into the wall and pinned there, more arms flashing out, locking onto my ankles, pressing me, starfish style, against the solid wall, and slowly increasing the pressure as it started to pull the rest of my limbs out of their sockets.

It clicked and buzzed at me, and I hissed in pain, then cried out, frantically heaving against the pressure it was gradually increasing, as the strain grew more and more painful.

"Shit!" I cried. "Stop! Fuck…what the hell do you want?!" It stopped, the buzzing changing pitch, then rolling up and down the register, going high enough it made my ears sting, then vanishing, before lowering all the way to a point that my teeth ached as it continued.

After a few seconds it started the pressure again and I shook my head.

"I don't understand!" I snapped, the pressure stopping at my words. "Are you…are you speaking?" The buzz was back, rolling up and down and I shook my head.

"I don't understand." I panted. "Words…can you speak? Wait, can you understand me?"

Buzz.

"Your head, can you nod your head if you understand me?" I said, and after a few seconds it nodded…its arm.

"Head," I tried again, waggling my head side to side.

After a second it did the same and I drew in a long breath. It understood.

It fucking *understood*. This was a specter that was thinking and responding to me!

"What do you want?" I tried again, and for a long second it paused, watching me, before slowly extending another arm from underneath the carapace.

I thought it was an arm anyway.

It'd presumably started out as one, judging from the mechanisms, but it'd long since been rebuilt and repurposed.

Now, it was damaged, new sections of shining chrome showing where it'd been rebuilt, a central post that everything was built around, with surrounding layers of armor that could be retracted—as they did before my eyes—or deployed to keep it safe.

The main point though, were the dozen or so medikits that were locked into position higher up on the arm.

They had tubes running from a central ring lower down, and then up to feed each of them, with spaces for dozens more to be attached.

I frowned trying to make sense of the thing. Was it some kind of massive medical system? A storage?

It looked more like it was meant to be used to harvest stuff the banshee passed over, like the arms would swing down and cut loose mods it wanted, collect whatever and then…maybe it pulled the medikits up and locked them onto there for later?

But the tubes, they were there to feed it, and to…

My eyes locked onto the hand. At the end of the arm there was a hand, brand new judging from the shine on it, with injection ports and needles replacing the ends of the fingers.

Right behind that, where tubes left the fingers…was an empty section. One that I suddenly knew should have a very specific bit of kit in place to cover.

I flinched and looked back at the skull, finding it watching me, ready.

It nodded the head up and down jerkily, signifying it'd fucking seen me jump and it damn well knew why.

"We recovered it," I admitted. "We killed goblins and found it. It's yours?"

Another jerk of the head.

"And let me guess, you want the fucker back?" I said, getting a vigorous nod. "Can you stop all this?" I jerked my head in the direction of the room overhead.

The skull shifted, moving and looking up, as if looking directly through the metal and seeing the area above, before shaking its head, and glancing down at the figures below us waiting in ordered rows.

I squinted down at them, at the torn sections of the floor, and the damaged cameras, the ghouls that were damaged, but intact, and yet not firing any more.

I took it all in, in an instant.

This section was supposed to be a place for us to bleed. Ghouls locked into the walls armed with shotguns and assault rifles that were in turn locked into welded frames.

If the banshee hadn't torn its way up through the floor, taking control of the specters here, this would have been a fucking bloodbath.

If the door had shut behind us, as it was set to do, with specters pouring up through the hole in the floor, and the ghouls firing at us? With the sheets of metal welded over them forming their prison and armoring?

We'd have lost at least a few people, and possibly the whole team trying to close off this section.

Instead, the banshee had presumably sensed the collection of specters and had come here, fucking hunting for *US*.

The way that it was watching me said it knew exactly what I was thinking, and it fucking wanted its stripper back. This was the creature that someone had stolen the device from originally.

Presumably, looking its clearly fresh repairs over, the fucker had barely survived the experience, and then whoever it'd fought with, had then been shanked by goblins.

Then we'd killed the fucking goblins, and this thing had been searching for its spare parts ever since.

"I don't have…" I started to say and it pulled hard on my arms and legs, making me scream in pain, Todds doing the same as he was apparently punished as well. "Stop!" I howled, and after a few seconds it relented.

"Fuck…" I panted, head sagging as I caught my breath. "I…was trying…to say, I don't have it HERE."

It nodded, the hand that had taken my helmet off making a point of tapping my bags and pockets as if to say 'I fucking know that, you dick'.

"I can get it," I assured it, and it nodded, hard. "This place, I need to get rid of the specters…my team and I are paid to get rid of them. We need to save my team, and I'll bring you the…the... whatever it is!" Realizing at the last minute that if it thought I didn't know what it was then there was a chance I'd actually survive this.

It turned, floating towards the exit, the specters below moving back, clearly about to leave and take us both wherever, and I shook my head.

"I need my team to get the device, the thing you want! I need them to get it, but we have to finish up here first! If we go before the whole site is clear of specters? Then…" I hesitated. I had no clue what this thing could understand.

Was it at human levels of comprehension? Did it understand debt, or honor? Was it like a dog, only understanding the immediate goal? Was it more intelligent than I was?

It wouldn't be that hard to be, I was well aware of my own shortcomings.

"The device, the thing you want?" I said slowly. "I can get it, we can trade! I'll get it, and give it to you, and in return…" It waited, and I felt a wave of relief wash over me. "My spinal mod," I said quickly.

It hesitated and I tried to twist, nodding my head in its direction as I spoke.

"I need a high end one, the best I can get, full spinal tap, do you understand? I need a tier…four!" I tried, knowing that it was fucking unlikely that it could get something like that, but that if anyone could it could.

I also knew that there was no way I was putting a mod from a fucking specter into myself, not willingly, but…

I was starting to figure that a serious portion of the mods in the various chop shops around the city were coming from these. Hell, one or more of those I already had might be.

That thought made my skin crawl, knowing I might be spiraling closer to the flame of madness, infected by my own mods, and never knowing.

The specter waited, and I watched it, not sure what I was waiting for, until it drove its head forwards suddenly at terrifying speed, making me screw my eyes shut, expecting it to smash the front of my skull in.

Instead, when I slowly reopened them a few seconds later, the gleaming eye sockets were millimeters from my own, and it waited.

"Uh…" I tried, until Todds spoke up hesitantly.

"Maybe…tell it where and when?" he suggested.

"Fuck!" I gasped, as the head nodded. "Uh, this time, tomorrow? Outside of here, outside of this building?" It waited for a second, I assumed considering, before it removed a small device from under its cloak, and showed it to me.

I stared at it, it was a disc, about six inches across, maybe two deep at the thickest point, and I held it before my face…before it twisted me around and slapped it onto my back.

I felt the solid click as it connected with the magnetic plate, then I was jerked back around, and a hand was held before my face. It formed a fist, then mimed an explosion, before finally waggling a finger at me in warning.

Clearly a message that if I fucked with it in any way? I'd regret it. If I didn't come with the device? If I tried to run, to hide, whatever? Kaboom.

I'd recognized it as some kind of pressure explosive, one of the ones that massively increased the local gravity field, possibly, like the reverse of the repulsors tech that let vehicles fly did.

I guessed that doing anything with it would be a very bad idea, possibly one that would result in me suddenly being an inch thick all over, but who fuckin' knew.

All I knew for sure right now, was that banshees were real, this one was fucking terrifying, had both Todds and I at its mercy, and the only way we were getting out of this, was if I basically gave up the one bit of tech that I thought could earn us serious credits.

It was a fucked if you do, fucked if you don't situation, and I didn't like it one bit.

I did like living though, and if this was how I got out of this situation I'd take it.

The banshee watched me for a long few seconds, then threw me across the room. I bounced off the wall, and then was hit by Todds, the pair of us falling to the ground in a groaning heap, and the banshee vanished into the ground, leaving the ghouls strapped in place.

We laid there, catching our breath, trying to deal with what had just happened, before Todds finally spoke in a low whisper, as we both popped a medikit and stabbed ourselves with the injectors

"Boss, you can tell me to fuck off if you want, but this is seriously the weirdest fucking team I've ever worked with."

"Yeah," I said, struggling to my feet, and wincing at the way the ghouls, now apparently free of the Banshee's control, were wrenching at the guns, trying to get them around to us. "This is just my fucking life mate." I drew the handgun, shot each of the ghouls in the head, one round each, then holstered it, offering him my hand and pulling him to his feet when he accepted it.

"You probably have some questions…" I winced.

"Oh, that's a fucking understatement." He shook his head. "How about we get the fuck outta here first though?"

"Deal."

CHAPTER SEVENTEEN

It took a few minutes to unlock the door, and by that time the first specters were starting to appear again, dragging themselves up through the damaged floor.

Todds worked his magic, unlocking it and getting us out, and I cut heads off as they appeared, punting them back into the hole, before grabbing and resituating my helmet.

"What the fuck happened in there?" Reign asked, as soon as I followed Todds out, and he got to work sealing the door again, welding it shut to make damn sure no more were getting in.

"I'll fill you all in properly later—"

"The boss is apparently on speaking terms with a fucking banshee," Todds said, "and he owes it some gear, now he's got a directional gravitation mine attached to his back, and I need a fucking drink."

"A banshee?" Reign asked, before looking up as though to pierce the levels overhead. "that what was controlling them?"

"A second one I'm betting," I said, thinking fast. "This place was clearly set up as a full-on fucking deathmatch gameshow. They had ghouls welded into armored recesses in there, set up for us to get slaughtered when the door shut. That banshee forced its way in and was waiting for us. I think it was tracking us specifically."

"Us?"

"It looked like it'd rebuilt itself a lot, but I'm betting it's the same one that came after us in the tunnels, and it wants the device we found." I waved off the looks they shot at Todds and me.

"I heard enough that I'm kinda all in now," he said. "Don't get me wrong, I'll not spread shit around if you boot me, but if you guys have more secrets on top of this shit? You won't be able to surprise me more than you just did."

"Wanna bet?" Luna asked with a grin.

I opened my mouth to add something, before a scream from overhead echoed down, then a sustained barrage of gunfire rang out.

There had been steady firing echoing down from above, and as soon as we'd left the trap box, there'd been plenty of evidence that Reign and the sisters had been fighting on this side while we'd been locked in...

But now?

The gunfire went from steady and controlled, to panicked. The controlled bursts to wild hammering, and another scream rang out, this time in fury.

"Fuck!" I snarled. "Right, we can catch up later, for now? Run like your ass is on fire!"

I did as I'd ordered, setting off running, my rifle up and ready.

The bottom of the stairwell was clear again—for now—of actively trying to kill us specters, but jam packed with dead ones, at least twenty bodies piled one atop the other were in the way, and I could see more trying to find a way down to us as I slid to a halt, released my rifle and grabbed the nearest body, dragging it backwards and out of the way. Luna moved in grabbing the next, and Gessh on her other side, as Reign and Todds took out the incoming few with headshots, making room as quickly as we could.

In under three minutes we were off again, running up another staircase, jumping and clearing two steps at a time, all of us switching to handguns so that we had a hand free to grab and pull and we leapt over bodies.

Floor by floor we ran, the cross-hatched pattern of the cages blurring as we raced past, finally making it back to the level we'd been on originally, and then moving higher.

Here and there we crossed paths with another specter, but after clearing away those lower down, they were few and far between.

As we made it to the next floor, and that much closer to the gunfire above, we saw why.

Specters, when they're not controlled, are desperate, brain dead scavengers of mods. When they are controlled? Sure they're different, but they're still not very bright.

Up ahead it was clear the default that they were working on was 'see it, kill it' as there were hundreds clambering over each other trying to get past a small barricade made of their own dead.

They were on the floor above us now, and the specters that had been filtering down after us? They'd presumably heard closer gunfire and signs of life, and had turned around, heading for that instead.

As we raced onto this floor—a single long corridor that ran from one stairwell to the next—we were greeted by the backs of at least two hundred specters, all pressing forwards, desperate to make it to the next level.

"My turn." Reign grinned, swinging the grazer around and firing a single solid burst at head height at the mass from behind.

Dozens collapsed silently, the flesh of their heads, necks and what was left of their brains simply cascading apart.

"Ten percent." She grinned, waiting for the bodies to drop, before doing the same again, and again. After the fourth burst, she fired a much shorter one, then stepped back, unslinging the battery and replacing it with a new one, but damn it'd been effective.

By rocking it left to right in a narrow arc, the beams had been soaked up by literally just the heads, killing at least a hundred, silently. The majority of the mass were still struggling forwards, unaware of the bodies behind them collapsing to the floor.

"Luna, Gessh," I ordered, as we all moved forwards, and the girls stepped into the lead, shotguns booming.

We lost the element of surprise, admittedly, but in doing so we drew the specters attention, giving the teams above a little relief, and letting them know that we were coming.

The shotguns fired, blasting into the packed mass, limbs flying loose, heads exploding, and bodies fell over and over. As soon as their magazines ran dry? They stepped aside, letting Todds and I through.

By this point we were clambering over the bodies, each of them laid haphazardly atop another, and our aim was suffering, a slip of the foot here, an angle to the stride there, a face squashed underfoot?

All of them combined to make me miss as many as I hit.

Fortunately there was a solution.

As they got a little closer, I released the rifle, and drew my sword.

The crackling wash of heat that rolled out from the self-contained sun, masquerading as a sword, was both welcome and seriously effective. The specters ran at me, and I extended the blade, essentially lunging, then staying at that extension, and flicking the blade left and right.

It was ridiculous.

It shouldn't have worked, hell it really shouldn't have worked, and against a 'living' opponent it wouldn't have.

Against the specters? These virtually mindless creatures, driven by hunger? It was insanely effective.

The only real issue was that there were so many I quickly had to start stepping back, clambering over the bodies. Going forwards, when I could see was difficult enough. Walking backwards was an order of magnitude more difficult at first.

Fortunately my team were as smart as I needed them to be, and in thirty seconds, despite me having almost fallen twice, I was holding the line while they cleared a path for me.

The press of bodies was difficult, but as the seconds became minutes, and then five became ten, the slaughter grew easier and easier.

After another five minutes beyond that, I powered down the sword and stepped back, letting Gessh and Luna take my place.

The gunfire overhead had returned to a steady pattern again, and as the sisters stepped up, firing over and over, the last of the throng filling the corridor fell.

We moved then, hurrying forwards. I realized that in my slow stepping retreat, beheading as I went, I'd been gradually pushed almost all the way back to the stairwell down, and as we moved up again, we clambered over fresh piles of bodies.

I glanced at the 'kill counter' I'd had the RI add to my vision what felt like months ago, but was in reality only a few days now.

"Fuck me sideways." I grunted.

"What's that?" Todds asked, at the same time as Reign piped up.

"Too busy right now, see me later," she said.

"Kill counter," I explained. "Have you guys got one? I got my RI to keep a record, group, as best as it can, and personal."

"And?"

"And you fuckers seriously need to start carrying your own weight, I've nearly got a solid third of the kills so far!" I joked. "Five hundred and seventeen, personal."

"How many for me?" Todds asked, and I shook my head.

"I don't have it monitoring individuals, and if I did I'd need access to your feeds—which is a point actually, we'll need to cut the banshee section from that— so the kills for the overall team?"

"Yeah?" Reign asked.

"One thousand, six hundred and forty-four."

"Holy shit," Todds exclaimed, and I nodded.

"How're we doing on ammo, boys and girls?" I had no clue just how many rounds, or even magazines I'd gone through so far.

Reign was the first to speak up.

"Two magazine for the solid slug sniper, each of twenty rounds, one battery for the grazer, one mag for the handgun."

"Uh…three mags for my rifle, three for the handgun…" Todds winced.

I had almost my full loadout for the shotgun, but I was down to a single mag for the handgun, and two for the rifle. Worst of all was that my plasma blade was down to a third of the charge. Both the electrical charge and the containment were heavily depleted, but that was a hell of a lot better off than I would have been if I'd been using a gun all day.

The sisters, when we got them to cycle back and let Todds and I take the lead, admitted that they were both down to a single magazine each in the shotgun.

Rifles weren't bad, and Gessh's rifle was a grazer as well, which was a relief, a good hundred shots there for her, but by the time we clambered up the stairs, and my tac-com finally overcame the localized jamming and connected to another outside of my team, we were grimly accepting that we needed to start scavenging as we went.

The first connection was to Timur, who was mid-way through a rant about 'proper fire discipline' over the local frequency to both his, and Liolet's teams.

"Really, that's what we get?" I asked, cutting in. "Not even a 'hi, how you doing'?"

"Who…*Kabutt*?" he asked, stunned.

"Yup, coming up the stairs, so you know, don't shoot me in the face, it tends to offend," I quipped tiredly, making one more revolution of the spiral staircase.

As I reached the top—and I climbed up the mound of bodies—I smiled at the sight of the two squads, as they maintained steady fire, taking down the seemingly endless stream of specters moving down the stairwell between us to head for them.

Whatever anyone might say about Liolet being a half goblin, or the rest of their teams specific mix, those fuckers were skilled at fortifications.

Sections of the gantry way had been cut through on either side of the corridor, right before the fortification, and additional plates had been sealed into place further narrowing the route.

They'd also angled sections of the corridor so that the specters basically must have been falling out and down regularly, rather than piling up right before the fortification, the ground and walls had been removed in staggered sections, and the bodies had been tumbling away through those gaps.

The more I looked, the more impressed I was, as well as understanding why so many of the fuckers I'd seen before had looked quite as battered as they had done, and where the stragglers had come from.

Where we'd been fighting our way down, then clearing the area, but still getting fuckers pop up now and then? They'd been using the situation to their advantage.

Bodies had been falling and hitting the cages, then bouncing off and off, the various levels breaking their fall until they hit the lowest level.

A living, sane being would have been screaming for help, and probably dying.

A specter? No reaction beyond a slight loss of functionality, it'd just get back up and try again, but it'd have to climb all those stairs on the way.

We'd been killing their tossed off victims for them, I realized.

"Oh you utter bastards," I grumbled, too tired and despite myself, *impressed*, to really be annoyed. I remembered the amount of times I'd seen, but not really consciously registered the bodies falling past, or the dents in the cage.

"Kabutt!" Timur greeted, actually looking pleased for the first time. "You're alive! And…and all your squad!"

"Yeah, we're here," I said, waving. "Hold up, we'll come to you…" I lifted my rifle and starting to thin the herd from my side with careful shots.

I lasted about five seconds before Reign tapped me on the shoulder and reached out expectantly.

"No room," Timur said flatly. "There's barely enough room for us to squat in here, and we had one lad fall already. No, I think it's time to advance."

"You do?" I muttered, shaking my head. "Well I think it's time for a fucking break first." I passed Reign my rifle, and moved to the side, leaning against the side of the corridor cage as she fired over and over, a single cycling shot, one round, one kill.

"We're being watched and recorded," Timur reminded me in a low voice on our private command channel. "Best not to show them anything they can use."

"They?"

"The fuckers who set this sick game up," he said. "This was well planned. We tried to cut our way out, the main doors were reinforced and molecular bonded. We'd need serious gear to get out."

"So we forged ahead with the clearance plan despite the bloody stupidity of it," Liolet growled. "I'm glad you're alive, Kabutt, we were wondering, but seriously, we need to hole up, brace ourselves and hold for rescue, you know that Julius will be coming for us…"

"Yeah, but he needs us to earn from this to keep things afloat," I said. "He'd probably have come straight for us under normal circumstances, but our contract is for clearance, there's nothing in it I bet that stops or makes this illegal. Yeah, there's dodgy shit going on, but they'll claim it's old stuff from when it was a deathmatch site. Hell, if Julius blasts his way in to rescue us? They'll probably sue him, and fucking win, for the damage to the building!"

Silence met my take on it, and I went on.

"I've sealed the lower floors, aside from the occasional asshole that fell off here, I think we've taken most of them down now, that we've not been hit much since I reached here?" I shrugged. "I think we need to push on, take the upper floors and then finish this, claim our wage and then…?"

"Then?" Timur asked, and I nodded.

"Then we find the organizers of this little party, and we 'discuss' their methods of generating credits with them."

"Sounds good to me," Liolet said grimly. "Two of my team are dead. I'll not let that slide."

"We came damn close a few times," I said, and Timur grunted in agreement.

"So, you hold that line at the bottom of the stairs, we're coming out," Timur said after a few seconds, and I passed the agreement onto the rest of the team.

Reign took over the suppressing detail, emptying magazine after magazine, as I broke out the spare ammo I'd had in my bag, letting the team reload as we waited on the others.

By the time they made it to us, and one of Timur's assault shotgunners took over, we were ready for a drink, some food, and to relax a little.

Not that any of that was going to happen for a while.

CHAPTER EIGHTEEN

The next section of the cooling tower was a lot more straightforward. With the overwhelming press of specters taken down, and all the teams dialed in, it took about fifteen minutes for us to clear our way up to the last third of the tower's height.

This section was again concrete, or something similar, reinforced with inlaid steel mesh and molecular bonding, meaning that without a lot more powerful explosives than we had, there was no way we were getting out without going all the way to the top.

The stairwell ended in a door, one that when it was opened exposed a reasonably wide corridor, with doors on both sides. As we moved deeper in, we checked the rooms, finding that aside from several specters that seemed to have gotten lost and trapped behind a couple of overturned desks, they were all empty.

"You think it's done?" Liolet asked softly, on the command line as we started up a set of stairs to the next level. "You think we might have finished them all?"

"Not likely," Timur growled. "Something was commanding them, something was making them a hell of a lot smarter than they usually are and…"

I opened my mouth, wondering if I should mention the basement. It probably wasn't a good idea, but maybe the trio of ghouls that had been—

My thoughts and Timur's mouth were cut off as a massive blade, spinning at an insane rate, dissected the short human, cutting through him, armor and all, across the chest, just below the nipples.

His body crashed to the floor in a fountain of blood, as a pair of ghouls stepped out of concealment at the top of the stairs, opening fire into the massed group of us with rifles.

We responded quickly, training overcoming the shock and horror, but it wasn't fast enough.

Timur was dead.

Even nanites, as magical as they were, couldn't stitch him back together when he'd been cut in two. Three others died in the stairwell as well, one of them Timur's partner, who'd been standing next to him, staring in shock, and then shot in the head by a ghoul.

The majority of us were protected by Timur's people, as they climbed the stairs ahead of us, but the stairwell erupted into pandemonium as we all tried to return fire, hide, or deal with the casualties.

The two ghouls were hit multiple times, but it wasn't until one of Timur's surviving assault shotgunners opened fire on full auto, that they were taken down.

These fuckers had been in body armor, with good helmets, and that had kept them in the fight far longer than they should have lasted.

The next floor was soon covered in blood, as we set up a triage section, eight of the group had been hit, four killed, including poor Timur.

Thankfully there weren't many specters waiting on this floor.

This time though, Todds set up his stealth gear and fucked off ahead, returning a few minutes later with news that the next stairwell had a similar blade, but that when we were ready he'd take it out.

There were also, he thought, two more ghouls waiting at the top of this stairwell.

So he'd set up a grenade on a remote trigger near the top of the stairs, 'just in case'.

As soon as we were all ready, I took the lead, and sent him ahead to disconnect the blade. The rest of us waited by the bottom of the stairs, with Reign braced and ready with her solid slug sniper rifle.

Todds disarmed the trigger for the blade, and returned to us, before I called out in a loud voice.

"OI DICKHEADS!"

That was all that was needed, any sound would have been enough I imagined, but as it was the pair stepped out, again in full body armor and helmets…but Reign shot the one on the right in the face before it could open fire, the high powered sniper rifle taking the back of its head off with a solid crack.

The one on the left was sent flying backwards as the frag grenade on a makeshift trigger was set off by Todds.

By the time we made it to the top of the stairs, the ghoul was almost on its feet, but due to the whole 'having no arms and only half a head' it really wasn't a threat.

Todds shot it in the head and finished it off, before quickly scavenging it for ammo.

We'd taken to doing that since we'd met the others, and we'd also cross loaded the ammo from the dead. It felt wrong, like taking Scott's battery had done, but it was also the right thing to do, and we all knew it.

An hour more, several dozen small encounters, a single specter here, a group there, and we could hear the wind and the rain from somewhere up ahead.

It wasn't exactly subtle, letting us know that once again, the final stage of this fight was going to be in the maze and no doubt broadcast to all comers.

"Before we reach the top people, remember that the client has paid for access to your feeds, all of them, bar anything that is covered by the legal exemptions, such as when I used the toilet at the bottom of the building…" I looked at Todds, who frowned, then nodded catching my meaning.

"I used it there as well. I'll remove that from the recording," he said quickly.

"So, anything like a toilet break, or a personal moment, if you remove it NOW, before the jammer is dropped, stays in your system buffer, it doesn't go to the client. Anything else? They get. Take a minute."

I did as I'd suggested, having my RI scan to the banshee encounter and erase it all, adding in a section of me moving towards a corner to take a shit and cutting out, before restarting as we left.

The conversations that mentioned the banshee were similarly wiped, and I made sure the others did the same, despite the longer time it took them to do so.

Reaching the top floor, and moving out into the flood light and neon lit top of the cooling tower, I was immediately hammered by a dozen access requests.

First was one marked by a vaguely familiar symbol, but as soon as it opened, I saw it was from some religious nutjob who started spouting off about a pogrom against all those who 'willfully injure the prophets of...'

I cut that one off and blocked the fucker, accepting the one from Julius next, figuring it said something that a religious nutjob had been the fastest to get a signal through.

"Kabutt!" Julius cried, clearly desperate for news. "Fuck's sake, man, what the hell is going on there?"

"We were setup," I said, checking the local area and cursing myself for being so overwhelmed I'd nearly let myself get distracted. There was nobody nearby, but the area here was huge, and with the panels of weather-beaten steel that ran everywhere cutting off any real sight ranges, we could be nigh on surrounded and we'd never know it.

"How?" he asked.

"The entire place is a deathtrap," I said, still looking around. "Maps were useless, doors welded shut and reinforced cages that were set up to trap us, spinning blades, ghouls trapped behind armoring so they could guide their specters and be a right fuck on to kill...all that good fun shit, you know?"

"Mother fuckers!" he hissed. "I'm getting telemetry...fuck! Timur? Ah man..." He broke off, shaking his head and clearly struggling for words.

"Yeah, that wasn't long ago as well, trap blade in the stairwell."

"Look, you're under contract to hand the recordings over at the end of the job, and they're being backed up even now to a server they have access to, so..."

"So they'll start streaming our people's final moments at any second," I growled. "Kids are going to find out their parents are dead by watching them literally die 'live'."

"Basically, yeah," he snarled. "Kabutt, this is an order, are you paying attention, operator?"

"Yessir," I ground out through clenched teeth.

"You need to lock all emotion down, especially about any plans for the future. Get our people out of there, keep them alive, and we can discuss possible *legal* options later..."

"*Legal*—"

"Shut it down, Sergeant!" Julius snapped. "To be discussed later, when there are less people fucking well listening, alright?"

"Yessir."

"Good man, finish the job and bring our people home. Julius out."

The line cut off, and I growled, seeing three more requests pop up trying to take his place, one using intrusion software that managed to activate my RI's autonomic defensive subroutines.

The line opened, and I recognized the same voice speaking that I'd heard earlier. It was one of the talking heads on the panel that was fucking broadcasting this debacle.

"...we might have access to one of the team leaders here now folks and..." he was saying as I growled, then grinned and tagged the intrusion software as a live terrorist intrusion attempt and reported it using an old internal APS privilege.

It wasn't, registering something as that when I was still an APS operative would have gotten me a fine, and possibly a demotion, but it was a *legal* option.

It was also sent directly to one of the city net's AI patrollers.

Where certain AI were literally general purpose workhorses, with wide ranging purviews, others were, by necessity, given insanely strict areas to work in because of the possible damage they did when unleashed.

The defensive AIs were in that second group, and they really, *really* didn't fuck around. Any danger, any possible risk to the city, and that met their limited tests?

The AI's tended to go nuclear, tearing the system apart and searching for anything, then move on, totally uncaring of the devastation they'd left behind. When people had reported things to the AI before, they'd taken down corporation cyber warfare departments 'accidentally', hence now there were fines and demerits if one of us reported something that wasn't really a terrorist attack…

…but I wasn't APS anymore, and I had the defense that I was attacked by a cracker—a system designed to force access to my implants—without warning, so had fallen back on my training.

I might get a message from the AI managers at some point telling me to not do that again, but considering they were a government entity charged with the security of the city, and this was an illegal hack? That was the worst I'd get.

"Hey…" One of Liolet's people called out suddenly. "The broadcast, its down!"

"For everyone?" I asked, and clearly something in my voice caught Reign's attention.

"Kabutt?" she asked, her voice low.

"Yes, Reign?" I replied calmly, just as someone else spoke up.

"The entire broadcast is cut, something about a terrorist threat?"

"What did you just do?" Reign asked me on a direct link.

"I don't know what you mean." I smiled. "Someone just tried to hack me, to force their way into my implants, and as I still have limited classified data in there? Well. I did what I had to do."

"And that was?"

"I might have reported it to the defensive AI's as a terrorist attack," I admitted. "After all, it might be, and I couldn't risk that data getting out." I sent her another smile, as my voice dropped to a purr of satisfaction as a thought occurred to me.

"In fact, I'm legally required to defend that data with my life, and report any attempts to access it to the proper authorities…"

"Oh," she said, clearly running the words and the unspoken meaning through in her mind, before sending me an image in return as she spoke. "I think that's a very good point Kabutt, you should make *very* sure that whoever did this is reported to the correct people…for the city's security."

The words she sent were entirely innocent, and publicly correct even.

The image she sent me, well…she apparently liked what I'd done and I'd be getting a little reward later for being a good boy.

I coughed and surreptitiously adjusted my pants as that image replayed over and over before me.

I quickly tagged the intrusion and dredged up the possible areas it infringed upon and while the others deployed, I sent a dozen messages in thirty seconds.

That done, I sent a compressed report to Julius, got a single image from him as a response—a Carcharodon smiling, thankfully, nothing sexual—and I locked down the external links again as much as I could.

I replaced the lockouts that I'd disabled earlier, my usual settings prevented any kind of contact in a fight after all, but I'd not realized that I'd overridden that earlier in trying to reach out as the jamming came online.

Well, you live and learn.

When you live, anyway.

"Reign, Liolet!" I barked out, connecting to them both. "What do we have?"

"My people are scouting," Liolet said distractedly. "I've two runners left out of four, and they're out there, telemetry is good, and they're stealthy."

"Reign?"

"I sent Todds," she said. "He's in full stealth, and going a lot slower, but between the three we're getting a decent image of the upper floor."

A partially filled out map appeared before us, and I growled as I saw the layout.

The rooftop was circular, we were atop the tower after all, and the lip of the tower came to around hip height on us where we currently stood at one edge.

The center stepped down into a bowl shaped depression though, leaving it protected from the constant wind that blew this high up between the buildings.

That wasn't the issue. The issue was that there were three things that promised that this was still all to fight for.

First and foremost, we'd not killed the last ghoul or banshee nor completed our sweep yet, and I seriously doubted that as the 'finale' for the broadcast area, this was intended as the easy part.

Next? There was a fuzzed intrusion shield operating above our heads.

I'd seen them before, a kind of shimmer to the air that made clear recordings almost impossible…unless you had the decoding key. That one was live and blocking out the view from above right now, as a good two dozen drones flitted and wove about up there, with more presumably on the way?

Not good.

Last of all, was the worst.

This place had supposedly had a maze, followed by a central area as the final deathmatch for people to bet on. I was assuming the maze was trapped to buggery, because it sure as shit was still there, and it looked freshly painted.

Metal walls with the occasional entrance could be seen, and from where we stood, we could see just over the top to make out interlocking plates further in. There was a central higher section that terminated right at the level of the intrusion field, so clearly we weren't supposed to find out what was waiting for us there. Clearly we were going to be the first, because while yes, according to the others nobody had managed it yet, but they were all people that were armed with melee weapons, against hunters that paid for the chance to hunt live people.

This time the prey had assault shotguns and grenades, not to mention a foul fucking temper.

It was time to go slaughter something.

CHAPTER NINETEEN

The first decision was the easiest to make, namely did we go in as a group, or split up.

Both possibilities had potential. Go in as a group, we were more likely to be able to support each other and make it past any enemies.

Go in as a half dozen or more small groups, or as three teams, and we had far less risk of all being taken out by a single well placed trap. We would also force the enemy to split their counters, rather than concentrate them.

Lastly, the space looked to be just wide enough for two abreast, if you were friendly. That seriously limited the options that we had for firepower concentration, and increased the likelihood of being taken down by grenades etc.

It was Liolet that came up with the counter to that.

"We move in pairs, but all follow the same route. Move a few meters apart, that way we're close enough to react, and far enough apart that a single mine can't get us all," he said. "My scouts will crawl across the top of the maze, yours leads."

"That works," I agreed, as Doul, the new leader of Timur's team nodded along gruffly as well. "How are we all doing on ammo?"

"Low." Doul grunted. "Couple hundred rounds between us all that's it."

"For the shotguns?" I asked.

"Aye." That was the only response I got and I shrugged.

"Fair enough, for the assault shotguns that's only a few seconds firing, so you bring up the rear, be ready though, if we need you, we'll really need you."

"Aye." Again, the same grim response, and I hesitated, before turning to Liolet.

"If your runners can stay on the tops of the walls? Great. I'm betting that's been tried before, so tell them to be ready for traps."

"They already know, and volunteered," Liolet replied, clearly not happy I was giving orders, and yet willing to take them as well.

"They volunteered?"

"They were volun-told," Liolet admitted after a few seconds of silence. "They'll do their job."

"Fair enough." I nodded. "Todds will lead the way in full stealth and watch out for traps. We find the center, we claim it and kill whatever they've got there, and then we fuck off home. Today has been enough of a clusterfuck as it is, so do me a favor and let's make sure all of our people survive from this point on."

"We've got the back," Doul agreed.

"My people on the tops and in the middle," Liolet said, and I nodded.

"And me and mine leading the way behind Todds." I finished the layout and gestured to the maze. "We take it slow and steady."

And we did.

The raised lip that we'd been standing on had a sloped runoff to get down to the lower level, and as soon as we all got to the bottom, people moved to fall into their place in line without complaint.

Luna and Gessh boosted two of the half gobbos up and onto the wall on either side of the entrance, and for a few seconds they stood, checking the route out.

"We take a left, then two rights, then a left, and that gets us about halfway to the center," one of them said after a few seconds pause. "Looks clear from here."

"Then let's go," I ordered, watching as the blur that was Todds vanished inside.

Stepping in, the walls seemed to tower over us, despite them being literally a half meter over our heads. They were close enough, and large enough that they cut us off from the rest of the city, and as soon as we took our first turn, the last flickering neon of the lights were extinguished again.

Helmets and optical implants took over, bathing the corridors of the maze in various colors, and I moved in staggered formation with Reign behind me to my left, and with Luna and Gessh ahead.

I could hear the muttered grumbling of the halflings behind me, goblins of any mixture were apparently unable to keep their fucking mouths shut, but as we took the next turn, and then the third, even their chatter died away.

The maze wasn't silent, not by any means, the distant sounds of the city still filtered in, as did the clanks and scrapes as something occasionally rubbed against the walls.

It was insanely oppressive though, the atmosphere, and as we came to the next section, one of the goblins on 'overwatch' on the left was forced to leap across the gap.

He'd clearly intended to land on the wall on the far side, but leapt a little too high.

He hit the interference field, and rather than pass through it, as we all expected…the entire field turned bright red, crackled, and suddenly contracted.

He screamed as hundreds of thousands of volts passed through him as a concealed shield flared to full life, knitting together with him half poking through it.

The shield jerked downwards, contracting towards the tops of the maze, and the second goblin screeched in fear, diving down and out of sight on the other side of the wall.

The unfortunate that was caught in the middle of the shield as it came fully to life, screeched as well, but not for long. The shield cut him in half, cooking the poor fucker as the bottom half of his body tumbled free, legs twitching to splat wetly onto the floor, intestines uncurling with a definite finality.

The top half? Well, the shield was slightly domed, and it slid—slowly—down the outside, crackling arcs of electrical discharge flickering over his remains as he charred, sliding from view.

As soon as it happened though? We were too busy to worry.

Here and there as we'd walked, we'd all noted tiny green LEDs, pin-prick lights that gleamed cheerily as we passed them.

They all, as one, clicked over to red, and the casual stroll through the maze came to an end.

Behind me I heard the bark of gunfire, but before I could look, a single horizontal line of light appeared before me, right behind Gessh, and crossing the corridor.

I blinked, then barked to the team. "Get down!"

The light had appeared at chest height, and as it burst to life, a track appeared, coverings sliding back to allow free movement.

The track was at the same height, but the blur as the laser projector slid along it, made it damn clear if I'd not been looking I'd have regretted it.

Probably for the rest of my life.

The laser was a thin red line, and as soon as it reached the end of the track just behind where I'd been standing, it shut off, the track covers sliding silently back up into place as I cursed.

"Move, MOVE!" I barked, knowing damn well the fucker would be resetting. I started running, Gessh and Luna were already past it and yet still moving, Reign at my shoulder and the teams behind me hurrying to keep up.

As I passed the last section, of this part of the wall, I saw the folding plates that signified the laser's reappearance…Then winced as someone behind us opened fire with a shotgun, blasting the wall.

At least half of the shot ricocheted off, some of it making Luna cry out in pain as several of the smaller pellets hit her, but at least the laser didn't trigger again.

Todds appeared around the edge of the next corner, hurrying back to us, then dove forwards, hitting the floor and rolling…as a nozzle behind him deployed, spraying the area with some kind of plasma weapon.

The wash of heat here was bad enough, but Todds cried out hurrying as quickly as he could to reach us.

"Next section…" he managed to get out through clenched teeth, dragging a medikit out and stabbing himself, the back of his plate carrier smoking on his armor, even as the stealth sections warped and crinkled, clearly now useless. "The walls are…oh gods that's better…the walls." He tried again as the medikit took hold. "They're moving, sliding into a new configuration and—"

"Get everyone up here!" I bellowed, a second too late as the nearby walls started to move too.

I had a split second view of the half goblin that had jumped down to the other side of the wall, as another wall slid sideways, revealing him creeping along on the other side…then the floor opened below him and he vanished, screaming.

The way the scream echoed before cutting off abruptly made me damn sure that he'd not fallen a short distance.

"Boss, they're shifting the entire maze," Luna snapped from my left. "This isn't what they did on the show, this is specially done. What do we do?" she asked, clearly rattled.

"Who has the fastest reactions?" I asked.

"Us, probably," Luna said, with Gessh nodding.

"And the fastest moving?" I asked with a grin.

"Me." Gessh said firmly. "My new legs…"

"And you're good with a sword," I said, reaching behind my back, and tugging the plasma sword free, before offering it to her. "Think you could take out the traps?"

"The lasers? The cutters and the plasma…" She hesitated, thinking about it. There were a few seconds as they went live, literally two seconds maybe, that was how we'd lasted this long, as the coverings needed to slide back, the mechanism needed to be exposed.

As fast as Gessh was, augmented as she was?

She reached into a pocket and pulled out a pair of stims, before getting another one from her sister.

Three of them, all expensive battlefield ones as near as I could tell, and the sisters exchanged a long look, before Gessh grinned, taking the blade from me.

"Always wanted one of these," she admitted, rolling her wrist as it flared to life.

I smiled tightly, having sent an unlocking code to the weapon, and even though I knew it was our best chance, hating the feeling of fear it gave me as I handed over one of my 'toys' for the first time.

"Just clear as far as you can, make a cut in the middle of each panel, by the ground as you run, that should stop them being able to move the fuckers later on as well," I ordered, getting a nod. "We'll follow along behind, anything that triggers but you don't get? Don't worry about it, just try and mark the wall and we'll take it out as we follow."

Todds spoke quickly, filling her in on what to look for, as she injected the first stim.

"Fuuuuuck!" She groaned, shaking her head and grinning, before tearing off down the corridor.

"She..." Todds cursed, cutting off. "Fuck's sake she barely knows what she's looking for!"

"She's not an idiot," Luna snapped, glaring at him, and then at me. "I know what you're doing boss."

"What's that?"

"Sending her ahead with her ass in the wind like that! You're playing fucking redshirt with her life!"

"Who has the best chance out of all of us to survive it?" I asked her grimly. "Because you damn well know I'd have done it if I could."

"Then why—"

"You and she were bred for war," Reign snapped. "Faster reactions, stronger, better stamina, all of it and—"

"Yeah, just like you were bred for fucking! I don't see him sending his favorite piece of ass ahead, do you!" Luna snarled, as the corridor went silent, Gessh already out of sight ahead and round the corner, a glowing scar fading on the wall as the plasma blade took the plasma jet out.

"Luna..." I started, knowing that she was both right and oh so wrong, and that this was coming from fear for her sister.

"No," Luna cut me off. "No, boss, sorry but you don't get to make this right, not now at least. If she survives, yeah, maybe, but if not? You just sent her to her death, and I can't keep up! That's the worst part!"

"I know," I said. "That's why its shit to be the boss. Sometimes you have to send a friend to die, to save the team. I hope I didn't just do that, but we'll see. For now? Todds, lead the way."

"Yes boss." He sighed, about facing and starting back down the corridor. The sections of wall that we passed that were scarred and cut seemed to roughly correspond to all of the traps, sure here and there, there was an extra one, either something that hadn't triggered in time, or that hadn't been seen at all, but damn, the girl did good.

Plasma jets were followed by a set of needlers, launchers on one wall that fired a barrage of tiny darts at the far wall, riddling anything that was passing at the time.

The launchers were spent when we found them, half cut apart with a burned trail across their surface as the blade had slashed them apart. The rest had fired, and judging from the number of barrels in the wall, and the number of darts broken on the floor? Gessh was seriously moving fast.

After the needlers was a trap floor, the middle panel of the floor still hanging there from one edge, and we quickly moved to one side of the corridor, inching our way past the lip.

After that we had several carved and broken panels, a collection of cracked and seemingly blown apart panels where something had exploded outwards, and then several twists and turns ahead—we were following the clearly damaged sections that she'd cleared for us—we found the razorwire section.

It was like a spiderweb of glistening razor sharp steel, here and there, there were splatters of blood, letting us know that here at least, Gessh had struggled, but by and large? She'd carved her way through them all without missing a beat.

There were two small medikits ahead, discarded on the floor, and I picked them up, pocketing them, noting the blood that covered one of them, and the blood trail ahead of us.

After a few meters though, it noticeably lessened, and then as the medikits took hold it almost vanished, much to the relief of all of us.

Two more sections were blank, before a shout from a passing corridor and a new heart attack for us all, resolved into a member of Liolet's team limping up.

Borrolet, as she introduced herself, had gotten disconnected from the rest of the team by a sliding wall, and had been panicking ever since, while still moving forwards.

She joined us, moving up to work next to Todds, and while she wasn't as fast as he was, she was still a relief to have. Half an hour we followed marks in the wall, cut as the trail went back and forth, and occasionally we caught a glimpse of Gessh in the distance.

Luna spent most of the time alternating between cursing me, cursing my 'fuck-toy that just sucks his fucking dick' and apologizing to us both, admitting that Gessh was doing an insanely effective job.

It wasn't until half an hour more had passed, as well as both the second discarded stim injector, and the third, before we heard heavy gunfire and screams rising from ahead.

That was it, until then we'd been able to take it slow and steady, but no more.

We set off running, full belt, all caution dismissed as we sprinted, a left, two rights, a third, then a fourth, another left, a stairwell that led down and under where I guessed we'd literally just ran a few seconds ago, and then a second stairwell up…

Then we burst out into the center of the maze, a much bigger area than I'd been expecting, with all hell breaking loose.

CHAPTER TWENTY

The center of the maze was a square, roughly, and where I stood on the outer face, we were raised up again over the middle.

There were four entrances into the square, then four sets of narrow, single step stairs leading down into a flat area, with a handful of small walls set up to shelter behind.

The center though?

Another banshee, as we'd guessed, a mass of arms and guns, firing in several directions at once, with specters running from cover to cover, and ghouls standing at the corners of the square using post mounted and welded on heavy machineguns.

Three were currently hammering into the walls that a half dozen of Liolet and Doul's people crouched behind, even as Gessh basically ran in drug induced mad circles dodging fire.

As soon as we entered, we were spotted, and the guns swiveled, opening fire as we broke up. I sprinted to the edge of the stair and leapt, arms windmilling, bullets glancing off my armor—and one hitting high on my helm and snapping my head back with a jerk—before I hit the deck a good five meters lower that we'd entered on.

I rolled, then swore and rolled again as a slug from a shotgun hit the back of my leg, tearing through the thinner armor and spraying the ground with blood as it punched through my calf.

I jerked behind the cover of the small wall, hissing in pain but not having the time to deal with it, as I edged my rifle around the corner, triggering the link to it and seeing the world from the barrel, as I opened fire.

Blind luck struck again as I lined up almost perfectly on a ghoul that'd been chasing Gessh with a machinegun, the heavy fire tearing into the walls right behind her, catching up as she sprinted.

She was back to leaving bloody footprints as she ran, a dozen small wounds trickling blood down her gleaming metal legs, the sword either dead or deactivated, but still clutched in one hand as she dodged gunfire.

Luna opened fire from behind me, the cycling of her shotgun by now familiar enough that I picked it straight out as she went full-auto, blasting into the banshee from behind.

It screamed, spinning, several of its dozens of arms twisting around to fire at us, before the boom of Reign's sniper rifle announced its arrival.

Almost before I heard the sound of the shot, I saw the banshee stagger, a repulsor exploding and sending it reeling sideways, as it drifted accidentally out of cover.

The others on the far side, at the twelve o clock and two o clock positions from us, had been hammering the enemy, and getting hammered in return, but our arrival at the back forced the specters to split their forces.

The specters all moved as one, the damage to the banshee overriding whatever else was going on as they all swung to fire on Reign.

She screamed, rolling to the side and frantically trying to get out of the line of sight as the doorway around her fractured and splintered under the barrage of heavy fire.

The opportunity granted by the distraction wasn't left unused though, as someone on Doul's side stood up and went full bore with the assault shotgun, the boom of each shot changing into a rolling sound almost like thunder as they took a good half dozen of the enemy down, ending with three shots directly into the back of the floating banshee.

It staggered, spinning and returned fire, literally shredding him, a good half dozen assault rifles all blasting the living shit out of the poor guy, before I cursed and screamed into the fight.

"EMP!" I bellowed, throwing the EMP grenade I had directly at the banshee.

It spun, seeing the grenade, and slapped it down, again proving the fuckers were intelligent. All the nearby specters dropped everything they were doing and dove on the grenade, as the banshee tried to put as much distance between it and the deadly blast as possible.

There was a moment of confusion, as they realized I'd thrown, but never primed the grenade, as I barked "NOW!" into the tac-net, and the others opened fire. Then the fucker realized it'd been had, as I went full auto on both my shotgun and assault rifle.

The pair lasted seconds, there was probably a joke in there somewhere over the speed of me ejecting the spent mags as well, the business done, as I dropped back to one knee behind the barrier.

It wasn't important though, because the loss of the suppressing fire and the fucker being out in the open was enough. Four other assault rifles chattered over and over at the banshee as it spun and twisted, bullets sparking off armoring, guns coming up and firing back, before the ear-splitting, bone deep thrum of the grazer filled the air.

Reign left the banshee alone, rolling the sustained fire over the collection of specters and ghouls as they tried to stand and the fuckers collapsed into a mass of dissociated rotted meat and metal in seconds.

The weapon cut off then, the battery drained all in one go, as Gessh, weaving from side to side dodged the barriers, vaulting over the last one, and threw herself down, sliding on her back under the banshee as two rifles and a clawed hand tracked her, the floor being chewed up, and the hand leaving gouges and a trail of sparks literally inches from her head in the steel.

She didn't miss though, as the plasma sword stuttered to life, extending upwards and carving through almost half of the fucker from below.

The banshee screamed, all electronics nearby freaking out as something interacted, the interference shield over and above us faltering and cutting off as the banshee crashed to the ground.

I was up and hobbling forwards both rifle and shotty discarded, handgun leaping into my right and vibro-blade filling the left as I raced forwards, seeing the banshee twisting, trying to bring a rifle around to point at Gessh.

I fired, two others doing the same, and the rifle spun loose, clattering on the floor, before Luna passed me, leaping on the banshee, her guns forgotten as she started to literally tear arms free, almost frothing at the mouth over the fury that this thing almost killed her sister.

My comms were going nuts, both local—with the teams, Liolet, Reign, and half the fuckers there—and with the one person who could get access to me in a fight now, Julius.

I accepted his comm—audio only—as I lined up the revolver and blew an arm free of the fucker, closing on it as Luna forced another arm back and snapped the rusted metal free, the banshee screaming in electronic pain and fury.

"DON'T!" Julius was screaming. "Fuck's sake, Kabutt! Stop!"

"What?" I growled, my arm in auto as I lined up on another arm, one that was already damaged but shaking as it tried to lift. I fired, the shot punching into the connector and blasting the lower half free in a spray of brackish fluid.

"Fucking stop, you lunatic!" That got through, as I slid to a stop over the banshee, and dropped to one knee. Ramming the revolver against the curved plate of the fuckers skull.

"Everybody freeze!" I barked out, and wonder of wonders, they did, even the banshee, who stared up at me, three optics in its face glowing a malevolent red.

We stared at each other as I spoke in a low voice.

"Dead man's trigger," I said. "You'll have something left as a last resort I'm sure, you do anything to me or them? This gun goes off regardless, and you die as well. So…stay very fucking still."

The optics blinked and I looked at it, wondering why the hell it'd removed the middle section of the skull, but kept the curved dome, cheeks and mandibles, then filled the nose and eye sockets with individual optical pickups.

"Now…what the hell do you want, Julius?" I asked slowly, removing the blocks I'd put on the commlink, and seeing his avatar appear in one half of my vision.

"The drones are broadcasting the banshee images across the city," he said. "We've got a bidding war going on from corpos and research centers that want that fucker for their R&D divisions, they're going nuts, and I fucking mean nuts!"

"The company that set this up?" I asked.

"Cored like a fucking apple." He snorted. "*Somebody* set a military grade AI on them looking for any possible terrorist connections…"

"Shame that."

"Yeah well, rats and sinking ships come to mind, the entire company basically just bailed. Nobody there is in any position to try and claim anything right now. You're there under my authority on a legal contract, which makes anything we find, as the company that hired us no longer exists…ours.

"The current bid is five million credits. I'm betting we can set a price of ten and get it. That's a hell of a payday for the entire team and the guild. This could totally save our asses, so please, don't kill the fucker. Take it alive. I'll make goddamn sure the credits are good before anything else happens, and get medics incoming, we'll be able to afford them now."

"Fine," I said after a few seconds, long ones in which I felt my trigger finger quivering, a single infinitesimal additional touch of pressure being laid on the metal, then another, before I finally forced myself to stop, and I cut the line.

"They want you for research," I said, staring into its optics. "Personally I'd rather kill you, remove the threat now, but it's not my call to make. I know you were captured, and were set up here for the 'show', it's the only thing that makes sense. That means that at least some fucker out there has a way to capture and contain you. They were willing to waste your lives in the same way they throw ours aside, so I guess we're the same in that.

"So, here's the deal. You come along nicely, no fighting, no attempts to escape. Once we hand you over? That's your business. You escape in an hour or a week, that's fine. You try to escape now? I'll kill you. I know you're as much of a fucking victim in this as we are, but you fuck with me right now? I'll kill you. This is the only warning you get."

We looked at each other for a few seconds, then its lights pulsed in a pattern, before apparently giving up on me as too fucking dense.

A knock rang out on my keystone, and I froze as I accepted it, reading the message that unfurled before my eyes.

TERMS ACCEPTED.

"Motherfucker," I whispered in shock, before clearing my throat and calling out to the rest of the survivors. "Medics are incoming, as is a transport for our friend here. Trust nothing. Patch yourselves up, reload, and be ready. They might decide to try and save the purchase price yet."

Various responses, from low and virulent swearing to approval rang out, but I didn't look away from the banshee, not until Reign stepped up and rested the barrel of her sniper rifle against the top of the dome of its skull, Todds starting to search and disarm it.

Then I finally lifted the handgun away, hissing as someone stabbed me in the leg at the same time with a medikit, and I glanced down, seeing the half-goblin Borrolet, smiling up at me in what she probably thought was an ingratiating way.

Considering her teeth looked like she was one step from dying of halitosis, and could give a shark a nightmare, it wasn't reassuring.

I forced myself to nod and thank her, reaching for a medium medikit on my belt to replace the one she'd just used on me…only to find she'd actually used mine.

I collected the empty one and slid it back into a pouch, waving off her request to join our team on a more permanent basis, and directing her back to her own group as I checked Luna and Gessh over.

They both had a dozen minor wounds, and Gessh…well. She'd already triggered two medium medikits, and was sitting shaking and panting as they worked to heal her injuries, repair the insane level of damage she had to have done to her internals through no less than three fucking stims in half an hour, and purge the remaining chemicals from her system.

She looked like shit, but the grin on her face was beautiful.

As was the one on Luna's when after hugging her sister she stood and pulled me to my feet.

I winced, the pain in my calf that I'm managed to ignore through the last minutes of the fight making damn sure I knew it was there.

Then she was hugging me, squeezing me tight enough that I felt ribs creaking under my armor, and I remembered the injuries from earlier, as she whispered into my ear.

"Thank you, Kabutt, for caring, and having the sheer brass balls to do what needed to be done."

I hugged her back. "I hated it, but it was right."

"Now…is Reign looking jealous yet, or do I need to get you to grab my ass?" she whispered, and I snorted, pushing her free.

I stepped around the banshee, seeing the rain running over it, hearing the spark and fizz as damaged electrical components shorted, even as Todds continued pulling weapons free and tossing them into a pile.

Most of them were empty, and almost all were the same make and mark as the rest of the specters had been carrying. A quick glance around the rain soaked plaza revealed a stack of boxes, clearly packing crates for the guns, and ammunition, making me shake my head in amazed disgust.

Whoever arranged this, really went all out. They must have been expecting serious credits from the pay-per-view. I joined the others, reloading, collecting my own discarded weapons, including the EMP, and winking when Liolet growled that he thought I'd fucked the entire day when I used that.

I showed him that I'd never even triggered it—it'd not, as he thought, failed to fire—and the look he gave me was one of sheer disbelief.

A few minutes passed before a transport tried to land to collect the banshee. Julius called us and grimly pointed out that this was NOT the client that'd paid us, it was some chancers trying to steal our payday, and thirty seconds later, my team was the owner of a lovely, if slightly battered, aircar.

Admittedly, there was a little blood here and there, but I'd had a bad enough day that I'd just confirmed it with Julius, stepped up, and had shot three of the occupants. The fourth had been more than happy to transfer his ownership of the vehicle to us as an apology, and had been directed to walk out of the maze through the left hand passage.

Ten seconds later there came a boom, a scream, and all was right with the world.

A minute or so after that, the actual client arrived for their property, as did a team of trauma docs.

That wasn't cheap, but clearly Julius could afford it now. We did some minor last minute jobs, including swiping a few arms and a rather nice left hand that concealed claws, then realized none of us were actually licensed to fly an aircar.

I was trained to, but only outside the city and under army rules, which basically translated as 'the shit has already hit the fan'.

Eventually a remote link was established to Dondo, the half orc that had done such a number on the sisters, and that worked for Oshbob. He took control and guided the aircar for us all the way back to the warehouse.

Unsurprisingly, when we landed he was there inside of thirty seconds, and in under a minute after that, both Luna and Gessh were in one of their rooms, apparently taking turns at the shower, and the muscular and well hung half-orc.

Reign told me to fuck right off when I made what I thought was a perfectly reasonable comment about joining her in the shower and I was forced to listen to the sound of Dondo apparently trying to drill for oil he was going that deep.

I couldn't even take my damn armor off, not properly. Not with that gravitational goddamn mine on it, and I was forced to make do with a handful of sanitation wipes.

The only consolation was that as the sun was coming up, and I was staring at the cheerful bastard lighting the sky, I got a personal message from Reign.

> Today we're getting my chip out, and tonight I'm getting your dick in.

I smiled at the beautiful sunrise, and sipped my coffee, sending an agreement symbol back to her, as I admired the world. Maybe it wasn't going to be such a bad day after all.

CHAPTER TWENTY-ONE

I sat in a small, shitty chair that was clearly designed to make the person sitting in it as uncomfortable as possible, while I shifted my weight, and pretended to work on the report of the tower mission.

I'd written hundreds of AAR's in my time, literally. Hell, I usually wrote them on autopilot, more than half of it coming from the RI and me just polishing the details as we watched the recording. It parsed relevant details out and locked them down.

Why the hell, when they had an AI go over the recording of the fucking fight, they had any need for an after action report, but they still did, apparently.

The waiting room I was sitting in, along with Luna and Gessh—Todds was taking his kids somewhere nice today apparently, treating them after the scare of them almost losing him live on a vid-cast—was that particular blend of rich and poor that only medical facilities and lawyers offices could manage.

The building was alright, well maintained, and the waiting area was clean. There were seats, and even a toilet. That was about it though. On the other side of the desk that the receptionist sat behind though? The quality was markedly different.

One glimpse through the door there when someone passed through revealed expensive seats and what looked like a full-on buffet bar for lunch being delivered.

On our side? A vending machine. A particularly shitty vending machine, that was both at least double the price I'd ever seen one before, *and* somehow managed to be out of stock of everything that wasn't apparently designed to be vomit inducing.

"This is taking the piss right boss?" Luna groaned, shifting on a chair that she barely fit on, and groaning in discomfort as she did. "I've never been so battered by a bit of furniture," she lamented.

"That's a new name for it," I said.

"Hey, I was fine before I sat on this. It's the chair's fault, not Dondo..."

"You were walking like you'd ridden across the wasteland on a bike with no suspension," I pointed out dryly.

"Hey, he knows what he's doing," Gessh interjected with a smile and a slight coloring of her cheeks.

"So I heard," I growled, shaking my head. "Can we change the subject?"

Luna sighed. "Touchy this morning aren't you?"

"Only because she didn't let him touch her," Gessh added, and I glared from one to the other, before resolutely looking back across the room at the door Reign had gone through.

When we'd shown up here this morning—four fucking hours ago—It'd been with the expectation that she'd be in and out inside of an hour. Hell, yes it was a brain mod, but a decent carver had that shit sorted in no time these days. She might have been a bit woozy, but I'd been planning on a nice aircar ride back, and I wasn't even going to try anything on the way.

Massage seats.

Maybe some music or something.

Definitely not going to try anything until she was a hundred and ten percent ready.

Probably.

But after three hours, when Gessh and Luna had messaged and asked where I was, I'd given in and told them, and they'd been steadily complaining about the seats, the décor, then lack of food and the horrible smell of the place for twenty minutes, and I wasn't sure if it was the grim-faced receptionist, who glared at us the entire time we were there, or the sisters that I wanted to shoot more.

That it'd taken four hours so far, and that according to a brief message from Reign an hour ago, nothing beyond a review of 'her circumstances and finances' had been done yet?

I was rapidly losing my limited fucking patience.

I'd just started to fantasize about shooting the receptionist in the face—she was genuinely glaring at me as if I was there to rob them of her children's inheritance or something—when the doors banged open and Reign stalked out, looking furious.

"Kabutt, I…Luna? Gessh? Brilliant. Get in here," she snapped, before about turning and marching back through the door.

We were up and moving before the squawk of protest could properly form in the receptionists mouth, and by the time we reached the doors—with her frantically hammering the 'door close' button and ordering us to back away, that we weren't allowed in there—it was too late.

Gessh grabbed one door and practically ripped it off the wall, while Luna drew her shotgun and smiled winningly at the security guard that came running out of the small office on one side.

He took one look at them, at me, and then at Reign walking away? Then shook his head, dumped his pass on the floor and headed for the door.

"Fuck this shit, ya'll don't pay me enough anyway!" he called over his shoulder as he left.

I followed Reign into a *very* nicely appointed office, to find a weaselly little man, presumably at least half goblin, sat behind the desk. He started sweating as soon as we entered, and that only increased as Reign took her guns back. She'd been forced to leave them with me as she went to discuss the matter with a 'counsellor' and hadn't been happy about it.

"What's the problem?" I asked. Standing behind Reign as she sat back down, both Luna and Gessh stepping up on either side and drawing guns.

An automated turret deployed from one wall, locking onto Luna, then switching to Gessh, then me, then Reign, clearly struggling to pick the most overt threat as it waited for an order to fire.

"You…you can't just…" the little bastard tried to say, when Reign cut him off.

"You've given me six different reasons why I can't be free of the mod since I arrived, and each one is shittier than the last," she growled. "So let's be clear on this. The reason you don't want to remove the mod isn't because you're afraid I'll relapse, or that I'm being used, that I'm trafficked for sex—my ass is great, but nobody will pay that for a go of it—and more. The real reason, is that I'm making decent creds, and you're taking forty percent of them, and you want to keep that going. Once I'm paid up? You're legally required to remove the claim on my account. So, we all know what's going on here, and considering that you're the fucking cockroach that fitted it, I don't believe for a minute that you can't remove it!"

"It's not that simple, we need to book in for the procedure, and—"

I lifted my plasma sword and triggered it.

The sight of the arm long bar of contained plasma, flickering and burning bright enough it hurt to look at cut him off quickly, and Reign started to speak again.

"Someone is getting operated on in a few minutes, Director Hughes, the choice is yours," she said almost patiently. "It can be me, paying my debt off, and you removing the implant, or it can be Kabutt here, a sergeant of the APS Corps, operating on you, with his plasma sword."

"Just to make it clear," Gessh said laconically, "we're all heavily modded. Your turret opens fire? It might kill one of us, most likely it'll just hurt. Then the rest of us will destroy it, and we'll force you to remove the implant without payment."

"Then we torture you until you transfer everything you own to us, and we kill the miserable bitch on the front desk, then we'll go have lunch."

"I could go for a burrito," Reign admitted, before smiling at the little bastard. "So. Last chance before I save a lot of money…"

"You…" he whispered, wincing before sagging, then waving a hand as the turret slid back into the wall, and he evidently made a call to the front desk.

"Prep theatre one…yes, yes, I know! Just do it, Dalla!"

A few seconds later and he'd clearly disconnected, as he glared at us. "Just so you know, the procedure is dangerous—"

"Very dangerous," Luna agreed. "If Reign isn't completely satisfied, then I foresee a 'complication' coming your way."

"One that involves a plasma sword being pressed against your asshole and triggered," I finished for her, cutting the power to the blade and holding the projector up, making it very clear where the blade would appear and go.

"No, I…I'm serious!" he tried.

"Oh believe me, so am I."

Reign smiled at him. "You fuck up and lobotomize me, 'doc'…" She shook her head. "…they'll kill you and everyone you've ever so much as looked at in passing. Do you understand this? You know that tower they broadcast the fight from? The team that went in and killed literally thousands of specters, that captured a banshee, that fought through insane traps and beat the old deathmatch?"

"Y…yes?"

"Want to make a comparison against the image of the ones that captured the banshee, and us?" she suggested.

A second later his face went even paler, and his ears started to shake as he forced a smile onto his face.

"You don't understand…I've *always* been motivated by what's best for my clients," he tried, to snorts around the room.

"Don't make me fucking laugh," Reign snapped, rising to her feet and glaring at the little fucker. "Let's get this done, and you'll get the transfer after I recover."

"We can't..." He started and she took the safety off the massive grazer rifle, letting the room fill with the ominous hum of the weapon going 'live'.

"If I die on the table, or get lobotomized, you'll die in there too," she said. "If not? You'll get your pay, like I came here to do in the first place. Now let's get to work."

"Uh..." He started and we all glared at him, watching him wither under the combined distrust and hatred. "Um, I've never removed one," he admitted in a small voice. "But..."

"BUT?" Reign snarled.

"Never?" Luna growled, shaking her head.

"If I remove it, there's going to be a gap in your cerebral cortex," he said. "It's that gap and space for infection that I've heard causes the majority of the port-removal terminations."

"So we put a new mod in?" Reign suggested as we all looked at each other in question.

"I don't have any, or any experience in..."

"Fuck it," I snarled. "Guess what you little bastard, today's your lucky day!"

"It is?" he asked, blinking.

"Oh, it really is," I assured him. "You get to learn a lot, and for such a reasonable price too..." I gestured to Luna. "Grab him, we're going to see Lion, he can watch over this little turd and make sure the job's done right."

"I...wait, what? No!" He shook his head. "There are trade secrets that..." He cut off as I lifted my sword projector and waggled it warningly.

"I'll get the cab," Reign said, as Luna grabbed the diminutive figure by the throat and lifted him with apparently little effort.

"Now there're two ways we can do this," Luna said with a smile. "One of them, you try to run and I get to kneecap you, the other you tell your bitch on the reception desk that this is your idea, and you make sure she believes it. Want to guess which one I'm hoping you choose?"

I smiled as Luna walked next to the director, and he led us all out of his office, passing the receptionist and speaking very quickly to her.

Whatever else was going on here, the receptionist was clearly either a shareholder, or thought she was, as she tried to complain that it wasn't right the director going anywhere, and certainly not to remove anything.

By the time the aircar arrived—a four seater, but which fortunately had a large trunk—we were all thoroughly sick of the pair of them.

By the time we landed outside of the chop-shop, and Lion wandered up, still eating his lunch, the director had apparently still not recovered his attitude.

Lion on the other hand wasn't as sanguine as we waved to him, then dragged the flustered and very well-dressed man out of the trunk of the aircar.

"What's he doing here?" Lion asked, taking another bite of his lunch—a wrap of some kind—then pointing it at the little man. "I don't do removals and strips, so if you kidnapped him..."

"Lion," I said, shaking my head in mock sorrow. "You wound me man, you really do. Thinking I'd stoop to that." I patted the smaller man we'd brought with us on the top of the head, almost driving him to his knees. "If I wanted a mod or two from him, you know me, I'd have torn it out myself, I'd never expect a friend to do something so bloody and violent."

"Yeah," he agreed, around a mouthful, before swallowing, then balling up what was left and tossing it into a nearby bin as he led us inside. "So, what's the deal then?"

"You know that shitty brain mod that Reign has in?" I asked.

"Yup."

"This is the fucker that installed it."

There was a minute of silence as Lion turned and glared at the little figure, who seemed to wither even more under that look.

"Go on." Lion invited after a few more seconds, clearly no longer worried about what was going to happen to our 'guest'.

"Turns out they only have the roughest of ideas of how to remove it," Reign said grimly. "And that if there's a space left over it'll cause issues, so we should apparently get a carver to add in a new brain mod."

"And you thought of me?" he asked, getting various nods.

"We wanted someone we can trust to do the work, and to make sure he doesn't fuck up. He's going to show you how it all works and how to remove it…"

"I can't! The guild will…"

"Your shitty little guild will never know you showed anyone, but the only two options you have here, are to remove it and hope we keep quiet, or to not remove it, in which case we kill you, and try and remove it ourselves. Now one of those outcomes is definitely fatal for you. Pick quickly." To everyone's surprise it was Lion that had spoken, and I nodded.

Clearly the carver that did special jobs for almost nothing to help his community disliked the vulture as much as the rest of us did.

That he had no ally in the carver apparently broke the director, who sagged, and nodded, before starting to speak.

The vast majority of the things he said were meaningless to the rest of us, only Lion seemingly understanding the words that fell from his lips.

For me it was like a someone had broken a language RI and it was spouting gibberish with extra vowels in, but fuck it. As long as Lion understood it, that was all that mattered to us.

Twenty minutes later and Reign was being 'prepped for surgery' which basically meant she gave me a single kiss, broken off before the rush of hope and pleasure hormones could make her sick, and she picked a new brain mod from the limited few that Lion recommended and could get there sharpish.

This one offered enhancements to all of her senses, supposedly enough to boost them all almost at will. It was a hundred and thirty grand, but I'd taken the little bastard to one side, and I'd explained to him that he was getting a class A education here for a cut price of only the exact amount that Reign owed on her debt. He was going to get to watch Lion do the operation, and then he'd know how to fix people in the future, wasn't that wonderful!

He also removed the claim on Reign's account, which she verified, and I explained the consequences of his actions, should he choose for example, to send an assassin after me for this.

Basically I made it clear that any attempt on any of our lives, would result in me coming after him. I didn't need evidence, so hiding it behind getting others to hire them and so on was pointless.

Any attempt, and I'd come and kill him. that was it.

When he pointed out that I was a mercenary and an APS operator, and that people must try to kill me all the time, I nodded, and agreed.

It really didn't appear to make him feel better for some reason.

Lion pulled out a tool called a nano-scalpel, and went over the details of it with the little bastard, while we all took up station a little off to the side.

Reign and I watched each other silently, as he injected her, and I swallowed hard, forcing a smile, as the woman I was slowly coming to care for most of all, sank into a drug induced slumber.

I watched those brilliant eyes flicker shut, and I sat there, knowing that she might never wake. That out of a desire to ride me, she was risking losing herself.

I felt terrible, suddenly wanting to stop it all. I didn't need the sex, hell neither did she, but…but that wasn't my call to make. It wasn't about the sex, not really. Sure we both wanted it, and yeah, it was definitely something that could grow to be an issue between us eventually, as apart from the sex, she could never experience real happiness with the damn implant in.

She couldn't enjoy food, drinks, real camaraderie, and yeah, sex. She couldn't go to a comedy night, or watch a favorite vid. She couldn't dance or sing or…or whatever she wanted, because she was trapped into a life of an emotionless automaton, all because of this little bastard taking advantage of her.

I hated him, and I forced myself to sit back, and stay quiet as Lion spoke about neural connectivity, and plasticity, and loads of words that just seemed weird to me.

I watched as the minutes became ten, then thirty.

After an hour, when Lion finally sighed and straightened from the job, I couldn't help it, watching her half laid there in a chair, eyes closed and seemingly asleep while he literally tinkered with her brain from behind.

"Is that it?" I asked, coming to me feet. "Is it done?"

"The mod is out," he confirmed, "The new one is ready to go in, so either sit down, or go for a walk, the less distraction the better here alright?"

I gritted my teeth and threw myself into the chair again, glaring as it nearly folded under me. After a few seconds, rather than laughing as they seemed to like to make people think they would do, both of the sisters moved as one.

A hand rested on either shoulder, and they both squeezed.

It was ridiculous, a show of sibling support that was meshed in who they were so deeply that they both reacted at exactly the same time, in the same way, and yet?

I reached up and laid my hand on theirs, squeezing back my thanks.

There was no need for words as we sat there, another hour coming and going, then a third, but eventually Lion stepped back and sighed, dunking his hands in a vat of some solution to one side, his tools sinking to the bottom as he lifted now clean hands free.

An injector was lowered on an arm, and positioned ready, as he gently smoothed the section of skull he'd cut free, back into place, and then did something with another tool, seeming to draw along to points of damage.

"I'm injecting a small portion of 'nites on the incision line," he explained, for the benefit of all of us, before he drew an elaborate pattern on the skull, then smoothed the scalp and her hair back into place, again, following the line.

"Did…did you just sign her skull?" Luna asked, and Lion snorted.

"No, I left a pattern of 'nites atop of the bone, they'll be sealing the skull to the scalp, helps healing." He shifted slightly, squinting and making a few last minute touches, then used the injector, and a medikit at the same time.

"The injector keeps her under for a few more minutes. The 'nites will flush her of the knock-out, but the time it takes to do that they'll be fixing more of her as well. I know it might seem like a waste, but without that, she'd have woken up with a splitting headache. As it is? Give her a few minutes and she'll wake naturally."

"That's it?" I asked, and he shrugged.

"I've done all I can, the rest is up to her," he admitted. "This is the worst part, memories are often lost in these kind of mods, and those memories? They might be nothing, playing with some childhood toy that you don't even really remember, or your parents arguing…or they might be a core facet of your personality. You just don't know."

I understood it all, intellectually, at least.

Reign and I had talked about it, on the way over to the facility, and we'd made the mistake of looking up the recovery rates…as well as the side-effects.

All of it went through my mind as I moved over and knelt next to her, holding one hand in mine as Lion moved off.

Where Lion had the common sense to give us a little space, it took Luna marching over and grabbing the director by the ear and physically dragging him away to get us a little privacy.

I stayed there, as my knee went numb, as my back started to ache, and as my fear of what might be rose. We'd talked about the worst case scenario as well.

Not death, as horrible as that was, but that she might be…less, or different. That she might not be able to work with us any more, that she might not be herself.

She might decide she hated me for some reason, or that I was loved 'like a brother'. She might not remember me, or she might be reduced to child-like in sensibility.

All of it ran through my mind, and my heart froze as her eyes finally flickered open.

We stared at each other seemingly for ages, before she tugged on my hand gently, and I moved in close to her, leaning in as she coughed, then wet her lips with a tongue and whispered to me.

"I'm going to rock your fucking world."

CHAPTER TWENTY-TWO

It wasn't that simple of course, as much as I'd have loved to jump on her right there in the chop-shop, we had witnesses, and the first time, well. It should be special.

Well over ninety percent of those 'first times' for me had been drunk, with very little memory of them, so yeah, maybe as we were both adults, we could put in a little effort.

Also, she was laid in a chop-shop, having just had her brain operated on, so me trying to cut off her airway with 'Mr Happy' probably wasn't the best thing for her right then anyway.

I helped her to her feet, then pulled her in close and held her for long seconds before finally kissing her deeply.

It was the best goddamn kiss I'd ever had, and that included the one she'd given me while seeing 'eye-to-ball' after I'd been seriously fucked up raiding the corpo pleasure tower.

I was eventually peeled off her as Luna and Gessh forced their way in, and then, surprisingly, Lion gave her a hug as well, telling her he was pleased she was alright.

"Is she?" I asked him as she spoke to Luna and Gessh excitedly about something.

"Her alpha and beta waves are good." He nodded, apparently seeing something that I couldn't, before jerking his head in the direction of the director, who was sidling towards the door. "Want to take care of that?" he suggested, and I nodded, sighing.

"So. Want to change how this comes out?" I asked the director, striding over to him.

"What do you mean?" he asked, slowly backing up, clearly ready to run.

"This is against my better judgement, but fuck it, it's for her, not me," I said, knocking on his ident, and offering fifty thousand credits.

"Why…" he whispered, his tongue darting out to lick dry lips as he waited.

"This way you get something out of this, far more than you fucking deserve," I growled, "But otherwise you end up walking away, then you start thinking that you deserved more from this, you end up drinking, and no doubt that's when the wonderful plan for revenge comes about. This way you get something, and we all go our separate ways. Mark my words though, if someone comes after us? The last sight you'll ever see will be me."

"So this is to keep quiet?" he asked, tongue darting nervously again.

"Call it what you will," I growled, already regretting it. "Last chance offered."

"Fine." He accepted it, then backed away a little, before turning and running.

I watched him go, feeling dirty for paying the little bastard, but also feeling like sort of shooting him in the face—which I really, really wanted to do, but shouldn't—he'd not actually broken the laws, he'd just weaseled his way around them. If that was illegal, all lawyers would be fair game.

As I walked back towards the others, I indulged in a few seconds of that fantasy, of being able to get bounties on lawyers and going round hunting them, then I dismissed it, and instead took Reign in my arms again.

This time the kiss was wonderful, but over too soon.

"How you feeling?" I asked her and she winced.

"You're not going to believe me, but…I have a headache?" she said, to the rising sound of laughter, and I snorted.

"Don't worry," I said. "I'll dip my dick in some painkillers…do you want it orally or as a suppository?"

Everyone laughed, and she grinned, then kissed me again and whispered in my ear for me to pick. I squeezed her tight and shook my head, before cursing as a connection request came up.

"Yes?" I asked, frowning as I approved it.

"Delivery?" a bored voice said, the image flickering into place of a smiling and professional greeter, sitting in a clean office, and supposedly controlling the various delivery drones that the company used.

In reality we both knew he was half slumped across his desk, probably in his own home using the net to direct things and sat there in his underwear eating chips…but that wasn't the point here.

The point was that I'd totally forgotten about the electronics set and bench that was being delivered, and that memory sparked another…and another.

"Fuck!" I snarled, then shook my head again, holding a hand up to stall the others as I stepped back from the embrace with Reign. "Okay, just give me a minute. I'll get someone to open the door, alright?"

"As per section twenty-seven, sub paragraph three, you have seven minutes from the connection time of this call before an additional delay fee will be added to your account sir. Please—"

"Yeah, yeah! Just wait!" I snarled at the bored operator, before blinking one eye free and focusing on Luna who was standing to one side. "Luna, call Dondo, I know that fucker or Oshbob will have access to the warehouse still, you know what they're like, we've got a delivery drone with the electronics gear hovering in the parking area…"

"I'll sort," she said, nodding quickly, eyes glazing over as she made a call. "Hey big…" She started and I cut back to the comm link, not needing to hear any more.

"There's a…there's someone coming to let you in, there's a cleared space inside on the right and…"

"As per the contract we are only permitted to…" He spoke over me boredom clear.

"Oh fuck it whatever," I snapped, ending the call and blinking as the real world settled back in for me. "We've got a problem."

"When don't we have a problem?" Reign snorted, but the smile was still clear on her face. "Seriously, Kabutt, I know it's been a while for you but a delivery? Is it really the electronics gear, or did you buy so much lube it needed a drone to deliver it?"

"Yeah, you keep laughing…" I growled in mock threat. "Just you wait till I forget the lube entirely!"

"Oh gods, seriously you two, get a room!" Lion groaned. "Look, is this a you lot problem, or a me as well problem?"

"Uh…us lot?" I said.

"That's great then! I like you all, but you're standing around in my workplace, and I've got another client, so how about you all fuck off?"

We all turned and saw a pair of young girls standing nervously in the door and Reign shook her head, snorting.

"Ah, I remember sneaking out to get my first mod as well. Right, come on you fuckers, let's give the man some room, then Kabutt can explain why we're fucked, and why I'm not going to be for a while."

We waved our goodbyes to Lion, even as we started heading out the door and past the two girls, the pair of them seemingly tiny and delicate in comparison to the merc sisters that towered over them in all their armor and loadout.

"So…" Reign prompted when we got away from any listeners. "How bad is it?"

"Fucking bad," I growled. "Remember Anthos Black?"

"Yeah?"

"Turns out that a site of his was hit, and his merchandise was lost, so he's taking a load of 'fresh' merchandise to a secondary site according to Stinger. Either we hit him today, or we miss our chance for at least a month."

"Merchandise?"

"We know he's a slaver and flesh trader," I said. "What do we think the odds are that the site we accidentally raided for specters was his?"

"The tower?" Gessh asked, frowning.

"No, you idiot!" Luna groaned, shaking her head and smacking her sister across the back of the head with an open palm. "The underground one! The water storage place that hadn't seen water in centuries!"

"Crap."

"Yeah exactly," I agreed, before shaking my head. "And that's not the worst of it."

"What is?"

"He's not the only job that we need to get done today."

"What?"

"You remember that banshee that dragged me into the box at the bottom of the tower?"

"Yeah?"

"We've got a meeting with it tonight, to hand over the tech we grabbed."

"Wait, what?" Luna growled, even as Reign spoke up quickly.

"No, we need that!" she said. "You said you could get it working. You said you needed it to harvest nanites to get us all into APS!"

"And we do," I said holding my hands up as all of them started complaining and arguing. "What we need though, is to not be at war with a fucking banshee as well…"

"Could we capture it?" Gessh asked, slowly smiling. "Sell that fucker, and split it four ways…?"

"Five," Reign interjected. "Either Todds is one of the team or he isn't, and he did well."

"Okay, five," Luna agreed, nodding her agreement to her sister.

"No," I said firmly.

"No we don't share?" Luna asked, shrugging. "Well if you're sure…"

"Right, fuck this. Shut it, all of you," I snapped. "This is how it's going to be!" I glared round at them all. "Right. We need to be able to harvest nanites, we fucking need that. Thing is? I've already canned the shit outta the invention. I need a full schematic download, but once that's done? Yeah. I can make a new one. I told the banshee I'd trade the kit back to it, for a tier FOUR spinal mod. If it can get that? We clean the fuck outta the mod and hey, maybe we sell it, maybe we use it, but either way its decent credits. With the schematic for the harvesting tool? I can make another. Once we've got the software download done? I can literally make it work, or at least we've got as good a chance as we ever had of getting that one working, alright?"

"So what, you meet it and hand it over? What's to stop it from killing you?" Reign asked.

"I'll be holding an EMP and you'll have my back," I pointed out. "Look, I don't like it much, but that fucker would have killed me. It tracked us across the city and was waiting in there for us. It didn't go after the gear, it went after *us*. Stop and think about that for a while. The banshee we handed over? It could use a keystone. It comm'd me directly.

"If we can do a deal and strike a balance with the banshee? There's nothing we can't do. You want to harvest the specters? They don't seem to give a shit. Maybe it can direct us to more concentrations. Maybe it'll trade with us, bring us tier four and five gear in exchange for whatever it needs. We've got an opportunity here, that's all I'm saying."

"And Anthos Black?" Reign asked after a few seconds of silence as they all looked at each other.

"We hit him as well. He'll be leaving the city tonight Stinger said. No way he'll be leaving while the sun is up, and his hidden way out of the city was captured, right? He lost it when we raided?"

"Yeah?"

"Well, we need to put some feelers out and find out what happened to that secret door don't we," I said grinning. "Because I'm betting that he's going to try and use it tonight. We find out if the wall guard have had it reported to them and it's been sealed up? We go looking elsewhere, but if it hasn't…"

"We go looking for the ACE team that are now selling a smuggling route in and out of the city," Reign groaned. "Fuck's sake is there anything those corrupt fucks won't do?"

"Right now I'm hoping I'm right," I admitted. "I might be totally wrong, and we'll have to go back to Stinger and ask for a handout for the location, or chase down Bowdoin and see if that sneaky fuck can find this guy, but honestly? It fits too neatly. If he's leaving the city tonight, it can't be by normal means, not with a fuck load of slaves and prisoners. Even the gate guards wouldn't let that happen."

"So it has to be a smugglers route," Luna agreed. "Why not use another?"

"He probably knows of one at least, and if the door was sealed? Then yeah, that'll be his play, but if some ACE team decided to make a little fun money on the side? I'm betting they'd turn a blind eye to him."

"I don't know," Reign said after a second. "Stealing anything not nailed down? Sure. Letting a bunch of people be carted off as slaves? That's not a striking off offense, that's a shooting offence. I don't know if they'd go that far."

"They might, they might not. Most likely though, I'm betting the dodgy fuckers won't ask nor care though. They won't have stationed someone by the door to stand and check people in and out. I bet they changed the door code and that's it, they'll be selling that."

"And there's less risk to them as well, as they're not there, so can't be fingered for a crime." Reign sighed. "Yeah, that fits."

"We need to make sure though, and for that we need to find out if the door was reported and sealed," I said. "I need to be downloading the settings and details for the harvester, then building our own, right? So…"

"So you need some wonderful, amazing people that are gifted with stealth and skill to do the dirty work." Luna sighed. "What do you think, Gessh?"

"I think that's exactly what he means," she agreed.

"You're right," Reign said. "Someone that's stealthy, trustworthy, skilled and able to blend in…"

Luna nodded, winking at her sister.

"I'll call Todds," Reign finished with an evil grin.

"Yeah, we can…what!" Gessh snarled.

"He's stealthier than any of us, he fought well, and he's in the team now I guess, might as well make use of him," Reign pointed out.

"You fucker," Luna grumped, before grinning. "Well I suppose I could call Dond—"

"No fucking chance," I growled. "I'm going to be making schematics and ordering parts from companies. I have to try and remake in hours what should take weeks! I don't need the worry he's going to fuck you through the wall while I work! You can give Todds backup!"

"So sad…" Gessh started.

"BOTH of you," I cut her off. "I'm going back to the warehouse, and I need to get the damn gear into place. We've got a day, literally, that's it. Don't waste it, and get to work."

"So much for fun…" Reign whispered in my ear as I called an air-cab to get us back as quickly as possible.

"You're going to bed," I told her, then raised my voice. "Yes, I know, and no I'm not playing favorites, or setting up so I can have some fun later. We're going to need Reign later, and she's literally just had her brain poked around with. She's going to bed TO SLEEP."

"I'll lock my door." Reign sighed, then smiled round. "Sorry girls, he's right. I need to rest."

"It's alright," Gessh said, putting one hand on Reign's shoulder. "I was only joking, and yeah, he's right as well. We've only got so long, we can make it all work, but only if we don't fuck about."

"Tomorrow," Luna said firmly, looking from one of us to the next. "Tomorrow we get a goddamn day off!"

"Deal!" we echoed.

CHAPTER TWENTY-THREE

Reign and I climbed into the air-cab about fifteen minutes later, one of those annoying situations where there were none available and then like six all at once had shown up, but that was life.

Luna and Gessh were on their way as well. Reign had called Todds who'd agreed to meet them in an hour, as he was still out with his kids—and their babysitter, who apparently had made it clear just how impressed she was that he wasn't just a nameless merc after all.

When he was named as one of the 'heroes' who'd 'saved the city' from a specter outbreak—that was how the media were spinning this for some reason, no doubt some credits had changed hands somewhere—he'd gotten back home to find his kids worshipping him.

He'd had some time with them, packed them off to bed, and then the babysitter had apparently nearly broken him demonstrating just how impressed she was.

He was single from necessity, not choice apparently, and had been barely surviving on the money he was pulling in. Now he was laughing, and I'd gotten a message from him confirming that he'd be ready for the next job whenever we needed him.

I watched the city flashing past the windows of the cab, then smiled, unable to help myself, as I felt Reign's fingers entwined with my own.

Turning to her, she smiled at me, tired, clearly exhausted in fact, judging from the rings around her beautiful eyes, and yeah, still with blood and cleaning solution matting her hair from the op.

She was still stunning though, and she leant in bumping me with a shoulder, before kissing me.

"Thank you," she said softly. "This wasn't what I was expecting when I joined you for that evaluation mission."

"Me neither," I admitted. "I'd not change it though, not for the world."

"Nope." She smiled and kissed me again. "So…when we get back…" She trailed off, quirking one eyebrow. "You think it'll take you long to sort the harvester out?"

"Most of the day," I said, "As much as I'd like to rush it off, we can't."

"I know." She laughed, then shook her head. "You know, it's stupid. I know we can't, and I know we shouldn't. But now that the only thing that's stopping us actually screwing each other's brains out is time? It's really hard not to just straddle you right now."

"That and we've got like ten minutes before we land, if that."

"Good catch." She nodded seriously. "So, we could go what, three times?"

"Cheeky bugger!" I laughed, before pulling her close for another kiss. This one went on for a lot longer, and was definitely getting more serious, when Reign eventually pushed back, breaking the kiss, and free of both our roaming hands.

"Okay," she said, her voice husky. "I'm going to sit on the other side of the cab, because one more kiss like that, and I'm riding you here and now, I'll pay the delay charge on the cab if it has to sit idle while we finish!"

"And the fouling charge?" I joked, getting a grin as she licked her lips.

"No risk there." She sighed, before moving to sit across from me, straightening her clothing, as I adjusted my own. "Right, let's think of something else…these electronics."

"What about them?" I asked.

"You're sure you can do this?"

"Yes and no. Inventing something like this from scratch? Fuck no." I shook my head. "As it is though, scanning the parts? Downloading the schematics and programming that were already done? Patching across what I was taught and using the versions that we had in the APS to replace any missing parts? Yeah, I can create a monster that'll probably do the trick."

"What about the missing or damaged parts?"

"Easy to replace most of them," I assured her. "It's literally a case of scan in the damaged bits, find a match, and send a drone order for them. I'll get a handful so I can test them, and then boom. The missing parts? That's going to be the awkward part, but that's life."

"How bad do you think?"

I shrugged. "Honestly, hopefully not too bad. It looked to all be there, besides the actual impact and storage sections. The real issue is the separation and cleaning process, and that's what we've got. If need be? I can use that hand that we salvaged earlier, build the system around it and…"

I broke off, my mind whirling as I considered things, then I grinned. "Oh yeah," I muttered. "Okay, give me some time, I need to work on this…" I told her absently, the desperate need to jump on her vanishing as my mind raced off down a new track.

"Men." She sighed, shaking her head fondly at me. "Such simple creatures."

"Hmmm," I agreed, not really listening. I was already miles away, linking back to Lion's shop, and scanning through the arms he had in stock.

None of them were right, but after a few seconds when I pinged him a notification, and he jumped in. Then we were deep in the data in seconds.

Turned out the girls had both chickened out, something about one looking for a sensitivity booster for sex, and the other looking for an audio enhancement, neither of which he had in stock, and certainly not for the handful of credits they had.

They'd been sent away to reconsider things, and Lion had been bored.

Now, I was sharing sections of my design with him, and he, being an actual cybernetic genius and carver, was racing ahead in leaps and bounds.

The original design had been on an extendable 'arm' more like a crappy post. Then there'd been medikits slotted into the arm to drain the clean nanites into.

That was great, I liked that section of it, but the arm? I'd either have to have a special unit built to wear an extra arm—and all the attendant problems that'd bring, from attention, to confusion and more—or I'd have to build it into a weapon, something at least the size of the rifles that Reign was always lugging about.

That meant limiting my offensive capability until I could get it built onto my APS, at the very least. I'd thought about my arm, attaching it there, but the fact it was a mid to low level one, and that I'd need so much work doing to another? It'd just seemed like something to look into later.

Fix the kit, then work out how it could be used.

Now though? Now I had limited time with the original, and I'd seen the missing parts?

My mind was leaping ahead again, even left in the dust by Lion.

He'd pulled up a tier three 'Aramid Armaments' model, a seriously nice one that was a hundred and seventeen thousand.

That was its price on OFFER, and I winced as I looked at it. Lion took the technical specs though, and put them into a program he 'just happened to have lying around'.

I grunted at Reign as she directed me out of the cab, stumbling along, barely paying attention as I was led into the warehouse and abandoned with a grumble.

The next thing I knew the arm was blown up before me, sections coming apart as layers were removed, wiring was rearranged and...

And the fucker removed the plasma launcher.

It was a one shot, emergency scattergun design, and it literally stored enough power for a single blast, but it was amazing, and I desperately wanted it to stay.

Lion scrapped it 'out of hand'...literally.

"Here," he said, twisting the hand that I'd tentatively shown him, and ripping out the claws and poison delivery system. "We reverse this. Sink the claws into the target, install exhaust ports in the heel of the hand, and you replace the pressurized pump for the poison, into a high power suction model."

"Specters aren't going to have blood that we can syphon," I pointed out. "Not most of them."

"No," he agreed. "But they'll have the 'nites, and that's what this magnetic separator is for, don't you see?"

He pulled the rough design apart before my eyes, bent it, folded it, and then fucking mutilated the design I'd had, replacing it with something that was both terrible and wondrous.

The nanites that we all loved that were deployed from medikits were basically kept in tubes, pressurized injection ports that forced the nanites out.

That was it. they were cheap as all hell to produce, and easily refilled.

This new system? It had sections on the arm to plug in empty medikits, sure, but it also had a section that was covered in ports, ports where the tubes the nanites came in could be pushed in.

The entire arm looked lethal anyway, it was all ridged steel and titanium muscles, hydraulic presses and more. Then on top of that, the internals required to produce a fucking scattershot plasma burst were ripped out, and replaced with a seriously high tech, botched together design to steal nanites.

I loved it.

Especially as to form the magnetic field, there would need to be rings of differing sizes implanted up and down the arm.

Between the copper coloring of the magnetic rings and the black of the arm?

The damn thing looked like it should be modelled by someone called Hugo on a catwalk.

"Can you do this?" I asked him after a few seconds.

"That?" He gestured to the tech side that I was providing. "Not a chance in hell. Can I put that into here though? Alter and butcher this into the device you want? Yeah, that I can do," he said. "You'd need a secondary power supply for this though, the arm wouldn't be able to power it normally."

"I can do that."

"You want me to do the work on that arm?" he asked, and I nodded fervently.

"Yeah, do it." I shunted the credits to him without being asked.

"If you can get this working…"

"Yeah?"

"We need to register the design."

"What? Fuck no," I snapped. "We've got the only shit that can do this, why the hell would we…"

"You're thinking short term," he interrupted. "You sell this design, and that tech? We'll earn a hundred times what the nanites are worth, that you can personally extract."

"And we'll be cut out of the deal in seconds, we'd be lucky to get paid at all, before the corpos have us stamped and branded, the device locked down and more. Fuck that."

"Seriously Kabutt," Lion growled. "Think about it, as soon as the wrong person sees you with this? Word will start to spread. Give it a week? You'll be dodging corpo head hunters, rather than selling it for a massive pile of credits."

"I…" I growled, then nodded. "I'll think about it, alright?"

"Deal," he said, before grinning at me. "I get half."

"You'll get an even split with the rest of the team," I corrected. "If there's six of us, we all get what, fifteen percent?"

"You all get fifteen percent," he tried. "I'll make do with whatever's left over and…"

"You'll be getting a flat fee at this rate you cheeky fuck." I growled. "I'm providing the arm, the body the damn thing will be mounted on for testing AND the tech. You're what? Plugging the fucker in?"

"I'm rebuilding the entire arm, and…" He argued, before breaking off and sighing, then nodding. "Alright, point taken, you'll all be on the shitty end of the testing, and you brought this to me. I'll drop any fees for installation, and I'll help with the work. What do you need?"

"You any good with electronics?" I asked, and got a flat stare in response. "Fine, get your arse to this address." I shot the warehouse address over to him. "Oh and Lion? If you, I don't know, 'forgot' and accidentally sold the location details to someone else? They better kill me, because I'll come for you if they don't."

"Anyone ever tell you, you've got real trust issues?" Lion asked me, grinning.

"Yeah, my last major," I grumbled. "And my old captain."

"What happened to them?" He joked.

"I tortured the captain, then dropped a building on him, and the major I'm still hunting. He's running a black ops APS unit."

"I…" he broke off, then nodded. "Alright. Point taken. I'm on my way, Kabutt, and yeah, don't worry. I know this is a hell of an opportunity. I won't fuck it up."

"Good man."

I cut the link, blinking at being in the now spotless warehouse, the sterilization drone making a slow pass on the far side, and the distant sound of Reign in the shower overhead.

I paused, seriously wondering if she'd have locked the door, and if she'd object to me joining her, just for a little bit…then shook my head.

"Work first, Kabutt, then kill people, then the sexy-time!" I promised myself.

CHAPTER TWENTY-FOUR

Lion didn't take long to reach the warehouse, and when he arrived it was with a fuck load of gear.

He caught me struggling to attach the legs onto a flatpack style electronics bench, and spent the next twenty minutes redoing what I'd done, cursing me for a fool, and ordering a new second bench for himself.

Once the bench was up, and his was on its way, we spread the actual kit out, and looked it over.

"Okay, first job is mapping the whole thing," he said. "We need to be damn sure how it came together, before we take it apart."

We imaged it from every angle, scanned it, and hooked it up to a tablet, downloading everything in the memory, before finally, starting to disassemble.

Most of the wiring was damaged, significant sections were coated in some kind of grease that I chose not to consider, while other areas…

"Why the hell was this coiled up?" Lion asked at one point, and I couldn't take it any longer, and I told him. "A potty," he said after a few seconds. "On a goblin's HEAD?"

"Yup."

"You let me taste that grease?" he said slowly.

"You said you needed to know what it was, and all you were getting from the scanner was 'organic'," I pointed out, entirely reasonably.

"I hate you."

"I get that a lot."

"He really does!" Reign called from above, stepping out on the metal landing. "You boys need feeding?"

"Always!" I called back.

"Pizza?" she suggested, and Lion nodded quickly. "I'll get a selection," she promised, before strolling from sight as we got back to work.

As we went, we ordered replacement parts. Some were easy, literally a box of some of the bits we needed was a credit. That was it. Others? The magnetic coils and separation system that we could order as part of a plumbing setup to remove contaminants was both better made, and cheaper to get than the original parts.

Some sections though had to be entirely rebuilt, painstakingly replicated according to the design some mad banshee had come up with.

Hours flashed past, as Lion and I examined, scanned, ordered and downloaded, then assembled on the second bench.

We ate, used the facilities, and Lion took delivery of the arm. Then started cutting and assembling sections into it, as I reassembled the stripper.

We power tested and cycled, drained and flushed both systems over and over.

The sun set, and still we worked, stopping only when Luna and Gessh virtually dragged us free of the tables.

"What?" I growled at them.

"We told you twice," Gessh snapped. "It's time to go!"

"What?" I asked, confused, shaking my head. "No, no it's…" I looked out of one of the windows, then blanched, realizing it was night, *again!*

"How long…?" I asked, glancing around.

"Five minutes, the driver is on his way," Reign said, smiling as she realized that I'd not been ignoring them, I'd just been so totally focused that I'd genuinely not realized.

"Fuck, I…" I looked around, before spotting all my gear, neatly arranged on a side table, the magazines loaded, grenades replaced, guns gleaming under a fresh coating of oil…

"Don't get used to it," Reign whispered into my ear, before kissing my cheek. "Seriously, I know you were working hard, and yeah, we need to get moving."

"Toilet." I groaned, only just realizing just how badly I needed it, as Lion wolfed down cold pizza on the other side of the room.

"I'll keep working," he grunted around a mouthful of pizza. "Another hour, no more, and it'll be done."

"Do we have that?" I asked, glancing at Reign, who shooed me towards the toilet.

When I returned, and quickly started loading my gear onto my armor, she finally filled me in.

"Luna got Dondo to do her a 'favor'." Reign grinned at me. "She's got him wrapped around her little finger now, and he was happy to pull some strings. *Somehow* he got access to the ACE records. The site we cleared was marked as old storage and a possible flesh market, nothing more, and that two officers, Darran and Garree would monitor it for any further criminal activity."

"So no mention of the door."

"Nope. Also *someone* has paid for ACE patrols and the wall guards to be away from that area tonight. That's enough that combined with us knowing that fucker is leaving the city tonight? I think its via that exit."

"The Banshee…" I started to say, and Reign nodded.

"The time they're guaranteed to be away from their posts?" she asked. "Two hours."

I glanced at my watch and did some quick working out, then nodded. "And it's five hours until we're due to meet the banshee, I told it 'this time tomorrow' when we were down there…"

"Exactly," Reign said firmly. "We've got just enough time, provided we air-car it across the city."

"It's costing us a damn fortune…" I started, and Luna spoke up.

"And that's why I might have 'hired' us a driver for the night."

"Hired?" I asked, as Gessh snorted.

"She promised Dondo he'd be getting laid when we get back, if he drove for us tonight."

"He's…wait, look not to be ungrateful…" I said, realizing that Reign had said earlier that the 'driver was on his way'. "But this fucker works for Oshbob, alright? He's an orc *crime lord*. Can we trust that one of his people just happens to be able to find all this shit out easily, and he can fly an aircar?"

"You underestimate the power…" Luna started in a deep voice.

"Of twins." Gessh finished for her, winking. "Believe me, he's more than happy to help, he's not asking any questions, and if he does? You already agreed to sell Oshbob parts, so that's what we're doing, alright?"

"Fine." I grunted, before looking over at Lion. "Can you get that thing working tonight?"

"The new one?" He asked and I nodded. "Possibly, but…"

"But?"

"It'll need a battery," he repeated. "An external one, preferably a…"

"Would one from the stealth suits work?" Reign asked, nodding to a pile off to one side. "They were delivered an hour ago, Todds is out testing his now, and we've got his old suit, its damaged, but the battery is fine?"

"It'll work, but not well," he said. "Mind you, the arm would need to be…"

"Fitted," I agreed. "Tonight."

"It's not ready for fitting, and your driver is here," he pointed out, and I cursed.

"Could you meet us later?" I suggested. "Then we could…"

"Better not to meet the banshee wearing its stolen tech I think," Lion said. "Believe me, field attachments are not a good idea. After all of this, come to the chop-shop tomorrow. We'll fit it, and do a test run, but for now?"

The door went below and the deep voice of Dondo called up.

"Dondo's servicing has arrived!"

"Promises, promises!" Luna called down, before grinning and grabbing her gear. "Come on then, let's go kill someone, free some slaves, and deal with a banshee. I need the boring stuff out of the way quick, we've got a date tonight!"

"Tomorrow," I corrected, before grinning as Reign bumped me with her shoulder.

"Later, how about breakfast, that shower, and we break in your new bed?" she whispered.

"Hell yes." I growled, the need rising in me despite the tiredness that also rose. "Although I'm going to need some stims," I reluctantly admitted.

"Getting floppy in your old age, eh?" Gessh called from below as we all headed down the stairs.

"No actually!" I replied. "Some fuckers were SO GODDAMN LOUD that nobody else could get any sleep!"

"Oh," she said, wincing as she looked back at us. "I'd apologize…"

"But we wouldn't mean it." Luna laughed. "We'll get some soundproofing sorted out!"

"Please for the sake of my damn ears, do!" I growled, gloomily sure that Reign and I would be settling down to sleep, the 'deed' done, long before those fuckers would be later.

Dondo flew us to the same site as before, the place looking pretty much as wonderful as it had last time, with the drag marks, the discarded bullets and shells and even the feeling of 'you shouldn't be here' still heavy in the air as he landed nearby.

We had taken a fast pass around the site from the air first, just to make sure, and then he'd landed us a block away, just in case.

"You kids have fun, you hear!" he joked, as we piled out, popping the trunk and quickly loading up on guns and our remaining armor.

"Just be ready when we call," I growled at him, before pulling my helmet on, and triggering the tac-net.

"Yes boss…" he replied, as the doors closed and the backblast shoved me aside, the car rising quickly.

I gritted my teeth, knowing that if the fucker had been able to fly the way he had? He'd meant to almost send me to the floor as well.

I growled, then shook myself free of it. Yes, he was undoubtedly reporting everything to 'that orc', and yes, he was keeping me awake by screwing the sisters all night long.

That wasn't a good enough reason to shoot him in the face yet though, not quite.

Maybe a light maiming?

Blow a finger or three off? Or his dick?

I shook that thought loose as well, it'd turn out to be armor plated or something.

Besides. He'd passed a message on from Oshbob earlier. The fucker had somehow managed to get ahold of the fusion core I needed, as well as the sensor package. I'd not be transferring the credits until I saw the fucking equipment with my own eyes, but I'd agreed to the price, and he was working on the rest.

By dawn I was grimly sure my nice credit balance would soon be wiped out, but that was the way my life seemed to be these days. A feast and a famine.

Currently I was just under seven hundred and forty thousand credits in my account, another quarter of a million to be split between us all once that fucker Anthos Black was dead, but I could feel the magnetic charge of that goddamn orc sucking on the balance already.

I set off jogging across the plaza we'd landed in, ignoring the snap of the awnings and canvas around the edges, as the wind tugged and tore at them, the broken lighting strips and mold that coated others, giving the area an eerie glow.

It didn't help that the only other light beyond shitty old glow sticks and light strips that were half filled with stagnant water and mold was the distant flickering neon brilliance of the city.

This close to the wall there were no stars, and the neon that reflected off walls brought such a multitude of flickering madness that anyone with epilepsy lasted seconds before collapsing and frothing.

The only way the locals could get any sleep, was to cover sections, great long constructions of old wood or plastic closing off areas, creating deep shadowed recesses.

Then the people were killed by monster incursions, by flesh market peddlers and slavers, and those very places they created to block out the light, to give them a little relief?

They became the homes of the creatures of the night.

Spiders that bred thick enough to carpet the walls, rats that battled the spiders, cats that tried to feed on the rats, and were preyed upon in turn.

These were the smallest and most genial of the inhabitants of the darkness, and every so often, when some genetic twist arose in their ranks? Something that fed upon the 'normal' creatures?

They grew to monstrous sizes indeed. They fed on both their mutated brethren, and the nanites that filled all life now, growing stronger and more terrible.

Eventually places like these became no-go areas indeed. Not just because of the proximity to the wall and the terrors that lived on the other side, constantly battling to enter.

No, it was because they developed increased intelligence.

Spiders that sent their lesser brethren in, through cracks in windows and under floors, to search for you, to make sure that there was fresh meat, when the bigger soldier castes came looking.

At least twice a year a housing area, usually a slum, was absorbed by a rolling wave of mutated death, the news reels all lamented it, railed at the corporations that 'someone should do something' and then some celebrity was caught with his dick somewhere it shouldn't be, and the lost were forgotten as well.

All of that rose in my mind as I saw the scuttle of multi-legged madness foaming across nearby walls, and Luna cried out.

"Swarm!" she bellowed, skidding to a halt and racing in the other direction.

"Wha..." Reign started, before we were both turning, boots skidding on the flagstones and tarmac. We ran, all of us, forget stealth, forget the fuckin mission, if that caught us?

It was all over.

We took the corner, racing out into the light, and then another, dipping into darkness again, then Todds screamed, twisting around and hacking with a blade at something that had caught onto one sleeve.

"Fucking webs!" he cried, cutting through it, as two more shot out of the darkness to splatter against his stealth coating. Clearly they had no issue penetrating it, and I cursed.

"Blades!" I bellowed, spinning and triggering my plasma sword, expecting to cut the webs down that were flashing out towards us, only to see the gleam of it reflected in a thousand, thousand eyes.

"Fuck this shit!" Reign screamed, ripping her grazer off her shoulder and slapping the safety off. The bone deep hum rippled out, and she jerked the weapon left and right ahead of us, walls that had appeared solid black with paint or more, suddenly exposed as coated in spiders.

Hundreds of thousands cascaded off the walls, crashing to the floor as Reign fired over and over, jerking the rifle in great arcs of destruction. Luna, Gessh—her rifle wasn't capable of the same and instead she ripped the battery free, holding it ready for Reign—Todds and myself fell in, going back to back, with blades out.

The spiders lasted seconds, the inexorable tide of death routed as they collapsed in their millions.

From spiders the size of a pinkie nail, to ones larger than any dog I'd ever seen, they crashed and fell all around us, as we gibbered and slashed.

The worst part, for me, was when she fired straight up, dragging the beam across the braced coverings that blocked out the light overhead.

The rain of bodies, twitching in death, was nightmare inducing.

When the largest finally showed itself, it was almost a relief.

They'd been coming in waves, trying to overwhelm us, then fleeing as the grazer swept across them. All the time, we danced and stomped, trying to keep them from climbing our boots, from dropping onto us, and we cried out as here and there a bite marked one that made it through.

Medikits were triggered and used, and more than once we screamed in utter fucking horror.

The queen, when she scuttled out into the open was as anticlimactic as it could be. The terror of millions of tiny spiders, all controlled, all guided and all fucking aiming for us, was too much.

When she appeared, and we all fired on her?

Well.

She practically detonated.

Cooked, by the grazer, riddled by holes, then stabbed, hacked and kicked to fuck?

It was over in seconds, as was the swarm.

Without the power of the queen to keep them all in check, they reverted to spiders, more or less, and broke away from the fight in all directions.

Thirty seconds later, we were running, still shaking, down a narrow alley way, then out into the middle of the next plaza.

Reign was in the lead, her grace and natural agility far surpassing ours, and she skidded to a halt, or tried to, as she ran full length into the group that was rushing past.

Luna, Gessh and I were right behind her, with Todds at the back, and while he triggered his stealth, vanishing, we screamed in reflex, and started fucking cutting.

It was only due to the spiders that we had the blades out, but in the narrow confines of the fight that we found ourselves in thirty seconds after running from the spiders?

They were the right weapons for the job.

We found ourselves in the middle of a group that had been running in the same direction we were, headed for the cleared area with its ruined temple at the end of the waste ground.

Here and there were dotted armed men along with several times their number in bound, gagged and obedience-collared people. Those that were armed though, were generally armed with low caliber pistols, basic rifles and electric whips or tridents.

We were armed with swords. Mono-molecular edged ones, and a plasma blade.

They tried to parry and block, and they were left with half a weapon, or frequently, half a head. The slaves and prisoners saw their chance and even screaming with the agony of rebelling, they grabbed and pinned their captors, making the fight easy for us.

Anthos Black, a huge man, clearly the leader of the group, raced back from the front, seeing what was going on, and barked at his men to stand firm, even as they collapsed under our blades.

He staggered, the hood that covered his head, shadowing the face suddenly torn free as a shot by Reign from her sniper rifle creased one of his cheeks, and removed an ear in the spray of blood.

He raised a hand, bellowing in pain and tried to say something else, before a scream was literally torn from him, as Todds appeared from stealth right behind him.

A dagger punched deep into Anthos' back, right where the body armor he wore ceased protecting his back, and the waist covering failed to cover.

He screamed as he lost a kidney, the blade ripping backwards and taking a section of organ, and a spray of blood with it. Then Gessh was there, leaping over a falling body and stabbing out, one smooth, graceful thrust that sank deep into the muscle of his right arm, severing it.

He screamed, then fell, his left knee exploding as Reign took it from him, the boom of the high powered sniper rifle echoing off the walls.

As he hit the floor, I skidded to a halt, spinning quickly, checking on all sides, and confirming that of all the slavers, only three, counting him still lived.

One was being beaten into the floor, a tiny red-headed woman slamming it into asphalt with such ferocity I could hear the cracks as the skull gave way.

Another was running, and he was moving like his arse was on fire. "Reign!" I called, and she spun, seeing the direction I was pointing, and raised her rifle in one smooth motion.

It barely seemed to pause before it barked, and he screamed, tumbling to the floor in a spray of blood.

"Luna!" I barked, gesturing roughly around me. "Free them!"

"Aye, boss!" she sang, clearly very happy to have something to vent her anger on after the spiders, as she dragged her blade free of a slumped body.

"Gessh, restrain him…remove anything you feel necessary."

"You…" The big man glared at me, his short blond and red beard shining with blood from the ear as he tried to shake his head. "You don't know what you've done... who I am…!" He ended with a growl.

"Anthos Black," I said, taking an image of him and sending it to Stinger.

"Aye…but…" He closed his eyes and steadied his voice, trying again. "You don't know who I work for," he managed to get out this time.

"No," I agreed, as Stinger called me, and I gave them a remote link to my optics, albeit a very limited and tightly controlled one. "I don't know who you work for, and I don't care. The people we work for gave us your name, that's all, and after seeing what a scumbag you are?"

I shrugged, then forced a smile. "I could finish you off quite happily, but…" I turned to face the crowd of now ex slaves, all being freed by Luna. "I think they have first call on you," I finished, before turning to the crowd.

"Feel free to kill him, but try not to mess the mods up too badly please, I need to sell them."

Anthos screamed as Todds appeared again, this time slashing the blade across the fingers of the hand that rose towards the grenades on Anthos' chest, cutting them, and then the body armor and weapons free.

"Are we good?" I asked Stinger, watching as the mass fell on the slaver, kicking, stomping, punching and gouging.

"We are. I recommend you ask them to leave the head more or less recognizable however, there is a substantial bounty on him, raised this morning."

"Really?" I asked, smiling.

"Yes, our payment stands, but the original price on his head went up by thirty thousand this morning."

"Very nice," I purred, moving in closer, taking a quick shot of his face and then submitting it for the bounty, tagging all five of us in the kill claim.

"We accept that Anthos Black is dead, and the contract is formally closed." Stinger said, smiling. "As such, our services are now available to you, for advice, for training, and of course, to act as your fixer, should you need a steady source of income."

"Thank you." I sighed in relief. "Right, these people…"

"Are most likely nobodies, but some may have missing person's bounties on their heads. I recommend scanning them all, then alerting the relevant charities to their presence."

"Will do." I stretched, cracking my back and wincing as I saw a nearby spider crawling across a wall. I ended the call, then started gathering everyone up, getting Reign to go person by person, scanning their face and ident, as she checked them over, making sure they were okay.

As soon as we were all a decent distance from the narrow alley that the spiders had chased us into, I started checking the bodies with Gessh and Luna, all three of us stripping them, while Todds got to play hero, speaking to the charities and arranging emergency collection.

It was insane that in a city as sick and twisted as Artem, there were still some people that ran charities rescuing and rehoming, but hey, I was just glad I didn't have to fuck with it all.

Twenty minutes after that, we were in our aircar again, ignoring whatever Luna and Dondo were doing in the front—the car dipped and nearly hit a tower at one point, just as Luna swore she was 'examining his belt'.

Soon after that, we landed at our warehouse, retrieving the old kit and waking Lion, who'd fallen asleep, then taking him with us as well as the arm.

We dropped him off at his shop—he apparently lived above it, somewhere in the old buildings—and I was dropped off with the gear for the banshee, as Dondo took off and landed a few hundred meters back, giving us room.

The cleanup was still ongoing apparently, floodlights lit the cooling tower, and dozens of goblins were clearly visible, laying out parts here and here, ready for cataloging and 'disposal'. Presumably via Oshbob.

I looked around, spotting the only area where the lights had failed off to one side, and an underpass next to that. An underpass that had not a single light nearby working.

I walked over to it, stopping at the edge of the light and waiting.

CHAPTER TWENTY-FIVE

The Banshee didn't take long to appear, floating forwards, the dim light of its repulsors baffled by the thick hanging anti-ballistic cloth.

It stopped at arm's reach, several of its own arms ending in hands that gripped guns and blades, one a hook and chain, which I really didn't like the look of, and I nodded to it.

"We made a deal last night, you and I," I said. "I took this as a spoil of war, as my loot when I killed the goblin that had it. You wanted it, and I agreed to trade you for it. Do you have the mod I asked for?"

There was a long minute of silence as we watched each other, and I started to panic, thinking that maybe, just maybe, I'd handed the only really sentient specter over to the highest bidder, and now I was about to pay the price.

Another arm slowly extended from under the cloth, and I let out a sharp breath, seeing the mod that it clutched there, the familiar bands and spinal sections of a standard mod, but hundreds of them where I was used to seeing dozens.

It held it there, where I could see it and I held the device, the harvester…and we both looked at each other, unsure of what the hell to do next.

After a long minute, I sighed and shook my head, muttering 'fuck it' under my breath, before starting forwards.

The banshee shifted its guns, tracking me, and I held the device up, moving to the halfway point between us, then laying it down on the floor and backing away.

Only once I was back to where I'd started from, did the banshee move, and this time it was slowly, slinking forwards. It reached the mass of electronics and reached down, dipping closer to the ground as more hands reached out, lifting the mass to where it could look it over and still see me.

It examined it for little while, before my keystone pinged.

Damaged.

That was all I got, and I nodded. It was after all. Some of it was from us examining it, and some no doubt, was from the goblin.

"It was damaged when I took it from the goblin," I said aloud. "I also examined it, trying to figure out what it was, before we met and you requested it back.

Why?

"Why what?"

Why trade with me?

"Honestly, because I need mods, and you might need something I can get. You can reach me now, communicate with me."

Why?

"Well…" I hesitated, then rubbed the back of my neck, thinking fast. "Maybe you need mods? Maybe you want electrical components? Some of those are pretty shit, boxes of those parts…" I sighed and moved in closer, walking right up close to the banshee, knowing that the fucker could kill me at any second.

"These ones, you see the rust?" I asked it, pointing at the damage. It nodded.

"Well, I could get you boxes of new ones of these. Whatever you're using it for, the power that this can pass through, it's not much, you understand? It'd drain batteries really quickly, right?"

Again a nod.

"Well, if you replaced these parts with new ones, and replaced the copper here with fresh, rather than corroded?" I reached out and touched sections. "Then you'd get the same effect for half the power cost, right?"

Why do you help?

"Honestly." I shrugged. "I wasn't expecting you to be able to speak and deal with me, I thought you were going to kill me. Now? I think you need some help, and I'm willing to give it." I held one hand up quickly, causing the banshee to back up a little, the guns locking onto that hand reflexively again.

"Don't get me wrong, I'm not helping for free, I need credits, I need mods I can trade for credits…and I need to stop specters from starting nests in certain areas…"

Mindless Ones.

"Yes!" I agreed, nodding. "The mindless ones, they keep causing problems, killing people, stealing mods…"

Need. Instinct. That is all.

"Right, well, I need to stop them doing that, uh…is there a way to get them back?"

Back?

"To make them self aware again, to make them sane, or to be able to speak, like you can."

No.

"Not at all?

Mindless are lost, nothing remains. Recovery not possible.

"Okay…what about you, what do you need?" I asked it, and it hesitated, before slipping the remains of the harvester back up under its robes.

Will consider.

That was it, and the fucker started slowly drifting backwards, before freezing and then reaching out with one hand, offering me the spinal mod.

I took it, fighting an almost irresistible urge to laugh at the absurdity, noting the fresh blood that still coated the mod. It gestured, a spiral with one hand, and I swallowed hard, slowly turning.

It did something, considering the speed and ease, it might have just lifted the fucking mine off me, hell, I guessed as it retracted it, that it might have never fully activated, but I wasn't sure.

Instead I nodded my thanks, then I backed away, moving up and back into the light. I walked as long as I could before the nerves got the better of me and I started to jog, as the aircar flashed across to me, landing and opening the door for me to jump in.

A few of the goblins stopped work, watching as we vaulted into the sky, but by then it was too late for anyone to ask questions, to wonder why we were there, and certainly to link up our departure, with the flickering of lights that started to work again.

We all looked at each other, stunned that the whole thing had come off so easily, before Reign started to laugh, and the others joined in.

"I'm sorry," she said after a few seconds, covering her mouth with the back of one hand while grinning at me. "The look on your face though, honestly, you were on the verge of terror!"

"Fucking right I was," I admitted, feeling no shame in that. "Did you see how big that fucker was? It's one thing to face it in a fight, to hold my gun and know that I might win or lose but whatever happened was down to me as much as luck, but that?"

I shook my head.

"Seriously that scared the absolute shit outta me. Its easily three times the size it was when we saw it in the tunnels, and the carapace?"

"It was familiar, but…"

"It's from an archaeon!" I said. "Seriously, that fucker rebuilt itself using parts from one of those…hell, the banshees might all *be* the archaeon! They might be rebuilding themselves under the city right now, and that thought friggin' terrifies me!"

"The…damn I remember them, the vids, the talking head panels…" Todds muttered, shaking his head. "They scared the shit outta me when I watched that stuff, but they're all dead right? We and the other cities destroyed them?"

"Supposedly," I said. "But they were a mix of neural circuitry and full on processors. You think that looked like it had much in the way of flesh involved in its construction? Take the head off, put it on a new body, or hell, just have it hide, make a mockup of one and remote control it around the battlefield?

"People were hitting them from range, massively overdoing it with the ordinance, they could have buried themselves, have a drone up that they could sacrifice and—"

"Have you two heard yourselves?" Reign snorted. "Seriously, there's enough mad shit going on without conspiracy theories! What about the one about the boss of m-corp and the alien probe? Want to throw that one in as well?"

"I don't think I've heard that one." Gessh replied, sounding bored.

"Supposedly the aliens came and tried to probe her. She liked it so much she kept them on staff and gets probed all day every day, but that's not the point here. The point is, we've just pulled off two things that couldn't be done, right after taking down that cooling tower, and we're fucking rich, alright?" She looked from one of us to the next, grinning giddily.

"Seriously, I've got more disposable creds than I've ever had in my life, I've got my mod out, and a new one in that not only makes me more in tune with the world around me when I want to be..." She reached down and squeezed my hand in hers, smiling. "...but it'll also let me tamp the world down when I need to focus, to block it all out when I have to make the perfect shot.

"We're rich, we've not got a mission we *need* to do, not like we've had, pretty much every day since we all met." She looked around the inside of the car and smiled. "Let's just fucking enjoy it, alright? Let's take the day, we're nearly back at OUR home...shit, sorry Todds, we'll drop you at the nearest mag-train or..."

"I've got an air-cab coming." He grinned at Reign. "Don't worry!"

"Well, anyway, we're nearly home. You go back and bang the shit outta the babysitter." Reign grinned at Todd as his face colored.

"She's twenty-three and works for a service, it's not like she's the neighbors kid or something!" he cut in quickly, defensively.

"Yeah, a 'special service.'" Gessh laughed, as Reign interrupted and spoke over everyone.

"I'm going to go and have a damn long shower—on my own Kabutt, you can wait half an hour—and then I'm going to work out some much needed frustrations alright? I suggest you all do the same, relax. Spend some money..."

"On sound proofing," I interjected and Luna laughed from the front.

"Hey, we're not the ones with the problem," she said and I winced.

"Please, for the love of the gods..." I mock begged.

"It's already on order." Gessh assured me. "Luna has no shame, I on the other hand...well, I'm not ashamed of it, certainly not, but if we recruit more people? I don't want the mental image of them getting off on us getting off, you know?"

"Any reason works for me, just stop those sounds!" I sighed as Reign took my hand in hers, then leaned in and whispered in my ear.

"Let's see who can outdo the other," she suggested, and I grinned.

"There's two of them."

"You'll just have to put in twice as much effort then."

"You too," I countered, and she laughed.

"Believe me, I'm going to break you," she assured me, and I settled back, grinning to myself as the aircar started to sink from the sky, the buildings around us seeming to flow past at dizzying speeds as windows and chimneys, solar panels and landing fields blurred past.

Dondo landed us in the enclosed front parking area, the fence surrounding the warehouse shivering and clattering in metal celebration under the down blast, as the engines cut off.

There were a brief few seconds as the hull settled on the landing gear, and the doors opened with a creak, then we were all piling out.

"We working tomorrow?" Todds asked me, offering a fist and I bumped it, nodding.

"We'll sort the details a bit later," I promised, "But for now view it as today…" I squinted up at the wine dark sky, lit by flashes of neon and the blur of aircars flashing back and forth. "…today is a day off, and we'll start tomorrow morning…"

"Lunchtime!" Luna called.

"Uh…did she mean we get together tomorrow lunchtime, or did she mean…" he asked and I sighed.

"Who fucking knows, mate. Honestly, it's like I'm babysitting at times. I'll be in touch tomorrow either way, but take the day and relax."

"Will do, boss." Todds grinned, started to walk away, then turned back and nodded to me. "Umm, boss?"

"Yeah?"

"Thanks, man," he said. "I know there's a lot going on, and some shit, yeah you still really need to explain, like that fucking banshee and more, but honestly? Thank you. Since you came for me in the pit, things have gotten a hell of a lot better for me and my family."

"Anytime." I smiled at him, then waved him off, turning to the warehouse, and walked inside after the others. "Dondo." I nodded to him. "Thanks for acting as driver for us."

"No problem." He grinned as Luna grabbed him by the collar, and tugged him in the direction of the stairs. "Hey, you know I need to go to work soon, right?" he said to her, and she snorted as she kept leading him up to her room.

"What, the big bad gangbanger has a bedtime? Or does he have to be standing at the front desk for a check in from his boss?" She joked.

"He *is* a crime lord, you get that right?"

"I have needs, and you're going to service them, you get *that* right?" she replied, and Dondo sighed, then grinned, vanishing into the living quarters section with her.

Reign was already gone, and I could hear the flow of water in the pipes, suggesting she was in the shower.

I had a few more minutes I guessed, before I hit the shower, and I checked on the arm, looking it over again, nodding to myself that it was pretty much perfect, before locking it in the transport container with my suit and the spinal mod.

No fucker was stealing this.

That done, I headed upstairs, quickly made sure the bed was clean and the room tidy, then stripped and hit the shower. Standing there, the water cascading down me, spray gels dissolving any dirt and working to relax my muscles, I sighed in relief.

I'd done it.

I'd done as much as I could be reasonably expected to have managed in any kind of a timescale since losing the others.

We had a new team, one that was ready to back me, and offer sanctuary to Richie and Sync. We had a base of operations, a setup that could grow with us, and hell, we had the local crime lord literally over the road.

As long as I could keep him on board with us, well, break ins were fucking unlikely.

Add to that once he understood that fucking with the APS meant pulling back a bloody stump with no body attached? He'd be a much more manageable neighbor as well.

Hell, with the way things were going we might be able to fold the guild in under us, raise some more funds and see about...

I'd been so engrossed in the play of the water and my reflection over recent events I'd missed the door to the cubicle opening, and so the first I knew of Reign being there, was the hand that slipped around me, holding me tight as she slid in to join me.

I turned—the shower really wasn't built for two, I had no idea how the half-orcs managed anything in here, but still—and I looked down into her beautiful green eyes, feeling her body as it pressed against mine, her warm, dry skin flooded with waters, growing wet as I reached out to her, pulling her in close.

We kissed, soft, gentle and almost hesitantly at first, and then rougher, more demanding and hungrily. I slid one hand down from the small of her back to rest on her firm ass, squeezing, as she moaned into my mouth.

My other hand slid to the front, cupping one small, firm breast as my thumb gently teased her hard nipple. Her right hand slid across my belly, then lower, wrapping around and gripping me, pumping me long and slow, making me groan in return as she broke off the kiss, and flicked her hair back.

"So where do you want me then, soldier?" she asked, her voice husky. "On the bed, or right here, on my knees, for the first round?"

"Yes," I agreed. "Fuck *yes...*"

CHAPTER TWENTY-SIX

The next few hours passed in a blur. Hell, it seemed like we were barely playing for minutes, and yet when I blinked next not only was the sun up, its distant warmth spreading across my lower legs where I lay on the bed, but it was high.

The room was almost sweltering, like the height of summer had come all at once, and yet it was nothing to do with the outside temperature, as I laid there, catching my breath.

"Okay," Reign whispered in my ear, settling back down next to me and pushing sweaty hair aside, spitting some out of her mouth, then curling a finger down her cheek and tugging that stray lock back, tossing it out of the way. "Wow, damn hair…okay though, yeah."

"Yeah?" I asked, brain well and truly fuzzed.

"Yeah."

"Yeah what?"

"Oh sorry, yes, you're fantastic, the biggest I ever had, yadda yadda," she replied in a blatantly fake breathless voice, before snorting and laughing. "Sorry, I couldn't resist. Yeah, I think Luna and Gessh know what we've been putting up with now."

"Really?" I hadn't been paying attention to the noise.

"Oh yeah." She grinned, then kissed me. "Good boy. You can stay."

"It's my room," I pointed out, shifting slightly as she snuggled in, the heat that was radiating off her skin making me both amazed, as my own body heat started to rise again, and then…I reached over, running my hand across her arm, up to the shoulder, then slowly down the front of her chest until…

"Ah, ah!" She laughed, taking my hand and lifting it free of her nipple. "Damn, Kabutt, let a girl catch her breath, alright?"

"Sorry." I grinned at her, not meaning it at all.

"No, you're not," she said, and I nodded. "Right, I need something to eat, besides you, that protein isn't going to fill my stomach…you know what, don't even go there." She put her fingers over my mouth as I opened it to make a comment, then she grinned and kissed me.

"You know what I mean," she said softly, and I nodded, our noses brushing against each other as we shifted, then relaxing again.

We ordered food, somehow it was my job to dress and go out of the room to fetch it, as well as drinks, and from the sounds of groans that rose from below, someone was making good use of the new electronics benches.

I retreated to what I guessed was now 'our' room, with the food and drinks, and reached out to the sterilization drone, programming in an hours delay, then a full and deep clean downstairs.

I didn't want to be leaning on those tables working until they'd been thoroughly fucking cleaned.

We had a quick call, by avatar, with Lion, discussed the new arm, and how close it would get me to my limit with the spinal mod we'd been looking at, and then I told him about the tier four mod we had.

He agreed to scan it and check the blood etc that was on it, make damn sure it wasn't infected with anything, and sterilize it. Then we could assess if we wanted to use it or not.

Normally I'd have never considered it, but more and more I was suspecting that the mods that were supplied from 'accidents' and 'upgrades' by other clients were as likely as not from specters.

That only made sense now that I knew Oshbob ran a dozen or more chop-shops, and was buying all the mods he could lay his oversized fucking fingers on.

I had a call with Oshbob, discussed the parts he had for me, the fusion powercell and the sensor pods he'd already gotten, but he was apparently chasing down a shipment that might contain some limbs, but I needed to pay for the stuff he already had first. I transferred him two hundred and fifty thousand credits, and he agreed to continue getting the rest.

Dondo was apparently more of a middleman than I knew, as he'd be delivering the parts later today I was told, as well as a list of secondary units that I'd asked for.

That set me back another hundred thousand, but there were apparently bonuses to working with shadowy crime lords, in that I wasn't expected to pay over the counter prices.

The five training swords that were coming had set me back five thousand a piece, and while that was expensive, they were the best to train with.

Matting, another cleaning bot, a full size and secure armory package—it was basically a flatpack unit that you built yourself, but comprised of heavy interlocking steel and titanium plates that overlapped as they slid into place—all these parts were ordered, and to my surprise, I got funds transfers.

I'd not really thought about it, I probably should have, but as the team lead, some things I just went ahead with, like the armory purchase, without asking the others. We'd all talked about needing it, and when Reign and I were on the call with Oshbob I just mentioned what we needed, and he told me to provide details to Dondo.

I did, and he got back to me saying they'd be delivered in a few hours.

The cost was far less than if I'd bought them over the counter, and I damn well knew they were being stolen to order, but I'd not considered asking the others for contributions towards the cost.

Just like I didn't for the parts for my suit. That was my expense, just like it was my suit.

That Reign apparently spoke to the rest of the team, and they all chipped in an equal share for the warehouse expenses was more than I ever expected.

As well as the call with Lion and Oshbob—he'd complained that I wasn't holding up my end of the bargain as well, and while he'd taken my assurances that the first mods and nanite deliveries would start soon, it was also made clear, that if they didn't? There'd be big fucking problems—I also had a call with Julius.

That one was both a great call and a bad one, on different points.

Apparently that fucking asshole Trees had made a scene, and a hell of a one. When he'd had his money thrown back at him, and the investment contract cancelled, he'd gone off in a huff. That was fine, it was about what we all expected, and because he was one of the teams that was supposed to be on the job, and he refused any call to go from Julius after the meeting, it made it legally him that was in the wrong.

Great, all that was a good thing as far as I was concerned.

The best bit, for me, was that as he'd had his 'investor' situation cancelled right before the job began, he'd also lost out on his percentage of the take.

The guild hadn't just done well out of that job, there had turned out to have been over four thousand specters on site, combined with the ghouls, and their increased bounties, and then the banshee?

Add in that there were a fuck load of weapons recovered, and all the little bonuses? The corpos that had been broadcasting the whole thing had apparently been seriously terrified when the AI came after them, and still hadn't come out of hiding.

Someone had made a thing of us being 'heroes' to the media, and because they were in a lull between corrupt politicians and media stars cheating, they went with it.

That meant that the guild was hit over and over again by the various media companies and a bidding war for the personal recordings had started.

It wasn't finished yet, but Julius had asked all of those on site to agree to sharing the feeds, and trusting him, most of us had.

Add in those to the job, and yeah.

The guild had gone from barely being able to cover the running costs and nowhere near enough members, to being inundated with mercs that needed to rehabilitate their images, and a bank account that was groaning at the seams.

The downside was that the asshole elf was trying to tie up the whole thing in a court case to stop Julius from paying us all, unless he got his portion of it.

Julius was moving as fast as he could, making damn sure the money was paid out, but that meant dealing with all the boring details and going over the AAR in depth when I really didn't want to, and Reign, because she wasn't the team lead, had bowed out of the call at that point.

Julius had basically then started hounding me as to when we were returning to work, because while we were all contractors, and unless the shit hit the fan we weren't required to work, he was also getting some very pointed requests from people that wanted us personally to deal with their incursions.

I'd agreed that for double the standard rate, we'd be back at work tomorrow, and that yes, we would totally dress, look and act professional, as the guild's reputation was obviously important.

I'd also quickly finished the call at that point, mainly because Reign had clearly gotten bored, and while I was ostensibly sitting at a desk in a virtual meeting room with Julius…

In reality I was laid naked on my bed, with who I guessed was now very much my girlfriend, and a certain part of my anatomy was being steadily and skillfully worked.

Yup. Whoever told her she was shit at that, *really* had no clue what the hell they were talking about.

By the time we'd finished playing again, I was red raw, bruised in the best of ways, and exhausted, not to mention suffering from borderline dehydration I suspected.

That night was one of the best I could remember in years, as Todds had made it over to the warehouse again, Dondo joined us and with Reign, Luna and Gessh, we all basically got hammered to fuck, drank way too much, ate really good food, had some great music playing and partied.

By the time we finally staggered to bed and passed out? It was like a 'refresh' button had been pressed on my heart. For the first time in months, I didn't feel like I'd failed my friends, like I'd lost the best parts of me on the battlefield and in the fingers, and that I was just going through the motions.

I felt alive again, and as I laid there, drunk, unable to stop smiling as a beautiful and lethal half-elven woman snored by my side, I couldn't believe my luck.

Then fucking Dondo started drilling for oil again, and I was forced to cover my ears with a fucking pillow.

CHAPTER TWENTY-SEVEN

The next morning dawned as most of them did, with the sun slowly edging its way up, the light searing its way around the edges of the blinds, and me wondering what the hell had crapped in my mouth, as clearly something was doing it, judging from the goddamn awful taste and dryness.

I slid out of bed, made it into the shower and woke myself up, scrubbed myself clean, and regarded Reign from the bathroom door, beautiful, long limbed, stark naked and fast asleep, and for just a few seconds I considered prodding her with it to wake her, then I thought better of it.

First of all, she didn't wake in a great mood, generally.

Secondly, I was bruised to buggery, and if I was to enjoy the experience I needed a medikit first—I was honest enough with myself that I accepted a 'small' one would do the job, but that wasn't important—and last of all?

There was an absolute shitload of things that needed to be done today to get things moving.

Yesterday had been needed, by the gods of chrome and blood it'd been insanely needed, and not just because I was at least a liter lighter on my feet.

I needed to get myself back on track, not just the team. For that, I needed to know exactly what I was dealing with, and we needed to run some tests.

We needed to know if I could actually accommodate the new arm and the spinal mod. If the new spinal mod, the tier four, was actually usable, and not riddled with viruses or whatever? I'd not checked the exact figures yet, but I was grimly sure that I was going to be either right up against my capacity for mods, or possibly over it.

The only good part about all of this, was that your capacity for mods was…fluid.

It was worked out on a combination of things, and none of them were exact guarantees.

For most people, the rule of thumb was that if you added your 'mental power' and 'toughness' stats together, they gave you your capacity.

For most people the scores of those two sections weren't that impressive, not blowing my own trumpet, but high mental power usually didn't come with high toughness.

That wasn't to say that smarter people weren't tough. Toughness was a mixture of many things, and it bled over into mental power quite a lot.

Mental power was all about how adaptable, how easily you learned, and how smart you were. That was one way of looking at it, and that toughness was all about how well you could take a beating, how long you lasted in a fight, and how much punishment you'd last through.

That wasn't it though.

Not entirely.

Mental power and toughness together were taken by some as *mental fortitude.*

It wasn't a term used much outside of special forces and operators, but mental fortitude was a lot more about that little voice that tells you to get back up.

The one that says yeah, you might have gotten your ass kicked, but you weren't down, nor out.

It was the little voice that made you never give up, that made a guy or a gal with bullet holes in them stand up and take another blow.

It was what made you damn well fight, and win, against all odds.

I should be dead.

Fuck I should have died on the fingers, I sure as shit shouldn't have thrown myself off them and let necrosis take my left arm. I shouldn't have fought and bled through all the shit I had, I shouldn't have been blown up, cooked, and fucking thrown out of buildings, without spending half my life in hospital.

I should have gotten put down, and damn well stayed down. I should have learned that my place was with the rest of the trash in the gutter, I wasn't smart, not really, and I certainly wasn't overly intelligent. I wasn't naturally tough like the orcs were, nor fast and graceful like the elves.

I wasn't sneaky like the goblins, nor fucking insanely skilled like the dwarves.

I was human. I was the average.

I was also the man that had stood toe to toe with an assault mech.

I'd dragged myself through the undercity, with a gun with one round in it, and I'd emerged broken, bloody and triumphant where ghouls had died.

I was the man that'd led a team of nobodies into the depths of that fucking arcology, and had killed off a gang. I was the man that'd fought fucking APS one on one, and carved them a new fucking asshole.

I was the man that'd faced and fought banshees, ghouls and specters, that had saved kids and that had led a team for more than half my adult life.

Maybe I was an asshole, sure, maybe as Fergie used to tell me, I was just plain fucking bad luck, and too dumb to accept it, but what I really was?

I was a stubborn fucker that not only didn't know when to quit, I didn't know fucking how. My toughness and mental score might be nineteen, when combined, but my mental fortitude?

That was a number that could smash steel down, and bend titanium.

Taking a deep breath, I summoned the standardized personal breakdown again, and I ordered the RI to run a full system re-evaluation, knowing just how fucking painful that was going to be.

It started at the tips of my fingers, a twitch, like a muscle that was on the verge of going into cramp, a quiver that ran down and up and back again a dozen times, even as a sensation like spiders crawling on me picked up across my body.

As it went, I felt my internal temperature spiking as the old 'grey matter' was massaged. There was no need for the times tables and shit like that, that we'd been taught in class as a kid. No this was a full on electrical surge and test, as synapses were fired over and over again, as muscles bunched and released.

My temperature grew higher and sweat poured down me. I started to pant, the effort doubling and redoubling as my heart raced faster and harder. My body stacked stress upon itself, over and over, my breath torn from me in great gasps like I was racing a marathon uphill with a fucking aircar on my back…and then it was over.

The change from the test beginning to the end was almost as great a shock as the abrupt start, and yet, as my heart stuttered, trying to regain a natural rhythm, I grinned to myself, watching as the sheet before me blurred.

The RI was the better method to track this kind of shit over the standard Keystone evaluation, because it saw everything. Literally everything that I went through all day every day, it saw, and so its evaluation of my stats wasn't as limited as the 'standard' version was.

To be fair though, the evaluation that I'd been working off until now was updated and refined by the RI, so it wasn't like it was massively out, but damn.

I'd been through some life changing shit since I last updated it alright.

Identification: Harry Kabutt				
Species: Human		**Bonus**: None		
Mod Capacity: 22		**Mod Capacity in use**: 13		
Stat	**Current Points**	**Description**	**Mods**	**Quality**
Dexterity	11	Governs agility and movement.	Left Arm Mod: 2 Cost: 2 (Dex: 12)	Basic
Mental Power	12	Governs swiftness and fortitude of the mind	Brain Mod: 3 Cost: 3	Professional
Perception	11	Governs an individuals senses and connection to the world around them.	Brain Mod: 4 Ocular Mod: 3 Cost: 4 (PER 12 + 14)	Basic
Strength	10	Governs physical strength and damage dealt	Left Arm Mod: 2 Cost: 1 (STR 14)	Basic
Toughness	10	Governs the body and internal fortitude	Basic Organelles: 3 Cost: 3 Spinal Reinforcement: 2 Cost: 2 Toughness: 11	Basic

Nine points! I had nine points remaining! I sighed like a fucking rocket hitting orbital, and sagged with relief. Nine points…that was plenty, well, for me it was, for now.

I didn't know how many points the new arm and the damn spinal mod were going to take up, hell the spinal mod that I'd been looking at was a tier three, and that had needed six points, which was concerning, but…

In putting the new one in, I'd be removing the old. That sounded obvious, but it wasn't to a lot of people. I'd be getting the two points that were taken up by the spinal reinforcement I had now, back. SO in effect, it'd cost me four more points than I had in use now.

That left me five points for the arm.

The arm was a custom job, as heavily modded as it was, but my current one was worth three points. I couldn't see it costing eight, not overall, not for a fucking arm, when the spinal cost was to allow for systemic integration of things like a fucking APS or a construction or war mech.

Hell, I'd heard of helo pilots that could deploy swarms of fucking drones while flying the damn things around buildings, thanks to their specialist mods.

I couldn't see a posh fucking vacuum cleaner with fingers coming to near enough the same cost as that kind of shit.

I blew out a long breath, nodding to myself that I needed certain things sorting out, and soon, such as the damn attaching, but before I could do that?

I needed a second goddamn shower.

Twenty minutes later—and Reign was still snoring—and I was downstairs, chewing on cold pizza, powering up the transport cradle for my suit.

These things were amazing, when you'd never seen them before, I reflected. Hell, as an experienced operator, using them was still a fucking impressive experience.

The cradle was higher than the suit was tall, fully laden, and was designed to provide a safe storage option for 'in the field'. Essentially it was a self-contained brace, armor stand, and storage unit, that had recesses for everything that the operator could need.

Replacement components, new armoring, hell spare fusion cores and containers for the gamma cannons and railgun mounts were included…

It was just a pain in the ass that the damn slots were all empty!

The fact that fucking asshole Tyrannus had stolen it before it could be equipped? That rankled.

Sure, when I considered the options, the major clearly never had any intention of me getting my damn suit, but to have it turn up like this? Instead of the titan of war it really was?

It *hurt.*

Well, I had new sensor nodes now, and pods and a suite to install, as well as the fusion chambers to fix and the core to power and test.

The suit towered over me, as the transport unit locked into position, the controls on the side closest to where I stood—I'd used these fuckers a time or three after all—and I manipulated the inbuilt restraint system to slowly turn the suit, lowering it to where I could climb up the side.

It was awkward, genuinely it was, they kinda assumed that you'd have operational gantries and hydraulic hoists, or at the very least a damn toolbelt with all your bits and bobs in, and I had none of those.

There were places to brace yourself though, and handholds, and with the suit being only a skeletal structure in places, that provided spaces as well.

Forty minutes it took me to install the first row of sensors, feeding the sections though, plugging in as I went, and making damn sure that the crystal matrix was perfectly polished for them

Back in the distant past, and the not so distant cheap ass maintenance past, they had used fiberoptics for this kinda shit. That was great and all, but the splicing process when they were damaged? It was inevitably shitty, and when it was done by the lowest bidder?

Yeah.

Crystal had changed all of that. They were either perfect, or they didn't work.

That had led to a massive upsurge in quality, when some components needed to be perfect and could be made so? Well, why the hell weren't the rest the same?

That had been a theory that had lasted at least a fortnight, hell maybe two.

That had been enough to massively improve the base line though, and then the centuries of slow degradation had resumed.

The crystals as I slid them in, locked into place with a solid click that gave me a warm feeling to my goddamn boots. It just felt right, as I rebuilt the suit, section by section.

An hour passed as I locked the next ring in place, and then allowed myself the luxury of climbing inside the suit. I slid down, the harness taking my weight as I slid into my familiar position. The fresh, brand new padding that weirdly had been put in place confused me for a moment.

That hadn't been damaged, and it'd taken me months of missions to wear the comfortable grooves into it, so why the hell replace that, and not put the real bits in first?

That the sensors, power systems and more weren't in, but the padding was? That gave me pause, and for the first time, I started searching the suit more minutely.

Checking the various sections I found what I was most concerned about.

Deployment pins.

Some fucker had triggered the deployment pins, that was why the fucking sections were all missing! I should have put it together instantly, never mind fucking moping around the damn suit all this time!

Some utter cockwomble had activated the emergency deployment pins, a safety cutout in case of a virus in the suit, one that forced the sections that were vulnerable out! A technician could easily reinstall them, we, as operators were trained to do it quickly in case of emergencies, but that someone had actually done it?

For a few seconds I raged internally, before I forced myself to calm. Tyrannus.

That utter cock had to have been the one that did this.

For a few seconds I'd suspected Oshbob, then I shook that off. That was ridiculous, sure there were ways to find the data online, and probably a way to figure out how to get access to the suit in the transport container, he'd had it popped open after all.

So, yeah, sure he *could* have someone that had figured out that when it was unpowered the right combination of sections to power, and to have found the controls for the deployment pins, but no.

There was also a theory that enough monkeys could write a fucking book, given enough time, and despite the evidence I'd seen, that was crazy talk.

No, it had to be Tyrannus.

That bastard had probably sold them to someone on the black market…

I paused, then started checking the various parts that Dondo had dropped off for me, and cursed even more.

They were in great condition sure, hell they were almost brand new…but that almost was the kicker. Here and there, if you know where to look, if you know which parts always jammed, and were always a bastard to remove?

I found matching scratches, both on the armor, *and* on the 'new' parts!

I was paying that fucking orc to buy my own suits goddamn parts off the black market!

For long minutes I sat there cushioned by the brand new bloody padding, and I seethed internally. Again, for a few seconds I considered if Oshbob could have somehow pulled this off, he was a sneaky shit after all, but…no.

No offence to him, nor to the girls, but orcs were generally dumb as shit. Sure, some of them were brighter than the rest, some were vastly more intelligent, freaks of nature, genetic mutations and all that, but no. All that I'd met of his crew so far were orcs, half orcs and goblins.

The exception was not the rule. For him to have people that could understand these systems, for them to figure their way around them? They'd need military experience, and at a classified level. No orc would be given that.

No, Tyrannus had been a desk jockey fuckhead, but he'd have had access to everything he needed to pull this off, and the motivation. I already knew he was a dick who'd sell his own mother given half a chance.

I dismissed the thought, and sat back, glaring at the systems before me, my reflection in the internal screens showing me just how much like a petulant child I looked right then.

After a few more minutes of anger—essentially spitting my fucking pacifier out—prompted by the sounds of the others moving around above me, I forced myself to focus on the good.

These parts I was getting would have all been checked for compatibility. They'd all have been tweaked to run with my particular suit, and the relevant coding patches that always needed to be done, despite the engineers assurances of 'correct tolerances' and such bullshit, they'd all have been done for me.

This was a good thing! It really was.

I managed to keep telling myself that for the rest of the next hour, until I added in the final sections to the power subsystems, and I triggered the primary boot.

CHAPTER TWENTY-EIGHT

The screens flickered to life, sections of the original coding flickering across the screen too fast to read, even as the gentle hum of the fusion cell grew, test firing as it readied for a deployment.

Systems flashed to life as the suit powered, and then, I felt the fucking clang as an integration needle hit my spine. A spine that was neither equipped with a port, nor ready for it.

I hissed in pain, the ports the integration needle was searching for now covered by synth-skin, and the pain faithfully replicated just as it would have been, was that my own.

I flicked the retraction lever as quick as I could, and the suit, finding no matching link in me, and no technicians override in place?

It powered back down, locking me back out.

My heart fell, my stomach clenching as I stared at my reflection, knowing the refusal of the system for the first time in my life, and feeling the panic that raced through me at the thought that maybe this would be permanent.

Maybe, just maybe, the spinal mods I'd get wouldn't be enough. They wouldn't help me to integrate the way I always had.

There'd been serious damage, when I'd thrown myself off that goddamn cliff, I'd taken real damage to my spine, as well as my arm.

Could that have…

I stopped that thought right there.

The use of an APS was like the use of your arms or leg. We were fully integrated into the suit, and I'd seen someone once that had a serious accident, and could no longer operate the suit.

The medics swore blind he could, and every single test said he could, but he just couldn't.

A seriously good operator had lost his career over what they later put down to him subconsciously believing he couldn't do it any more. It was stupid, genuinely it was, and yet it'd put the fear of chrome and blood into us.

If you could have a dream where you couldn't operate the suit any more, and then wake up to find it was true?

It didn't bear thinking about.

Instead, I flicked the final switches, approved the locks, and clambered out of the suit, gathering the gear on the way out and down, before standing by the base of the unit and ordering the full lock.

As the suit slowly retracted, the sides of the container sealing up again and locking down, I watched the suit vanish, determination flooding me as I moved back to the nearest bench, and the two mods that were laid atop it.

The spinal tap and the harvesting arm.

It was time to get shit done.

I gathered them up and walked up the stairs, heading to the main kitchen and towards the low buzz of voices, finding the others were all awake, and the coffee was all gone.

I forced myself to not let that get me down, and I made a fresh pot, ignoring the way the vultures all swooped and tried to steal it from me before I'd even poured my own.

"What's the plan then boss?" Reign asked, smiling at me over the rim of her coffee cup.

"We've two choices," I said to the group, noting the way that silence fell as I spoke. "First and foremost, we need to earn more creds…"

"You guys have a gambling problem or something?" Todds asked, shaking his head. "Seriously, I've got kids and a house to run, and—"

"And a baby-sitter," Luna coughed into the back of her hand.

"—And I'm good for cash for weeks, maybe a month from now," he finished, glaring at her.

"We have more expenses than we've been letting on, and frankly, it's a story that none of you know. So, we might as well get this out in the open, as you already know most of it, Todds, but the rest of the team need to hear all of it anyway."

"So, to understand this, I guess I need to tell you all about my old team." I sat on the edge of the table, facing them, as I started, and I felt every wound as if fresh made, as I described them.

Fergie, Scott, Barnes, Richie and Sync lived and breathed again for a few brief minutes as I described them, their style, their personalities.

I told them about Fergie and Scott's band, and Richie's tech genius. I told them of Sync, and the quiet way she watched over us all, alternating between shy around Richie, and exasperated as a mother-hen as we all did stupid stuff.

I described Barnes, the bravery he'd shown in running in and locking to Fergie, offering up his fusion plant to form the 'Heavy-Soldier' symbiote unit, and the way the Shark drone had blown him to shit.

I described the cold of the fingers, and the joy of finding Richie and Sync, of the fear of hiding them, and then the sheer stupidity of throwing myself off a cliff to make sure I couldn't lead anyone to them.

I talked about the major, and the bean counting fucking corpo asshat that saddled me with shitty mods.

I spoke about Lucky, and about Gunther, I told them about the APS unit, and the potential of it, as well as the reasons they were 'locked' to a single user, as well as the ways that I thought the corpo black ops teams were getting around that.

I told them everything, including that my friends were in cryosleep, buried in the mountains, and that Julius knew about it, and was going to arrange the transport.

I told them about the need for Bowdoin, and the fake registration. I told them all of it, and I apologized for not doing it sooner, explaining why I'd told Julius, before them, and the grip that gave us over the guild, and finally?

The opportunity that offered.

I explained that the suits could—I believed—be bonded to people other than those originally intended. That we could get my suit working, that we could rescue Sync and Richie, and that as soon as the Major found out, there would, without a doubt, be consequences.

That he'd send his tame APS black ops after us.

Then I told them that if we pulled this off right? We'd have APS suits. Damaged ones, sure, but we'd have them, and given some time, and some credits? We could repair them, then I could train them to be operators.

From that point, they knew exactly what I was offering. We already had a guild, one that we liked, more to the point, and a guild master we trusted. Add in a team of possibly eight APS operators? The guild would be catapulted almost overnight from a low to mid ranks, to right up near the top.

Once we were there? We'd be able to set our prices. If we wanted to do specter clearance still—unlikely but hey, maybe—then we'd be rounding up great masses of them and slaughtering them wholesale.

There'd always been the rumor of banshees, but aside from the ghouls? We'd never had any solid evidence of a sentient class.

For all we knew they were the equivalent of the corporals and sergeants in the specters ranks, and there were everything from sergeant-majors to fucking captains, generals and more buried under the city.

Hell, for all we knew they were building a massive army, and Tuesday was the end of the world for us all.

Or maybe there was nothing above the banshees, and there'd only been two of them. One was now getting experimented on, and one was off harvesting for shits and giggles.

Who fucking knew.

The point was though, that after all of this shit was finally out in the open, the rest of the group had a chance to really understand the stakes we were playing for, and to decide if they wanted to stay 'in'.

When Luna asked the carefully casual question that 'would we get the same shares in kills' I knew I had them.

"We'll share everything equally," I said. "We'll probably have to set up a formal fund for shit, like ammo and repairs, and channel a set amount from each of us into that, but beyond that, I've no problem sharing the take equally."

"No," Todds said, and we all turned to look at him in surprise. "Not 'no' to the deal, fuck yes to the deal, and yeah, okay, I totally want to be an APS operator, if your pet hacker can sort out fake IDs that get us registered? Fuck yeah. No, what I'm saying 'no' to is the equal shares bit."

"You think you deserve more than an APS..." Gessh asked, confused.

"No," he said, glaring round. "So how about you listen for a second, alright?" He waited, getting nods from us all before going on. "So, we go and we kill what you tell us to boss, you come up with the overall strategic plan, and let's face it, on top of actually leading the group and negotiating all this shit, you're going to be the one training us, and basically being out on point.

"When the job's done, and we're all cracking open a cold one—"

"Or a hot babysitter." Luna coughed into her hand again, getting a grin from most of the team.

"—Then you're still working doing AARs and shit," he finished glaring at Luna. "All I'm saying is that for the next year or two, we're going to be carried by you and your friends, right? You're going to be training us, teaching us, basically taking us by the hand and making sure we don't crap in the suit, as well as teaching us how to clean the fuckers and maintain them. While yeah, I *want* the credits? I think the boss should be on at least ten percent more than the grunts."

"I agree," Reign said. "And not just for the obvious reasons. We're also celebrating, spending our credits on the shit we want…you're repairing your suit and getting the upgrades you need to carry out the plan aren't you?" she asked, and I nodded.

"Okay, then I suggest this," Reign said as the others looked at each other. "For now, until the other APS are here and pulling their weight, we pool our upcoming earnings. We each get ten percent of the overall pot, I know it feels like we're handing over our creds, but seriously? I didn't expect to pay my debt off this side of ten years. In a week of working with Kabutt I've earned more than I ever thought possible.

"So we pool our earnings from this point on, what we've already got? That's ours. When it comes into the pot, we each take ten percent, that's four of us, so forty percent…"

"We can do basic math," Gessh groaned.

"Okay, well, Kabutt gets twenty, he's the boss, right?"

A round of agreement for that, and I nodded my thanks.

"So, that leaves forty percent. Forty percent to pay for this place, to restock the ammo cabinets, to go towards buying the parts we need on the black market for the suit, and to repair the others. It'd be to pay for upgrades to this place, and for the security we're going to need, unless you think us leaving suits here all alone will be safe?"

"Not in the fucking slightest," I agreed. "My suit has been safe so far because no fucker knows about it. Once they do? We'll need a perimeter defense and turrets at the least, probably military grade."

"So, we split the credits, as an investment?" Reign repeated, looking around the room and waiting to see what everyone thought. "Honestly? In the long term, its massively worth it, as is probably buying this place from Oshbob, *before* we do all the work on securing it."

"If he'll sell it," I pointed out.

"Oh I think he will, if we go to him with a good enough deal. It was a derelict warehouse in a slum industrial zone, its only value at the minute is that we want it. If we offer to buy it, or we're moving and buying somewhere else?" Reign shrugged. "Remember, he's a crime lord, as much as he's a big bad fish around here, and even if he'd never admit it, he'll have enemies and some of them will be a lot bigger than him. Having a team of allied APS operators that live next door?" She shrugged, then grinned. "I think we can persuade him to see the advantage of that."

"That's one for you to sort then," I said. "If you're to be second in command of our little enterprise, then you're also quartermaster. You'll have control of the funds…" I saw the alarmed look that Luna and Gessh gave each other at that suggestion, well aware I was suggesting giving an ex drug addict access to what would hopefully be massive funds. "…*but*, you'd need oversight."

"You do strategic, I'll do local level." She nodded. "Okay, who would have oversight over the funds? I'm not offended people, I agree that I made some horrific mistakes in the past."

"I could, if you want?" Todds offered. "Maybe make it a two person release for company funds? So either the boss or I have to approve any larger expenditure for the pot, and anything under say, a thousand we don't? That covers all the usual day-to-day stuff like food and bills, ammo and air-cabs and shit, but for things like heavy weapons, turrets and so on? We'd need two to approve?"

"That works," Luna agreed, as Gessh nodded. "Sorry Reign, we trust you but..."

"But I fucked up in the past," she agreed. "Massively so." She nodded, smiling sadly. "Believe me, I know, and I'll always be paying for it as part of life. It's fine."

"So..." I said after a few seconds. "Lion."

"What about him?" Gessh asked. "I mean, he's cute and he's skilled, but you know, Dondo is..."

"That's between you and Dondo!" I cut her off, shaking my head at her grin. "Fuck's sake, I mean he's helped to fix up the harvester arm, and we need him to keep his goddamn mouth shut. Do we recruit him, or keep him as a contractor, or what?"

"As a contractor there was no contract or anything to keep him quiet about what we've got was there?" Reign asked, and I shook my head. "Dammit."

"Exactly," I said. "Limited time, and to make it all work, we involved him too deep, too fast. Now we're left with a mess to clean up. Hence do we recruit him, or boot him."

"Would he want to be recruited?" Gessh asked. "I mean, he's all about helping his local community, right?"

"True, but he might see selling that tech and the location of the arm as the best way to do that," I countered. "If he can see real credits coming in, and in the short term? He'll probably shut up."

"What about his shop? And what does he bring to the team?" Reign said musingly. "I mean, having our own pet carver would be great, especially as he's good mechanically, between him and Todds..."

"We've got the start of a good tech team," I agreed. "As APS Operators we're taught to maintain and repair our suits, but honestly, we don't do it, we have engineering teams for that, armory squads who specialize in it, rather than understanding that if we pull this lever, that happens."

"So we'd need him anyway, further down the line..." Luna said. "What if we gave him the gist of what's happening...?"

"Not about Richie and Sync, not yet," I said. "I'm not risking them."

"No, not that, but we tell him about the way we can sort the APS suits that are out in the city and..."

"He'd never bet on us in that fight, much more likely we all end up squashed than winning."

"If you look at the odds, yeah probably," I grunted.

"And then the arm is lost," Reign finished. "What if we agree to sell the tech?"

"What?" I asked, shocked.

"I mean, it's what he wants right? Or what he will want?"

"Yeah, but..."

"But we agree that it needs to undergo testing, prototyping, fixing the minor details, and then we sell it, and he gets an equal share. We say that we don't sell it until its ready, and we make sure he knows that's not going to be tomorrow, but what, six months? That's do-able? Then it'll vanish into a lab somewhere, and the corpos make a fortune. We make a nice pile, and we move on with our lives."

"I…" I didn't like it, not at all, handing this tech over to have it vanish into a corpo research lab? Hell, they might already have this shit, dozens of such things, all hidden because they needed to keep their finger on the profit margin.

"Realistically, did you see yourself using the arm once the APS units were up and running?" Reign asked me gently, seeing that I was struggling with it. "Would you still be harvesting, or would you be too busy for that?"

"I'd probably be too busy." I agreed.

"It wouldn't be worth our time." She nodded. "Better that we sell the tech, maybe we make a version that's carriable by a normal team, and we have the goblin clean-up crews carry them?"

"Hell, sell them the drawings, the data and shit, and keep the arm, you don't have to give that up," Luna offered, and I paused, before shaking my head.

"They'd want a working prototype." I sighed. "I hate the corpo scumbags, but…"

"But it's their world." Gessh finished for me. "We just live in it, and we can either profit from it, or not. This way Lion isn't tempted to fuck us over and sell it, and us to the corpos, we can keep him as a contractor, and when we're ready? We can fold him in if we want."

"Everyone happy with that?" I asked, getting nods all around. "Fine. In that case we need to get shit moving then, I know Julius has missions he wants us on today, and we need to test the arm, so I'm thinking we split up."

"Some to restock and reload?" Reign asked, and I nodded.

"We need it, we bought a fuck load of ammo the other day, and we used almost all of it. We need a load of ammo here, for all our weapons. We need the rest of those stealth suits cleaned and repaired, and we need a decent selection of armor for us all, as well as clothes I guess…" I looked down at the only semi-clean clothes I had left, before sighing and shaking my head.

"I need to get that arm in place. I know Julius wants us back out and earning but…"

"But he owes us," Reign finished for me. "Everyone else happy to spend today on a restock and rearm, fix our gear and so on, start afresh tomorrow?"

Nods all round.

"Then I'll call him for you, boss, fill him in," she suggested, as I stood and finished my coffee.

"Thank you, but no…I need to do that one. You sort the rest please, and I'll go get a new arm…"

"And get that spinal checked out," Luna suggested, before biting her lip.

"Out with it." I ordered her, knowing her tells well enough by now.

"Is this a good idea?" she said bluntly. "Not the breakup of jobs and so on, or the future, I mean you going on your own to Lion. That's putting temptation in his way, when he doesn't need it."

"That's a good point," Gessh agreed. "Boss, one of us should go with you today, watch over you while that gets done, and make sure you're not fucked over. No offence, but if Lion's going to do it? That'd be the time. You're out cold, or restrained, the tech is all there ready, and we're not about?"

"And it's totally not to get out of cleaning and restocking," Luna said seriously, before ruining it all with a wink. "Honest."

"Fuck's sake," I groaned. "Alright, it's a fair point, one of you, heavily armed...and no, Luna, there's even odds you'd be trying to ride him the entire time...Todds?" I suggested.

He grinned. "I'm in, boss."

"Great." I nodded my thanks, before looking at Reign, who smiled, knowing me all too well by now.

"Air-cab is incoming," she said, before sipping the last of her coffee, and offering me the empty cup. "Four minutes out, so be a dear and refill that, would you?"

CHAPTER TWENTY-NINE

The ride to the chop-shop was easy enough, most of it spent on the call to Julius. He wasn't happy about us not doing any missions today, but he was also swamped arranging missions here there and everywhere, and apparently liked the idea of dangling my team out as a possible solution to a few problem areas for tomorrow.

He also understood both that we took missions as a team and when as mercs, and that he'd better not fuck with us too much, as we could very easily go to a competitor.

That we needed time to integrate the new mods and upgrades? That was something he could sell to the clients as a bonus, rather than an apology.

The rest of the flight was calm and relaxed as Todds and I chatted about his past and family life, before touching down outside the shop.

My first impression as I clambered out of the cab was that we'd made a mistake, the area was abandoned, and my instincts went into overdrive, fully expecting that we were too late and that Lion had already sold us out...

But on getting down into the actual chop-shop?

Nope.

We walked in on three gangers apparently trying to negotiate with him for 'protection'.

That the dumb fucks had chased everyone away, and were now all gathered around him, explaining that either they got their mods done free in exchange for their 'protection' from now on, or he lost the ability to do any mods? Along with his hands?

"Yeah, that's not going to work for us lads," I said bluntly walking into the middle of the room, and drawing the plasma sword.

They spun, guns coming up, and I rolled my wrist, sending the crackling blade into a wide arc.

Two of the three guns fell to the floor, carved through, the third? Well, the wielder had been threatening Lion personally, the other two were stood back closer to the door, and when he spun around, he found my revolver already leveled between his eyes.

That froze him in place. What ended his interest in anything else though? It was when Lion grabbed his nano-scalpel, and snarled about 'teaching them a lesson'.

Eight minutes later, and the three of them were helping each other to stagger out of the chop-shop, each of them having to help the others, as their missing mods—shite though lion assured me they were—were now floating in sterilization fluid baths.

Their little attempt at a protection racket had literally cost them an arm and a leg, although in this case, there were two eyes and a hand to add to the tally.

"So…" Lion said, once he was done, drying his hands with a cloth as he looked over the bag I had with me. "Thanks for your help there, and I assume that's our little special project?"

"It is," I agreed. "Time to get it installed, and to start doing test runs."

"And have you thought any more about the future?" he asked carefully, as he gestured to the table nearby.

"We have." I outlined the conversation we'd had about the harvesting tool, not the rest of the things I'd shared with the team though.

"You're serious?" he asked after a few seconds thought. "Equal shares, for each of us?"

"I am," I said. "Within the confines of this deal, and I'll be in control of it. We keep this under wraps until we're damn sure that we've got it working, and that we can prove it, we make use of it for a few months, make sure that it doesn't burn out, nor fail. We get our use out of the system first, line our pockets in case they fuck us over somehow."

"But…"

"But we do sell it, and I'm thinking within six months." I finished, seeing the relief on his face.

"Oh thank fuck, I thought you were going to say like five years or something," he said. "Look, I'm fine with six months, I can wait that long, probably, it's just…"

"Just what?" I asked.

"Since you killed Lucky? I'm getting assholes like these every few days," he admitted. "They scare my other customers away, and to be honest? I was borderline anyway before this shit started. I need protection, I just can't get it from these assholes…"

"And you want it from us?" I asked, surprised.

"We already have a deal on me giving you all discounts, so yeah, basically, I need you guys to hold up your end of the bargain." He sighed, making me snort.

"There was never a promise of protection." I pointed out, but seeing the look on his face I relented. "I'll think about it. So…how about you check these fuckers over?" I pulled the arm, and the spinal mod out of the bag, laying them on the top, before stepping back.

Lion's eyes lit up, literally, a steady bright blue radiance as the optics went fully powered, and Todds and I waited. I'd tried using my system to identify the mods already, and I'd gotten precisely dick for it.

The arm was still showing as the same model that he'd ordered for us to build the system into, and the spinal tap?

Well that just showed as 'Classified: Experimental' when I looked at it.

Lion though, clearly saw a fuck load more.

"S5 to S1 are configured for storage, possibly military?" he muttered, moving his hands in the air as he apparently tried to manipulate the image in different ways. "L1 to L5 are all standard, but high interface, maybe a dual sheath? No that can't be right, there's sections here for integration between the neurons, and a spider path of symbiosis…"

"That sounds great…" I interrupted him. "But for the rest of us?"

He flicked his fingers towards me and Todds and I received a knock, followed by the data for the mod, and I realized why the hell he was working through the individual parts instead.

There was basically fuck all in the way of information about this mod anywhere.

[Redacted]	Tier: Four
The [Redacted] Spinal Tap Mod is [Redacted] and provides [Redacted]. This model integrates through [Redacted]. **Note**: *Unconfirmed reports of up to 97mps have been recorded, although this carries with it the risk of [Redacted].* **Warranty**: [Redacted] **Toughness**: 12 **Dexterity**: 12	
Durability: 97/100	**Slot Cost**: 8
Availability: Classified	**Credit Cost**: N/A

The last two sections though, that it granted a boost to both Dexterity AND Toughness of twelve? That was insane. That would basically mean after a decent time acclimatizing to the mod? I could integrate more fucking mods down the line!

I wasn't one of those nutters that wanted to go all cyber and into the machine, no, but seriously? Knowing I had the option, if I was to lose my other arm, or my leg or something to replace it? It was a massive relief.

This though? I didn't know for sure what it did, and I still wanted it. I'd wanted it as soon as I saw how many connective sections it had.

This was kit that was designed to fully integrate you into your suit, most likely? It wasn't intended for APS operators. Being realistic, even as I knew that officially we were the cutting edge of tech, the most lethal weapon out there…

I also knew that as soon as a design was finalized and began production, even with the amazingly efficient production methods we had today, it was still obsolete.

This was designed for the next, *next* gen suit I was betting. The APS systems had sections that could be replaced. They had sections built in for expansion, and areas where we were told frankly that we didn't need to know what they were for.

The spinal tap section was like that. We used two main insertion nodes, two connectors, that slid into the back of our spinal tap systems, and then connected from there. The actual connective sections in us were spread out over a lot more space, but they compressed down to a single pair of plugs that extended into the ports in our back, and connected us up.

If this was what I thought it was, then this could accept at least five ports, looking at the relevant sections.

If I could install two more plugs into my suit?

This was dangerous territory, seriously so, but hey, Lion was a carver, and Todds a mechanic, with my knowledge of the systems, and the background? If we could do that?

The biggest limiting factor on the speed of an APS wasn't the motor, the power core or even the weight. It was inbuilt into the operators ability to use the suit.

Some were naturally faster, able to overcome the natural limits that our bodies enforced. Most though? We were all around the same level. The guy I'd known who could practically blur past us all, and that I now seriously suspected the major had stolen for his black ops team?

He'd had a better spinal tap than the rest of us.

This was the next step down that line.

If this was able to sync me up with the suit even more than I could already? If it could spread the distribution of commands from my brain, across *four* insertion nodes instead?

The lag that was the limit was caused in part by the bunching up of signals, or that was the theory. We'd always wondered why full on assault mechs got six ports in their back and we got two, while flyboys got another number?

We'd been told it was just how it was, and not to question it, but when the current gen suits, like mine, were delivered, and we spotted the expansion slots ready to use more nodes? We'd wondered.

Now?

If we could use the nodes, it might be a game changer.

"So..." I started, and Lion turned to me, seeing my wide eyes, and presumably the hunger on my face.

"I don't know," he said.

"What?"

"I don't know," he repeated. "I don't know what it does, I don't know why it has so many connective sections, I don't know if this system is better for you or worse than the one we were already considering. You're trained to use the nodes in your back, sure, but think about when you first started using the suits, how hard was it to learn to walk?"

"It was a fucking nightmare," I admitted.

"Well, this would be like that all over again. Sure you're sending the same signals, so it wouldn't be exactly the same, but different nodes picking up different things? It could break you. You could be literally crippled by this, also, it had fresh blood on it. Dwarf blood, specifically."

"Right?"

"It might be designed only for a dwarf to use, their neural connective tissues are thicker than a humans. This might burn you out, it might interface with you without a single issue and turn you into a fucking specter in a week, or a second. You might be able to fart flames and piss glitter. I. DON'T. KNOW." That last section was said with a finality that made his feelings clear.

"Okay, so it's a fucking risk," I said slowly.

"It's a hell of a risk," he agreed. "This is a risk that frankly, I don't know if you need to take. I can get the other mod, and we can install that, if there's problems? Hell we can call in their support team and sure, it'll cost, but they'll tweak the package until it works. This? we don't know who made it, we don't know if anyone's looking for it, and we don't know what it'll do to you. Hell, this is designed to access spinal vertebrae that you don't have! I'd have to install spacers to make it line up with a human system..."

He paused, then sighed.

"You're going to do this anyway aren't you?" he said and I grinned at him, then nodded to the arm. "Oh for fucks…you mean to do them both? Today?"

"No time like the present."

"You know this takes you to your limit, or near enough right? And that modding at that level isn't guaranteed? The limit isn't a hard thing, it's a combination of dozens of factors, you might go under for the op, and wake up a fucking specter, you know that, right?"

"I do," I said. "Be realistic, is it going to make any real difference if I wait a few days before installing the spinal? And is it definitely clean?"

"Clean of infection?" He dumped it into a tube of gently bubbling blue liquid. "It will be in thirty seconds," he assured me. "As to clean of specter infections? No fucking idea."

"No…" I started to ask, shocked.

"This is a mod I barely understand," he said sternly. "Can I link it all up? Yes, though it'll take most of the day, and it's not going to be cheap…"

"But you don't know if its infected."

"No I don't," he said. "You remember those old school jets that we all learned about in classes? The ones before the nanites bonded us into tech and that had like a bajillion lines of codes in them, that people didn't really understand and they just added more onto until things worked?"

"Yeah?"

"This is like that. there's code here that I can understand and parse out, no worries, I had to learn the very basics with this kinda shit to be able to do brain and spinal mods anyway. But the rest? There's shit here that might be viruses on top of viruses, it might turn your entire spine into a fucking broadcast point for a walking specter maker, I. Don't. Know."

"So what do you recommend?" I asked after a few seconds.

"Weigh up the pros and the cons," he said. "You got it from a fucking banshee. It got what it wanted out of the deal, presumably, but what does it gain by fucking you over further?"

"Nothing really." I admitted. "I told it I'd trade more with it if it needed shit, I can't see it being able to make many deals like that, so…"

"So it's unlikely to waste that possible bonus, to make one more specter," he said, nodding. "That's great, but remember, it's a specter at heart, even if it's more or less sane. It won't think the way we do."

"So…your advice is to weigh up the pros and cons on something that might not think the way we do?"

"Just…look. Why do you need this experimental mod over another? This is clearly a test system, you could sell this to a corporation for a decent wedge, and you know that they'd not ask any questions. Add this to the arm and…"

"Install it," I said shaking my head. "Just, trust me. I need them both."

"I…" He hesitated, watching me, then sighed and nodded. "Alright, it's your funeral. It's a hundred thousand credits though." He saw the way I looked at him and he went on. "It's not just for the work, there's going to be a fuck load of that, and yeah it's not something that most carvers would fucking do. This is seriously skilled shit, and it's only thanks to all the work I've done on reattaching living organs that I'd consider this. the real cost is to cover the risk. I think you're mad, and I'm going to be ready to shoot you in the fucking face after this, so be ready for that."

"Just do it," I said, psyching myself up for it. Yes it was a risk, a hell of a one, and yeah, I might be fucked by all this, or I might never be able to get the connected nodes working in the damn suit either.

If I could though? This would give us a hell of an edge, and frankly we needed it.

The best case scenario with the black ops team, had them attacking me in a location I chose, with Richie and Sync in APS, and the rest of the team on foot, against not corpo security putzes, but against fellow APS operators. Ones that would have been given additional training, the best upgrades and no doubt kept hungry for the fight.

They were unlikely to simply rock up and fight us one on one, and even if they did, Scott used to frequently kick my fucking arse in the dojo.

I wasn't the best fighter. I was good, but I was a team lead. I saw the battlefield and manipulated it, guiding my team to beat the other fuckers. That meant I needed to know the strengths and weaknesses of my operatives. I needed something to really even the odds, or we were boned.

The chair was fucking cold, sod's law, as I stripped and lay down on it, face poking through the cut out section so that I could stare at the filthy floor under the operating chair, as Lion prepped me.

Feeling the fucker pouring cold gel onto my back, rubbing it into the skin all the way across, and the subtle differences between the synth-skin and my own in the sensation, before he laid something against the back of my neck.

"You sure about this?" he asked me, one last time, and I nodded as best I could, restrained there.

"Do it," I ordered him, confirming the hundred thousand transfer.

"Well, here goes. Sharp scratch incoming in three...two...one..."The fucker lied.

They always do, it's not a fucking 'sharp scratch', its bastard stabbing me with a needle and then injecting fuck knew what cocktail of drugs to wipe me out, but as the world vanished, I knew that Todds was there, watching over Lion.

The last thought before the world slid sideways, was that maybe, just maybe, I'd never wake up again, and I should have said something to Reign, beyond ordering specialty ammo for my damn weapons.

Chance missed there.

CHAPTER THIRTY

When I woke, seemingly seconds later, my vision was overcome with scrolling code, flashing past at a speed that was incredible. For long seconds I stared, lost to the mass, confused, and yet awed, until finally a shouted word made it through the mass.

"—chance!"

"Wha…what?" I asked, blinking and trying to clear my vision, confused as all hell.

"This is your last chance!" Lion snapped, holding the paper out before my eyes, shaking it, even as he held a shotgun leveled at my head, and on the table next to me…

A container of nanites.

I'd never before seen just how mesmerizing they were, the way they streamed, the flowing intertwining mass of code that they broadcast while they physically swarmed in a mass too small to pick out individuals and…

"Kabutt!"

I blinked, then looked at the paper again and started to read.

"In Grangemouth there's an oil refinery, a port, a canal and a winery, and to thrill you to bits, all the girls have ten tits, that is if you count them in binary…" I snorted, shaking my head as I finished, blinking as the world seemed to settle slightly, the sounds of the other two rising in volume as the flow of images and code faded still further.

"Kabutt?" Lion asked slowly, and I nodded.

"Who the hell were you expecting?" I asked. "I couldn't damn well focus as my eyes were updating!"

"Updating?" he asked slowly. "I didn't install an update."

"Reboot." I lied. "Not sure why, but they were rebooting, and I guess an update or something must have been queued?"

"Fuck." He groaned, resting the shotgun barrel down and shaking his head. "I thought you were going fucking specter on me…"

"Give a man a damn chance!" I growled. "I literally woke up, you're shouting, my eyes are going nuts…the drugs are still in my system…"

"Yeah well, you can't blame me! Alright, try moving," he said, leaning over and snapping loose the straps that bound me to the chair.

I did. Laid there, I started with my toes, then my feet, and then my legs, just little movements, as Lion monitored the system, playing with something.

"Try the left knee again," he ordered, fingers flashing as if beating out a rhythm in the air, and I dutifully flexed that knee, then the other at his urging, before moving back and forth.

I lifted my arms, and waved them. flexed fingers and more, stood and walked, then turned and squatted, did a forward roll at his insistence, and didn't miss the stifled smile as the fucker clearly enjoyed how awkward I was.

"Anything else?" I asked, trying to keep the growl from my voice. "I'm sore as shit you know."

"Don't be such a baby," he replied absently. "The inflammation will die down in a few hours, the flesh is already knit, and the nerves are responding well. All you're feeling are ghost impulses from the excised sections, and misfiring neurons. It'll fade."

"Anyone ever tell you your bedside manner sucks ass?" I grumbled at him, and he grinned.

"Yeah, you did last time, and a few others. Mind you, this isn't a bed, and I'm sick of your face, so do me a favor and go test that arm out."

The arm! I'd been so focused on the spinal mod, on making sure I could still run and bend and shit, that I'd barely thought about the arm!

I extended it out before me, marveling at the sheer artistry of the manufacture. It was perfect, the individual locking plates gave the impression of flowing sculpted muscle, the bands of magnetic relays were high points of color in bronze, copper and gold that contrasted against the solid, gleaming black. I shook my head in disbelief.

I was gonna be beating mod fashionistas off with a fucking shitty stick.

"How do I use it?" I asked.

"Its integrated into you now, so it's down to you to learn to use it mate, probably going to take a while to actually get it to work properly, so…"

I felt fluctuations in the arm as the power flooded it, in the way that sections seemed to raise and shiver, the new sensation of the world around me, and yeah, the nanites.

This was coming from the mod on the arm, I realized, not the one in my spine, which was a bit of a relief. I'd worried that the sudden fixation on nanites was the first sign of going specter, but as I focused on the container of nanites that Lion was carrying, I could feel distance opening up between us.

I reached out instinctively, despite them being well over a meter out of my reach already, and heading away, and I 'pulled'.

"What the…?" Lion grunted, stopping dead, then twisting to look at me. "Was…was that you?"

"I don't know," I admitted. "I think so?"

"Do it again," he said quickly, holding the container up.

I did…or at least I tried to.

Suddenly 'pulling' at the nanites through the air the way I had? It seemed about as possible as lifting my feet off the ground, and staying up.

No longer could I feel the 'nites, not their metal, nor their code, not the way I had, and yet…

I tried again, a dozen different ways, flexing and pulling, pushing, summoning, hell, fucking *demanding* both aloud and silently, and still nothing worked.

Only when I snarled in frustration and flexed my hand, did anything change, and that was because the installed claws, the filtration system we'd built in, suddenly awoke, sliding out, ready.

"Fuck!" Lion jumped back, and even Todds took a step back out of range as I stared in wonder at the gleaming black claws.

"Right," I said eventually, flexing my hand—it was like relaxing my fingers, but not quite the same—and the claws retracted, then out, then back again. "I think this is going to take a while…"

"Most likely weeks." Lion sighed. "Look, let's review it in a month, alright? If you've made no progress then, well maybe…"

"Six months," I said. "We review it in three, but we're not selling before six months are up. We need to know how it works, and we need to recoup the costs."

"Yeah well, we'll see." He grunted, waving us off as Todds and I left the shop.

The cab ride back to the warehouse was a longer one, but it was also a chance to relax. With us not planning on doing anything this evening, and Todds having already spent the entire day watching over me while Lion operated, he was done, and so was I.

He went home to his kids and new partner, and I grabbed a cheap ass ground cab, sitting there in the back as it bounced and rumbled along, taking three times as long to get to the warehouse, as I sat and plotted.

The arm, and the sense of nanites was weird. I'd certainly not expected to be able to sense them after the install, but hey, equally I'd not be complaining.

I needed to train this new sense, but if I could master it? Flashbangs were going to be far less of an issue that was for sure.

When the cab finally pulled up and I crawled out of the rear, stretching my back and groaning as the doors locked and it pulled away, I swore that never again would I 'not waste money' on me. I'd taken the cheaper ground cab because hey, we're going to be saving money where we could and pooling it all soon, so I might as well start now, it was only me after all, and it wasn't that much slower…

It was a fuck load slower, and it was also a fuck load more uncomfortable.

I'd passed through a section of the city that was having a shift change, and the road essentially became gridlocked. It was normal, it happened literally around the clock, always had and always would, but when you were in an aircar? It changed the designated lane, and boom, you were past it. You never even noticed.

Twenty minutes in the aircar, an hour and fifteen in the ground. No fucking more.

I strode through the front gate and into the compound, still grumbling, as I saw Gessh heaving on a box, dragging it inside, and I hurried to help her.

"What's up?" I asked, grabbing one end and helping to shift it around, as we 'walked it' on the edges of the box along the ground.

"Oh hey…" She groaned, as we shifted it, and then set it down to rest. "Our glorious leader returns eh?"

"Yup, I'm back…what's this?" I asked.

"Turrets," she said. "Reign got great deal on a shipment from—"

"Don't say Oshbob!"

"—Oshbob."

"Fuck!" I groaned.

"What's up boss?" Gessh asked frowning. "Is it because—"

"No, it's not because he's an orc," I said. "It's because every goddamn time I turn around that fucker just made more money off us! I thought we were going to try and buy the damn place first!"

"I asked, he's working out a deal for us, said he likes Luna and Gessh, that they're 'good kids' and he'll look after them," Reign said, jogging down the stairs, then half throwing herself into my arms for a kiss.

"Hello?" I said, surprised, but enthusiastic as she reached around me…then slipped a hand up under my top and felt my back.

"He did!" she called out loud. "Told you!"

"Fuck!" Gessh growled. "That's not a different spinal is it? Something different to the one that the banshee gave you…?" she asked hopefully, and I shook my head.

"It's too good to pass up and…wait, what the…!" I broke off as Reign started laughing, then kissed my cheek.

"Thanks lover, easiest twenty credits I ever earned!" She grinned, as Gessh rolled her eyes, and apparently made a funds transfer.

"Wait, you bet I'd…" I broke off, shaking my head and refusing to look at them. "Fuckers."

"We just know you, that's all, boss," Luna called out. "I bet with Reign by the way. Gessh thought you'd be more self-controlled than that, but I heard Reign nearly get nailed through my wall last night, so I know you've got none!"

"I get so much respect," I muttered under my breath, shaking my head. "So much."

"You love us all really." Reign grinned. "Come on then, let's see it."

I paused then grinned, and nodded, unable to help myself. I'd been wearing a long sleeved jacket when I went out today, body armor—because after a while in the army you felt naked without it—and a long sleeved top underneath that meant that from dressing at Lion's chop-shop, I'd hidden my mods away.

Now I pulled that all off, standing there in just my combat pants.

There were several seconds of silence, then Gessh clapped, before shaking her head and grinning. "I never really showed you mine did I?" she asked Reign and I, before stripping down to her underwear to show her new legs off.

We compared the gleam of the metal and the workmanship of her legs, to my new arm, and in minutes the room was changed into the four of us in our underwear showing off various tattoo, mods and scars, followed by drinking and pizza, as Luna got her new legs booked in with Lion.

That sobered us up more, when Reign started to go through the job we had arranged for first thing in the morning.

CHAPTER THIRTY-ONE

The next morning dawned clear and cold, a bite in the air that wasn't expected, and to feel the cold in the city like this? With all of the fusion plants, the factories and more, all surrounded by the wall?

That meant it was fucking freezing out on the plains of the wasteland.

That made little difference to us though, beyond that the coffee was more in demand, and the site we were booked for was surrounded by swirling clouds of steam, the vents along the edge of the building bleeding off excess heat in maddening patterns.

Visibility might be shit, but we were heavily armed, and that had a habit of evening things out in my experience.

The office block we'd been called to was long abandoned, supposedly, but of late it'd been overrun by homeless. That in itself wasn't a problem, hell everyone needed somewhere to get their head down, and I certainly didn't begrudge them that, no the issue was that the group that owned the site, had come looking to move them on, and they'd been attacked by a specter.

The description was that it was big, black with massive bulky shoulders, red eyes, and it was heavily armed.

When Julius had put it on the board as one of the early jobs that needed doing—the owners wanted it dealt with before the reno team arrived—he'd been surprised when Reign had claimed it.

"You sure?" he'd asked. "It's a single specter, I was going to send one of the inexperienced squads out and…"

"We'll take it, its next to uh…this one!" she'd said quickly, picking up another, a much bigger job in the building at the edge of a block a few further down the road from the first one. Julius had been overjoyed apparently, and had confirmed the job with the clients, who insisted on a photo op at the beginning of the job.

That the developers insisted on the same thing? It was a pain in the arse, to say the least, but at least it was done quickly. Reign and I were in full face helmets, Gessh, Luna and Todds weren't, and apparently that was enough. I refused to take my helmet off, knowing that while I'd almost certainly been identified by the major on the cooling tower job, I didn't need to make it any fucking easier for him.

The job was a letdown.

First and foremost, we'd thought it was the banshee. That for some reason it was dealing with these people, and that was why it'd attacked the developers.

It wasn't. Hell, it wasn't even a fucking specter. It was a heavily modded homeless guy who'd apparently traded his face plate for some angel dust to some gangers, and now he was literally 'faceless'.

His eyes were glowing red optics, and apart from his lower jaw and his temple? His face was down to the supporting structures. Add on that he'd once been a particularly large guy, and had worked as a bouncer in a load of places before getting thrown on the street?

He was just wearing a damn big coat, and carrying two—empty—guns. He'd scared the shit outta the developers, and nearly got shot for it, but a quick discussion with him and the other homeless, and the developers paid them a few credits each to move on.

It wasn't worth our time, not in terms of the cost, but we'd saved some innocents from what could have been a nasty situation, and we all felt a little better about that.

The second job? That was a lot trickier.

The client site was 'Future Enterprises Inc' and advertised that they provided 'a capsule to carry you into the next life'.

That was more or less true, as well, if you were a fucking idiot. The company had floor after floor of the building converted to hold anti-entropy pods and cryo-chambers. They were two of the latest fads to come around again, and were sold to those who wanted an escape, but didn't want to take the final option of eating a bullet.

Instead, there were the two options—cryogenics and anti-entropy. Cryogenics was exactly what it sounded like, they froze your ass—and the rest of you—and kept you on ice, until the destination date you'd selected came round. For example, three hundred years from today.

Then—again in theory—the company would unfreeze you, and using the more advanced technology of that time, return you to a pristine new body.

Hooray, all the old rich farts that couldn't afford to actually rejuvenate their bodies, would get to palm it off for a while in the vague hope of 'new tech' down the line. All the while their trust funds and more would be 'maintained' by the company, to cover the costs of housing them.

Swap out maintained, and add in raided, and the advert was suddenly a lot more accurate.

The other option was anti-entropy.

This was a LOT more expensive, and it involved the entire body being preserved in a null-field. This was actually new tech, and when the field was switched on, you simply ceased to register for reality as we knew it. Turn it off a week, a month or a millennium later? For you it'd been the blink of an eye, and that was it.

The big advantage of this was that your body was intact, so rather than possibly being told that as a brain in a jar—with frostbite—there was nothing the company could do for you, you could actually walk around and deal with things as you wanted.

Maybe you go again, maybe you don't.

You'd have the choice though. The issue with it was the cost, the entropy pods were horrifically expensive to maintain, but it'd been discovered that there were advantages to it.

If the field wasn't turned off, but instead was lessened, you could activate lower functioning areas of the brain, crucially without bringing the client to full consciousness.

That gave you access to a full neural loadout that was essentially doing nothing.

Considering that the best way to train an AI was to interact with it and let it read living, active brains? Well. The company suddenly had an extremely lucrative sideline.

The once struggling 'Future Enterprises Inc' was suddenly looking for more investors, as they needed to buy extra space for all the space-cadet clients. They even dropped the prices of the anti-entropy pods to below that of their competitors, and were busy as hell, with a waiting list of over three years.

The clients had no clue they were being brain harvested, and essentially, if they wanted to complain about it? The first one that was due to be unloaded wasn't for another century and a half, so fuck it. Someone else's problem, that.

This was where we came in, just as the ledger was looking fantastic for the company, a member of staff had noticed a scratching noise in the basement, and had opened an old door.

The influx of long dormant specters was both merciless and lethal, and when they found the virtual smorgasbord of high tech equipment? Well.

The survivors of the massacre of the lower floors were traumatized to fuck, and that was just the staff. The actual clients hadn't found out the truth about the incursion until the specters managed to turn the pods off, and by then they were both surrounded, and looking very tasty.

I was standing at the top of the steps glaring at the weaselly little man that was both trying to justify the situation, and its potential—he'd decided that as we had sold the banshee, word had gotten around about that after all, then we had disposable funds to invest in his business—and on the other side, he was trying to make damn sure we didn't damage anything.

We were to clean out the specters—and dispose of any bodies—without damaging the pods, as they were highly sensitive and expensive equipment.

I'd asked if there were cameras on the floor, and had been told that there weren't unfortunately. It'd been judged 'best for privacy reasons' by some utter idiot.

On the upside, when the door closed behind us, and all of us 'accidentally' forgot to activate our recording devices? Well. Any damage that was incurred at the site had definitely been done by the specters.

We didn't, we were recording, just in case, but they didn't need to know that.

We exited the small airlock style door at the foot of the stairs into the actual floor 'proper' and I shook my head in disgust. Clearly it'd been designed to appeal to people with more money than common sense, things like hangers by the pods for dressing robes and a comfy pair of slippers were sat neatly at the head of each pod.

That the previous occupants had put so much thought into their long term napping situation, and so little into the realities of life was obvious.

They were laid here and there like discarded cordwood. Mods ripped free, and the majority of the elderly had been cut apart to get at functioning systems inside them, such as organelles and bio-hearts.

Bloody handprints were slap-dashed across previously pristine pastel painted doors and polished floors. Meat and dripping, congealed blood covered the walls, and as soon as we walked in? the proverbial dinner bell rang out for the next course.

There weren't many of them, not really, maybe thirty, and most of them came straight to us, drawn by our high levels of electromagnetism and the coded signals the nanites broadcasted.

For me, the experience was insane.

As soon as we stepped inside I could feel them, like a shimmering chime from a tuning fork, the song of the 'pure' nanites, but where that soared and lifted, underneath it, was the song of the dead. A crackling, warbling 'wrongness' that slunk along the bottom of the register.

I'd hesitated, stunned by the onslaught of wrongness, until Gessh had shouldered me aside and snap kicked a specter in the face.

She wore shoes, and trousers, not because she needed to hide her gleaming alloy legs, but because she hated cleaning all the crap out of them when we were on missions.

Despite that, the sheer impact of her foot was enough to tear the rotting skull free of the neck, and the body collapsed. She twisted, hopped to land in the foot as it came back down, and spun. Her head going low as she swung her center of gravity around, and her other foot blurred by high, taking another down to the floor with a crash.

In the two seconds it'd taken her to do that? I was back, the song was suppressed, as much as I could manage, and my rifle was up, barking over and over, single shots as we started down the corridor, Gessh and I in the lead, Luna and Todds checking the side rooms as we passed them, and Reign floating in the middle, ready to help out wherever she was needed.

Fifteen minutes it took, that was all, and we were at the door to the undercity, checking our weapons and readying, before slipping out.

The click of our optics flickering from full 'standard' to 'dark-mode' was always jarring, but the more you did it? The easier the change became.

Looking around the section that we emerged into, it was clear we'd found another of the old escape tunnels that were built into the underside of Artem long ago. The arced ceiling, the mosaic tiles where some long dead city planner thought that what was important was preserving some fucking advert for eternity, and the deep funk of the air made all of that damn clear.

The deeper we went down the slightly sloping tunnel, the danker the air became, until I was seriously glad for the full face helm and air purification system, while Luna, Gessh and Todds complained vociferously.

Todds ended up sealing his stealth suit helm and shimmering out of existence not long before we reached the bottom, and the reason for the funk was revealed.

The city, like most I guessed, had very strict rules on the kind of pets that were allowed inside the walls, and that should the citizens decide to get rid of said pets? Well this is how it needed to be done.

There were disposal services, both for the living pets and the dead bodies, and despite jokes to the contrary, I was fairly sure it wasn't actually the same company with different colors on their vans.

Neither, again despite the urban legends, did they provide said pets remains to be turned into the 'elephant legs' that rotated on a spit in the late night food joints frequented only by the exceedingly drunk.

What this meant, was that there were ways to dispose of the animals, and that they were both simple and easily available. That was why when we reached the bottom on the decline and splashed out into the huge cavern before us, I was exceedingly pissed off to see a fight between two massive bull-gators.

CHAPTER THIRTY-TWO

Bull-gators were one of the many mutated species that we were 'blessed' with by the old world, essentially a form of reptile that stood fully two meters high at the shoulder, weighed in excess of two tons, and had a generally foul fucking temper for anything that wasn't the actual beast in question.

The females, from what I could remember of the single class I'd had on them in the army, were the more colorful, with a collection of yellow strips that ran their length, providing warning that yes they were dangerous enough they didn't give a shit about hiding, and yes they were venomous.

The stronger the venom? The redder the lines.

Interestingly in one of those 'fuck you's' that only Mother Nature's twisted cousin Mother Mutation could come up with, they also developed those red lines when they were ready to breed.

I guessed that made their sex-lives an interesting experience.

The fact that we were unfortunately knee deep in brackish water, with dozens of infant bull-gators swimming towards us, a pair of the massive males battling it out directly ahead and what looked like an entire herd mooching around the outside of the cavern?

Yeah.

"Let's back it up people!" I said quickly, matching words to action, when Todds screamed.

Apparently as well as the fucking giant bull-gators, there was some breed of 'fisher' here too, as I'd heard them referred to, and due to the fact that they flattened themselves against the cavern roof high overhead and essentially 'reeled in' whatever they could catch in their 'nets'?

Yeah.

Todds was being dragged up into the air, his screams ringing out as instead of silencing him, the steady electric charge that the fucking thing apparently deployed was burning him as the stealth suit was overloaded.

That scream was enough to break the rest of the cavern out of watching the two alpha males battling it out, and to seemingly ring the dinner bell, as Reign lifted her rifle and opened fire on the fisher.

The damn thing seemed to absorb the bullets, and she quickly cursed and swapped from the solid slug model to her grazer.

While she did that, Luna raced forwards, leaping into the air, and snagging Todds' leg. The charge flowed through to her as well, and she cried out in pain, but the combined weight was enough to stop them being reeled in, as Gessh swapped to her grazer rifle, and started firing at the nearest closing infants.

I was firing non-stop already, the bullets from my rifle sinking into the flanks of the big bastards as they turned and charged at us.

"Now we know why the hell the specters were all in there!" Reign called out. "They were fucking trapped and neither they nor these beasties had anything that the other wanted!"

"We…" I broke off as a second 'line' smacked into Luna and started hauling her and Todds upwards again, and I reoriented, zooming in and in, holding my stance…

The fisher's face leapt into focus through my rifle's scope, magnified again and again, until I could see the two bulbous eyes atop thin stalks, and the up-down, as opposed to left-right aligned maw.

It opened wider, salivating as it sensed the prey it was reeling in, long fangs angling outwards, ready to bite down and inject a powerful paralytic and dissolver…when I pulled the trigger.

The shot was dead on, slamming into the section where both eyes connected back to the head, barreling straight through and into the wall behind, before causing even more damage as it ricocheted off, burying itself somewhere in the back of the head.

It was enough, probably it was enough to kill the fucker outright, but either way it was enough to send paroxysms of conflicting signals through the body, and when said body is devoting every possible effort to hauling a great struggling weight upwards, and desperately clinging to the roof at the same time?

It ended badly for it, with Todds crashing down to land in the knee deep waters, the electrical and burning damage he was taking shorting out, replaced by impact and the shock of the water.

He hit hard, the angle he'd been at meaning he was unable to catch himself, and he went under, even as I switched my aim to the second fisher, seeing more scuttling dimly across the ceiling.

This one was bigger, long spindly legs that clung to the underside of the cavern roof, the head weaving as it moved backwards, intent on dragging its prize from the field of battle. Its body was long, almost stick-like, as were its limbs, but the spray of glue, the lure and fishing line both, came from the center of the chest, with smaller secondary limbs working the line, dragging Luna upwards as she struggled and jerked, being hit over and over with electrical shocks.

I fired, missing by an inch or less, and the damn thing flinched, picking up speed, scuttling across the roof and dragging Luna directly into the path of the oncoming bull-gators.

I went to fire again, only to curse and shift my aim, firing a shot at a charging behemoth's eye instead.

The frustration almost made me miss, but luck was with me as the round penetrated, the head twisting sideways as it roared in pain, and it hit the creature next to it, who immediately swung for it, teeth snapping at the back of the target's foreleg.

The two of them went down, multi-tons of charging ferocity suddenly back to snapping and snarling at each other, as I recentered on Luna, cursing as Gessh stitched the fisher with grazer rounds.

"Wait till she's clear of the gators!" I snapped. "If she falls in there…"

"Fuck!" Gessh cried, twisting and opening fire on another as they closed, Reign switching to high powered solid beams of grazer fire as she stepped up between us and dragged the beam across the rippling scum-frothed waters ahead of us.

The beam hit dozens of smaller bull-gators, most of which I'd not even seen, as they went into full screeching thrashing spasming death.

Some would probably have survived, just being badly cooked, but that they were trying to scream while underwater?

Yeah, it turned out that semi-aquatic was not the same as aquatic when it came to respiration.

Those fuckers that didn't cook, drowned.

We killed dozens of the little ones, and the two biggest were back to savaging each other, uninterested in the interlopers, which was wonderful, but Luna had ceased her struggling, Todds was barely struggling to his feet, frantically coughing and retching as he yanking the charging handle on his rifle and cleared the barrel, and dozens more of 'smaller' ones were racing at us.

That they were 'smaller' was a bit of a misnomer, they still weighed anywhere from half a ton to two, were basically mobile tanks, and were heavily armed in the old 'teeth, claws and foul mental attitude' stakes.

We'd been back pedaling to the corridor we'd entered from, then we'd been forced to stop that, when Todds was captured, now Luna was being dragged away through the air, by a wounded fisher, and several other, smaller ones, were firing attacking lines to her, starting to tug her this way and that as they tried to steal the meal from their injured matriarch.

Todds splashed his way back to us, firing as he went, Gessh was screaming at Luna to 'fucking stop laying around' and firing at one then another of the charging monsters. I tried to slow the fuckers claiming her, firing a shot into this one, then that, trying to force the lines that were attached to her to break strategically and swing her off to the side, away from the incoming wall of muscly death.

She was still thrashing though, letting us know that she was alive at least, but for how long we didn't know.

"Fuck it!" I snarled, grabbing Reign's high powered sniper rifle from her back. She was still keeping the waters near us clear, essentially frying them with overlapping beams of lethal gamma radiation, then managing a quick shot at the incoming tanks.

We had seconds before they were going to be too close and we'd be forced to retreat into the corridor behind, and we all knew that if we did that? Luna was dead.

I barely bothered to aim the rifle, they were that close. The slugs were designed to penetrate armor, the kind that old world tanks had hidden beneath, and that modern ceramics and alloys had made possible for 'normal' people to wear as a deterrent.

Against a weapon designed for that? Even the thick plates of bone that were evolved to absorb the damage as it headbutted other giants was insufficient.

The shot slammed into the nearest creature just above the orbit of the eye, hitting some bony protrusion and ricocheting downwards into the small glaring organ.

Where the bullet came to rest eventually in the massive monstrosities head, nobody knew, but the fountain of blood that suddenly burst from its mouth and nose, as it face planted the water all at once made it clear it wasn't getting back up.

As big and bulky as the creature was, when it went down, it cut off an entire section of the approach, two others smacking into it with squeals and roars of frustration. Frustration that became tearing and feasting as they fought over the suddenly available corpse of their sibling.

The world descended into a screaming, roaring flashing madhouse as we tried to keep things going, firing over and over, twisting this way and that as here and there smaller spawn managed to make it through Reign's cleansing.

The first that surged up made the mistake of sinking its teeth into Gessh's leg. Or it tried anyway. It was about the length of a large rat, the mouth was almost a third of the length of its body and full of teeth, and the confusion it must have felt when the elation of 'gotcha' became 'this is hard to chew' must have been immense.

It was probably even worse when Gessh kept standing on that leg, raised the other, and stomped on the little fuckers back.

The crunch of breaking bone and the abrupt squawk of pain, before it drowned beneath the murky waters made it clear those legs were paying dividends.

I moved left and right firing, chambering another round and firing again, barely aiming, they were that close, but where Gessh's shots caused pain and distress, mine shattered skulls.

Todds and Gessh fired on the big fuckers after I did, aiming for roughly the same location, and where cracks and occasionally worse were left in their skulls, the pounding of 'small' arms fire over and over took them down.

Reign switched from local area suppression to medium range, the beam reaching out and touching the fishers, burning them from the rock they tenaciously clung to, no longer dragging Luna up, they were suddenly falling limp and adding to the weight the remaining creatures struggled with.

In another minute, it was over, Luna going silent and falling through the air to land with a splash, sinking beneath the waters as Gessh crouched and leapt, landing atop one of the corpses, then leaping to another, racing to her fallen sister's side.

Todds, Reign and I focused on the least wounded of the two alphas, concentrating fire as we took the big fucker down, followed by its injured opponent.

Gessh landed in the water, thrashing her hands this way and that before dragging her unconscious and half drowned sibling free, then racing back to us, as we pulled medikits and more, backing up the corridor.

A few minutes passed while we checked ourselves and each other over, reloaded our weapons and figured out what the hell had just happened, before slowly returning to the bottom of the corridor into the water.

We stood there for long seconds, looking around the cavern, trying to figure out how the hell these creatures had gotten down here, and more to the point why such massive carnivores would congregate here of all places, when a section of the roof clanked open.

Meat, maybe real, maybe not, but looking real enough, cascaded from the gap into the middle of the room, hitting the water with a resounding series of splashes, as Todds snarled something nearby.

"What?" I asked, having missed it.

"They're pets!"

"What are?" I asked, confused to fuck.

"The bull-gators! Some fucker kept them here, look at the size of them, and then at the doors to get in and out!"

I looked, scanning the distant intact walls quickly, blinking as I took in what I'd missed before.

There were three exits, counting the one we'd used to get in, and aside from a set of massive sealed steel doors that clearly hadn't been used in centuries…they were all way too small for the creatures to have come along.

"They were probably brought in as pups, then fed!" Todds snarled, and I stared at him in confusion. "As guard dogs!" He explained. "Think about them as a line of defense, sure it's illegal, but who's going to care, or even report it, anyone that finds them? They're a meal most likely."

"And the fishers?"

"They're not common in the undercity, but not that rare either." Reign sighed, checking her grazer, then slinging it back over her shoulder and reclaiming her sniper rifle from me, checking it for damage, reloading and stowing it over her shoulder.

"So, what, we just killed those assholes pets?" I asked, disbelievingly.

"Probably not," Todds said. "There's three exits here, want to bet that one of the leads to the owners of this little nightmare show?"

"I…I don't care," I said after a few seconds. "Fuck this shit. Does anyone care?"

"Not beyond a need to kick someone's face in." Luna grunted, injecting herself again with a medikit.

"Then fuck it," I said. "Anyone recording?"

"Turning it off, job's done," Reign said, the others echoing her with smiles.

I moved to the nearest corpse, and reached out, slotting one of the empty medikits we had into the port in my new left arm, taking a deep breath, and relaxing.

This time the sensation of the nanites was harder to sense, coming and going as it had been on our way over was weird, the sensation of them in my companions didn't bother me, but here?

The nanites sang softly, the vibrations of them inside the bodies made me respond without thought. The claws, formerly retracted on my left hand, slid out, and I sank them into the body of the nearest beastie, burrowing inwards until I found a decent vein, then sinking into it.

The magnetic rings in my arm pulsed, like I was drinking something thick and viscous, but through my arm as the ports in the heel of my hand opened and blood jetted out.

I swallowed hard, the feeling being weird, and sure as shit the experience was as well, the shaking and pulsing as I tried to get the rings in my arm to react in smooth relaying instead of a pull, then a pull, then a pull, each barely seeming connected…

I forced myself to stop thinking, to stop *interfering*.

The software, the programming was all done already, and Lion had integrated it as best he could into the arm. My RI was trying to make it work with me, but I was basically focusing on it and forcing myself into every step along the way.

It wasn't the way to damn well do this, and I knew it.

When moving the arm of my suit I didn't fire each motor and actuator individually, just like I didn't move the muscles of my arm individually.

I did them all on instinct, instinct that that was partially developed over years as a child, learning to control my muscles, and partially was hard-coded into my brain.

That same hard-coding that was used for the muscles, was there in the arm, but used to control the rings and harvesting device, I just needed to learn to let it do its job.

I relaxed, focused on the overall aim, on harvesting the pure nanites, on separating and storing them, and discarding the rest, focusing on the end goal, and 'pulling' all at once instead, and the difference was night and day.

At first it was like a stutter, as the RI stepped in and smoothed things, the subconscious fight I'd been having with it as I mentally ordered it to help, then tried to do it myself each time, suddenly falling away.

Then it just…worked.

It was weird, like breathing, if I tried to guide my breathing it slipped out of the natural rhythm and I got a weird feeling in my chest, if instead I just ignored it and let my body do it on autopilot?

Boom, no issue.

The harvesting was like that, the more I left it to do it itself, the more efficiently it worked.

"Fuck!" Reign gasped suddenly, and I jerked unthinkingly, before looking over at her, and seeing the wide grin on her face as she doffed her helmet.

"What?" I asked, frowning.

"It's working!" she said, grinning widely, as we all turned to look at the formerly empty medikit attached to the port on my arm. It was already a third full, and the creature I was harvesting?

Everything had nanites, by now. They were pervasive across the entire planet, and had been for centuries, the air we breathed, the water, the food, us, everything had nanites on it, from the soil to the seas, but they were almost all contaminated, failed nanites.

Out of every thousand nanites, there were, according to estimates I'd seen years ago, two or three active, pure nanites. That was it.

But when you considered that we all have billions in us? That was both a huge number of pure ones waiting to be collected, and a tiny, tiny fraction that actively was.

I'd seen plans that were floated by idiot friends to build floating scoops that would trawl the seas, like they once had to dispose of the plastic that nearly killed us all, they would now repurpose those old dredges to instead separate the nanites, harvesting and destroying the corrupt, and recovering the pure.

It was a fucking pipe dream.

The same people that swore they could do this, also spent their entire wages each month on a combination of hookers, drink and drugs, as well as buying novelty masks, giant movie prop hammers and so on.

How they intended to develop tech that the world's best scientists couldn't? Well that was a minor detail, often ignored.

Now though? As the small medikit attached to my arm slowly filed with gleaming quicksilver nanites? All those plans came back to me, making me grin.

We had the tech. We literally had it here, attached to my fucking arm!

If we were to buy one of those fucked up old dredges and attach this to the intake jets? They could syphon off billions of gallons of water an hour, at top speed. That would in turn fill great vats of nanites!

My mind raced ahead, until a strange almost bloated feeling started to rise in me. I checked the arm, finding the medikit was almost full, and as I reached for another empty, Reign was there already.

My arm had been designed with slots for holding kit, or for installing the overall boosts that high end prosthetics could bring you, from hidden weapons to storage areas for strength, speed or perception enhancing drugs and hormones.

Lion had instead used those section that weren't needed for the harvesting process to provide attachment ports for the medikits, as well as for the actual containers that sat inside the medikits.

I took the empty medium kit from Reign and plugged the port on it to the port on my arm, hearing a satisfying solid 'click' as the two ports mated, then pulled the small kit free, passing it to her to keep in a special bag we'd brought along just for this.

The theory was that the medikits were now filled with pure nanites, but there'd been a few incidents over the years where dodgy batches of medikits had been released, mainly by gangs, although when a Corp had tried it, they'd been forced to provide a solution, as part of the rehabilitation of their image.

Basically here and there, scattered across the city, were vending machines. You could go to them, plug your medikit in, and they'd verify the kits authenticity, charge and purity.

Well, ours would fail the 'authenticity' straight away, we had no legal right to be refilling these after all, but if they passed the other tests? Then we could use, sell and supply them.

The creature was emptied before the medium kit was filled, but that was fine, there wasn't exactly a shortage of them after all, and I simply moved to the next.

An hour and forty minutes later, and we were making our way back into the main building, stifling grins when we looked at each other over the sheer volume we'd been able to harvest.

The specters, on the whole, had been fairly unimpressive, individually at least. It was working out as an average of five to six specters to fill a single small medikit, with ten to twelve for a medium, and twenty to twenty-five for a large.

That wasn't that impressive, but considering a medikit, a small one, was about a thousand credits? There was a damn reason that most places still used stitches, bandages and more.

If five specter kills got us a couple of bits of loot, like a few mags or a bit of jewelry and so on, it was barely noticeable in the grand scheme of things. They were brain dead after all, they tended to drop shit and forget about it.

That they had mods that we could sell? Well, that increased their value. Most of them were crappy tier one shit, some twos. The ghouls and occasional specters that had tier threes? Well, there was real value.

On average though, the parts once they were stripped, if we could do it properly, were worth maybe a few hundred per specter.

That the specter themselves were worth another hundred, from the government and the contractor?

Then add on that if it cost us five specters to fill a thousand credit medikit, so we were looking at another two hundred credits per specter there?

The potential credits were getting into crazy levels.

The real question was beginning to be, did we stay with the guild once we'd gotten the team all together again. If we hired our own 'cleaners' to strip the parts and give them to us, rather than the little bastards that were working for the guild currently and pocketing the mods?

That would be a game changer.

As it was though, we were happy.

We gave the owners of the 'brain farm' some photo ops on the way out, left them one of the creatures heads that Luna had decided she wanted as a trophy, then got bored of carrying, and went on our merry way with a quick explanation, and an agreement that the door below could now be sealed up tight.

The owners weren't particularly bothered about the loss of their 'clients' as they had full control over the trust funds, and had been merrily plundering them for 'maintenance fees' anyway, so now a few minor repairs were needed and they had an entire floor available to resell.

CHAPTER THIRTY-THREE

It took us twenty minutes to cross a good section of the city by air-cab to find a testing station, and when we did find it, we arrived just as some idiots were testing theirs.

They'd apparently bought a batch from a seller that was 'going out of business and needed the money, so offered a deal of a lifetime'.

They'd bought a hundred medikits for ten thousand credits. Ten thousand credits that they'd borrowed from a gang, and now owed interest on, and considering that the medikits were filled with what looked like red jam paste?

I wasn't hopeful for their chances.

After twenty minutes of us waiting as they argued over whose fault it was and fed in the same medikit over and over, Gessh, being the soul of subtly started kicking them and their shite out of the way, then drew her sword when they complained.

"Fuck about on your own time, dickheads!" She snarled at the pair, before sniffing the 'medikit' that she pulled out of the machine.

"Egonberry," she snapped, shaking it. "It's an egonberry mix, looks like shit, smells like shit, and its gonna do fuck all for a wound except infect it! Go hunt the fucks down that sold you this or fuck off but…"

"Now there's a point," Luna virtually purred, putting her hand on her sister's shoulder and drawing her back from the terrified youngsters. "They had to get the empty kits from somewhere, and we could do with them…"

I ignored them all, Reign standing by my side, Todds watching our back as we fed in the first of the medikits, and waited.

Authenticity: Failed, no registered tag attached

Charge: Full

Purity: 97%

"Ninety-seven," I muttered. "Is that good?"

"Oh yeah." Reign snorted. "Seriously, usually they're in the eighties. Some 'filler' being used is the best guess, padding them out when they sell the mass to the chop-shops, and then they probably add a bit as well."

"Pessimistic much?" Todds said, grinning over his shoulder.

"Am I wrong?" Reign countered.

"No, just, well, you know." He laughed.

"Right, let's check the others," I said, checking through the bag full we had, over the next few minutes, before packing them all away and stepping over to where Gessh was still arguing with the idiots.

"…just so you can make a killing!" one of them was saying.

"What's this?" I asked the group at large.

"They don't want to tell us who their supplier is, as they think the medikits are real, and that we're somehow pulling a fast one on them now. They think they can contact the seller and get more, but they want to charge us more than the filled medikits are worth, that's about it."

"Look, we're not afraid of you…" One of the youths sneered, their body language giving the lie to the statement, as they both stood shoulder to shoulder, shaking like shitting dogs under Gessh's glare.

"Happy for you," I said unsympathetically. "We need to speak to your supplier, so give us their details, and we'll stop their little scam. If you're honest and we catch them in time, maybe we'll give you your credits back. If you lie? Gessh here gets to beat the truth out of you."

"Wait…no you can't!" The one on the left, wearing a hand-me-down suit and a Mohican cried. "We've not done nuffin!"

"You're trying to rip off my companion," I said clearly. "One of you test your medikits in the machine, right now. Pick one at random."

The one on the right pulled one out, the red liquid inside swirling slowly, lumps clear in it as he moved gingerly around us, and pressed it into the injection port of the machine.

A tiny sample was taken, and the screen lit up.

Authenticity: Failed, no registered tag attached

Charge: Empty

Purity: 0%

"Right, now try this." I ordered, passing him one of ours.

The difference was clear, for a start ours was filled with the quicksilver of active nanites, and his…well.

Jam that had gone off a few years ago was the nicest comparison.

They tested it, saw the difference, then insisted on testing theirs again…then tried to switch them over and hand back theirs instead of ours, at which point Gessh drew her sword and levelled it at them.

"Give me the fuckin' contact details for the shitbag that ripped you off, or I start cutting bits off you that you don't need. Like your balls, because there's no way you two should be allowed to breed!"

Ten minutes later and a quick call, and we were on our way to meet the salesman, his shop was apparently shutting down due to 'gang activity', and he just needed to get back 'something to cover his losses'.

We'd been assured we would get the 'deal of the century' as well.

When our aircab landed in the dilapidated market area, the locals started moving instantly.

Anyone stupid enough to come to such an area, especially with credit chips, as he'd asked Gessh to have the creds loaded onto? Well, they were clearly too dumb to live.

When the door opened and we all climbed out, heavily armed, locked and loaded and clearly ready to shoot first and ask questions never?

Well. The jerky movements as the incoming thugs decided that they'd really always wanted to examine this stall, or grab a bite from that one? It was comical.

We were clearly not in the mood to be fucked with, and the locator ping that had been guiding us to the market to do the deal suddenly blinked off, as an elf saw us through the window and panicked.

He tried to close, and then lock the front door, Luna kicked it inwards. He then tried sprinting for the back of the building, only to find as he made it out of the door, that Gessh was a fuck load faster than he was, and could leap incredible distances.

She'd jumped up to the first floor, grabbed a windowsill and kicked off, made it to the fire escape, up and onto the roof of the small two story building, then across and leapt off, all before he managed to get from the front, through the backroom and out into the alley behind.

He ran into her, bounced off, landed on his arse, and then tripped up the two that were running behind him.

Luna was there then as well, and the pair dragged the three back inside, while Reign, Todds and I did a quick inventory of their goods.

"A hundred and forty-seven medikits," I said nodding at how hard they'd clearly worked to collect them all. "Plus a giant fucking container of red gloop and a syphon. You've been busy, lads."

"There's no law against collecting old medikits, nor having a red...liquid?" the elf tried, forcing a smile, his eyes darting from side to side as he tried to figure out an escape route, before relaxing noticeably.

That he'd done it at the same time as the other three?

He just got a message from his boss, be ready for a gang or enforcers arriving soon.

I sent the message to the others, while maintaining eye contact with the now much more relaxed figure before me.

"Now, there's three reasons we're here, and one of them, well, we'll get to that last, as frankly, it kind of changes the tone of the conversation," I said with a smile. "So, first! You've been selling medikits to idiots as a get rich scheme."

"I don't know what you're talking about," he said, feigning innocence and looking shocked. "We found this building empty, and came to have a look inside, that you ran at us the way you did? Well, you scared us, that's all, that's why we ran."

"So they're not yours?" I asked, nodding to the medikits sitting in a series of boxes off to one side.

"No, certainly not."

"You just said you were collecting them," I pointed out.

"I said there was no law against collecting them, not that we had been," he corrected quickly smiling apologetically as he spread his hands.

"Ah, well that's fortunate then." I smiled as well. "Because we own them."

"You own what?"

"The medikits," I said firmly. "They're ours."

"No they're not."

"You said they weren't yours. There's only two groups here, and you admitted you didn't know who owned them, so its fortunate that we're here now isn't it! We don't have to shoot you in the face for trying to steal from us."

At that unsubtle point, Gessh stepped forward, her shotgun in hand and smiled at them.

"Of course…" the elf said after a few seconds of silence. "And you'd be able to prove you own them, no doubt?"

"Of course," I agreed, pulling a bullet out of one of the magazines and tossing it to him. "You'll find that provides all the proof you need."

"I…don't understand," he said after a few seconds, handing it back.

"My point is that this bullet, when I return it to you, fired from the barrel of this rifle, will stop any such stupid fucking questions being asked again," I said, dropping all pretenses. "That's point two, by the way."

"Ah…"

"So, let's be fucking clear here. You're running a scam, ripping off idiots, selling them medikits full of red gloop and laughing your arse off. I am an APS operator, do you know what our primary job outside of the city is?"

"To protect…?" he started, eyes darting again and I shook my head.

"To protect the city? I suppose that's one interpretation, but no, not really. We're the only form of law out there. If I say you're guilty of committing a crime? I don't need to bring you in for processing. In fact, I'm fairly sure that if I tried that, the regular legal pukes wouldn't know what to fucking do about it. The only people I've ever had to hand over, were always those who surrendered to military justice." I leant forwards, shaking my head slightly from side to side as I dropped my voice.

"Believe me, there's very little justice, and absolutely zero fucking mercy in that system, so I don't recommend it." I sat back and relaxed a little, still waiting for what we all knew was incoming.

"So, as I was saying, I didn't take people back to be punished, I was generally out there to do a specific job, and when I encountered those guilty of breaking a law, the only sentence was death. Issued from the barrel of my gun."

"Right…?" He forced a smile, sweat clear on his brow now, as his clearly painted hair—a fad a few years ago—started to smear under the liquid ingress.

"You'll also note, there's no room for doubt in the system. There's no appeal, no concern on my side that maybe there's a mistrial of justice. There's also no levels. Guilty equals death. That's it." I smiled, then shrugged, settling back in the chair and looking from the elf to his companions.

"You don't get the death sentence for a lot of things in the city these days, politicians like to speak about how progressive they are, while doing absolutely nothing to stop the corporations doing what they want of course, but I digress. Out of the city, if I say you're guilty, then you are. That's it. My judgement? You're guilty, therefore you deserve death."

I noted the silence that had fallen as everyone around the room listened with baited breath, my own team finally starting to understand the reason that the APS were so feared wasn't so much the tech, although that was impressive and terrifying all on its own.

No we were terrifying because we were the final arbitrator. If we said you were guilty, then we were not only within our power to, but were legally required, to dispense justice. And that justice came from the barrel of the gun we held.

"So, you are running a scam, one that preys on the stupid—we won't say innocent, because they're too dumb for that—but you're selling them fake medikits. To sell something that's the difference between life and death? That I take exception to. That you're selling them is proven beyond a doubt as far as I'm concerned." I smiled. "You're guilty." I repeated.

"Boss," Reign said from behind me, looking out of the door. "Looks like his back up is here."

"How many?" I asked, tensing slightly, but doing my best to hide it.

"Seven, all armed, low level wanna-be gangers it looks like. Minimal body armor, and hell, they've only got small arms," she said, snorting in derision.

"Let them come in, spread out, order them to stand down and surrender or—"

"We know you're in there!" one of them shouted from outside. "Throw out your guns or we're coming in."

"Come on in!" Reign called out to them, smiling and waving at them through the doorway.

I smiled at the elf who sat ever more visibly terrified before me as I spoke to my team. "Disarm them and see what they have to say for themselves." I ordered Reign, not even turning around.

"And if they refuse to stand down?" she asked, knowing damn well what was coming.

"Execute them," I said. "They're guilty."

"No, you don't understand…" the elf started to explain, as the gangers walked into the room behind me.

The door, if the building was seen from above, was in the upper, left-most corner, and they filed in through it. They were gangers, used to asserting control over the weak and frightened, and clearly thinking they were in control here.

They sauntered in…and froze.

Reign had taken up position at the top right of the room, her grazer loaded, held in position to be dragged across them all, even as Todds and Luna stood by her side with guns levelled and ready.

Gessh was behind the idiots sitting before me and facing the group that came in, while I didn't bother to turn around.

"Drop your weapons," Reign said, the unsubtle hum of the grazer cutting through the air like god's own buzzsaw. I smiled at the elf before me, saying nothing, and noting the panic on his face as he went from 'I'm in danger' to 'I'm safe' to 'oh fuckfuckfuck I'm so much more worse off than I thought'.

It was actually more enjoyable to watch than I thought it'd be, even after all these years of seeing it.

Admittedly, it was usually on the face of some petty slaver, and I was seeing it through my camera as I tore the roof off their transport, but still, seeing it face to face like this?

Yeah. I could live with the change.

"So…" I said to the elf, as Reign opened fire behind me, the single long loud burst filling the air, before cutting off, a short staccato burst of fire echoing from Todds and Luna as Gessh gently rested the barrel of her shotgun against the back of the elf's head. "…where were we?"

CHAPTER THIRTY-FOUR

Needless to say, the situation didn't improve for the asshole scammers, but it did for us, quite nicely.

It turned out that the gang had been running this scam for a few weeks at least, and had hundreds of small medikits, and nearly seventy of the medium and large ones.

The elf and his friends—those who survived at least—were more than happy to spend a little time scrubbing and purging the kits they'd contaminated with their muck, and in a miraculous burst of conscience even volunteered all their credits to make up for the situation they'd created.

Luna tried contacting the kids that had started this whole chain of events for us, but considering she was reaching out to them to arrange to transfer the credits over, and they started demanding more? Saying that we owed them half of everything we got, as we'd never have gotten anything if not for them?

Luna told them to get fucked and enjoy paying off the gang.

When she shared out the credits between us all, I totally agreed, little shits seemed to think we owed them something for them being stupid enough to be scammed like that. Sure, it wasn't nice, but out of all of it, they'd gone into it thinking they were ripping off the merchant, so they deserved whatever came to them.

We took the filled kits we'd gotten so far, minus a selection for ourselves of course, and sold the majority to Oshbob, then headed over to a place the Lion recommended, having the entire collection of empty and supposedly 'clean' kits scrubbed again by a service that actually did it properly.

It cost a grand total of a credit per kit, and considering the gunk they ejected? It was worth it.

From there, we hit up two more minor jobs for the guild, clearing out a few dozen specters at each of them, and harvesting the bodies afterwards.

It was beginning to look like a 'rinse and repeat' day, when Reign sent a general call through the small group tac-net.

"Behind us, where the piled mattresses and the plastic sheeting is thickest, don't look, but we have an issue."

"What's up?" I asked, slowly rising from the crouch I'd been sitting in, the claws of my left hand retracting as I stopped the syphon, expecting an attack.

"Remember Borrolet?" Reign asked, and I frowned.

"The name's vaguely familiar…" I admitted, running a search, and grunting a second later. "The half goblin from the cooling tower run, from Liolet's team?"

"Yeah," Reign spat. "Liolet kicked her out, caught her trying to threaten one of the new hires, and didn't take it well."

"So?"

"So I think she followed us here," Reign growled, sending us all a still shot from her cameras.

The face peeking out of the pile of gear wasn't that familiar to me, hell, a lot of goblins looked the same, and while she was a half goblin, she was also hiding as best she could, had filth smeared on her face, and I'd seen only a handful of times.

I ran a comparison though—thank the gods of blood and chrome for my RI— and grunted again as it came back. "Ninety-six percent likelihood that it's her." I sent in the group. "RI did a comparison based on my previous visuals of her. You think she saw me harvesting the specters?"

"I'm sure of it, and she's talking to someone right now."

"Shit." I snarled. That was all we needed, to have word get out before we were ready.

"How do we deal with this?" Luna asked. "She'd followed us, recorded us, as I'm betting that's what the device is, and she's reporting on us?"

"We confront her and find out what the shit is going on," I ordered, turned to face Borrolet in her hiding place.

As soon as she saw she'd been seen, rather than do the sensible thing, and come out, she ran for it.

That was the worst of all possible outcomes for me, even as I ordered Gessh to catch her. If she'd been doing anything that she thought was even slightly defensible? She'd not have fucking run.

Considering she was apparently recording us, yeah it was weird, but that was it. Nothing illegal about it, and at worst, she'd have had to just say that she was curious about our methods and wanted to study them.

Hell, she could have just told us to fuck off, that there were no laws against her recording us. She'd have been right.

Instead she ran for it like her arse was on fire, and as Gessh closed the distance? She pulled out a flashbang.

"Don't do it!" Luna roared at the goblin, only a handful of strides behind her sister, but it was too late.

Borrolet triggered the grenade, dumped it a few seconds later and took a corner, darting out of sight.

A second later the grenade went off, and those of us giving chase were momentarily blinded and deafened, the grenade giving off a low level chaff field that made it difficult for electronic measure to get though.

I was still reeling from it, when gunfire rang out somewhere ahead, followed by an answering burst from Gessh's shotgun.

"Fuck!" I snarled, shaking my head to free it of the lingering effects of that shit, and picking up the pace again, racing after the sisters.

The corner that they'd gone down was a right, followed by a left pretty much straight away, then a second right, the doglegs of corridors down here under a clothing shop making damn sure there was little space.

I took the final corner, and found Gessh hissing in pain, as Luna stabbed her in the shoulder with a small medikit, the crumpled body of Borrolet laid in the middle of the corridor, her gun still in her hand.

"Bitch shot me when I took the corner." Gessh groaned, as Luna held the skin together for the nanites, glaring down at the little body of Borrolet.

"Why?" I wondered, a sinking feeling in my stomach. "And are you alright?"

"Yeah, it's a through and through," Luna replied grimly. "Armor piercing round, no guesses why she was loaded with them."

I checked on Gessh, getting a grunt and being waved away as I stepped around her, moving to the body that was even now leaking blood into the corridor.

I turned her over, seeing the pain and fear that was now etched into her face as well as the hole that had passed through the middle of her chest, destroying the heart entirely. Gessh had gone for her own gun, that was understandable, being fired upon, but the difference between the small but admittedly high powered handgun round, and the shotgun solid slug, were light years apart.

I picked up the recording device, then flicked off the broadcast button, severing the link to who, or whatever it'd been sending it to, before trying to play it back.

The recording asked for authorization, and when I hesitated, then tried Borrolet's thumb? It wiped itself. It wasn't even subtle about it, there was a crackle, then then entire device grew insanely hot. I threw it aside, and smoke started to rise, wafting around the narrow confines.

"Now what the hell do we do?" I asked the group, totally confused, as I started searching her little body.

"We report it," Reign said grimly.

"To ACE?"

"Fuck no!" Reign snorted. "Why the hell would we involve those bastards? No, we need to report this to Julius, he needs to know about it, and whatever was going on here? It's best it comes from us."

"You don't think she was working for him?" I asked.

"What, to see what we were doing?" She shook her head. "He gets access to the recordings and knows what we're doing anyway, more or less. It's not like he needed to spy on us, hell he could just ask and he knows we're invested enough we'd just tell him. If anything? He wants to know *less* about the shit we're up to."

"You want to tell him?" I tried, looking at Reign. "You're his friend after all."

"And you're the team lead," she pointed out, shaking her head. "No this needs to come from you."

"I know." I groaned, straightening up, then triggering the call, and hoping, just praying, that we were too deep to get a signal, and that maybe…nope.

The call went straight through, and my last hopes were dashed, as I accepted that whatever she'd been doing, it'd been done.

"Sarge!" Julius answered, grinning in my virtual vision as the connection went through. "Tell me you're calling for another job? I've just had one reported and…"

"Julius?" I interrupted.

"…it's a good one, you know? It's by an ex-military store that—yeah?" He broke off, finally seeing my face and realizing this wasn't going to be a good call. "Fuck Kabutt, what's wrong?"

"Borrolet," I said. "Did you send her to follow us?"

"Who?" He asked frowning. "Wait, half goblin Borrolet? Little sneaky fucker?"

"Yeah." I sighed, knowing what was coming, and believing him.

"No, why would I send her to do anything? Hell, she's been booted from Liolet's crew, and she's back in the reserves, why?"

"She followed us," I said. "Reign spotted her recording us stripping the specters..."

"Crap."

"...and when she realized we'd spotted her? She ran for it."

"You didn't hurt her did you?" Julius asked. "Look Kabutt, I know it's bad form but..."

"She's dead." I cut him off. "She ran, then dropped a flashbang, then hid around a corner and fired on us, point blank with armor piercing. One of my team shot back, in self defense."

"Fuck!" he cursed, shaking his head in disbelief. "Ah shit man that's screwed it."

"She fired first!" I snapped.

"Yeah, she did, but you've been with the guild less than a fucking week, Kabutt, and you've shot and killed another guild member. There's going to be an investigation."

"You're shitting me!"

"I'm not," he snapped back. "Fuck's sake man, if it's as you say? Sure, nothing to come of it, but you've still been with us less than a week! You kill another guild member and I wave it off? What does that say about the guild? That as long as the boss trusts you it doesn't matter? No, not in my guild, not on my watch." He glared at me, then shook his head. "Tell me you were still recording."

"Not sure to be honest...," I admitted. "I know I'd stopped mine, I'll have to check the others."

"Right." He growled. "So all I've got is your word then? For all I know you took her down there with you and shot her to get rid of her and hide something she saw..."

"Julius," I said quietly, but he paused, clearly getting the tone. "We were testing hardware."

"Fuck, on a client site? This is so gonna get messy. What was it?"

"I'm not saying, but she was recording us, and when she died? The recording caught fire. Someone sent her after us, filming us, and was fucking after something. They got it, whatever it was."

"You're sure they got it?" he asked, after a few seconds of quiet.

"Yeah, fairly," I admitted. "I'm calling you from right by her body now, so the broadcast got out, unless she wasn't backing it up, but you know. My luck's so fantastic I'm not even going to hope for that."

"So what we've got is a situation where one guild crew, who are already getting complained about, by the way—"

"What? By who?"

"—that getting complained about as getting juicy assignments and let off for things, have killed a member of the recruits," he finished shaking his head that he wasn't going to answer my question. "Now yeah, Borrolet was on a warning, and yeah, she was a goblin. Let's look at this from another point of view though, and maybe you'll understand why I want you to hand over your entire recording to me. Not just the guild one you stopped."

"Isn't happening," I said.

"It is, because if it doesn't." he said, "you're out of the guild." He let that sink in for a few seconds. "Sure, you can do without us, hell, you'd be picked up on your first call right now I bet, but they're not going to give you the cover you need to recover your friends from the fingers now, are they? You need me and my guild, Kabutt, so listen up.

"The reason I need to do an investigation? It's not that I don't trust you. It's not that when, not if, but *when* Trees and his friends find out and cause a stink about it, we need to be totally above board. It's because a slightly different point of view on what's happened is this. Maybe—and to be clear I don't believe this, but someone will suggest it if we don't, and we need to be able to prove it wasn't this—you took her down there as a trial. Maybe you decided you wanted services she wasn't willing to give you, and maybe you and your team had a little fun, then shot her."

"Fuck's sake, Julius," I growled, shaking my head. "You know…"

"I know Reign wouldn't," he said. "I've known her for years. For the record? I don't think you, Todds or the sisters would either, but I have to see it from all angles. You want me to sort this out and get you and the team reinstated and fast?"

"Yeah." I growled, furious, and yet when he'd suggested it that way, knowing that there had to have been incidents that gave rise to such a detailed description of the possibilities, I couldn't blame him as well. "Just…tell me that its only you that'll see what we were doing?"

"Nope," he said. "It'll be a tribunal, three team leaders with me seeing the file, and they'll be volunteers. You better believe Trees will volunteer after your history with him, so unless there's three others that do, expect him to be watching it. If I can avoid him applying? Great, but if I have to do a second call for volunteers?" He shook his head.

"Great. Can you cut out…?"

"No, I need the entire recording," he said grimly. "No sections cut, no sections blurred, the entire thing."

"Fuck." I growled, shaking my head. "Honestly, I don't know if I can," I said after a few seconds, and stifling the urge to kick the pathetic little corpse laid on the floor before me. "What we're testing…its under NDA's. Like 'cut your own throat after reading' level of NDAs."

"Shit. Who with?"

"Can't say," I said. "Look I can share most of the recordings, not the sections near the specters corpses for the testing we're doing, but the sections all around it, including Reign spotting Borrolet, and then her using the grenade, then chase, all up to this conversation."

"I…" He hung his head. "Send me what you've got and get out of there. I'm on my way over, or I will be in two minutes, as soon as I've got another team lead to act as a witness. I hope we get a friendly group, Kabutt, because if we don't? You're out, and we're all fucked again."

"Understood. I'll scrub the sections you can't see and send it now."

With that I cut the call, and turned to the others, explaining the situation as quickly and concisely as I could, before using my RI to doctor the recording, tactically blurring the sections around the specters, making sure it was clear that literally everything else was there, and that the only section that was hidden was the specters.

I didn't have any great hopes that it would be helpful, but at least it was as hidden as it was.

We left the site, leaving the mods as well—we'd not harvested them yet, so that was a relief, at least there was less effort required there—and we summoned a cab, heading back to the warehouse, dropping Todds off on the way.

"So now what?" Luna asked eventually.

"I don't know," I said. "Until this blows over, I guess if we're specter hunting, it's on our own time."

"Shit, I was liking how much we were getting." Gessh groaned. "So we're off duty while they figure this shit out?"

"Basically," I sighed. "Maybe we could…"

"Damn!" Reign groaned, covering her face with her hands. "That's it!"

"What?"

"With us benched and at least three team leads involved in an inquiry? That's Julius down four teams. It's not like he can send those teams out without their leads after all."

"So?"

"So it's fucking Trees!" she snapped. "Or someone else that's trying to fuck the guild over. We just went through the roof with contracts, and they have to be honored, take four teams out of the rotation after they've just accepted the contracts? Smaller teams need to step in and take the load, if they get taken down? The guild looks shit again, and the debts that Julius was paying off? There'll be non-completion fines and more. Hell, I bet if he checks some of the contracts, there'll be insanely high fines for not doing the job."

"So, you're saying we were set up, and Borrolet was a tactical sacrifice?" I groaned, rubbing the bridge of my nose. "I fucking hate this shit, can't he just fuck off and go back to drowning kittens or whatever he did for shits and giggles?"

"And if you go after him now? He's covered. You'd be banned, as would we, and you better believe he's hoping you do," Reign added, jumping ahead as I started fantasizing about beating the fucker to death in a dark alley.

"I know." I sighed. "Right, we're nearly back at the warehouse, I need to check on things with the suit and…"

"Dondo messaged," Luna said suddenly, wincing that she'd clearly forgotten to include this. "He says they've tracked down the right arm for the suit. He says the price is a hundred and seventy thousand."

"Tell him to bring it over," I forced out between gritted teeth, knowing damn well that it'd be the fucking arm that the suit had been fitted with. Again, for just a second, I wondered if Oshbob's people had stolen it, then dismissed it again, there was just no way, not realistically.

I was just damn lucky that the orc was smart enough to see the advantage of working with me, rather than trying to steal the suit and selling it.

Speaking of which, I'd been paying for the parts he'd brought to us so far, mainly because we'd not had the gear ready yet, but the deal was that he'd run a tab for the parts, that I'd pay it with nanites and specter or merc targets we harvested the parts from.

It was time to get ourselves back on track.

CHAPTER THIRTY-FIVE

The first step, while also boring, was for the team to damn well get ready for an extended harvesting trip.

We needed to get the suit sorted, we needed to get the bank filled with credits again, as despite the others all agreeing that from now on we'd pool our takings, until the suits were up and running, we'd only done a handful of minor jobs.

Most of all? We needed to get ready.

I was getting that itchy feeling between my shoulder blades that something was wrong, very wrong, and that was never good. Sitting there as the air-cab flew us across the city, I worried away at it, until I found the niggle that was eating at me.

It felt like we'd just been on the verge of earning real credits and something had hit to stop it. As much as I joked around and laughingly cursed the gods of blood and chrome, I didn't really believe in them, and neither did I believe in the gods of the old world, or any world for that matter.

I believed there was such a thing as luck, but I also believed that it was what you made of it that counted.

We had the medikits ready, we were ready, we had the gear, and the suit, we had a home, and a plan.

All of that was from not taking any shit and from continually forging forwards. Now though? I felt like we were being held back. Held back to slow us down, like we'd been moving too fast, too successfully.

Well, looking at that, if there was someone out to get us, I didn't believe it was Oshbob and his crew, despite their dodginess, and I didn't believe we had a mole.

That left two avenues. First was Trees, he was a dickhead, and he deserved his face kicking in but the question of if he was smart enough to have set all of this up?

No. He'd take advantage of the situation, certainly, but I didn't believe he could set it all up. That meant that there was another party involved, or this was a lucky coincidence and he was just taking the opportunity as it came.

That third party? That was the problem. If, as I was worrying, it was the major and his people? The only reason they'd not be hitting me and taking my suit right now, would be if they had limited resources themselves.

If they didn't have access to the spares they needed, not easily, then they'd be leaving us to get the suit repaired. As soon as the suit was ready? That's when they'd hit us, or near enough.

While the suit was stripped? They'd leave me to do that work. That was if they even knew about it and I wasn't being paranoid.

Paranoia was a soldier's friend though, right up until it wasn't, and I resolved to make the most of it.

So. With the plan that the major knew what we were doing, and was fucking us over, maybe paying Trees to do it, then we needed to move, and fast, he'd either be waiting for us to fix the suit or…

Or he'd be busy, his team laying low, and he was planning to hit us soon.

If I was wrong, and all of this was a little low-grade paranoia? Worst case scenario, we ended up tired out from working our arses off.

If I was right? We'd make damn sure he got a nasty surprise when he came for us.

"Luna," I said aloud, coming to a decision.

"Yeah boss?" she asked, turning from the window.

"Are you still getting those legs?" I nodded to Gessh's ones, the black gloss hidden by her trousers currently.

"As soon as we've got the time, yeah?" She said, nodding.

"Get them now then." I ordered. "We're moving the schedule up, as of now people, we're on full-on mode. If you need any work doing? Get it done NOW. Tomorrow we're going dungeon diving."

"Dungeon diving?" Reign asked, grinning. "You mean we're going deep?"

"Oh yeah, and not just in your kinky fantasies." I winked at her. "Seriously people, we use the rest of the day and tomorrow morning to prepare. We load up, get all the gear, all the mods and all the rest we can, because tomorrow we're going deep into the Undercity, and we're not coming back up until we've got enough high end mods and nanites to pay for the fucking suit entirely. We're going all out."

"Why now?" Reign sent me on singular mode through the tac-net, subvocalizing as Luna called Lion, and Gessh started shopping for replacement gear.

"I think we're being slowed down deliberately, that dickhead Trees is either doing his best to get us out of the guild, or at least cost us a few days earnings and damage the guild. If I'm right and its deliberate? Then the major and his pets are coming for us, and soon."

"So what do we do?"

"We get my suit ready, and we go get Richie and Sync, then we lay a trap."

That was it, that was all I needed to say, and I was damn fortunate that they took me at that, everyone stepping up, as I made the plans.

We were suspended from the guild, but not booted out.

That meant we were still in, as far as the system cared.

I started plotting points of convergence on the map, searching for common outbreak points, and feeding them into my RI, searching for likely underground clusters.

By the time we'd landed I had four possible zones already worked out, and the almost certainly out of date Artem undercity maps, which all swore there was no way into those zones.

Reign and I splashed through the light afternoon rain shower and into the warehouse, while Gessh and Luna stayed in the air-cab, lifting off and heading straight for Lion's chop-shop, along with a load of nanites, just in case.

Reign made herself useful organizing replacement parts, additional batteries, grenades, survival kits and more. Then she spent over forty thousand credits just on ammunition.

I had an altogether less fun conversation with Dondo, reminding him that my deal with Oshbob—who'd refused my call, Dondo had called me, making it obvious who my 'contact' was—was built on the understanding I'd be bringing in specter parts and a fuck load of nanites.

Well, tomorrow I'd be delivering them, and we needed the missing sections of the suit. He wasn't happy. Apparently somewhere along the line, presumably when I'd started handing over great masses of credits, the deal had happily changed to me buying them, but that wasn't going to continue.

I also had a quick call with Julius, who basically told me off the record that I was up shit creek. Three volunteers had indeed stood up to be involved in the examination of the facts. One of them was Trees, and one was his closest ally.

That Liolet had stood up as well, was a slight bonus, we'd gotten on well, but…Borrolet was previously a member of his team, and that wasn't good.

Basically Julius was on our side. He'd watched the clips I'd sent him, including the one from Gessh—fortunately her recording was still going—as she'd taken the corner, and been shot at close range, at no point threatening the little fucker until that gun was used.

The best I could hope for at this point, was that the investigation was a tie, as Liolet was undecided, and Trees and his mate were out to get me.

If there was a tie? Then the guild leader's decision was final.

The good news however, when Julius asked why I'd been remotely checking out the jobs board and specter locations, was that as a registered member of the guild, if we went out and killed specters that weren't on a job? Like we found them as we were hoping to, and slaughtered them?

We still got paid.

It wasn't as much, the corporate payment that came from the hiring company was lost after all, but the original hundred credits from the city? That was still paid, providing we could prove the kill.

The recording was deemed enough evidence, provided it was fed through a verified guild AI. As long as the guild was getting their fifty credits per specter killed? Julius was onboard with the deal.

He refused to let us use the guild services before that though, so my hopes of buying up any discounted spare gear were smashed.

After the calls?

Well, Reign and I trained.

Dondo and co. hadn't managed to get any more plasma swords, not yet, but I had two, the one I'd been using and the spare, as well as some training swords, and I made the most of the next two hours teaching Reign to use them.

After two hours?

It was clear that Reign was NOT getting a plasma sword when we got more.

She was frankly crap and would have managed to cut her own foot off twice if not for the fact we were using training imitation blades.

The rest of the afternoon was divided between maintenance, Reign working on our weapons and me on my suit, and finally, on me actually powering up my suit fully.

The system slowly began the power up cycle as I sat in the harness, a low level of utter sheer fucking terror that I was going to find the suit's internals, the computer, the storage, all of it had been stripped out and replaced?

It was utterly misplaced as the first sight that greeted me, as the port in my back fired, sliding into my spinal slot and deploying, was the boot up screen that Richie had 'fixed' for me.

I'd made the mistake once of saying how boring the launch checklist was, and needless to say, that fucker had fixed it.

A giant lizard appeared before me, screamed and vomited out the data I needed, the overlay of the lizard suddenly battling some old word monkey making it almost impossible to read the questions that I knew were there, and I tabbed to them on instinct.

There were four systems available on boot. First and foremost was the 'full' boot. Basically was I ready to use my suit, and needed it to be working?

That was a no for today. I moved to the second in line.

System Diagnostic. This was a simple header that concealed the billion or so tests that could be run on the suit, including the one I needed to do most of all.

I flicked through several, pinging them and ordering they be done as soon as the priority one tasks were done.

The only one of those I ordered?

The dating of memory components.

Then I sat there for long minutes, unable to do anything else, forcing myself to watch as the system checked for the installation date, coding cycle and lifespan of the memory crystals, as well as when they were last accessed.

I stared at the blank screen wiling it to answer, to share the data to…

It flickered up, lines of code streaming into a single row of data, one that made me actually sag in relief.

The data cores, the crystals, all of it, it was original!

I'd been shitting myself that the location of Richie and Sync, that Richie had hard encoded into the computer, supposedly so deeply that nobody not a hacker could get it, besides me, would have been discarded.

I'd imagined technicians removing the carefully hidden sections of crystal and deciding that there was a blemish on it. Maybe swapping it out for a blank, crushing the original and moving on, having no clue that they'd killed my friends as well.

Instead? Laziness and the fastest solution won again.

I took a deep breath, then moved on, flicking the diagnostics to continue, but moving to the integration tests, ordering the system to run compatibility tests and more, as well as on my spinal tap.

An hour of me working through the selections, doing the tests and mentally commanding the suit—it was still held tight in the cradle, with the restraining bolt fitted, making it unable to move externally, but allowing all the impulses to be checked—and low and behold, it passed.

For long seconds after I'd tested everything I could, I simply couldn't believe it. The system had passed the tests, my spinal tap had passed the tests, and despite it being heavily redacted? I'd even got confirmation that the model wasn't just compatible, it was perfect for my suit.

I sat there, the final test before me, as I focused, reaching out not with any particular system, but with *desire*. Not the 'I'm gonna get my end away' kind either. No, I focused. I concentrated on what I needed, what I wanted most of all, and then I pushed that at the system I was attached to.

> *Ping*
> Encoded data download has begun.
> *Ping*
> Download complete.

I froze, reading the messages, then took a deep breath and made the call.

CHAPTER THIRTY-SIX

The call with Bowdoin was anti-climactic in just about all possible ways. He accepted the file, laughed his arse off for a solid minute, then sent me the locational data for Richie and Sync.

I asked him what was so funny and he laughed harder. The bastard.

"Fine, whatever," I growled at him. "Look, I need another job doing."

"Sounds interesting." He shrugged. "What do you need?"

"You know how the APS are registered? When we're free of the army I mean, any suit that's in the city has a registered locational tag, as well as a hardwired explosive in the suit that the government can detonate if we act up, or you know, go corpo hunting?"

"Vaguely, yeah?" he agreed, nodding and seemingly playing with something else, not really paying a great deal of attention.

"Well, I need that."

"What?"

"The registration, just hack it or whatever."

"Yeah look, when we talked about that before, well I've looked into it a bit. You want me to hack into a secure server, something that's designed to keep the most lethal machines in the city under surveillance and from running amok, and you just want me to 'hack it or whatever'."

"So, let me guess. This is where you tell me that nobody else could do it, and that you're a genius, and triple whatever cost it was going to be?" I asked him sarcastically.

"No, seriously man, this is where I tell you it can't be fucking done."

"It can," I assured him.

"It can't," he replied just as seriously. "You don't know what you're asking, this is a system that's maintained by AI's, a system that searches the city constantly, every single goddamn camera that's connected to the city systems, all traffic cams, surveillance, security cams, weather trackers, hell the fucking rodent and research systems, ALL of them are linked to this! There's no way a suit can move in the city without being instantly picked up on one of those and then cross referenced! As soon as that's done? They'd know, and there's no way to spoof it."

"Wait, no you don't understand—"

"No, Kabutt, you fucking dinosaur, *you* don't understand! There's no way to get the system not to report you! I'd have to hack all three AI, watch them around the clock, maybe code more AI to watch them, they're that fast and then…"

"Bowdoin, it's been done before!" I said firmly.

"No it's—"

"That walking turd Major Marcial has an entire black ops team that get by without, and M-Corp had one as well, so…?"

"Yeah but…wait, no that doesn't work." Bowdoin said after a few seconds of thought. "That *can't* work."

"Just because you don't know how they're doing it, doesn't mean it can't be done. Figure it out!" I suggested, and he totally ignored me, staring off into space.

"It's not possible," he said. "Genuinely, I mean, it can't be, right?"

"What's that?" I asked.

"Nobody's that stupid." Bowdoin mumbled after a few seconds of staring into the distance, before sitting up and smiling at me, making me both confident he'd figured out a way to do it, and fear for my wallet.

Then he spoke up again. "So, here's the deal. I have an idea of how things may work. However, since you are a fucking suicide risk *for me*, and this is so damn far beyond my paygrade I should be presented the keys to the fucking Living Earth tower any day now...I'm going to turn you down."

"Bowdoin. You're not fucking—"

"Except... because I *am* that nice, and because you'll be paying me a lovely finder's fee, I'll be presenting you to a *friend* of mine, who is almost as crazy as you and almost as talented as me. And I will tell him which hunch I just had."

"Fuck, no look, I don't need 'nearly as talented', I need…"

"Tough!"

That was it, that fucking hacker dickhead Bowdoin said he'd get back to me with the other guy's details and soon, as well as that as soon as I knew when I needed it all in place, I was to call him, giving him as much notice as possible.

He and I knew damn well that the way my life was I'd give him as much notice as was *possible*, which meant most likely I'd call him and demand it be done 'now bitch now'.

That being done, and unable to resist it, I'd powered the suit fully, then sat there for a few minutes, my eyes closed, feeling the hum of the power cells and the comforting presence of the suit all around me.

All my personal stuff had been stripped out, the stored memory files by Richie, to keep them safe, and the actual personal physical bits, like the stupid things like the stickers and the stink bomb that Fergie had stuck into one boot—it'd driven me mad for a fortnight—were all gone from the rebuild.

Eventually, I couldn't put it off any longer, and rather than physically keying anything, I did the final test. I closed my eyes, and I 'felt' the system through my nerve ports.

It was the last fear, and it was justified. As soon as I closed my eyes, it all changed.

Until now I'd been commanding the system through my implants partially, running tests with them, and through the various 'normal' system processes. Moving my arms, or thinking to, and the padding mimicking the feeling of the outside world so that it matched.

Now though, I stopped all of that and did a full mental linkup.

There were issues.

I'd expected that there would be, and sod's law, I was 'out' of the system now, which meant that I couldn't get a patch that would just fix things.

My RI began cataloging the various issues, and I winced as the list hit over a thousand sectors. In IT and system issues that was nothing, not for the *billions* of lines of code that made the APS usable. Hell there were sections that were designed to only kick in if the code had issues, or if limbs were removed.

I pulled up the code in my mind, suddenly standing alone on a beach, water lapping nearby in my mental construct as screens surrounded me, code streaming as I focused and parsed the meaning out.

There were sections that were written to account for seismic shifts in the ground, in specific latitudes, in specific depths of water, ranging from a puddle to deep water ops.

A thousand lines of errors? That was practically the gold standard!

The problem was, I didn't know if these errors were the usual fuckups, if they were a new patch that had been applied and rushed, and now my legs worked backwards or whatever—I'd not be getting a replacement patch after all—or if these were specific to my situation.

My new spinal tap system was rigged for four inputs. The suit had done one main insert, the weapons systems would be run through the secondary line normally, and until the system registered that there were weapons attached that wouldn't be inserted.

So that might account for the errors as well, but maybe…

A knock sounded on the exterior of the suit, and I blinked my eyes open, the massive walls of code that I'd been scouring through vanishing as I focused on the 'real' world again.

I also focused on Reign.

She was standing right before the suit, in a fucking tiny little red outfit, one that did nothing to hide and everything to enhance.

The escape bolts slid free and the suit began to open to my unstated command, as Reign stepped back, smiling when she saw the look on my face.

"We've got about an hour before the girls get back here, and we have to put up with Dondo and the pair of them trying to fuck the walls down," she said. "I thought you might like to make the most of some private time with me?"

"Oh my gods, yes." I breathed, disconnecting and ordering the transport container to seal itself up before I was even out fully. I barely made it out of the harness and down to ground level before the handholds had retracted, the corners drawing in and sealing the container shut.

Reign walked up the stairs to the apartment area, and I almost fell over myself hurrying after, admiring that elven ass as she cleared the top of the stairs ahead of me.

I hit the door without slowing, almost taking it off the hinges, and swept her up in my arms, tearing a burst of laughter from her, then kissed her soundly.

She put her arms around my neck and returned the kiss, then somehow she twisted and was wrapped around me fully, hands undoing my buttons and tugging me free, before whispering a question into my ear, and making me groan with need.

The next hour passed in a blur, the backblast of the aircar outside taking off as Dondo presumably took it to get the girls—although it could have been stolen for all I cared right there and then—and then the blast seemingly far too soon again, as it returned, warning us to shift rooms, the main room bench having been the perfect height, and the table? Well.

It was both sturdy and had just a little give that meant it rocked in the most delightful of ways at times.

We barely made it into the bedroom before Luna and Gessh entered, and the laughter that followed us when they found some of the clothes we'd missed out there?

There were various catcalls and shouts of recommendations, before they went quiet, presumably having had enough fun and decided to move onto 'making their own entertainment'.

We fell asleep in each other's arms eventually, the pair of us exhausted, sweaty and both determined we'd get up and get a shower in just a minute…

…then we were out, fast asleep.

…

When I woke the next morning, it was to the sensation of Reign slipping from my bed, a gentle kiss placed on my forehead as I laid there drifting, not quite awake, and not quite asleep, and then she was gone.

I sank back into a lighter sleep for a little while, then forced myself to get up, having a long shower, dressing slowly, still feeling relaxed.

Leaving my room I closed the door softly, seeing that the sun was barely risen, and smiling to myself as I smelt the coffee in the machine.

Reign was sitting at the table, sipping at her own cup, and smiling at me over the rim as I moved in.

"Morning," she whispered, and I stole a quick kiss, her lips tasting like the juice of the gods, before I got my own mug. Sitting with her I couldn't help but smile at the way she slid a hand almost hesitantly across the table, half way to me, and I reached out and took it, holding it in mine.

We were so similar, and so different in many ways, but the feeling of her slender, small hand in my mine made me smile so easily. For a few minutes we simply sat there, not saying anything, just enjoying each other's presence as we watched the sun coming up over the distant chimneys and buildings, the long shadows being cast by the wall meaning that 'sunrise' was a misnomer in the city, but still.

It was the company that mattered.

Twenty minutes later the first sounds of stirring from the others filtered through to us, and I finished my second cup, before standing. "Are you ready?" I asked Reign, and she nodded.

"What's the first job?" she asked, setting her cup aside and squaring her shoulders, pushing our romantic morning and fun night aside, making room for the paid professional killers we were.

"Reload, check the gear we've got, then load up. We need to make the most of this. We're going deep today, and we won't be coming back until we're out of ammo, we're out of specters, or we physically can't loot anymore."

"Sounds fun," she said, smiling at me, before nodding towards the steps down to the warehouse floor. "You get started, I'll organize some food to arrive soon and check on the others, get everyone moving."

Another hour had passed before the last of us—Todds—arrived, and by then? We were mainly ready.

We'd taken the lessons learned from the cooling tower mission, and applied them here. Not only did we have spares for most things—and I had a spare fuckin' helmet, because they *always* get trashed—but we also had enough food for three meals each, a container of water, four small and two medium medikits each. A length of lightweight chain, because it was a fuck load easier to climb than rope, and strong as shit, a welding torch—a small one that had an integrated battery and filament dispenser—and lastly our standard loadout.

All the things like a 'normal' medikit, a blanket, a change of clothes, a spare knife, a windup torch, just in case of EMP's, and most importantly?

An utter fuckload of ammo and razorwire.

We literally had a buttload of ammo for everything, so much I hadn't even counted it, there was enough to fill every mag we had, then an ammo case, a heavy duty case filled to the brim with ammo, probably enough to reload everything from scratch at least once over, as well as directional mines, grenades, collapsible bags, and last of all?

A pair of big bags that were filled to the brim with spent medikits, ready to be refilled.

If we managed to fill all of them? Individual small medikits were a thousand each, and we had more than two hundred. If we just filled all these fuckers up, not counting the damn kills, not counting the looted mods?

That was going to be a hundred thousand or more, considering that Oshbob had agreed to pay half the market value for them.

Loading it all into our aircar took all the space it had, and we had to get a second cab for ourselves, but hey, that was life, nothing was ever fucking easy after all.

Clambering out of the cab at the other end, loading each other up, we got some seriously weird looks from the locals, considering where we were?

There was nothing dodgy going on, specter-wise here, besides us anyway.

"You sure this is the place, boss?" Luna asked as we set off walking, the sections we needed to pass through to get to the nearest entrance to the undercity were too narrow for the cabs.

"I am." I told her, using the tac-net.

"Good, because you know we're fucking surrounded already, right?" Gessh added in, and I nodded. "Just, you know. This is a bit of a bad area, that's all…"

"I know," I said, smiling as we passed a symbol etched into one wall, glowing with a mixture of imprinted metallic hues and photoluminescent paint making it gleam in the dim alley.

Where we were was one of the most congested, dodgy and dangerous areas I possibly could have found. The buildings here were ancient, old housing slums that had started out as blocks of flats and individual houses, but over hundreds of years they'd grown into each other.

The building code for the larger blocks and the arcologies was very specific, the insane weight of such structures meaning that they had to be spread out, and certainly not in any area that was as structurally unsound underground as this was.

As such? Investments were focused elsewhere.

Areas declined gradually, as more and more buildings were converted without any consideration for the rules, and when a city as corrupt as Artem thought that an area was bad?

It was really bad.

Hundreds of meters of streets, parks, shopping areas and more had been gradually cut off from the sky as people extended their apartments out and up.

Soon the parks were lost to gangs, then the shops were replaced with more slums, and before long you had a level of living quarters in an area that approached that of the worst arcologies, but without the common sense approach to building and spacing.

The result was this.

An area that corpos ignored, that ACE patrols avoided and actively turned around, giving up on chases inside of, and that the only real way to deal with, besides ceding it to the gangs as they had, was with a flamethrower and wrecking balls.

"You're way too cheerful for this boss," Todds said, trying to watch in all areas at once. "We're walking into a trap, you know that?"

"Nope," I said. "If we were trying to pass through here? Sure. They'd be setting up an ambush ahead, but we're taking the next left, then we should find a covered entry, that's our path."

"To the undercity?"

"Yup."

"Why the hell did we come into this section to do it?" he asked nervously. "Seriously boss, we're carrying more disposable wealth in one of these bags than this entire area is worth, and there's five of us. This is not a good place to be, alright?"

"We're going to need a nice safe exit…"

Luna snorted. "Boss, I know we see some shit slightly differently, but this is fucking Reaper territory, this is NOT a safe area."

"True, but if you cheerful fuckers will let me finish?" I said, as we took the planned left, then all stopped dead for a second. I sighed as we started pulling free the piles of dumped rubbish and boxes I should have been expecting, before gathering around the sealed entrance. "Todds, get the door, be ready to seal it after us."

"Yes, boss." He pulled out the plasma cutter and welding torch, then starting to check the entrance out.

It was old, clearly dating back to when this was a respectable area and people worked, instead of thieved for a living. The old entrance to the undercity was arched, once wide and more or less inviting, and no doubt tiled inside as those areas we'd seen elsewhere had been.

This was wide enough that I had to guess there'd be a mass transit hub nearby as well, not far from the surface, but it's clearly been given up on as too dangerous when the rest was abandoned.

The wide entrance was filled with solid metal doors, with a massive locking bolt and cover. There were also laminated overlapping warnings that the inside was dangerous, subject to collapse without warning and infested, and were in turn covered with centuries of graffiti.

Now it was all reduced to the point that all that you could say for sure was that Sharon wasn't going to be happy about what had been written here about her, and that Donald was likely to be long dead.

"Right, we need a safe place to exit with our loot, okay? Anywhere we enter this section is either too close to the gang territory, or too far away to be lugging all this gear in. If people see us enter with all this, and then a few hours later leaving again by the same entrance, we'll be hit. As it is? Likely they'll come after us regardless. That's why we brought directional mines, and the MADD grenades as a last resort.

"Instead we enter by one of the more dangerous routes, we mine the area behind us, set up a nice little secure position, and we get ready for any fuckers that try to hunt us, namely the gangs. You all with me so far?"

"Yeah?" Luna said. "Won't this draw the specters though?"

"I certainly fucking hope so. And just in case it doesn't?"

"Yeah?"

"That's what the gang is for," I finished, and waited.

"Why…oh, you evil bastard," Reign said, and I could hear the smile in her voice. "You're not leading us in here unaware of the gang, you're killing two birds with one stone."

"What?" Todds asked, crouching down by the grate, checking the seal on it. "Sorry, I'm missing something, but you all need to be aware this was sealed and then opened again, this has a recent lock applied, it'll cut easily enough with this, but someone's going to be pissed."

"That's fine, like I say, seal it again after us, we don't want it to be too easy, but also not impossible."

"And the reason you want a fucking gang chasing us?" he asked.

"Nice and simple," I said watching the street behind us, gun ready, and making note of the number of eyes watching us from the crossing streets, as well as the small drones that flitted overhead.

"We need specter bait."

CHAPTER THIRTY-SEVEN

The gang showed up fairly soon after Todds started cutting, people strolling past the end of the street looking in and seeing the sheer massed firepower pointed at them?

They moved on again, and damn sharp.

The miniature drones that hovered about the end of the alley, watching us, were getting so numerous that even with their automatic station-keeping features and anti-collision protocols, they kept bouncing off one another and every so often one would clatter to the ground.

By the time Todds had the door open and we were filing in? The local street kids were looting the crashed drones and running for it.

We saw the gangers starting in after us even as we pulled the damn doors closed, and Todds made only a cursory attempt at sealing the entrance behind us, knowing that if we made it too hard?

They'd just find another way down.

No, we wanted them following us, and desperate.

The passage ahead ended barely a handful of meters inside the doors, well-worn ancient steps leading down quickly, the passage bracketed by ornate handrails once, no doubt.

Now there were holes in the wall where the metal had been ripped free. Shattered tiles showed the bracing that had held on too long, and here and there piles of debris marked where something else had been torn free.

The lights were long gone, as were the accessible airflow systems, holes left in the ceiling and dangling wires all that marked their prior regularity.

The steps passed by under our feet as we jogged downwards, the bags clattering and pulling us off balance, the group spreading out to give each other room, as we ignored the scuttle of spiders the size of small dogs, and the hisses from nests that we passed.

Here and there corpses lay, long forgotten and festering, and I shook my head at the state of them, wondering what the hell had possessed them to come down here?

After a few back and forth flights of stairs, we reached a north/south passage, and set off along it after pausing just long enough for Todds to lay both a tripwire at the top of the last flight of steps, and a razorwire at the bottom.

It was evil, but we could already hear the shouts from above, and we needed the fuckers to slow down enough that we could set up an ambush.

A hundred meters down the passage it split into four, heading off in all directions, and we picked the left at random, pausing again as Todds attached a new razorwire across the passage, this time at neck height on an average man, and we were off again.

A minute or so later? The first screams rang out behind, and I grinned to myself in the darkness. There was utterly no reason for anyone to be down here under innocent circumstances, and I had no concerns that the razorwire would last long enough to be a problem to any possible future people.

Once deployed it was coated with a specialist coating that slowly evaporated. It was designed so that after a period of time, it could be seen easily, but for the first few days?

It was damn hard to spot, and they tended to break after a dozen impacts anyway, so fuck it.

If anyone blundered into it that wasn't a gang member actively hunting me? Well, they were also actively roaming around in what I believed to be a specter spawning or collection zone.

The fast death would be preferable and a lot more merciful than they were likely to receive under any other circumstances.

We took two more turns in the passage, weaving left and right and passing long sealed crossing corridors, before we finally came to a perfect spot to set up for the ambush I knew we needed.

The last few minutes we'd been passing bodies fairly regularly, the deeper we went the more frequent, and most of them had stupid things like clubs or home-made spears as their only weapon.

Few of them had more than a single mod, and some had none, but they were all alike in one way.

Besides the mods being ripped out, and vermin having fed on them anyway.

They were all dressed in a mixture of local overalls, factory worker garb and scruffy pants and top combos that screamed that they were on the bones of their arse financially, and were forced into accepting stupid deals.

The section we'd moved into now was an old mass transit system, with a collection of passages all terminating on a single platform.

The passage we'd come down was at one end, and opened out at one end, the next passage was sealed, and the one after had been as well, but something had broken through at some point.

The dried bloodstains on the floor, as well as the handprints and drag marks suggested whoever had gone into the broken section hadn't done it willingly either, which made it perfect.

We set up at the other end of the platform, facing the entrance we'd entered by, and we'd cut the various seals on the passages leading up to here as we went.

We cut sections of each of the covers free and dragged them with us, leaning them into makeshift barriers to hide behind. There wasn't a huge amount we could do, not when we had literally a few minutes if that, but still, it was the best we could manage, and as we quickly made our defenses, Todds attached more and more tethers of razorwire at weird angles as lethal surprises for our pursuers.

Shouting echoed down the corridors to us, as gangers panicked and tried to find us in the dark, all the while fighting over who got to go first.

We created a simple little triangle of barricades, each overlapping the other, and coming up to our waists, the barricade behind us and leading deeper into the tunnels was solid mainly, as were the ones we were hiding behind, but we didn't have the time to set up properly.

The best we managed was to fast weld three points to another section and clamber in, getting the guns in place and waiting, trying to ignore the fact that right to the left was the old mass transit tunnel, and absolutely anything could be living in it.

A minute passed, then a second, as we tried to make sense of the clanging noise we kept hearing from the gangers, until eventually, along with a load of shouted encouragement, a single figure came around the corner, swinging a long metal pole over and over in a constant windmill, as others behind him carried flaming torches.

"It's ingenuous," Luna whispered as he made it out onto the platform, pausing to catch his breath and looking around in all directions.

"It's annoying," I corrected, before sighting on him and waiting as he turned and shouted back behind him that he'd reached the end, and which way now?

A small gaggle of gangers gathered up around him, four or five, all arguing over which way to go, as they spotted cleared entrances to the other passages.

One of them was stupid enough to walk up and look into the nearest passage, waving his torch into it to make sure there wasn't any razorwire in the way.

He called to the others that it was clear, turned and took two steps towards the next one, and beheaded himself on the next wire that he'd totally missed.

More shouts rang out, and the idiot with the metal pole raised it, clearly intent on smacking it into the cable to free it, when I shot him in the head.

It wasn't a hard shot, hell the distance was short, there was no wind, they were utterly unprepared as well, having apparently forgotten that they were chasing a group of heavily armed mercs into the darkness, but the shot was beautiful.

It rang out at the same time as one of the idiots dropped something, and when we stayed hidden? The sudden collapse of the pole wielder was thought to be from something else at first.

Another of the group grabbed the pole, laughing at the dead man, before starting swinging it generally, clearly trying to get used to the weight. I couldn't help myself, and sighted in carefully, timing it just right…

As he banged one end of the pole off the edge of the platform, I fired. The bullet taking him in what might have been referred to as his 'pride and joy' if he'd had any pride in himself that was.

Instead he screeched in agony, clutched at his crotch, and tumbled out over the edge of the platform to smash face first into what looked to be knee deep water.

He coughed and spluttered, screaming and panting in pain, trying to get his words out as his 'friends' laughed and jeered, before one of them saw the first hints of movement.

The screams started in earnest then, as short, fat creatures I tried not to look at too carefully streamed up and out of the water, clambering onto the thrashing body and biting down, tearing chunks free.

They were short bodied, like a fat rat, but had six long limbs like a spider's, and a head that only a nightmare could love. It had a trio of eyes on stalks and tearing mandibles. The ganger started convulsing and frothing at the mouth as his friends pointed their guns and opened fire, blowing the shit out of him and his attackers.

A minute later, and the gunfire was echoing away, not a one of them having noticed that Reign had taken the opportunity to shoot three of their number that had been at the back of the group.

By the time that they did?

Well, out of at least ten that had walked out onto the platform, there were only five left, their super sneaky way of finding the razorwire was out of reach, and only one of them had a torch now.

We watched the dawning fear on their faces as they saw their friends bodies all around them, saw it in the way they twisted and spun, searching, cursing, for the threat, only to finally meet the first of the specters.

It stumbled out of the darkness, mouth agape, arms reaching, one leg dragging. It was filthy, covered in cobwebs, a spider the size of my goddamn hand scuttled across his back and froze as the torch was fixed on it, before hissing at them.

More came boiling out of crevices in the ambulatory corpse, from under tattered clothing, and we watched in horror. One of the number had the presence of mind to use a shotgun, pumping it and blasting half the specter apart with a single burst of buckshot, but all that did was release a plague of the spiders from their grisly home.

More raced free, and the gangers fired with abandon, one pulling out a canister of something as soon as his shotgun was empty, backing up and firing it as the spiders closed on him.

Then he collapsed to the floor as glittering dust cascaded down, more than half of it having shot up his nose, his choice of ways to go 'out' clearly being 'drugged up to the eyeballs, literally!

More were coming, both gangers and specters, as the last of the first group fell, and gunfire rang from the joining passages, tearing into the mass. Luna and Gessh stood silently, even as Reign fired once, then twice, sweeping the grazer across to make sure none of the spider infestation survived.

The sisters drew their swords and started quickly and silently killing any of the specters that drew close, clearly sensing and being drawn by our active mods, but where the majority of specters seemed utterly brainless, even they avoided the remains of the one that had become a walking spider nursery.

More staggered out slowly, after a few minutes, the sisters moved into the center of the platform, standing with a narrow gap on either side, as they stabbed out over and over again, the gunfire from the gangers dwindling as they were slowly overtaken.

Minutes passed as their gunfire died away entirely, and the specters kept coming, they moved in fits and starts, sporadic in their appearances, ten or twenty, then one or two, then another great wash of them, as they filtered along.

The sisters stepped back and Reign, Todds and I took a turn, steady firing over and over, then quickly pushing bodies back out of the way as we got a break in the onslaught. The fight was reasonably steady for the next fifteen or twenty minutes, with over two hundred eventually falling.

"Well, that was fun," Luna growled, cleaning her blade on a body, and looking around. "I think we need to seal that corridor back up," she said, and I nodded.

One of the connecting corridors had spat out only three specters in all of the fight, the vast, *vast* majority coming from two others, but those three? All walking spider nurseries.

Reign had been forced to sterilize the area each time with the grazer to make damn sure it was as clear as could be of the multi-legged little bastards.

Todds was moving already, none of us wanted to know what was down that passageway, the sight of the specters that it'd birthed, all with draukka spiders crawling in and out of them as they staggered along would give me nightmares for years to come.

As he sealed the previously blocked off entrance back up with some more scrap metal, making goddamn sure that it was as tight as possible, I started harvesting, while Reign, Luna and Gessh stripped and looted.

The bodies that is.

They stripped and looted the *bodies* of anything that was worth taking, valuables, tech, mods and belongings, as well as guns, ammo and the occasional grenade.

It took the better part of two hours for the full harvesting process, but in that time we'd cut free nearly sixty mods that were tier two, four mods that were tier three, and a fuck load of guns and ammo.

The gangers were almost all tier ones, but they at least had decent guns here and there. We took down the razorwire as we worked as well, seeing no reason to leave it up when it'd served its purpose. By the time we were ready to move deeper? We had a bag of mods for Oshbob, a half full bag of medikits, and a fuck load more guns.

Being realistic, we all knew that we'd have to be a bit pickier moving forwards, otherwise we'd end up bogged down by the sheer mass of crappy mods, but we decided to work until we couldn't collect any more, and then we'd filter the collection before returning to the surface.

We were feeling quietly confident, lugging the great mass of loot around with us, as we set off down the next passage, following the gradual decline, for a few minutes.

Reaching the bottom we took a right, then a left, Todds slinking ahead in one of the stealth suits, and we followed him, slowly heading deeper and deeper until we reached a section where a building project had sealed off the passage, a single door in the abrupt wall of steel before us being marked as 'emergency exit only'.

"Well boss?" Todds asked, and I shrugged, trying to contact the city datanet to query the building, only to find we were too deep to get a response.

"Fuck it, can you open it without damaging it too badly?" I asked, noting the thick mold, the deep sludge around the bottom of the door and the cobwebs etc. that made it clear that the door wasn't normally used.

Hopefully it'd be long abandoned, but when I'd checked this area there'd been nothing to suggest anything working here, so if it was? It was unlikely to be busy, and a bunch of specter hunters were likely to be greeted well, and pointed in the right direction to clean out any local threats. That was what I was betting on anyway.

Shame really, that I was totally fucking wrong.

CHAPTER THIRTY-EIGHT

The door was a nightmare to open, slow to unseal, and when it did? Something was propped up against it, making it a pain in the ass to see around.

Todds had needed to cut into the wall itself to deactivate the locking mechanism, and when he'd reached the section he needed, despite the distant noises that we could hear filtering down to us, he swore that whatever was going on in there, the door at least, was long abandoned.

When it finally swung open, rust cascading off in flakes and a squeal fit to wake the dead echoing around the space, the sight before us was the last thing I'd ever expected to see, as piled debris collapsed to the right and left, freeing the entryway.

The five of us stood there, trying to make sense of it at first, considering how deep underground we were, but this place?

We'd exited the passage into this new room about halfway up, the door we'd entered through leading to gantry that in turn lead up to the next level to our left, and down to the level below to the right.

That was fine, hell, that was practically *normal*. What wasn't fine? The central hollow mass of the structure we found ourselves in was filled with rows upon rows of bodies attached together on a slowly rotating gantry that reminded me of the old pictures of chickens on rotisseries.

From where we were, we could see hundreds, possibly thousands of bodies, and they were alive, or at least active. They twitched in undulating rhythms, masks over their heads, cables and hoses leading into the masks and plugged in over and over across their bodies, siphoning out some liquids, forcing in more.

They were spread out like starfish, head upright, arms out to the sides, legs spread, connecting posts running from one limb to the next, keeping them on their 'mount' as it gently swung, a connection at the top and bottom locking each into place with inches to spare before the next body in line.

This wasn't what I'd been expecting, this was a thing of nightmares! Hundreds, probably thousands of people were connected to the great construction, with a solid thrum of power filing the air, hoses were humming liquid being harvested…I moved forwards to the edge of the gantry, looking out over and down, seeing at least five more levels disappearing downwards from here, and three more leading up, the air was suddenly hot and humid I realized, and here and there below us, I saw automated machines moving on rails, selecting a 'frame' with its humanoid occupant and removing it, replacing it with one that thrashed and gargled as they tried to escape the tubes.

"What the absolute fuck is this place?" Reign asked in a hushed whisper.

"I have no idea," I admitted. "The signs were that there was a major infestation, but this?"

"An infestation of…?" Luna asked.

"Specters," I said. "It looked like specters, what the hell do you think I'd be bringing us here for? This is…"

There was a sound from above, and we all looked up, seeing another machine, this one though? It wasn't here to change the frames.

It saw us, and its guns opened up.

"Fuck, run!" I barked, lifting my rifle and opening fire as it did, bullets slamming into its armoring as it closed on us, its own fire sparking and ricocheting around us. Todds twisted, ready to race back into the passage we'd come from, only to have a secondary door, one suspended over the first, slide down with a clang as the structure sealed itself.

I had moved too, and barely managed to stop from hitting the now sealed door, turning and racing for the pile of debris we shoved aside to enter.

There were piles of steel, sheeting and more there, and it'd at least absorb a few of the bullets for us.

The machine though? I had no idea if it was sentient, if it was a defender and running on automation or what the hell it was, but the damn thing had more limbs than any spider, it was climbing down the wall towards us using the rails, the tubes, piping and wall supports.

It had an ovoid central body, two upper and two lower mounts each with what looked like standard assault rifles attached, but belt-fed rather than magazine, a dozen or more eyes on the front, long tentacle-like arms and as it flowed down the wall, alarms started up all around.

The clangs of more doors being sealed rang out distantly, as the assault rifles chattered, bullets tracing the path behind us as the machine navigated obstructions, clearly used to the paths it needed, as we ran, dodging hails of fire, sliding under the piled scrap.

Turrets spun up around us on the walls, one managing to tag me on the left side, denting an armor plate and making me gasp in pain as I returned fire and took the fucker down.

I barely made it under cover as more opened up, Reign ahead of me, slinging her grazer, clearly deciding that there was fuck all flesh to effect on this thing, and dragging her sniper rifle into place instead.

Luna and Gessh backed up, firing at the machine, peppering it with dozens of rounds, and Todds was frantically searching for a more defensible location, while taking down turrets as fast as he could.

"Reign, fuck that shit up!" I ordered her, before wincing as one of the ricocheted bullets from the girls sparked off and hammered into a frame loaded body.

The bullet passed straight through, leaving a spray of blood on the one behind it, as the first sagged, then started thrashing.

"Fuck!" I snarled, knowing damn well we should be rescuing these people, but that we could only do that if we won this fight.

I searched the area, quick as I could, taking two more turrets down as I leant aside, then ducked, avoiding return fire. I saw two options, first, we stayed where we were, fired on the damn thing—Reign was even now lining up a shot—until it was dead, and then we dealt with whatever else came along, or we moved.

We had limited cover where we were, sheets of tubing and more, clearly used in repairs and in forming the interior of this place were piled here, but that was it, we were already hiding behind it, and it wasn't like it was light enough we could hide beneath it.

The machine was clambering out as much as down, clearly moving to put itself in a position where it could get at us without the limited cover we had.

Luna cried out then, falling as she failed to dodge fast enough, and several shots landed at once, hitting her in one of her modified legs.

She hit the floor, falling out of cover, and I cursed, all of us opening fire at once, peppering the outside of the machine with small arms fire, as Gessh dragged her sister back into cover.

"Fucking come on Reign!" I barked, dropping my rifle and dragging the shotgun free, pumping it and firing a solid slug at the thing.

It twisted, the slug glancing off, making it clear that the armoring was heavy enough to ignore just about anything, when Reign *finally* fired.

The machine was halfway down to us, braced atop an outrunning post that helped to hold the forms in place, and clinging to the underside of a crossing gantry, when she shot it.

She'd clearly been taking her time, knowing she'd only get one chance before she was identified as the main threat, and whoo-boy was she the main threat.

The solid round was both armor piercing by dint of being fired from a fucking sniper rifle, and being a specially designed round to do maximum penetrative damage, and it showed.

One of the creature's eyes exploded, the round punching through the camera system and burrowing deep inside, taking out who knew how many other systems before it ran out of energy, but the effect was clear.

One side of the machine simply shut down, the arms releasing, and it fell. The other side wasn't strong enough, or wasn't ready at any effect, and the sudden shift threw off both its aim, and its timing.

It'd been moving forwards, multiple arms releasing and clinging onto things at the same time. When half simply released all at once?

It fell, a single arm trying to cling on and only succeeding in sending it swinging into the wall, head first.

It hit with a crash of breaking glass and resounding steel on steel, before tumbling free, hitting the gantry way below and bouncing off, plunging downwards.

"Luna!" I grunted, forcing myself to move, jogging around the corner, slinging my shotgun and reloading my rifle as I went. "You alright? Everyone okay?" I called out, getting a mixed response from the team, even as I cursed, checking my side and wincing over what I damn well knew were broken ribs.

"I will be!" Todds growled, squinting and firing a trio of rounds into another turret, before cursing. "We've got movement up above boss!"

"What is it?" I called back, making it to Luna's side and cutting the pants leg away, looking over the damage to the prosthetic. It wasn't bad, some dents and scratches, along with a section where a bullet had lodged, and was currently releasing repeated electrical shocks.

"What the fuck?" I dragged it free with the edge of my knife, then dropping it when it shocked me. "Capture and containment rounds!" I called out, finally realizing what it was. "The turrets aren't firing full on either!"

I'd known I was lucky when I took the hit to my side full on and got away with just pain, instead of a hole through-and-through as I would have had if it was an armor piercing round. Now I knew why.

"We need to get the fuck out of here," I said definitely. "Todds, what've you seen?"

"Nothing you're going to like," he replied grimly. "Two more of those things down there, one looks like it's been getting worked on, the other? Heavy machine guns."

"Grenades," I replied almost conversationally. "I think this is a situation that calls for grenades."

"Only if you don't mind killing the poor bastards in the frames!" Gessh pointed out.

"Fuck's sake," I muttered under my breath, looking at the body that was strung out nearest to us. It was, as previously noted spread out and locked into place, but...

The more I looked at it the more convinced I was that something was insanely wrong here. More so than the fact the fucker was locked into place like a Winter's Night ornament, but that the bodies were locked into place, with tubes inserted, feeding, draining and doing who knew what else. The victims' faces were covered, the majority of their heads were in fact, and they were all modded, as near as could be seen, arms and legs, torsos...

"Are they alive?" I asked as Reign shocked me out of my stupor.

"What?" she snapped absently, sighting down her rifle and tracking the target below as it wound its way between stacks of equipment. "Come on you fucker, look up...just look up at me..."

"Are they dead?" I asked again, pointing at the nearby bodies.

"They're moving, boss," Luna replied. "Look, you want grenades or not?"

"Fuck's sake, no, not until we know for sure what they are." I countered the order. "But Luna, Gessh. One of you fuckers get closer to the bodies, find out what the hell they are."

"Now?" Gessh asked, disbelievingly.

"Yes, fucking right now," I ordered. "Head upwards, everyone, if they're sending those fuckers from below lets head up, but if we know they're all brain dead, or whatever, then it gives us options, alright? Otherwise we should be rescuing these people!"

"Yeah...we're not rescuing them," Luna replied. "Boss, these people have had serious levels of surgery done, whatever the system they're connected to? I don't see them surviving being disconnected without a LOT of credits being spent on them."

"Just fucking do it!" I snarled, swapping the standard magazine out for an armor piercing one, then sighting in with my rifle as Reign finally let loose with a shot.

It hit the machine in the middle of the back, where two plates overlapped, denting it, but ricocheting off into the darkness. I sighted in on that same spot, as best I could down five levels and between pipes and outcroppings, and fired.

I squinted, leading the target, and fired.

I also totally missed as it twisted at the last minute, squeezing between two sections as it angled itself up towards us, the reaching metal tentacles grabbing onto protrusions and pulling the body through the gap.

My second shot rang out, along with two more as I switched to triple shot, aiming at the upturned optical sensors, as Reign fired again and again, the boom of the sniper rifle overpowering my own lesser barks.

Where my shots were powerful, and they were, it was a good fucking rifle after all, hers did considerably more damage.

The front of the machine jerked and shivered as it rocked under the impacts, before the twin miniguns on its back opened up.

Where the assault rifles of the other had been bad enough, firing at that speed, the miniguns? They were a whole new level of fucking nasty.

The rounds that flashed across the distance between us were practically a solid line of lead, and fuck they hammered into the pathetic shit we'd been hiding behind.

The steel piping was sent flying, the walls grew dents and the air was filled with glowing ricocheting rounds.

If that wasn't enough as we ran and dodged, panicking under the insane levels of fire? The weapons tracked us. Lines of solid light drew across the gap as Reign, Todds and I frantically ran across the gantry, and the metalwork was slowly sawn apart behind us.

We'd not get far, we knew that, but as soon as we sprinted around the spiraling walkway, we came under more and more turret fire as well, hitting us and sending us staggering.

I looked up, hissing in pain as my left arm died, the electrical charge the round embedded in it was discharging, finally made sense.

They were containment rounds, and while the machine that was chasing us was tearing the room apart with its concentrated fire? It too, was firing the same kind of rounds, just the sheer level of them was causing crazy levels of damage as it chased us.

There were three levels leading up and every revolution that took us out of the line of sight of the insane machine below, instead brought us into sight of the turrets!

I dragged the rifle around, firing on the turrets, stitching lines of destruction across the wall, even as they fired back at me. I side-stepped and dodged, ducked and wove, my left arm quivering over and over, until the charge dissipated.

It came back online, twitching, the muscles realigning as the arm returned to factory default, rebooting…and I twisted, bring it up as I saw a new turret ahead.

It fired and I couldn't dodge in time, not running as I was.

Three hits, shoulder, lower arm, then stomach, and I hissed. My armor was doing fuck all to resist these, the tips coated in some kind of impact glue, discharging shock upon shock, freezing my cybernetics.

And the hit to the stomach?

Too close to my spine.

My legs gave out and I tumbled to the floor, crashing on the steel framing, bouncing, the rifle trapped under me as I thrashed.

Gessh and Luna were nowhere in sight, hell they must have gone a different way to avoid the turrets, but nearby I could see Reign was down as well, shaking, convulsing as the turrets hit us both again, and again, single shot now, clearly a suppression round until we could be captured, but fuck!

Todds…

I forced my right hand to release the grip of the rifle, curling the fingers through the gaps in the metal walkway and dragging myself forward, hissing in pain as the turret switched from 'he's down, keep him down' into 'shoot that motherfucker again and again' mode.

I cried out, then convulsed as three rounds hit me near on simultaneously and I bit down on my tongue, shaking as the muscles tensed.

After a few seconds as the latest rounds ran out of the fast releasing charges, I regained control, letting out a bloody sigh and a gurgle, my teeth having chewed the shit outta my tongue in that last round…but the convulsing and my fingers being laced through the walkway had an unexpected bonus.

I'd dragged myself out of the line of fire entirely without knowing it. My left arm began the reboot process, as did my spinal taps, but I didn't have the luxury of time…

I could hear heavy firing still going on below and somewhere off to the side, rounds were hitting the walkway nearby, sending weak pulses through the metal as I dragged a medium medikit free—I didn't need a medium, hell a small would have probably done, but I didn't have the luxury of time to fuck around.

This was what came to hand, this was what was getting used.

I jabbed it into my tongue, keeping myself pressed as far into the corner as I could as I tried not to scream and let the stream of nanites fall free.

They poured into the chewed tongue, and then out and over it. A small portion was used in a flash, rebuilding and repairing, while the majority searched my body for more damage.

I dumped the injector, and dragged my hurricane revolver free, twisting and lining up on the nearest turret, firing one shot before taking a hit to the side of the head that had me crashing down again.

This time the surge of electricity was dampened by the helmet—a feature I'd not needed before, but fucking loved already—but the sheer impact had almost knocked me out.

I struggled back into my tiny safe zone, shaking my head, then trying again, this time aiming for the fucker that was keeping Reign down.

That one I got, the cascade of sparks and the explosion as something detonated in the wall under the turret making that clear, even as more fire rang out, and voices rose.

"Boss! Reign!" Todds shouted out. "If you can hear me, you need to move to the bodies!"

I shook myself, twisting and squinting through the metal at the slowly turning massive rack filed with them, then down, noting that the big fucker was in sight again, and it'd soon get its guns on us again.

I might have survived the suppression rounds so far, but there was no chance that if that fucker hit me I was just going for a nap. That was dirt-nap territory right there.

Possibly in a small box due to the loss of limbs.

"Turret!" I barked out, shifting slightly and trying to hit the one that had me pinned again, failing miserably. "We're pinned by a turret…"

"I'm coming!" Luna called, and I twisted, my heart in my mouth as I saw her swing into sight, literally clinging to the outside of the frame that held someone.

"Get back!" I screamed. "The turret…"

I leant out of cover again, ignoring the shots that rang out straight away, firing at the turret over and over until it took me down, spasming, and Reign dragged me into cover again.

"You crazy bastard!" She groaned, shaking her hands free of the wash of electricity from touching me. "Stay down!"

"The turrets…" I groaned, and she shook her head.

"They won't fire on the bodies!" She cut me off, and I stared at her confused. "The turrets and the tank thing!" she explained. "Gessh and Luna got too close to the bodies, and they stopped being tracked! Whoever controls this place doesn't want their 'farm' damaged!"

"Shit, seriously?" I groaned, shaking my hand and trying to get some feeling back into it.

"Yeah, you crazy brave bastard," she said, a smile of pride clear in her voice as she reloaded her sniper rifle. "Get ready, Todds is…"

She broke off as Todds opened fire, the turret exploding, before he called out to us.

"All clear, now move!"

Reign scrambled to her feet before I could make sense of the world, sniper rifle slung onto her back as she backed up, squinting at the edge of the walkway, and the distance to the gently swinging bodies.

Then she ran and leapt off the side.

CHAPTER THIRTY-NINE

I twisted around, dragging myself to my feet and staring after her, my heart in my mouth as Reign flew out over six stories of metal and pursuing monster machines…

Only to catch onto a post between one of the slowly swinging bodies, connected to their ankles, and then flipped herself up.

She was like a lanton, leaping from brace to brace, not a care for the drop below, until she could stand comfortably atop a slowly rising section of bodies.

The one that she'd grabbed first was shaking and making gargling noises, but beyond the shock, didn't seem too badly disturbed, and I winced, imagining what the impact of me, fully armed and armored would do to those chains and braces.

I squinted left and right, searching for a solid link to jump to, afraid I'd snap someone's sodding feet off and have the brace come free, but there was nothing.

I backed up, still searching…

…then the whine of the miniguns spinning up rose from below and I was running before my mind finished processing it. I jumped, bracing one foot on a corner section and the other on the top of the gantry, then flung myself out into space, my arms reaching desperately as the scream of minigun rounds tracked after me, carving the gantry apart.

My hands reached out, fingers extending and…I fucking missed.

Where Reign had leapt across like a goddamn lanton, I plunged past, my fingers inches from the post I'd been aiming for.

I hit the next level a few meters further on and down, smashing full bodied into the gently swaying and unsuspecting victim before me, the weight, the unprepared impact alone causing bones to break.

I grabbed onto them, half sliding down their torso, ripping cables and tubing free, liquids and solids cascaded from the broken connections, as did electricity, sparking wildly as I dragged myself up the unfortunate figure, hissing as I tried to ignore the possibly fatal damage I'd done them.

Shots rang out again, the miniguns falling silent as more and more rounds were fired downrange, and I hissed and cursed, dragging myself up, reaching…

And a hand appeared from a sudden blur as Todds stealth field dropped, the mad bastard standing atop two of the swinging forms with a handgun in one hand, firing down past me, as he helped me up with the other one.

"Fucking fucks…" I groaned, dragging myself up and planting a boot on the shoulder of the spread eagled figure below me, using that to level myself up and onto the frame, figuring the faster I was off them the better. "…shit am so, so—" I started to apologize, only to have Todds shift for a second and shoot my unwilling climbing assistant in the side of the head.

"What the hell?" I asked him, shocked.

"What?" he asked, confused, then grinning. "You thought they were alive?"

"They're fucking moving."

"Specters after all, boss," he assured me, shaking his head. "The whole farm, specters being hooked up and drained, the machines protect it and it looks like the others load it and keep them going. No clue what's going on, but it's a fucking weird place!"

"The machines…?" I asked, looking down and swaying as I tried to catch my balance, shifting and grabbing the rotating system overhead.

"You need catch the rhythm, boss," Todds said. "This row is going up and back, they're on wheels or something, so the level above are going clockwise, but you're seeing the bottom, they're going past you and back behind as they lift, while the one we're on is at the top of its arc, heading ahead. Just work like they're monkey-bars from when you were in basic."

"Swing from them?" I asked, vaguely getting the gist, even if I didn't know the name.

"You move from one to the other, feet going in one direction, arms the other, it'll take you a minute, we had them in the scout obstacle courses, so I'm ahead of you that's all!"

He stepped down onto the rising next form, took the time to shoot the occupant in the head, then resumed firing on the machine below.

It was still coming, the miniguns tracking us, but unable or unwilling to fire while we hid amongst its charges.

Reign's rifle boomed from somewhere overhead and it staggered, sparks rising, before it started to climb again, another round slamming into it a few seconds later and starting black smoke curling up from somewhere deep inside.

The machine clambered two more meters, as the smoke grew thicker, before it shut down, sagging and hanging from the section of gantry it'd been traversing.

A final shot from Reign, this time at a tentacle, and the body fell, three stories, straight down to land atop its half built companion.

Both laid there, silent, as I shifted slowly, keeping my balance as our row slid further and further back.

"This way, boss," Todds called to me, stepping into the middle of the two 'wheels' of forms, and grabbing onto a rising post. He clung to it, lifting up into the air, grinning down at me as he was carried higher.

I looked about for an alternative, then sighed and moved to the same spot, grabbing the next post and clinging on, trying to ignore the figure who I literally dangled below.

They thrashed and made muffled noises, but as close as I was now, and paying attention?

They were clearly not alive, not in the usual sense.

The body was grey, not the somewhat solid healthy grey that some orcs had either, more the 'I'm a single step from rotting' grey.

While they were clean, more or less, presumably they were jetted down before they were loaded into the system, they were still bodies, and I was damn thankful for the helmet's air filters.

I dangled for about thirty seconds as I was lifted out and around, before I managed to brace my feet atop the next frame, and then Gessh was there, her hand reaching down to grab mine as I rolled round.

One more level we 'rode' the specters for, until we were at the roof, and the turrets all around us were dead. Here handholds, presumably 'just in case' were readily available and once again I gritted my teeth and dragged myself across.

Dropping onto the walkway next to Luna, I shook my head, blowing out a long breath and moving quickly back from the edge, a sick feeling rising steadily in me as I tried not to look over the side.

"You okay, boss?" she asked, and I nodded and tried to wave her off. "Boss?"

"I'm fine." I lied. "I just…" I took a deep breath, then looked around, seeing the others were watching me as well. "Fuck's sake, alright look, I threw myself off a cliff in my armor alright? When I was shot down in the fingers, to make sure nobody found my friends? I powered down my armor and wiped the locational data, then rebooted and threw myself off a cliff to hide it."

"Right?" Reign said, having heard this before.

"Well, there was a storm going on and I didn't realize that the ground below was another cliff, and another. I fell and bounced for a long way, a hell of a long way, and that's why my mods all needed replacing. I was seriously broken up, my suit was trashed, hell they almost left the suit on the mountainside, destroyed it with thermite grenades, that's how badly I miscalculated, and after that?"

I shrugged and gestured to the space below us. "I don't have an issue in an aircab, but like this?" I shook my head. "I don't like it, that's all."

"Understandable." Todds whistled. "If I fell off a cliff and almost died I think I'd stay away from high places too."

"Yeah, well." I shrugged, before squeezing Reign's hand, as it found its way into my own. "Thanks everyone, but we need to find out what the fuck is going on here."

We looked around, finding a seriously thick and well protected door at the very end of the walkway, previously flanked by two turrets, but now very much alone.

"Todds," I said. "Open that door."

"Yessir," he said, moving ahead, pulling out a small scanner and getting to work on the door.

"You okay?" Reign asked me quietly, moving in close as I leant against the wall, pointedly not looking down.

"Yeah," I assured her, getting control of myself and nodding. "Honestly, don't worry."

"I am," she told me. "So are the others, Luna and Gessh sent me direct messages asking me to distract you."

"I'm fine." I pushed off the wall and moved to the edge, gripping the handrail and looking out over the slowly rotating mass before us. "Who the fuck would do something like this?" I muttered. "And more to the point, fucking *why?*"

"Specter research groups." Reign shrugged. "Sure it's weird, but there's a few of them."

"Like the ones we sold the Banshee to," I said. "But why this?"

"Let's find out," Todds said from a few feet away, and I realized I'd said that last bit on the team, tac-net, rather than in private to Reign.

The door clunked as locks disengaged, and slid back, alarms going off again, as someone tried to stop the door opening, but Todds snorted and overrode it.

Seconds later the massive door, clearly designed to hold off an army of specters, slid back easily, and we stepped in, moving into a clean, well-lit corridor that led to…

…to a small apartment complex.

An apartment complex filled with terrified lab-tech types, and a single security guard who nodded a greeting to us from the floor, his guns set aside neatly as he waited.

"What the fuck is this shit?" I asked walking in and looking around.

"It's not worth my fucking life is what it is," the security guard said. "I surrender. Under Artem City Law, as a formally surrendered…"

"Yeah, yeah." I waved at him. "You didn't shoot at me, you're fine." I hesitated. "Wait, were you controlling the…"

"We woke up when the alarms went off," he said quickly. "The whole system is automated, we're here to monitor it and to make sure that the traps are emptied daily."

"Traps?" I asked, glancing at one wall of the main office, then shaking my head in disbelief. There were dozens of capture traps along the lower sections on screens, and a handful of them were flashing as 'full' with a machine like the ones we'd fought earlier moving between them, firing on the helpless specters that were caught in a pit, before dragging them out with a tentacle and locking them down onto its back.

I shook my head in disgust as the screens showed more being captured, while still other machines loaded them into frames, attaching them to the lower levels.

"What the absolute fuckery is going on here?" I whispered in disbelief.

"How long have you got?" one of the researchers asked, biting his lower lip and looking from one of us to the next. "Look, I'm sorry you were fired on, but you broke in here, and…"

"In an abandoned section of the Undercity," I pointed out. "We're specter hunters."

"Hunters?" one of them piped up. "Why?"

"Because they're fucking dangerous?" I replied, non-plussed. "You know, the whole 'rip your mods out and eat your face' thing?"

"That's a myth," the speaker snapped, moving forwards, dressed in long pants, a black floor length lab coat and a bright red top that read 'ask me about my…' and was then crossed out as he glared at us. "You people are only adding to the problems faced by the Ambulatory Confused! With the problems they face already? You spreading misinformation about them so you can be paid for murder disgusts me!"

"Murder?" I muttered, stunned, as Reign started to laugh.

"The fucking 'Ambulatory Confused'…" she barked out, before shaking her head. "Are you for fucking real?"

"Jared, we've discussed this…" one of the others said and the idiot cut them off.

"Yes, we have and your bigotry disgusts me! They're confused, that's all, they're only dangerous if you startle them, who knows what still lives inside there, and these…these *jack-booted thugs* have been executing them as if they were rabid animals!"

"You need a fucking reality check, my son," I said.

"You mind if I get up off the floor?" the security guard asked calmly, and I looked to Gessh and nodded towards him.

"Up you get friend." Gessh said cheerfully, checking him over and making sure he had no other weapons on him, before collecting his up and she went to sit on a seat in the corner, killing the alarms as he passed the main console.

"So, okay, you're doing research on specters," I said, dismissing the foaming idiot as unimportant, and speaking to the first of the researchers to talk. "You look like you're a bright lad with a sensible head on his shoulders, care to fill me in?"

"It's classified!" Jared snapped.

"It's an NDA," a woman said with a sigh, rubbing at the bridge of her nose as she removed a pair of goggles. "Look, you don't seem like you're murderers and rapists, which is great, because I had neither of those on my to-do list for today. Can we assume you're civilized and this can be written off to a misunderstanding?"

"We were shot," Reign pointed out. "Repeatedly."

"You broke in," she countered.

"We're working for the city of Artem, conducting a licensed sweep of the area, searching for specters," Reign fired back. "We're supposed to be here, are you?"

"We're registered," she replied, then winced. "But I think the project was supposed to be a lot smaller than it grew to, and yeah, it's under an NDA, so it's not on the public servers, so whoever sent you probably didn't know about it."

She bit her lip, then nodded.

"How about this, we've got a load of specters that are deemed too damaged to be of use, they're stunned and sealed in the vault, we didn't want to kill them, but we can't use them either. How about a compromise?"

"We're listening," I said, leaning against the wall.

"You clean them out, do…you know. What you do," she said, wincing as Jared drew a deep breath, only to go quiet as Luna drew her pistol and inserted it into his mouth.

"Oh, I'm sorry, did you have something you wanted to say?" she asked, glaring at him.

"-Gno-" He choked on the barrel.

"Good boy. Remember that feeling, next time there'll be more, and you're already running a serious risk of heavy metal poisoning."

He frowned as she removed the gun and Gessh helpfully added in the details.

"She means you keep your fucking mouth shut while the adults are talking, or she's going to shoot you."

"Ummmm." Jared closed his eyes and nodded, shaking a little.

"And no pissing on the floor," I snapped. "I hate it when people do that." I shook my head, sighing, then pulled my helmet off, setting it down on the table nearby as I took a seat. "Alright, explain the vault and what the fuck is going on down here, do that, and maybe some coffee, and we'll see."

CHAPTER FORTY

All told it took two hours for us to drink several cups of coffee each, to visit the facilities, to visit the vault and then to finally leave the research base.

They were conducting experiments there on the interface between nanites and the mods, and the reasons that specters came about. Basically looking for a silver bullet, something that was there in all of them.

They'd found fuck all so far, but knowing the world the way I did, I guessed this was some corpo tax write off more than a serious research plan.

The slow rotation on the racks apparently calmed the specters, they'd tried keeping them in various different ways over the years, but this was the latest, best version.

The majority of the staff bore us absolutely no ill will for neither the damage to the security bots—they were there to stop the specters if they broke loose somehow—nor for the specters we'd killed.

They had drones which would repair the facility, and enough security drones still that the ones that we'd destroyed were a loss they could take, and their leader had contacted the sponsoring corporation.

They apparently didn't care that we were down there, though they weren't happy about the damage to the facility and viewed the whole thing as a governmental botch job when we explained—bullshitting for all we were worth—that we were being paid to sweep the area.

They warmed up to us a lot though when they realized that it was our team that had caught the banshee. Suddenly, provided we agreed to give 'Hari-BalliGag-Systems' first refusal at any banshee data or banshees themselves that we got access to, then we were considered 'fellow professionals'

An agreement was struck that we would keep our mouth shut, and they would let us kill the 'broken' specters they couldn't make use of, in the vault, and claim them as 'free range' specters.

Reign, in a stroke of fucking genius, claimed we were being paid to retrieve any mods at tier three or above for research into the models, looking for commonality or some such shit.

We demanded those, and were told that the corpo didn't give two fucks officially, and that for a small fee we could remove a certain percentage of the bodies in the racks that held tier three.

We settled on ten thousand as a 'thank you' to cover the restocking costs, and the corpo dickhead cut the line as soon as the payment was received through his system.

The end result was that we emerged from the hunt on the far side with few medikits filled—we couldn't risk them seeing what we were doing and so hadn't dared to use the harvester—but with no less than fifteen tier three and four tier four mods in the bag.

That would have made it worthwhile in itself, but we deliberately moved off through the tunnels on the far side of the lab, and spent the next who knew how many hours harvesting where we could.

The first location was a disappointment, apparently the traps were working well, and the usual wandering idiot brigade—that weren't snapped up to be politicians or lawyers—had already been caught and loaded onto frames.

That meant that when we found them, the specters were few and far between, with Todds eventually slinking off ahead of us, leaving sections of the wall scratched to show which way he'd gone, while we set up a kill zone.

It wasn't hard to be fair, the sheer amount of random rubbish that had somehow found its way down here meant that there were literally more building materials than we knew what to do with.

We made small trip hazards, strung razorwire here and there, and made killing fields by strategically placing barriers to funnel the specters into certain areas.

The next hour was notable mainly by the fucking boredom we all felt, Todds roamed far and wide finding the specters and dragging them back in small groups for us to kill, and mainly Reign, Luna and Gessh and I talked and joked.

"Seriously, you've never heard anything like it." I sighed. "The noise that the little bastard made when Fergie caught him trying to steal that double bass and punted him in the balls? Ah good times." I grinned sadly, shaking my head in fond remembrance.

"Sounds like your experience of the army was a lot different from ours," Luna grunted. "Seriously, even half orcs don't get the level of respect of 'normal' troops, we were generally sent on the shittiest missions, over and over again, I'd have happily stabbed our C/O any day of the week."

"I think most of us feel that way, when we're in service." I muttered, dragging the latest body over to the pile and starting work on it.

"You feel any differently now you're out?" Reign asked curiously and I snorted.

"Don't be daft. I'd shoot Tyrannus in the face right now if I could, even knowing the major was behind all that shit, shooting us down and sending us out there to get killed in the first place I mean. That he wasn't quite as much of a shit as I thought he was? Well, you've gotta remember that he was—"

"Incoming!" Todds bellowed into the tac-net, and we could hear him pounding the ground as he came.

"Todds?" I asked quickly. "What's going on?"

"Something changed!" he snapped. "I took a corner and found a fucking wall of them coming at me!"

"How many?" I asked, gesturing the others to take their places.

"Fucking hundreds!"

"How the hell?" I grunted. "Fuck it, just get back here asap, we'll be ready," I said, glancing at the others. "Get ready people, you heard the same shit I did."

"Ready," Gessh said, nodding and grinning to her sister. "Sooner we kill these fuckers, sooner we get some Dondo."

"He's no longer a person then?" Reign laughed. "You two planning on being 'Dondo'd' tonight?"

"He was never a person," Luna assured her. "Believe me, he's a walking delivery system for a weapon of mass pleasure, that's it."

"Well, I wasn't going to comment on how little conversation you guys enjoy together, you know besides 'do me like that' and so on," Reign replied grinning.

"Honestly, are we just meat to you?" I asked, shaking my head in mock sadness.

"No, don't worry dear," Reign assured me, racking a round in the sniper rifle and checking the line of sight as we got ready. "We only treat certain people like that."

"Just the ones that are really, really good at it," Luna pointed out. "You know they could prescribe him as a cure for depression? 'Take Dondo twice a day, you'll be fine' and shit like that."

"Yeah, except you'd never be able to walk it off." Gessh shook her head. "Seriously boss, don't beat yourself up about it, Reign likes you for more than just that, personality, and…well…other stuff. Probably."

"I'd have to really," Reign agreed, setting her gear out.

"You know, it's a good job I'm not self-conscious," I growled. "You fuckers could give me issues."

"You love us really." Reign laughed. "So Luna, how much does an anti-depression treatment cost, you know, for a friend."

"Todds," I said into the tac-net, speaking over the chuckles. "I'm really in need of something to kill, alright?"

"I've got you there boss!" He assured me, his breath whistling as he tore along distant passages.

Two minutes later he finally made it out ahead of us, weaving in and out of the cleared lines of approach. He'd barely reached us, skidding to a halt and bent over, hands on his knees panting as he tried to get his breath back, when the first of those that were chasing him came into view in the distance.

"What the hell did you do?" I asked, stunned, as Reign opened fire, taking a ghoul in the distance down before it could direct those around it,

"Nothing!" Todds swore, straightening and pointing. "I literally…took a corner…and boom, there they were…right in front of me…hundreds walking in lines."

"Lines?"

"They were…searching for something…I'm betting," he forced out.

"Searching for…" I broke off, looking at my left arm as I put the pieces together. "The banshee. It was tracking the original tech, maybe us harvesting the specters does something, gives off a signal or something?" I guessed, before shaking my head and dismissing it.

"Well, maybe that'll make the harvesting easier then!" Reign suggested. "Less searching around?"

"Or more dangerous," I said, starting firing, single shots, leading the target and firing as the specters ran at us.

There were enough that when I missed one, a second behind them tended to 'catch' the round for me instead.

Luna and Gessh opened fire, as did Todds, and the real job for the day started all over again.

When we finally trooped out into the dim morning light, filthy, stinking and exhausted? We'd filled our medikits, we'd emptied most of our magazines and we were the proud—if temporary—owners of a hundred and seven mods, ranging from tier two to four.

The flight from where we emerged, back to the warehouse was mainly in silence, we'd spread out, myself and Reign in the one with all the mods and medikits, the girls and Todds in our own aircar, with Dondo flying them.

When we landed, all of us headed together over to see Oshbob, Dondo making us wait in the warehouse as he apparently discussed things with his boss, and I took it that the fact we'd shown up with a fuck load of gear ready for him was a bit of a surprise, all things considered.

Just over two hundred small medikits were full, ready to be handed over, and because I wasn't goddamn stupid, a further thirty-seven were full in another bag, ready for us to store them, along with all the medium and large kits, as I was fucked if I was handing them over.

Between the seventeen hundred and eighty-six specters we'd managed to kill over almost an entire goddamn day in the depths, we'd earned a grand total of fifty credits per specter, which came to eighty-nine thousand, three hundred credits.

That the guild was receiving the same amount as we were registered through them was a pain in the ass, but at least it made damn sure that Julius was going to be on our side over everything.

Then add on the hundred grand in medikits, at half the retail value to Oshbob that was, and finally, the guns and mods? I was very sure that I was going to be walking away with the parts I needed for my suit one way or the other.

The orc eventually made his way down to meet us in the warehouse, ignoring me entirely, as he smiled at and spoke to the sisters first.

Knowing that the arrogant fuckstick hated humans, I'd already suggested I take a step back, and Gessh was running point on this now, separating the arms out from the legs, laying them side by side on the floor where Oshbob could see them.

He moved through the pile, checking things over, occasionally muttering things to a pair that followed him along, some crazy looking goblin and a carver, the pair seemingly inches away from utter madness as they picked and kicked the goods.

"Where?" the goblin asked suddenly, looking at me.

"Where what?" I asked, despite my previous determination to leave this to the girls to sort.

"Where the rest?"

"The rest of what?" I asked, confused.

"Rest of bodies!" He sighed, shaking his head. "You leave? This many bodies just left?"

"There's a few thousand of them," I said. "We spent a full goddamn day in the depths, we left the bodies, and we left the shitty mods, no sense in hauling them around."

"He's got a point," the carver added, straightening with a hand held in his, looking over the connectors as he spoke absently. "That many corpses moldering under a section of the city will bring disease. I hope you reported the location to a clean-up crew?"

"Totally," I lied.

"Give location," the goblin said quickly. "We go, make sure, for good of city."

"You've not got the time to be dealing with that." Oshbob grunted at the goblin.

"Old d—" the goblin started to complain, before shutting up at the glare the orc gave him, then glaring at me as if I was somehow to blame for all of this.

"So," Oshbob growled. "You expect me to just what? Magic more parts up for your suit out of my arse?"

"You said you could do it, that it'd cost a hundred thousand per section. I'm missing from both legs the main actuators, the jump jets and lower shielding. Then the exterior main armoring, both railguns on shoulder swivel mounts, the standard assault rifle and ammo feeds, rear storage compartment, one arm and the cluster bomb dispensers, as well as three plasma swords."

I saw the squint as he worked through that lot in his head and I spoke up quickly. "The legs will be together," I told him. "That fucker Tyrannus must have stripped it for parts before arranging transport, nobody else could have done this. The legs are complete units, so they'd be kept together."

I made the point that I knew how this had happened and that he was essentially buying back my own fucking parts from whoever Tyrannus had sold them to, because I had no doubt the sneaky orc would be adding on a cut for himself. I didn't need him charging a hundred grand per part, not when they were sections of the same thing.

"So the legs are two hundred," he said, counting on one hand, as if to mock me. "The exterior armoring, the railguns, the rifle…"

"With its feed, it's all interlinked, they'd not be selling it as a separate unit," I lied.

"That's five hundred thousand so far, plus the arm, the storage compartment, then—"

"The cluster-bomb dispensers are less than twenty grand a pair, so they won't be expensive," I added grimly.

"The cluster-bombs, we'll see what the price is on those, plus three swords…" He paused, scratching at his chin and pretending to be lost in thought. "We'll call it eight hundred thousand."

"You're fucking kidding me." I growled. "Eight hundred grand? I've already paid—"

"Nothing compared to what the suit's worth, never mind the parts." He cut me off. "You want to go to someone else for this? Fine, fuck off. See how far you get." He sneered.

I took a step forward, hand dropping to my side, the hilt of the plasma sword feeling warm against my palm as he held a hand out to the side, presumably stopping someone, though I didn't know or care who.

"Listen you fucking asshole, we made a deal…"

"Yeah, we did," he agreed. "You'd provide me with parts and with nanites, now you finally turn up with them, and I tell you how much I'm charging? The price was a couple of hundred grand, depending on the parts, remember? You keep this shit up? It's a million."

"I'm not paying that." I growled at him.

"Then fuck off and buy from someone else."

"Fine," I said grimly. "Luna, Gessh…"

"These stay here." Oshbob ordered. "As do the nanites, call it compensation for breaking the deal."

"I'm not breaking the fucking deal! You…"

"You want to renegotiate?" He snorted. "Not happening. Now, you want these parts or not?"

"Yeah, I do." I growled at him, and he nodded, turning to speak to the carver again.

I had no idea what his problem was, he moved from telling me to fuck off, to selling me shit, to warning me, to seemingly dismissing me, while Dondo and some Goblins carrying a bunch of boxes out from the back of the room.

He set them down on the table with a grunt, making me look over as I saw Dondo pull a covering off the box, showing parts of the railgun mountings to me, as I nodded my thanks to him.

"The parts are worth half a mil to me," Oshbob said eventually, and I glared at him.

"The lowest spec is a tier two at fourteen grand. The tier fours?" I shook my head. "I don't even know what the fuck they're worth, but its more than that!"

"Sure, but I can't sell them at that price. Ex-Specter parts, remember?" He shrugged.

"And if I go to one of your chop-shops and see these on sale they'll be clearly marked as that, and discounted will they?" I asked, glaring at him.

"I'm just a supplier." He smiled crookedly. "I don't force the shops to sell their gear my way…"

"Bullshit."

"You taking it or not?"

"Half a million," I agreed, furious but knowing the big fuck held all the cards here. "Plus two hundred more for the medikits and nanites.

"A hundred," he snapped, back at me. "That puts you in my debt for, oh two hundred grand. Got it handy?" He smiled, clearly expecting the answer to be no.

"I do." I replied. "And once I've seen the rest of the gear you'll get it."

He blinked, then growled, indicating I was to open the boxes and check it out.

Most of the parts were scratched and battered, bright fresh paint marred in sections where they'd been dumped one atop the other, and I cursed under my breath as I worked, borrowing a handheld console from Todds and plugging into the units, one by one.

After a few minutes I turned back, staring at the orc.

"How much are you charging me for the plasma swords?" I asked.

"Ninety," he replied, looking up from an argument with the goblin again. "Why?"

"Because they're not here."

"The…" He broke off, looking at the goblin who shook his head. "Seems they've not arrived yet," he growled. "Next time you tell me that shit, you little bastard."

"Well, till they're here I'm not paying for them," I said, and he waved me off, uncaring. I reached out, 'knocking' and getting the response from his account as I transferred a hundred and ten thousand, then reached for the nearest box. "Tell me when they arrive and I'll pay then."

"Whatever." He shrugged. "Dondo will give you the list," he said casually, turning away and stalking across the floor as he left us.

"List?" I called after him.

"Remember the deal, human! You deliver the nanites where I say!"

I turned to Dondo, seeing the wide grin on his face, as he transferred the list to me.

Checking it over, I started swearing under my breath, then gave up on that and cursed that goblin-fucker loud and proud.

He had me literally travelling over half the goddamn city! Some of these chop-shops were literally getting a single small medikit from me, a single kit, and I just knew it was deliberate, done only for the fucking pleasure of that bastard sending me running all over the place!

"Luna, Gessh," I said, turning to them, only to have Dondo cut me off.

"I'll help you carry these parts over to the warehouse you're renting if you want. I know Oshbob wants you to deliver these kits personally, so you'd not want him to double the price of the swords because you got others to do it for you, would you?"

I glared at him, knowing the fucker was making sure he could get his end away while I was working, but I swallowed it, when I saw the looks on Gessh and Luna's faces.

They'd helped me to do this, all of them, and now they were really hoping for the downtime I'd promised them. They'd worked and fought all day to earn all of this to pay for my suit, I couldn't take that away from them.

"Of course not," I snarled, grabbing one of the bags. "That was the deal."

CHAPTER FORTY-ONE

By the time I made it back it'd cost me eleven hundred credits in cabs, mag-train fees, food and drinks, and I was exhausted, the general crud of the sewers and undercity was well and truly baked in now, and I was exhausted.

Reign and the others were asleep, and I was forced to shower as quietly as possible, before climbing into bed and collapsing.

I was well and truly goddamn done with the day!

I managed a handful of hours before waking and checking my messages, finding that Bowdoin had been as good as his word, thankfully, and he'd passed the details to some lunatic called Skeeter. I'd had a call with him from the back of a cab while I was out delivering medikits, and fuck I distrusted him instantly.

He had a face that only a mother could love, and she'd have to have a thing about rodents with lopsided teeth, not to mention a twitch that made me want to know what the hell he was doing to make him so…wrong.

I was also absolutely certain I didn't want to know.

He'd sworn blind he could get me the passes and have us all registered as permitted and loaded with the required explosive charges, signed affidavits and checks performed etc. for a mere fifty thousand credits.

Each.

I'd told him who and what I was, and he'd been utterly unimpressed, telling me that he basically didn't give a shit, and that he did deals with people more dangerous than me every day.

Then he'd asked me if I liked the warehouse I was living in, and had sent me a live feed of Reign who was oiling her rifle.

I'd warned him off, and he'd just smiled, agreeing that he'd keep his mouth shut about our location and anything else that I contracted him for, but that the price was the price.

I offered him thirty thousand and told him to take it or fuck off.

He'd apparently been willing to accept less than that, as he grinned and took the ten thousand deposit, agreeing that he'd provide the passes and data tomorrow.

One of the passes was in my inbox now, and I transferred the rest of the money, getting the other passes literally seconds later.

The relief when I checked the registered city systems and found all three passes were live and mixed in with the rest as having been issued at various times over the last two years was immense.

Of slightly more concern was the easily found 'minor' detail that one of the upper management of the department had a break-in last night. They were screaming blue murder in all the news reels over how they'd find the fucker that did it. Apparently they left 'DNA evidence' in the form of a turd of improbable dimensions inside of one of the bugger's real silk pillows.

I just hoped that the ID was secure for now at least, and I planned to sort a backup as soon as I could.

The knowledge of quite how fucking many suits were registered? That on the other hand *terrified* me. I knew logically that the vast majority were corpo drones, doing bodyguard duty and other shit, but still.

That the AI's checked the registration on all suits constantly and cross referenced constantly meant that even black ops suits had to be registered in one way or another, or as soon as they were out on a job, they'd be reported. Sure they might be hiding in a van and painted and so on, but that wouldn't stop an AI from spotting them.

No, they had to be showing on the system as permitted, and when I'd spoken to Skeeter, he'd been adamant that it was easily fixed.

Now, he'd apparently proven he was right, and I had no choice but to shrug and move on.

I checked the various other messages I'd gotten, finding that I had apparently been discovered as some long lost prince's son and there were a million credits in an account just waiting for me to connect my account to it, sure, right. I had a subscription for 'horse cock enhancement pills' approved and more.

Hell, some fucker had even tracked down the aircar and seen that the extended warranty had expired on it.

There were twenty-seven messages from that bastard in four hours.

The rest of the messages were crap mainly, and I sorted through them as I dressed and made a coffee, having Reign steal it, then Luna and Gessh come out, filling their mugs and taking one for Dondo, before going back to bed.

Then I made a second pot of coffee and actually got to drink some of this one, as Reign and I made small talk. Then I moved down into the warehouse section properly and checked on the parts, laying them out as I checked for damage and missing sections.

"How long to fix it?" Reign asked, having followed me down and was leaning against the door jam with a coffee in one hand and wearing just her underwear and a smile, which definitely made me want to drag her off to bed as soon as possible.

"Two, maybe three days," I said, checking things over. "I also need to get some more parts, and I don't trust Oshbob to get them for me."

"Like what?"

"Ammo, for a start," I said. "Fuel rods, filters for the air filtration systems…all the little consumables that you never think of I guess. They were always just 'there' in storage when I needed them."

"And you've got none?" she asked, straightening up.

"No, there's a standard loadout in the transport case," I assured her. "But that's it, once it's gone it's gone. The rest of it I'd need to get the parts in and store until we need them. Most I can probably get from Gunther, he's got a mil-tech surplus store, but some parts, like the fuel rods? He won't be able to get, and I don't want to be in Oshbob's pocket for the normal day to day running gear."

"No, definitely not," she agreed. "Give him that kind of power over us all and we might as well just start working for him."

"Exactly," I said absently, checking a circuit board and crystal connector. "I'm thinking Stinger…"

"Sounds like something they could get," she said. "Look, do you need me for the next few days while you do this?" She gestured at the suit and I shook my head, frowning over at her.

"No, why?" I asked, a little surprised.

"I'm thinking we take them up on the offer of training," she said. "Todds is a stealth specialist, sure, but Gessh, Luna and me?" She shrugged. "We're not so much specialists as…well."

"You're a hell of a sniper," I assured her.

"And am I as good a shot as this Sync we're going to rescue?" She asked bluntly.

"Well…" I broke off and winced as I thought about how to put it.

"Just fucking say it, Harry." She sighed, and I knew I was in trouble when she was using my first name.

"No," I said after a few seconds. "Reign you're fucking good, genuinely you are, but Sync was a sniper elite in the APS for years, she trained and upgraded her mods to be able to kill anything that lives. If you had the same training, I've no doubt that…"

"So unless I want my job to be 'chief sucker of Kabutt's cock' I need to improve," she said grimly. "I'm second in the team, I run all the various bits and bobs, and I'm good at that, you give me the list of the shit you need and I'll sort it, but unless I'm to be made a mascot, I need to be as good as I can be. That means taking advantage of the offer of training by elite assassins. The girls feel the same way, and I'm sure Todds won't turn down the kind of experience these people have."

"Look, Richie and Sync…" I started, then winced. "Richie is a tech, sure he's lethal in and out of his suit, but he's all about the drones and the hacks, he wouldn't want your slot, and…"

"And Sync is a sniper," she said nodding. "You've said it before, that's all she's interested in, but how long until she or he decides they want my slot, or they just start doing the job because they know what you need and because they've worked with you for years longer than us? No." She set her coffee cup down and walked over, taking my hand and pulling me to my feet.

"I'm not a pet, and I'm not a charity case, nor your toy," she said, staring into my eyes, searching for the right words. "I *earned* this slot as your second, and they'll take it from me over my dead body."

"You did," I agreed, shutting up and she put her hand over my lips.

"And so, part of the responsibility of the second, is looking after the team," she said. "We need things, as a team I mean. We need equipment, we need training, and we need a heavy. That's my new slot."

"As a heavy?" I asked, stunned, looking at the slim, beautiful woman before me, as the image of Fergie swam up in my mind. They couldn't be more different, and not just because he was seven feet virtually of solid muscle and ginger beard.

He weighed damn near as much as the suit, and carried the massive heavy weapons of his station with pride. Reign was a sniper at heart, waiting for the perfect shot, while Fergie would take great pleasure in turning a square mile into a zone that still wouldn't sustain life in our grandkids lifetimes.

The contrast was insane, and yet…Reign was a hell of a shot. If she could bring that fixed perfection to the role of a heavy? It was frankly terrifying.

The heavy in any squad was a position of excessive concern to everyone. Nobody sane wanted a plasma caster strapped to their back, the power to melt the fucking planet and set fire to its atmosphere was a terrible thing, and they spent at least as much time checking the 'do not' details as they did the 'do'. Because of that, generally their targeting?

Well.

There was a reason that a heavy operatives chosen style was referred to as a 'to whom it concerns' weapon, rather than the intensely personal experience that is a sniped round, but if Reign could overcome that?

I was torn between utter terror and a sense of wonder.

"Okay..." I said after a few seconds, "So you're going to see Stinger and what? Get training for a few days?"

"That and more," she said honestly. "Luna and Gessh and I talked about it while you were out playing delivery boy, and we've talked about it a few times before as well, ever since the mission at the tower really. She shrugged, moving over and hopping up to sit on an empty bench nearby.

"That's cold," she complained, frowning down at the metal under her bare legs, then shaking her head as she went on, dismissing the chill. "So, at the tower, we basically hid in the van, that was it. Most of the mission we were less use than a chocolate fireguard. No, don't try to sugar coat it, seriously, we were." She held a hand up when I opened my mouth to respond.

"That's the nature of some missions," I said. "For assassination runs? Let's face it, I'm crap at stealth, I tend to just shoot every fucker in the face, Luna and Gessh are much the same, but you? You'll be sniping at extreme distance and then we drive off. I'll be useless on those missions."

"Yeah, that's true, and its fair, but my point is that unless the job went sideways, us girls couldn't have helped you. Todds? If he'd been in the squad then he could have, but only up to a point. We're going to have a lot more strength and depth with Richie as a hacker—"

"Tech," I corrected. "He runs drones and interference, mostly electronic warfare, spying and countering the other teams, he can hack stuff, but he's not that great at it."

"So we'll still need a hacker?"

"Yeah," I said. "If we're to grow into the kind of team I'm hoping we can? I'd prefer a dedicated hacking team in the office behind us, with Richie acting as liaison and link. That's for the future though, and sorry for interrupting." I winced as I realized I derailed the conversation, again.

"Yeah, so anyway." She sighed. "We'll have a lot more options in the team, but unless there's a need for standard soldiers? The girls are going to be massively outclassed, and I'm just the second rate sniper in the team then as well. We don't want to be the mascots, or the pets."

"There's always a need for the 'standard' soldier," I said. "I lead my team, and yet I'm not carrying any heavy weapons, I'm carrying the same loadout as Two..." I broke off, shaking my head that I'd automatically slid into thinking of the roles in the squad as I used to.

"Okay, look as team lead? I'm 'One' we might want to start using those monikers again for our missions in future actually, just in case, keeps our identities safe from at least some people. Two is a 'standard' soldier's billet, same as I carry, heavy assault rifle, spare ammo, and an expanded battery compartment, as well as additional loadout for the team in case we need it. My armor usually carried the 'mission pack' which was whatever we needed, be that a retrieval unit for radioactives or whatever.

"Two and I carried the same weapons, and so did Four and Five, all four of us able to swap ammo. The difference was that while I was lead, and Four, Scott, was the assault and melee advance, with Richie as Tech, Two, Barnes on our last few missions, didn't have a specialist role.

"So he was a standard soldier," Reign said nodding.

"Yes and no." I shook my head. "He was a generalist, which is what I think you're meaning. He wasn't a specialist in any one area, but he was a damn good shot, he could run a basic hack, he could reload, repair and use the heavy weapons. His expanded battery? It was to form the Soldier/Heavy symbiote. When Fergie—Three—was up shit creek and deployed his really heavy weapons? He needed to lock his armor, to stay in place as the power core charged them."

"That's…"

"It's a design flaw," I said. "We all hated it, but it meant that the firepower he could lay down was horrific. He'd drain his core to the dregs, and anything that he didn't like he'd shred. The flip side of that was that as he charged and his systems came fully online, he was vulnerable in ways the rest of us weren't. One of the reasons the 'heavy' operator stands out in any crowd is that their armor is fucking *heavy,* okay? Like its half again as thick as a normal operator.

"They still die on a regular basis because they're seen as the highest threat unit on the board. That's where the symbiote comes in. The soldier billet is also one that needs serious balls, because they don't have that expanded armor, or the insane levels of firepower to defend them, but they do have an enhanced battery, and they can link up to the heavy and overcharge their shields."

"So, what are you saying here? That we should become the sacrifice pawns?"

"No," I said quickly, then sighed. "At least, that's not my intention. What I'm trying to say, and doing a piss-poor job of it, is that every single role in the squad is needed. The 'standard' soldier as you call it, is fucking needed, they're a generalist, but they don't have the weaknesses that each of the specialist classes do. The sniper that waits for the perfect shot?"

I got a nod from her, to confirm she understood that example.

"Well, they can only do that, if they're really well hidden, or if they're backed up by the soldiers. Otherwise, as they're waiting for their perfect shot, others stumble over them and fucking kill them. As team lead, I can't be watching the overview and planning the objectives, or having Five work on hacking and drone control without knowing that there's someone watching over us. All the billets are needed. For us that means that we'll need soldiers."

"Like me and the girls?" Reign asked and I shook my head.

"No, honestly, I think Luna and Gessh will fall into the 'Four' role perfectly. It's an advanced melee and close combat role, primarily focused on martial arts—as much as they can be performed in a suit—sword wielding and close in slaughter. You send the Fours in when something needs fucking up badly and fast. That's perfect for the sisters."

"It is, I guess. So you're saying don't focus on things like hacking and stealth or whatever for them when we go to the Stingers, instead ask for close combat training?"

"Definitely," I said. "If we can get everyone suits? Then we'll kit them out to carry expanded power cores most likely, they're certainly brave enough for the role, but we'll need to talk about that further down the road. It's not something we need to focus on now. If they're going to go and train though? There's wooden training swords in that box over there…" I gestured to the right box on the rack nearby.

"I'd like them to work with those, I know they're bigger than the swords the girls have currently, but hopefully Oshbob comes through with the plasma blades soon, and if nothing else we'll take the fuckers from the black ops teams' dead bodies. I'd like the girls to get used to the size and weight of the plasma sword, they're a lot different to the 'normal' swords they're used to," I finished.

"Okay, I'll talk to them," Reign promised. "We were getting a bit worried about that, so it's a relief we'll actually be needed. So…"

"Yeah?"

She winced. "What about me?"

"Honestly?" I asked. "I'd been damn happy with the idea of you as my second and as a sniper along with Sync. She could teach you some insane tricks, but you're very different, I was happy with the idea of you both in that role, with her specializing in it and you focusing on life as my second."

"And now?"

"I think you're right," I said. "I think we need a heavy…but I'm not sure if you could do it." I saw the look on her face at that and I moved on quickly. "I don't doubt your skill or dedication, I mean physically first of all. Your body is magnificent, and listen to what I'm saying before you hurt me, okay?"

"Go on," she said in 'that' tone, and I winced, knowing that when a woman invites you to 'go on' like that, it's an invitation to bury yourself as deep as possible before she murders you.

"You know I love your body, and I worship it given the chance," I repeated. "But physically? You'd need to at least double your muscle mass, carrying the full 'heavy' loadout weighs as much as the armor. The operator needs to be massively strong. Again, your body is wonderful, but I don't know if you could do that." I saw the flinty look in her eyes, and I moved on quickly. "Also, the reality of the heavy's weapons are that they're area of effect a lot of the time. You spent years learning to be an amazing shot, while the heavy role is more about reducing an entire area to blackened cinders."

"Right," she said, but I saw a little waver in her resolve.

"I think you could do it, again, just like you probably could pile on all the muscle you'd need, probably. I don't think you'd like it though. In fact? I think once you got past the love of the firepower? You'd be bored. You're a sniper at heart."

"So what? We just do without a heavy?" she asked, and I shook my head, then grinned at her.

"Oh no, I'm just thinking that you specialize even more," I admitted. "There's a single crossover between the sniper and heavy roles, a singular point of convergence, and they're elite."

"I'm listening."

"Railguns."

"Railguns?" she asked non-plussed. "I carry a railgun, it's basically what every slug thrower is at heart, that's my usual sniper weapon a—"

"No," I said. "Not like this. Your slug thrower is a powerful sniper rifle, but its built on the sniper rifle frame, it's a 'normal' gun, just specialized for accuracy and a little additional force, right?"

"A lot of additional force," she corrected.

"Sure," I agreed. "A lot of force, but that's it. A heavy sniper though? Very, very few of them, it's a sort of joke in the APS corps…" I hurried on, seeing that look in her face as I misspoke. "…not that the role is a joke of course, just that because all of us are heavy compared to normal soldiers, it's like saying the 'heavy' role with heavy weapons is actually that of a 'heavy, heavy, heavy soldier'. Its seen as overkill, right up until you damn well need it."

"And you need it when?" she asked, clearly not sure what I was getting at.

"The heavy railgun is a weapon that ends battles," I said. "Every single round is individually loaded and designed for that specific railgun. Tailored to perfection. Fergie and Scott died when we fought an assault mech, literally, because most of our weapons couldn't do much damage to that much heavy armoring. They were the titans of the battlefield for a reason, right?"

"Yeah?"

"Well, had we known that there was going to be one there? Fergie would have taken the heavy railgun instead. One shot, one kill," I said. "A single round would have torn through the heavily armored pilot's compartment and that would have been it. Game over for them. The scavs that were hiding behind masses of metal and firing over the top? No problem. Fire straight through, kill them all," I explained.

"Then why the hell didn't he carry that normally then?"

"Because they're slow to reload, limited ammo and he was shit with it. Sync could use it, more or less, but she hated it, liked the utility of the normal model of sniper railgun, like you do, not the heavy, as well as the stealth field coating and the mobility of the sniper role as she did it, rather than the additional armoring of the 'heavy'."

"So you're saying…"

"I'm saying you will still be my second," I said. "That isn't in question, and neither Richie nor Sync would contest that, believe me, team leadership is not one of their goals, not in any of the conversations we had. Hell I had to practically order Fergie to undergo the second slot training. None of them wanted the responsibility."

"And the role?"

"Heavy sniper," I clarified. "Get a railgun, a *real* one, not a standard sniper rifle, Stinger can arrange it. Learn with that, then, if you're happy with it? We'll start on the exercise routine you'll need to carry the heavy version."

"How bad is it?"

"The exercise?" I asked, and she nodded. "At least an hour a day, every day, in the gym. Cardio and so on won't cut it, you'll need specialist weight training, as well as possibly internal augments later on. I know Fergie had to have his heart and lungs replaced to be able to power that frame. Something to think about further down the line.

Also, if you're going to train with Stinger? If they have a melee specialist, take advantage of that, it'll be easier for me to build on it for the plasma blades if they train you as well."

"Okay, thank you." She sighed, smiling a little sheepishly. "We were getting a bit worried that when you got your old team back…" She shrugged.

"That I'd not want you?" I smiled, moving in close and kissing her gently, then deeper. "Believe me, I want you alright."

"As your second?" She kissed me back, then wrapped her legs around me and pulled me in closer. "Or as chief cocksucker?"

"Well…" I breathed, "I'd hate to have to pick one skill over the other, but clearly if it has to be one…" I waggled my eyebrows and ran my fingers down her sides.

"Well, I suppose you've made me feel a little better, and you did do all the running around for us with the medikits…" She breathed into my ear, gently kissing my neck. "Why don't we go upstairs and share a quick shower? Before I take the girls to go see Stinger I mean?"

"Hell *yes*," I agreed fervently, grinning and I stepped back and she hopped down from the bench, then took me by the hand and led me back up the stairs like we were teenagers.

CHAPTER FORTY-TWO

An hour later and I was sitting smiling to myself as I played with the armor, each and every part I needed spread out around me like a childhood connection toy.

All in all the morning was going well, all things considered.

I'd had coffee, some great sex, nobody had shot at me, and I had a 'little' building project to keep me busy for a few days.

Also, Reign and the girls were planning on doing as many assassination and bounty missions as they could over the next few days, so it meant we had credits coming in, they got more 'real world' experience and I got peace and quiet.

"That looks complicated." The voice from behind me almost made me drop the crystal matrix in shock, I'd been so absorbed in it as he moved in I'd not noticed the bugger's approach.

"It is," I assured Dondo, looking over at him and frowning. "No offence, Dondo, but usually the only time I see you, you're swinging that chair leg you pretend is a knob around, and dragging the girls off, or you're here to ruin my day with Oshbob wanting something, so which is it?"

"Neither," he said, a little smile on his face as he took a sip of his coffee. "I'm not busy, usually Oshbob has jobs for me, today he doesn't, so I'm relaxing, thought I'd come and have a look at this."

"Well, just don't touch anything," I ordered. "No offence, but unless you know what you're doing…"

"It's an expensive mistake waiting to happen—like that ANN, if it's not kept cool, it'll degrade," he pointed out.

I frowned, looking around, searching for the…fuck.

"Shit…" I started to get up, and he waved me back, already striding over to reconnect the loose power connection to the ANN. As soon as it was plugged back in, he flicked a few of the connections, then picked up a sensor and connected it to the output, checking the readings before nodding.

"Solid green," he assured me. "No degradation, yet."

"I'll need a new connector putting on that then."

"Looks like a factory fault." He rubbed at it with a calloused thumb. "You can see the way it flexes, cheap crystal."

"You know your stuff," I agreed grudgingly.

"Oshbob likes us to learn the basics."

"The basics?" I said, a little surprised. "You recognized an ANN and knew it needed the connector checked. That's not 'basic'."

"Depends on your point of view." He grunted, amused. "I deal with a lot of things for Oshbob. I get an Artificial Neural Network out and I break it? I'll be looking in the gutter for my teeth, so yeah, keeping a unit like that fit for use is a basic thing."

"Interesting," I said slowly. "So, if you know what an ANN is, you'd know how to integrate units to each other?"

"Some, not sure about this, I heard it's a lot of crystal integration, that's why I wanted a look at it," he said, leaning against the wall and sipping his coffee again.

"Still, you can run a link and set up turrets?" I asked, and he nodded as if that was nothing. "Well, we've got six." I nodded to the turrets in boxes on the far side of the room. "I need them setting up with overlapping fields of fire."

"Where?" he asked, moving over to the boxes and glancing in. "And these the ones we got you?"

"Yeah." I swallowed my desire to snarl at the fact that it was always fucking Oshbob at the bottom of any dodgy dealing. "And they need setting up in here and outside. We need…"

I explained the locations I'd picked out, and the reasons; four outside, each with at least one overlapping field of fire, and sensors that were rigged and hardened, a central basic node to run everything off and a simple RI to manage it. The remaining two turrets were to be set up inside the warehouse, both in strategic locations, hidden from casual observation.

He agreed to help with the installation of them all, provided he got a few nice little details in exchange.

He'd apparently had his eyes on a plasma sword for a long time, as well as wanting the training to use it properly. He'd seen the monomolecular blades that the various nutters about the city wielded—as did Gessh and Luna for that matter—but he wanted the god fucking standard.

I hesitated, then shrugged at his price. The blades weren't cheap, but if he could actually get them? It was worth agreeing to teach him a little of fighting with it, in exchange for making sure the fucker actually chased Oshbob up to get us the ones we needed.

I was also fairly sure that nothing that was going on here was without that bastards approval, so he wanted Dondo to know the inside of the suits, and how to use a plasma sword. Probably in case I ever went after Oshbob.

Some might think that having a potentially untrustworthy ally like Dondo set up my turrets was a mistake, and they'd be right, if not for the fact that I still had, stored away in my RI, the settings I was going to be using for the control RI.

It'd be linked to me, personally, and my RI as the primary owner. Dondo could insert whatever shitty little hacks he wanted, and when my RI installed that? He'd have wasted his time.

It might be that I was a little paranoid, but that was life.

The morning morphed into the afternoon quicker than I expected, and Dondo proved to be better company than I thought, the rough jokes, and surprising insights as we worked, as well as having someone to bounce a technical question off now and then was a relief.

Most of the time he didn't have a clue, this was APS tech after all, and it was head and shoulders above the levels of most engineers and mechanics. I only knew what I was doing through rigorous training, but there was something about explaining the technical steps to someone else that helped you to see the issue yourself.

An old training sarge had called it 'rubber ducking' after a supposedly ancient custom of explaining your system to a literal rubber duck, as saying it out loud helped you to find the issues.

Being a training sarge, he had an actual rubber duck with an eyepatch that when you explained your mistakes to it, was programmed to give you constructive abuse for an hour solid.

'Constructive' being things like pointing out you were too dumb to breed and so on. Still, by the time the girls finally returned, I'd managed to get the skeleton of the suit fully operational again, the legs were fully enclosed and the jump-jets attached, although the power still needed routing for them, and the arms were attached fully again, both undergoing integration tests.

Dondo had pretty much earned his place in the sword training that I was planning on giving, and the turrets were in place, even if not fully active yet.

Reign, Luna, Gessh and Todds had carried out two minor hits, literally only a few hundred credits each, but they'd also had three quarters of the day in specialist training with the Stinger collective.

That wasn't cheap either, notably, but it was seriously effective.

There'd been some attempts years ago to 'upload' skills to people's brains directly, to take someone fresh into bootcamp and to make a lethal soldier out of them, an all-rounder that could be a sniper specialist, a hacker extraordinaire and more. The first stages had apparently been so promising that the tech vanished and so did the class they were training.

Someone had apparently thought they could make perfect spies and so on like that, and had gone all out.

Unfortunately the imprinting was short term and seriously damaging, the entire batch of trainees ended up brain-burned and wiped out, forgetting skills in combat, forgetting the combat itself and just flopping down to play in the mud and more.

The entire project had been shelved.

It was something that was brought up every fifty years or so, tried and failed, then dismissed over and over.

Instead they'd all spent most of the day in Aug-World, with their sensory input linked up to full.

They'd been in flat, featureless rooms with unloaded weapons, but to them, they'd crept around massive military complexes, they'd carried out assassinations that required them to climb to the top of buildings, and they'd fought hundreds of enemies in waves, dancing from form to form, one hand tied behind their back.

It was one of the few things I agreed that Aug-world was useful for, even more so than a 'normal' training building, because you could tailor make it.

If you had the technical specs for a building? If you could get access to it and do a walk around? Maybe hack the cameras? You could build an exact replica in a different building, an abandoned one, and run a thousand dry runs.

If you had the time.

The only issue with that kind of training?

Consequences.

Specifically, the lack of them. You get used to doing a mission over and over without any long term consequences if you fuck up? You grow complacent, even when you know you shouldn't.

That was why we were given highly limited access to Aug-World for training in the army, and we had our pain receptors turned up to maximum, so any simulated bullet wound?

It felt worse than the real thing.

That apparently was how the Stinger collective liked to run it as well, against members of the collective playing the part of guards and countering teams, and they'd had a great time kicking the shit out of my team.

Luna and Gessh especially were a mass of bruises from a day spent in martial arts training.

Fortunately we had a nice supply of medikits, and could afford the luxury of using some up on this.

Reign had spent the day with the massive bastard that had insisted on Anthos Black's death as the price of us 'killing' Stinger and claiming the bounty.

He'd not offered a name, beyond 'Stinger', but he was apparently a heavy-weapons enthusiast, and when Reign had come to him with her desire to learn to use a 'real' railgun, he'd taken her off to one side and shown her his collection.

She'd come back with a new respect for ultra-heavy weaponry, and a love of the possible levels of destruction she'd be able to unleash with an APS Heavy Railgun. Todds on the other hand, was absolutely knackered, and while the others were mainly happy about the idea, he was ready to go home to his kids.

And apparently his nice warm baby-sitter, as the girls had spent all day ribbing him about a message he'd gotten when they were having lunch.

The baby-sitter was expecting to stay at his tonight, again, and while they couldn't hear the message, the bright red cheeks and the awkward adjusting of his pants as he got up suggested it was a good one.

He'd really wanted to go home sooner, rather than later, and me stopping that wasn't popular.

Especially not to discuss sword forms, and certainly not ones that were so different to the ones they were taught today with Stinger. They'd had a joint hour long training session with the sword, as I'd asked earlier, and now I was teaching them something so totally different it was almost a dance.

I couldn't help but smile, I'd done these katas with my old squad, and alone, and it felt so strange to do them now, to be the one guiding as a group fumbled and cursed their way through the slow, graceful movements.

Mushin, as I'd experienced it only a few days ago in the depths of the water storage tanks, surrounded by hundreds of specters, and as it'd come to me again and again through the cooling towers?

It'd changed things for me.

I'd felt that exactly as Scott had described it, I had it, as much as I ever would.

Now I knew that I'd only scratched the surface. This was a pursuit of decades, of your entire life, I realized, but as I started to teach, sliding my mind back to those days in the dojo?

I felt a calm envelop me.

The simplest forms were all we did for now, standing and sweeping right and left, ignore the arms, focus on the legs, on the placement of the feet, glide, not step.

Feet stayed close to the ground, smooth arcs that flowed constantly, starting with feet shoulder-width apart, we then swept the left foot back, facing outwards at a forty-five degree angle from the forward facing foot, and sink slightly, dip the knees, and hold.

This was the resting stance, the most basic of them all, and learning to keep the weight on the balls of your feet was insanely important.

Teaching the 'passing step' got me a load of sighs and glares, shakes of the head and more, but I stuck to it, the basics were important for a goddamn reason.

The front foot stayed in place, shifting out to forty-five degrees, and the back foot slid forwards, planting to face directly ahead, or at roughly ninety degrees.

I made them copy this over and over, watching as they grew more and more frustrated, until finally I told them to stand however they felt was right.

Then I told them to keep their feet still, locked in place, and I moved from one to another and shoved them.

Each and every one of them, had shifted from the new stance, to stand 'normally' and each and every one of them fell over.

Then I stood—in the correct stance—and told them to take turns at me.

When they couldn't push me over, they slowly started to see the damn point.

The next half an hour was literally shifting stances, dancing forwards then back on the balls of the feet, before I let them take the swords up and 'play'.

Dividing the group would have probably been the best way to do it, especially as the sisters regularly fought with their blades, and had spent the afternoon getting their asses kicked by Stinger, and so had received some interesting new training.

That wasn't my style though.

All six of us faced off in a rough circle, wooden training swords ready, with Luna and Gessh on opposite sides so they couldn't team up straight away.

"Go!" I barked, and I stepped back, falling into stance and waiting.

Reign was the first to see it, and I'd half expected that, with her ease of taking the second position in the team I knew she had good instincts.

We both waited as Dondo launched an attack on Todds, who in turn attacked Gessh. Luna paused, switching from her first target of Reign, and instead striking at Todds' back, as he was distracted taking him out, when Reign struck at the back of Dondo's knee.

Then I and Reign attacked at once, standing on opposite sides of the melee and striking at the most distracted, taking them down.

In seconds, Dondo and Todds were out, and Luna and Gessh were facing Reign and I respectively, the sisters moving to fight side by side as Reign and I did as well.

I smiled, watching Reign out of the corner of my eye, as I waited.

Luna stabbed forwards, risking it all when she dropped to one knee and stabbed across, ignoring her nearest opponent to try and take me, of all people, in the crotch.

It was uncalled for I felt, and I whacked her blade aside then smacked her in the temple, taking her down.

Gessh had struck at Reign, the pair of the sisters swapping targets in an unspoken attempt to confuse us. It partially worked, as Reign, swinging at Luna overbalanced and missed, then took Gessh's blade to the stomach.

I rolled my wrist and brought my blade back up and across, taking Gessh in the underarms, and effectively disarming her.

It was close enough a fight though, that I felt there needed to be more of an example. With that in mind, I paired the others up, Dondo on his own against me first, then Reign and Luna, and Gessh and Todds.

I had them attack me, and I disarmed and beat them once each, hard.

Dondo was the simplest, thrusting at me as if to try and skewer me—had the fucker landed it would have damn well hurt, he put that much force behind it—so I returned the favor by parrying, slapping the blade aside then spinning and bringing my own across the back of his head.

As he went down in a crumpled heap, Reign and Luna attacked. They ran at me, blades swinging, one high, one low, and I stepped to the left, slapping Reign's blade aside, then shoved her, hard, in the shoulder.

She tumbled into Luna, who tried to catch her, then thought better of it, dancing aside…only to have me step in and sweep her legs out from under her as well.

She hit the floor, rolled…and felt my blade smack off her ass, ending her fight.

Reign had stayed down, tired enough and knowing that if she moved it was over, and I tapped her lightly on the sternum, before picking up her sword.

Now armed with two blades, I stepped up parrying the combined attack from Todds and Gessh, before kicking his knee when he tried to plant it wrong, sending him staggering as I blocked Gessh again, then dropped to a knee myself and swept both blades across my chest in a downward 'X' as she tried to stab me.

Her blade slammed into the floor and I rose, keeping her sword trapped between mine as I twisted and rolled to the right, rolling my blades down hers.

She had the choice of have her hand 'chopped off' or release it, and she dropped the sword, leaping at me in a midriff tackle instead.

I took it, driven back two steps before I smacked her across the back and 'killed' her, then disarmed Todds easily.

The example made, that none of them had managed to land even a single hit on me, I spoke, giving them some constructive feedback, some criticism and sent them on their merry ways.

Todds was out the door almost before I was finished talking, while Dondo grinned at me and set off straight for the stairs up and after the sisters.

"That was cruel you know," Reign said, coming over for a kiss. "We know that you're better than us, you really should have…"

"Toned it down?" I asked, snorting as she paused.

"You did?" she asked, and I nodded.

"Sorry, Reign, but yeah, I did," I admitted. "Give it a few weeks and we can start training properly, tonight was a tester, just to show the basics."

"Now I feel even worse," she muttered.

"And if I was to try and outshoot you?" I pointed out. "You'd kick my ass every time. It's about training and experience, when you all have a little more under your belt then you'll feel better, but until then, the plasma swords will be kept firmly out of reach."

"Are they that different?" she asked and I nodded.

"You saw the two sword parry?" I asked "Where I blocked Gessh?"

"Yeah?"

"Totally pointless with a plasma sword, its *plasma*, it'd go straight through and disrupt the containment field. The blade would have taken me in the face, and mine would have carved her leg off. She'd have won that one, but she'd be down a leg, and you'd all be down a team lead. You need to learn the basics first, then you can learn which rules are fixed and which can be bent, or broken."

"Without killing each other."

"Without killing each other," I agreed.

"So, now what?" she asked, as I picked the blades up and put them in a storage box, then kissed her again. "Too early for a shower?"

"It's never too early for a shower," I said firmly, it was rapidly becoming my favorite place after all.

"Or…" she suggested with a smile. "We could have a starter of pizza?"

"If you're my main course, then I'm in," I assured her, grinning.

That set the pattern for the next few days, the mornings were a little slower with coffee and unfortunately no more early morning 'fun', as when you'd recently had sex, you tended to be crap at fighting, the killer instinct missing, or it was in most men's case at least.

Once we'd all had one form or another of breakfast, I started work on repairing my APS, Dondo got to work installing the turrets and syncing them up in between doing jobs for Oshbob, and the others went to see the Stingers.

Todds invested his earnings in a new grade of stealth-suit, something much more powerful, as well as more appropriately armored.

Reign fell in love all over again, her 'one true love' of the grazer sniper rifle almost neglected as she began training at the knee of the heavy weapons expert. She carried out several solo hits, the pair of them travelling the city to find their target, then 'one shot, one kill' was the order of the day, each from increasingly further distances.

Minor details like wind and rain weren't really a concern for a railgun, but additional unintended casualties massively were.

The charge was adjusted on the fly, and she was trained with specialist goggles that could be tuned to identify materials and shielding. They spent hours on rooftops, discussing the material resistance and shield level that would need to be overcome to shoot through a wall, burst a shield and kill a target, and yet have the round stop there, rather than punch through the building, racking up collateral damage and deaths.

Luna and Gessh focused on melee and team fighting, working side by side, taking down incoming swarms of enemies, everything from beasts and monsters to corpo scumbags and drones.

There were set exercises to move through a projected building, trying to achieve different aims, rescuing someone, killing them, taking down a location, or protecting it.

Hour after hour they slogged at it, before being guided in hand to hand and martial arts by three of the stingers.

Todds was back on full stealth training, learning to use the equipment he had, moving through buildings and across various sites ranging from a shopping mall to a corporate headquarters.

He was tasked to get to 'x' floor without being seen, and if he was seen? He had to eliminate them.

By the time they made it back to train with me for the last two hours of the day, they were exhausted, and frequently pissy about the need to do so.

I stood firm though, knowing that sooner or later, the training with the plasma swords would have to be real.

It took four more days in the end, before we finally got approval from Julius, and confirmation that we were good to return to the guild.

Liolet had apparently been offered a fuck load of credits to make sure we couldn't return, as Trees tried to keep the guild tied up. It was all aimed at ruining the guild's burgeoning reputation, Julius had told me when he'd turned up one night, swearing that he wasn't there. He came to fill us in, to get us on board for the plan and to drink all my goddamn rum 'before he died', he was that soaked, having been caught in a sudden downpour as he exited the cab.

Liolet had gone to Julius when the deal was offered, not liking or trusting Trees, and the pair of them had hatched a plan.

Liolet took the money, things were dragged out, several jobs got redlined and there were fines being threatened…and then Liolet had voted to reinstate me and my team.

Trees had been furious, and had quit the guild, taking three of the more senior teams with him, and practically gutting the guild in what was obviously a well-planned and funded coup attempt.

Julius came begging, and we answered.

"Seriously, if we can't take the nest down that's developing in the Suburban Heights district? We're fucked as a guild. We've got forty-eight hours, after that?" He shook his head. "We get a ten thousand credit fine, and the contract is 'open' again. I've got it on good authority Trees was promised it, and he and his three teams will be there, waiting and ready to storm straight in."

"And?" I'd asked, still pissed.

"And then you don't get your pass, and I don't get to keep my guild together as the shit hits the fan, alright? We're making good credits, but losing four of our main teams all in a day? We can't hold our contracts, not all of them. Liolet is running around like a blue arsed fly, trying to make up for it, I've been out on specter hunts for fuck's sake, and my skills are in administration and organization, not shooting!"

"Why'd you let it drag on so long?" Reign asked him.

"Because it made sure that any that were going to him, went. Those that stayed are loyal, and they didn't give me that much of a choice, if Liolet hadn't kept playing along with them, they'd have used the same tricks, but I'd not have been in control. As it was, when he switched sides? It caught them flatfooted."

I'd hesitated, not liking that the guild was constantly running from disaster to disaster, but hey, I guessed this was the best chance we were ever going to get.

"I know what you're going to ask for," he said, glaring at me. "You want a position of power in the guild."

"Shares, actually," I said.

"That's a position of power, considering that there's only so many shares available to sell. I'd normally have to sell you my shares, but considering the bloodletting that's going on?" He looked sick as he stared at the glass in his hand.

"After the cooling tower, we looked stable as an investment, and they came running. I sold forty-nine percent of my guild in shares, keeping control by a single percentage point."

"And now?" I asked.

"Now those same investors are trying to sell their shares."

"And what did you do with the money?"

"What money?"

"The money that they gave you for the shares," I asked bluntly. "Fuck's sake man, you didn't spend it all on angel dust and hookers did you?"

"Ha!" He snorted, shaking his head. "No, I invested most of it in the guild, fixing some of the machines, upgrading equipment and more, the rest?"

"Yeah?"

"It's not enough to pay off the debts that'll come if this goes fucking wrong," he admitted. "I kept the rest of the money, just in case, and now I need your help, Kabutt. I'll sell you shares, I'll use my savings and buy them from the investors that are willing to sell, but I need a miracle from you."

It was tempting to give him a totally different answer, given that he'd let us cool our heels so long, but the look on his face was priceless when we agreed to take a thirty percent stake in the guild, in exchange for the full earnings of the next nest job and saving their asses.

"Keep him up here till I give you the signal, then bring him down," I told Reign when he went to the loo, and I jogged down the stairs, grinning to myself.

The suit was as finished as I could make it in the short term, with only a hundred rounds for the shoulder mounted railguns, ten cluster bombs in either dispenser, and three hundred rounds in the rifle.

It was however, fully operational, including the cold weather seals attached, and when Reign brought him down to the warehouse, unlike when he'd arrived, I'd opened the transport crate, and was in my APS.

He was chatting to her amiably about how much of a surprise Trees would get when we showed up to the nest, when the lights in the warehouse turned on fully, and he froze, staring up in a comical mixture of terror and wonder, at my APS.

"Holy fucking gods of chrome and blood…" he whispered, unable to keep from shaking his head in wonder. "…you did it?"

"We're back in business," I admitted, my voice coming through the speakers, the suit's inbuilt systems adjusting the harmonics slightly to induce a subliminal level of near bed-wetting terror in those we faced. "How do you like your miracle?"

CHAPTER FORTY-THREE

It was sunrise the next morning as the helo transport landed, the rest of the team standing by to watch me leave as I boarded it, in all my APS glory, the storage pack on my back packed with everything I thought I might need, dozens of large medikits, power cells I knew I could drain into an APS unit, clothing, food, anything and everything.

It was time to recover my friends, and as much as I'd love the help from Reign and the others, the simple truth was that the Fingers weren't a place for any living creature out of full armor, and the storm that was raging there was predicted to last the next three days.

That was both a boon and a nightmare.

A boon because the electrical storm was fully preventing any kind of observation missions there, meaning that nobody that saw us going in, could tell what the fuck we were doing.

The nightmare side, was that there were horrific winds going in all directions, and while I had a plot to the location of Richie and Sync, if the helo was trashed by a crosswind, we were all fucked, and it seriously decreased the time on station we had.

We had thirty-six hours before the guild was going to be fucked up though, and that gave us two choices. First, we could go to the nest today, all of us, including me in my APS, and we could clear it—if I was on foot, the odds of success dropped significantly but it was possible, we'd just lose most of the teams doing it—that dealt with the immediate problem, but left Trees out there, playing silly games.

It would also most likely start the fight off that we couldn't afford yet, with the major and his people, especially when they saw me vanish into the nest, considering it was in the undercity.

They'd send the ghost team in, and probably pay Trees as well, and I'd get absolutely pounded, with my team being caught in the crossfire as the major took me down.

On the other side though? We'd carefully disabled any cams anywhere near the warehouse for my takeoff, and while I and my companions were marked as boarded on the manifest of the helo, there were thousands of such vessels in action around the city at any one time.

If the major was looking for me? He'd already know where I was, and chances were that if he knew my suit was working? He'd have attacked already.

Instead the three of us—myself and Richie and Sync—were boarded under our pseudonyms, the handles we'd inevitably used when gaming, and that was our best chance.

"LDS aboard," I confirmed to the pilot who flashed the 'ready' and 'take off' lights twice, clearly giving me all the warning I was getting.

The helo lifted, shifting under the additional weight as I forced myself into the sections set aside for me. It was an old transport helo, heavily reinforced, and the usual deployment pods I would have been in weren't in this model, meaning I was reduced to holding tight to the seats, kneeling between them as it pitched and rolled, taking the gaps between the skyscrapers and arcologies at a rate that was frankly terrifying.

I kept hearing everything from collision warnings from drones as we blurred past, to air cabs and more screaming around us. I gritted my teeth, holding on tight and praying that the pilot didn't fucking pancake us into the side of a building, as a sudden comm request came through.

It was an unknown ID, I almost denied it, then in a fit of contrariness, I accepted it instead, pulling it up and connecting, grateful for the distraction.

The connection was grainy, deliberately so, and the figure that spoke was as broken a figure as Stinger was originally, deliberately using tech to hide who and what they were.

I almost killed the connection then, expecting to be sold some shitty sob story or wild ass attempt at hacking, when they spoke.

"We. Know." That was it. A shitty threat, if ever there was one, but before I could tell them to fuck off? A vid started to play. It was crappy quality, but it was clear who and what it was. It was Borrolet, filming me draining the nanites out of the specters and harvesting the remains. "You will pay us one hundred thousand credits a month, and quit the Vigilant Heart immediately."

I stared at the figure before me, we were, in the simulation, sat across a table from each other, the chair under me small and uncomfortable, the table slightly bigger than it would be really, and the figure on the far side looming over me in a shitty attempt at intimidation.

They were an outline only, black as pitch and filled with a thousand swirling stars designed to make identifying them impossible.

"And if I don't?" I asked, feeling a surprising wave of relief running through me as the blackmailer I'd been expecting finally showed themselves…more or less.

"Then we release the recording. You will have the technology claimed by the city, losing everything, and be executed when the truth that you were attempting to infect innocents with contaminated specter parts comes out."

"Whatever." I snorted. "I'm a little busy right now. Want to give me some details?"

"Details…?" he asked sounding confused.

"To pay you for fuck's sake," I lied, biting down on a rising need to vomit as the flyboy fucker in charge of the helo took another corner at a ridiculous speed.

"You have twenty-four hours, before…" they started, the ID showing up as Finn Tekk, which I assumed was bullshit, unless they were tremendously stupid and had actually shared their real name. But hey! I cut him off and made a call to Dondo, who answered surprisingly quickly.

"You miss me more than Reign, eh?" The half orc grinned at me, and I glared at him, swallowing my bile again.

"Fuck right off," I said. "You know our deal for me to supply your boss with nanites?"

"Yeah?" he asked warily. "You better not be trying to back out of that shit, Kabutt, Oshbob doesn't like—"

"He doesn't like *me*, never mind people that try to fuck him with deals, I get it don't worry. Some dickhead knows about it though and is trying to blackmail me…" I paused for a split second then went on, lying through my teeth. "…and he knows your boss is using the nanites, he's planning on spreading the word and put him out of business."

"You got any details on him?" he growled.

"He gave me an account to pay into, that's all, not sure if the name is real."

"Good enough, gimmie." He nodded, and I sent the details over, trying not to smile as Dondo ended the call with a curt 'we'll deal with it'.

I couldn't help but grin, knowing someone was in for a world of hurt now.

Clinging to the seats in the back of the old transport, I cursed, shifting my grip and moving as far towards the middle of the helo as possible.

I'd broken one of the seats accidentally, two rows ran up the middle of the helo, seats facing into the middle, with a space between them, and a row on either side, back to back, facing outwards, with the sides of the helo able to be cranked back to a huge degree.

Clearly it'd been designed to drop the maximum number of troops in one go, unloading from both sides at once, but as it was? With me in the middle in full armor I was being rocked from side to side constantly, then up and dipping down as the mad bastard pilot played at flying.

I'd never liked those goddamn flyboys, but fuck me, right now I was wishing for the arrogant fuck stains of the army helo divisions.

My fingers had left dented, crushed metal behind as I gingerly lifted them free, wincing at the damage done to the old craft, before shaking my head.

There wasn't so much as an integrated anchor point back here, just small metal eye-links to run cables through, strapping or clipping your gear down.

They were obviously designed for infantry packs and so on, not multi-ton mecha, and fuck me it showed. I started to slide to the right, the scraping sound of my armor against the floor of the helo loud even to my ears inside my armor, as the squeal of tortured metal rang out.

I tried grabbing a link, managed to get a finger through it, and snapped it off.

This was going to be a *long* goddamn flight.

After twenty minutes I couldn't take any more, and comm'd the flight deck, asking for a status update, then cursed roundly as I found we'd only just crossed the outer wall.

That was it.

After all that time we'd literally just crossed the wall of Artem, and were out into the wilderness.

The ETA to the Fingers? Five hours. Five fucking hours. The maximum range for the helo? Twelve hours, or so the pilot thought.

He *thought*.

I gave in to my mounting rage and called Julius before we were too far out. Needless to say the helo didn't have a dedicated comm node available.

"Kabutt?" Julius asked, looking harassed. "What the hell man, you there already? Give me good news!"

"There?" I growled. "Fuck's sake, Julius, I'm not even properly out of the bastard city yet! There's five more hours of flight time, six hours almost each way..."

"Long flight I guess, but that's life..." he started and I cut him off.

"The pilot thinks the helo can manage a maximum range of twelve hours, Julius," I snarled. "What's six hours each way? He's saying he'll land on site if the weather isn't too bad and I run off and collect, then come back to him? You think my people are going to be able to climb a mountain after being in cryo? They'll barely be able to walk!"

"Tw- oh." He winced. "Look, Kabutt, seriously, it was the best I could do, I'm sorry. Heavy lift helos outside of the army? They're just not needed, there's less than fifty in the city that I could find, and most of them? They're corpo owned. You want a corpo drone watching as you retrieve your friends?"

"There must have been better options than this, come on man." I sighed, bouncing and shaking from side to side as we hit some turbulence. Seriously, it feels like I'm going to fall out of the fucker at any minute."

"There's seven options for non-corpo affiliated heavy lift helos in the city," Julius said bluntly. "Seven. Of those? Two were undergoing maintenance and are out of action for the next three or four days, so count them out. One is rated for a fifty ton lift, and is a three rotor 'Battlefield support' model, wide storage and so on, heavily armed..."

"Perfect..." I started and he nodded.

"For the trip out there and back? Seven hundred thousand credits. That's the fuel cell usage more than anything else, but it also requires a flight plan be filed with the city, an independent observer from the city be aboard, and a background check on anyone that hires it. It's *heavily* armed Kabutt. I know you're a walking fucking weapon, but add in the ability to fly? That fucker could take down an arcology if it wanted to, they don't let that shit fly without a damn good reason."

"Okay, fair enough, but—"

"Of the remaining four, two are already booked, that puts us down to two options, one of the pilots swore blind his bird was perfect for our needs."

"Okay..."

"He was also off his face on angel dust and naked when he took the call, not to mention painted blue, and kept telling me to call him 'His Royal Majesty Paulus Hazelnuts, Patron Saint of Ribs, and Lord of the Banana hammock'. I decided that even considering the stable nature of most pilots, it was probably best to take the last option."

"Fuck." I groaned, shaking my head inside my armor. "Pilots man, why the hell are they all either mad or assholes?"

"Why pick one?" He snorted. "Half of them are ex racers and lunatics that escape the army for crashing their birds, you know what they say. If you can walk away from a landing it's a good one, if you can use the bird again?"

"It's a great landing." I finished for him, nodding and cursing. "Seriously, what the fuck is wrong with my life."

"Is that a serious question?" He snorted. "Look Kabutt, you're in the latest and greatest death machine the army can build, you're armed to the teeth, and if the worst comes to the worst? Get him to fly close to the ground and when he runs out of fuel, jump out. You'll be fine, he'll crash and die, and I'll save half the flight fee. Now, no offence, but I've got a load of shit going on here, and I'm with a team of newbies, hunting specters. I kinda need to focus on how many of them I brought down with me, or I'll take less out than I should."

"Fair point." I sighed. "Good luck with that, and shoot straight man."

"You too."

With that, he was gone, and I was back to rocking side to side, buffeted over and over by the wild winds out in the wastes.

I contemplated calling Reign, more out of a need for distraction than anything else, and quickly dismissed that as well. Instead I pulled up a story I'd started reading ages ago, and settled in, forcing myself to relax, focusing on that, as my RI read it aloud in my mind.

Hours passed in a sick feeling blur as I constantly moved from attempts at distraction, checking out everything from the schematics for the harvester, to the internal records for the arm, to watching out of the single tiny window.

I was quickly cursed and ordered to get back into the middle of the helo, as I was throwing the weight distribution off, and I did as I was told, having seen what I always did out there, a fat load of nothing.

Miles upon miles of scrubland flashed past under the belly of the helo, long dead and arid, blasted by everything from conventional munitions, to the sun, to radiation and chemical leaks.

There were entire sections of the wilds that while they were a wasteland, were full to overflowing with life, but there was nothing you'd want to go near.

Landing near to more than half of them would be a death sentence, even for me in my armor, and here and there flying creatures could be seen distantly tracking us.

I head the occasional click and whirr of the helos onboard guns, automated turrets that locked onto targets, waiting for a firing solution, and a command, but fortunately nothing closed the distance.

By the time we closed with the Fingers, finally, the sky had gone from leaden all the way to roiling, with thunder and lightning shaking the little craft from side to side and hailstones hitting the fusillade like constant machine-gun fire.

"I can't get you too close!" The pilot finally deigned to speak to me, connecting as he battled the weather. "The winds…its crazy here!"

"It's the Fingers!" I snapped. "It's always crazy!"

"I don't fly here," he replied flatly, the air filled with flashing lights, warning beeps and more. "Nobody with any sense flies here, you know there was an army helo lost here only a few weeks back?"

"Yeah!" I snapped. "I was on the fucker!"

I pinged him the directional data again, checking our altitude and distance, and saw we were over two miles from it, when he shook his head.

"Can't do it!" he declared. "Sorry and all, but this is costing us fuel like crazy, I keep this up? We're not flying back."

"What the fuck do you mean…" I started, only to have him speak over me, professionalism and experience coming clearly through as he spoke, even as he was clearly distracted.

"For every hundred meters we fly deeper into the storm, It's costing us the equivalent of three hundred meters worth of fuel, I've got a reserve that should have given me an hour on site—"

"You said we didn't have enough fuel before!"

"I was making sure you understood not to fuck around," he snapped back. "Right, that hour on site? It's now forty minutes. Sure that should be plenty, but at this rate? We'll have less than ten minutes, and that'll be if you can find me somewhere flat and stable to land. You want me to hold while you climb up, or keep station off a cliff in these winds? You're down to a single flyby, you miss that? We're not getting back. That's on top of the risk we're running of flying into the side of a fucking mountain, you know, because we're literally blind here!"

"Electromagnetic…"

"The distortion is too strong! According to the sensors? We should be *in* a cliff right now, or splattered across it. No, you've got a choice, either we turn around right now, and we come back in a few days when the storm blows itself out?"

"Or?"

"Or I drop you off on a plateau somewhere here, and you use your Lidar as you go on foot. You map the section out, and I drop back, land and conserve fuel. That's gonna cost me fuel to go out and come back, then go out again, so you'll need to get whatever you're getting, and bring it as far out as you can on foot. You'll get one chance, a single pass, so you'll need to be ready!"

"You're fucking kidding me!" I snarled, my stomach dropping and my asshole trying to make neutronium at the thought of walking the fucking mountains again. "Seriously, there's entire sections here that there's no way up!"

"Or down," he agreed. "And a couple of miles in this might be dozens more on foot, but the choice is I drop you here, and return for you in an hour, or I don't, and I turn us around right now!"

"Fucking flyboys!" I snarled, shaking my head as I searched for a way out, a solution, anything that wasn't such a goddamn fuckup of a plan.

I had nothing.

"Last chance!" he called. "Turning now!"

"Drop me!" I ordered, grimly, mentally swearing I'd never fly in a fucking helo again. "Drop me now!"

"Use the winch!" he called, as a section of the ceiling clattered back revealing a filthy old winch and chain setup, that I quickly locked into place on the connectors on my shoulders and back, glad of the arm articulation.

"Can it hold my weight?" I yelled over the sudden sound of the howling wind, the floor directly below the winch starting to split, snow and screaming gales filling the compartment as flashing lights went off, warning of cabin depressurization.

"We're gonna find out!" The pilot laughed, an edge of madness in his voice as he tried to hold the helo steady, the floor cranking back wider and wider as the seats, clearly fixed to the front and back of the superstructure were left dangling.

"I fucking *hate* pilots," I whispered to myself as I felt the connections start a slow spin, the world starting to rotate for me, as I slid lower, my legs dangling into the snow and storm tossed void.

CHAPTER FORTY-FIVE

The descent was bloody awful.

It would forever more reside in the back of my mind, the helo vanishing above me, whited out as soon as it was more than a few dozen meters away, and the howl of the storm making it impossible to maintain a stable electronic connection.

I'd shot him the location of the cliff, one of the few fixed points of reference I had, and I had a solid hour to get there, two and a half miles away, through the blizzard, the storm, the fucking nightmare that was a mountainside frozen hell.

It should be easy.

I was in a goddamn armored suit that could run at a solid sixty miles an hour without any issue, two miles? A piece of piss.

Hell, Part of the basic APS training schedule included walking five miles in the armor on 'low power mode'. It was basically like walking while naked and wearing a suit made from a cheese grater, and weighted to fuck, but it proved that even when most of the power had failed, we could still fight.

Two miles was insanely easy.

Or it would have been, if I could see any land.

"Go!" Came the transmission from the wanker in the helo above me, as he released my connections.

One minor issue became readily apparent, as he banked sideways and the cable vanished into the wind…He'd not gotten a solid fix on the cliffside.

I fell maybe ten meters, slamming into the ground on a twenty degree angle and falling over instantly, the servos in both legs creaking and screaming under the weight and impact.

My mind filled with warning symbols, projected half strength pain to let me know what—and where—had just been fucked up, and diagnostics that flashed warning me that the landing had just done serious damage to my lower legs.

The short-range jump jets were down to forty percent capacity.

I cursed, no, I didn't just curse, if I'd been able to speak old world Latin I'd have fucking summoned half the demons in hell, I screamed that fuck abuse after the fucking helo pilot as they flew off on their merry way, but after a minute, I accepted my fate, and turned, locking in the Lidar and boosting the signal as far as I could.

The fingers had been partially mapped in places over the years, of course it had.

It was ridiculous to think that somewhere so close to the city, and frankly so fucking weird, as a mountain that had been chewed to shit by a load of experimental orbital weapons, and that people would just nod and leave it alone.

People had tried to explore it. Corporations had tried to map it and mine the metals that were left here, all that remained of the mighty engines of war that battled so long ago. Scientists had come exploring, students had studied here, and yeah, lunatics had tried to climb the fucking fingers, 'conquering' the mountains over and over.

Almost all of them had given up in short order, or they'd died.

What they'd done was contribute tiny fragments to the maps that were freely available, and that was wonderful, but without points of fixed reference, until I was actually on the ground, those maps were useless.

There were also massive black zones on the maps where things just didn't link up, and where there were only the tiniest fractions actually explored.

That meant I had a half useful, and half fucking use*less* map. One that I was adding to as I started hobbling along, teeth gritted as I stumbled over hidden rocks in the snow.

The only consolation, in this white landscape, surrounded by white snow, and a heavy, leaden, goddamn snow-filled sky, was that the wind hadn't given up.

It was scouring the rocky landscape clear almost as fast as the storm could lay more, keeping the ground more or less in a constant state of covering and uncovering.

I picked up the speed, the pain gradually decreasing as I jogged, the directional indicator clicking away merrily as I wove around boulders and leapt across small crevices, triggering the jump-jets over and over, gritting my teeth as I barely managed to clear the distance each time.

Minute by minute I closed on the virtual beacon, and hope slowly rose in me…until the ground started to angle downwards.

Steeper and steeper it went, until for every meter forward, I was going at least one more down, skidding and sliding.

Cascades of frozen rocks clattered past me as I dug my hands into the side of the mountain, the angle getting worse as I picked up speed, until I was forced to trigger the jets again, this time to slow myself.

I skidded to a halt, bare inches from the edge of a cliff, a second cliff a six or seven meters ahead angling back out and over me, as I stared up in dismay.

Looking down? There was a definite drop that I didn't like, and looking upwards? I didn't like that much either. I squinted, wondering if the patterns in the rocks nearby, and the combinations of broken and scoured mountainside were my imagination or…

"Fucking bastard luck!" I cursed in disbelief a minute later, crouching and tearing at the ground, pulling a battered and broken shield projector free shortly after.

I twisted it around, searching for the tell-tale marking on the back, and while the identification tag was too badly damaged to make out, I was sure.

This was my fucking shield generator that I'd lost on the mountain.

That meant…

I looked down into the dark crevasse, squinting, then nodding to myself as I spotted sections here and there, even with the limited visibility.

No wonder I'd been so messed up when the SARS had found me, it looked like the cliff I'd thrown myself down in my idiocy had ended in a crevasse, that partially slalomed down the fucking mountainside.

I mean, sure, I'd wanted some distance between me and the cave where I'd left the others, but fuck me sideways with a vibrating peacock, I must have made it halfway down the mountain!

It was blind luck they'd actually found me instead of giving up and fucking off for their supper!

That meant…

I looked across and up, then cursed.

It meant I needed to climb the fucking cliff-face, to get to where I'd jumped from. A vertical overhang cliff-face, in a storm, in a suit of power armor that weighed several tons.

I couldn't even test the goddamn handholds because the bottom of the cliff was over the crevasse!

I shook my head in disbelief, sincerely believing that whatever god controlled my fate with his die, was rolling fucking snake-eyes every damn time.

Looking across I hesitated only a brief second, searching, and glad that I'd secured my rifle to the magnetic plates on my back earlier.

I folded back the railguns with a silent order, both shoulder mounted systems twitching before turning around to face behind me, and then folding down, leaving me with two short pinions like wings laid down my back.

That done, I locked the cluster-bomb ports—not like I was going to need them on a mountainside, best not to let the likely flying stone and ice get into there—and took a few steps back, crouching and spreading 'my' fingers wide.

The suit faithfully replicated the gesture, clicking the stubby talons together as I checked they deployed, and then I ran at the edge, leaping out, and reaching for the cliff.

I crashed into it, hands scrabbling for purchase, and immediately bounced back, starting to fall, when I triggered the jump jets. Normally I could have used them in fast, high powered bursts, and I could have made it to the top of the cliff in short order. Normally of course, I'd have been on a specialist obstacle course if I was trying this shit, and if some sadistic drill sergeant *bastard* had come up with this?

I'd have been cursing his name for the entire time.

Which was kinda what gave them the warm and fuzzies, a tiny calm part of my mind commented, while the rest of me frantically kicked, scratched, gouged and leapt my way up the cliff.

Entire sections of the cliff came away, and still more radiated sparks like fireflies as I tore my way upwards, scratching and tearing.

It wouldn't have been possible without the jump-jets, not even slightly. As it was, every time I slid, I slipped, I missed a handhold or whatever, with my boots practically tearing through the cliff wall, my fingers tearing in and heaving, I'd still have fallen to my gory death.

Instead each time I fucked up a hold, or I didn't have the grip to climb 'properly' I'd trigger the jets, pushing me up and ahead, then cut them.

If they were fully working? I'd have run up it and cursed the sadistic bastard that came up with this all fucking day long. Instead?

By the time I made it, triggering a final burst of power to get me over the edge, I was exhausted. The jump jets were radiating warning signs like crazy about being overstressed to all buggery, and my chest was heaving as I tried to gulp down enough air.

There'd been no chance to rest, to catch my breath nor to slow at all really. If I'd done that I'd have fallen to my gory death at worst, and at best had to have started all over again.

No instead I was broken now, laid here in the swirling snow, blinking up at the howling leaden sky, lit from within by flashes of lightning.

"Wonder if they're going to be a problem?" I mumbled, thinking about the helo being fried over and over by them, before grunting and rolling onto my stomach, then pushing up, forcing myself to move again.

The landscape was as bland as could be, white snow and shattered rock, ancient wrecked steels and the hulls of war machines—okay, maybe not the standard bland, okay, so sue me—but still bland in that there was nothing but snow in all directions.

Certainly nothing to identify one way as better than another, if I discounted the cliff edge behind me. Setting off with that there, and following the marker on my HUD, I started climbing again, this time up a steep slope on the far side of the narrow little plateau.

I winced as I passed heavily dented armor plating that looked like it'd once belonged to an Osprey attack drone. It was roughly the same size as a small helo, carried enough munitions to level a small city and were armored to hell.

I'd watched vids about them in the great wars, the final RI war machines that were ever produced.

They were designed and built by a combination of rudimentary AI and RI, and piloted by individual RI's that were created from the base of dead soldier's brains.

Much as the Archaeon had been utterly insane and terrible ideas, the Osprey had been a boon and a blessing. They were like the old world nukes, where they were supposedly used as a deterrent, because nobody would actually be stupid enough to awaken and deploy them.

Once out, between their gravitation lens, the gamma cannons, the various lasers and their power generation? Where their physical weapons might run dry, their launch cradles were designed to accept almost any munitions, so they'd loot the bodies of the fallen and keep going.

They understood nothing but the slaughter, and they were incapable of mercy.

That they'd been used in the Fingers at some point I vaguely remembered, they'd been talked about after all, but they were almost never seen, so I quickly tagged the wreckage with a marker in my HUD, wondering if I was going to be able to sell the location to some research team.

It'd caught my eye because they were easily identifiable, massive as they were, and almost organic looking in the way they arced here and there.

It also had a massive dent in the side of it that I was fairly sure I remembered making, at high speed, coming down this very mountain.

I couldn't see, at the time, but I'd damn well felt that fucker.

That I'd hit this hard enough to dent layered titan-weave armor, then I'd slid off the cliff I'd just climbed up?

How fucking far had I ended up away from Richie and Sync by the end of all this shit?

I skirted around the massive hulk, and kept going, feeling the hairs on the back of my neck rising as I did, my innate paranoia from a hundred vids of how damn near impossible to kill these fuckers had been, rising as I presented my back to it.

Nothing happened of course, how could it, the damn thing had been here for hundreds of years, but still. It felt like I was tip-toeing past a sleeping dragon.

The mountain rose on and on ahead of me. I slogged up and on, forcing myself to pick up the speed as I took switchback and battered snow-buried trail after trail.

The only thing that let me know that the boulders were there at all was the slight angle of the protruding edges and the Lidar punching through to flicker over the ground.

I was starting to lose all sense of reality as I went deeper and deeper, paying more and more attention to the Lidar as I climbed.

The snow was building up on my frame by the second as I went, making it impossible to 'see' through the cameras, but the Lidar?

It was mapping out more and more, and as I went, diverting more power to it, the mountainside was revealed for what it really was.

It was a graveyard, and one of epic proportions.

Tens of thousands of machines had battled over every square mile of the mountains when they'd been hit by the orbital bombardments.

One of the treatise that we'd been shown in the army when I reached the APS, had argued that some of the old maps didn't show a mountain range here at all, and that the reason the range was so fucked up?

It'd been created by a gravitational 'last resort' weapon. Something that had driven the various automated systems mad, and the war leaders back then had been forced to corral everything in close through magnetics somehow, before bombarding their own armies—both the living and automated—with everything they had left.

They'd then hidden the truth, in their shame.

We were taught about it in the APS as a warning as to why the suits were highly limited in their RI/AI interfaces.

We didn't know how much was true, how much was bullshit and how much was corpo propaganda lying about the past to try and claim that they were so much better now, while spending as little on us as was possible.

Hell it could all be bullshit.

The mountainside I was climbing up right now though? If not for the insane storms of the area and the even more insane and dangerous beasts lower down, the corpos would have mined this place flat.

Everywhere I looked at least half of everything was wreckage. Armored hulls laid atop remains, sandwiched between overlapping fractured and settled rock, and here and there?

Caves.

Caves that the Lidar picked up as running deep.

I had no idea how they'd have factored into everything, but that they were here just showed how fucked up the place was.

Continuing up the mountainside, I gritted my teeth and pushed harder, following routes that lead upwards back and forth, picking my way over centuries of rusty debris, until at last, I was hit full in the face by the howling wind again, as I came out from the lee of some rocks.

The beacon was throbbing in my vision, as was the timer for pickup, and it was getting scarily close to the time.

How the hell had two miles taken me forty-seven minutes?

I broke into a lumbering run, crossing the last dozen meters, and increasing the power to the Lidar. It pulsed and pounded the mountainside ahead of me, easily finding the entrance to the cave we'd buried, now reburied by a snowdrift.

I set to work, scraping, digging and throwing boulders aside, grabbing them like they were nothing, tossing them here and there, blindly behind me, the crack and distant booms from below telling me that some I'd thrown were bouncing over the edges and probably setting off minor avalanches.

I didn't care.

In under a minute I had a gap wide enough, and I struggled through it, paint scraping and sparks flying as I shouldered my way inside, until finally I stood there before them.

Two suits the same as my own, still showing the scrapes and battering's, not to mention the Red Team markers on their shoulders and chest, the occasional flickers of slowly decreasing power markers showing as I pinged them, sharing my ID and reconnecting.

The suits stood side by side, hands entwined as if toddlers seeking reassurance from one another, the horrific cold of the mountain nothing compared to the cold of cryosleep that both bodies radiated, and I stood there, staring at the markers in horror.

They were alive, sure, and thank the gods for that, but?

They were also deeper in cryo than had been the plan. Something must have gone wrong, because there was no way they were moving in the next hour, maybe two or three.

Hell, I'd be lucky if we were moving by morning!

This fucked everything, all our plans were dead in the water, especially the rescue here, the escape by helo and the nest clearance tomorrow.

I briefly contemplated leaving them here, turning around and running for the helo meet, planning on coming back for them later…and I dismissed it before the thought had fully formed. Staring at my two friends, fast asleep in their armor, encased in glittering frost, I knew what I had to do.

Moving over to Richie and Sync, I used my command overrides—thank fuck the systems still accepted my authority on my keystone, and hadn't been updated that I was no longer part of the APS—to start the 'defrost' cycle.

I also plugged into Richie's suit, set the system, and deployed one of his drones, flying it out of the entrance to the cave and settling it down on the ground atop some scrap metal.

Fortunately, the sheer fucking amount of it that was available here abouts was going to play into my hands for this. Metal, when used right, and with the correct tech, could boost a signal tremendously, and I was going to damn well need it.

Linking the comm gear I had, feeding in the helo details and then routing through Richie's *much* more powerful gear, I linked up to the pilot, who was totally not expecting my call.

He was due to collect us, literally any minute, and according to the signal degradation on the meter, and the directional sweep? He was five miles away, and heading in the opposite direction.

He was also singing about 'easy-come, easy-go' a recently popular song about losing a job, and finding another and not caring.

The bastard wasn't even subtle about the fact he'd hung around for a bit and was now fucking off, rather than coming to collect us.

"Helo this is LDS," I said grimly. "I have you on escape vector, not, repeat, not recovery. Advise."

"Uh...yeah, ah LDS...right!" He grunted, cut off from his shitty singing as he tried to cover his ass. "Ummm right, you know, this storm, and the fuel..."

"You're heading back to the city to refuel," I finished for him. "I understand, don't worry."

"You do?" he asked, unsure. "I am? I mean, yeah! Yeah that's it, but you fuel cost..."

"You got half upfront for the job, and you built the fuel into the deal, so I'll go to ten percent higher. Considering the amount of fuel you're saving, you know, with the helo being at a third of the weight on the way out with just me in, and without any of us at all on the way back."

"Yeah...but you know..."

"Because the other option, if that's not what's going on here, is that you're abandoning us out here. And I *know* that's not the case, because then I'd be firing a hellfire at you, to make my displeasure known."

"Ah..."

"And even if you managed to escape that, you'd be left landing in the city, having only taken half the money, because the other half wouldn't be paid out. then when I complete the days of walking to get back to the city, with my companions? You'd have three fully armed and armored APS operators visiting to explain why you don't fuck with us. We'd be getting our money back, from your corpse, after ripping your little helo into shreds."

"Now wait a fucking..."

"But that's not the case!" I said firmly. "Because you'll be back here to meet us at 0400 sharp, and you'll be monitoring this frequency, in case there are issues, isn't that right?" I asked bitingly, getting a subdued confirmation from him.

I didn't have great hopes about his reliability, but that was life. Basically if I pushed too hard at this point, he'd soon find out I didn't have a hellfire missile, and then my only option was walk back.

I left it at that, and disconnected, ordering the drone back to Richie's armor, then looked at my two friends, and sighed, shaking my head as I looked over the jobs ahead of me. This wasn't going to be a fun night.

CHAPTER FORTY-SIX

The next few hours were spent in general 'clean-up' duties, doing maintenance on their suits, powering them up and plugging in the battery relay.

These were shitty batteries, literally, not full on fusion cores like the suits ran on properly, but they still held a fuck load of power, and they needed that after two missions, a crash and then an emergency cryo procedure.

I hooked them up, one by one to their suits and watched as the batteries were drained like a soldier with a beer, each of the dozens of batteries only adding a few percentage points to their systems, but even one point could be the difference between life and death.

I also reloaded their nanites, ordering their systems to start using the nanites to repair the damage done as they started the defrost cycle, plugging in more and more of the medikits as each hour passed.

That was my night—monitor them, unplug the old unit, plug in the new unit, wait, drain the system, repeat.

The suits were efficient fuckers, forcing the discarded flesh and parts, the dead nanites and so on into the clearance cycle, forming those, like they did all bodily wastes, into compressed carbon pellets that were stored.

I then had to order them to be ejected, and basically kick them away, as I didn't think they'd appreciate waking up with their containment full and surrounded by shit.

Hour after hour passed as I monitored them, amusing myself by sending Lidar pulses into the back of the cave, where at some point a collapse had closed off the rest of the cave system from this one.

I looked over the resulting maps, checking them against the little I knew about geology, and the little I knew about the fingers, along with the evidence seen so far.

The result was that I thought I was starting to get a clue about the area, and why it was so insanely fucked up.

If—and this was a big if—but if the entire area had been ground zero for a gravitational lens or something, a seismic weapon that created the Fingers, then the whole area was hammered over and over with orbital weapons?

The end result wasn't a mountain at all.

Not in the classical sense anyway. The end result was a massive pile of debris, rock, random building materials and warmachines, all piled atop each other.

That could be justified as a mountain, sure, fuck load of rock and metal, boom.

But the warmachines were also using nuclear and fusion plants, there was an insane amount of radiation here, add in the layered metals and more, roll the stones and more across all of this, and leave it to settle?

Then let the weather be pulled in by whatever weird elemental shit that caused all of that—I didn't understand it much more than the water cycle—but I knew that mountains seemed to drag in storms and that was definitely happening here.

The end result was that over hundreds of years, as the mountains settled, spaces would develop, not so much from standard erosion by millennia of water and ice and so on, but because those gaps were left in the forming. There'd be pockets of open spaces, and then as the water ran down the mountains they'd smooth these places out.

The random bits and pieces that took up most of the space inside say a battleship might be washed away, but the overall superstructure would last long enough for sediment and more to coat it. Over centuries the result would be caves…

They'd link up as the rainwater and snowmelt ran down the mountains, and then…

I moved to the back of the cave and locked everything down that I could, using the Lidar one last time, running a test, no longer amusing myself, but deadly serious.

The result when it came back? It made me grin.

We had a way down the mountain. Probably.

Two more hours passed before the first of them—Sync of course, Richie was notorious for being slow to wake normally, never mind when frozen—began to wake.

An hour after that, and the pair of them were almost able to speak again, making me reassess my plan of getting them up and out as fast I'd expected to, as a bloody stupid one.

Maybe I'd actually lucked out with the helo pilot, because if I'd have had to physically carry them out and load them onto the helo? There was no way, realistically that I could have done it with the helo being battered by the storm.

As much as I didn't want to admit it, in this regard I was a total novice. Next time I'd book the helo myself and have a damn good conversation with the pilot about the realities of life as well.

For now though?

My friends were back.

"Ka…butt?" Sync mumbled and I nodded, unable to keep from grinning widely at her being alive and awake. I sent them both a virtual link, the three of us sharing operating and processing power to create a virtual location that we could all be in, instead of sitting in the armor.

In a blink, we were sitting around 'our' table in our favorite bar. Fergie and Scott were playing on the stage with their band, and there was beer in front of us.

It was virtual, and did fuck all to quench the thirst that we all felt at seeing it, but it was part of the overall image.

We all sat there for a few minutes, watching the pair with the rest of their band, before I forced myself to turn away. There was a risk to virtual like this, to recreating dead friends and having them act from memories.

It was a balm to the soul at times, but you knew, and if you let yourself forget, really? You suffered all over again from scratch when you let yourself feel again. I waved a hand and the band appeared as if on a screen instead, obviously not live and right before us.

It hurt, but seeing the looks on the other two's faces, I should have thought to load in a blocker. My RI had built this virtual from my orders, and had fleshed it out with subconscious desires. Scott had once made a HELL of a mistake when he'd created one of these, and we'd never let him live down the 'serving staff' that he'd had wandering around.

It'd been weeks, maybe a month for me, and I'd been insanely busy all the time. I'd had time to come to terms with losing Scott and Fergie, but for the other two? It was literally yesterday.

"I'm sorry," I said softly, shaking my head.

"It's okay," Sync said, her head hanging a little, before she looked across at the vid and smiled, despite the heartache.

"They really were good weren't they?" she said wistfully. "In the old world they'd have gone all the way…"

"The band?" I asked, and she nodded.

"If they'd stop chasing ass long enough, then yeah, but they lived for the life, not the fame," Richie corrected, smiling and shaking his head. "Fergie smoked anything he could, drank more than four men, and shagged anything that moved, and Scott? He'd be distracted by a pretty girl or a new martial art every five minutes! In the old days when bands were real and toured the world? They'd have spent half of each day tracking the pair down and dragging them back onto the transport."

"It'd be wonderful to have seen though," I admitted.

"It would." Richie sighed, before coughing and straightening, clearly burying his emotions as he tried to get himself under control. "So, how long then boss? Are we free? Are we fucked? How we doing?"

I snorted. "We're doing about as well as we usually are."

"That bad?" Sync asked, wincing. "Come on boss, give us some good news…"

"I beat the shit out of Tyrannus," I said, picking an image out of my memory and displaying it on the screen before us, then starting it playing from memory, as they watched me beat the absolute shit out of him.

Richie winced when I cut through his hand, and even Sync looked at me sideways as my beating him to death went on. Watching it again, from the recording the RI made automatically, I had to admit it made me slightly uncomfortable.

Without that rage against him, without the adrenaline, the anger and everything else? Sure he deserved to die for the shit he'd pulled, but…

The truth was he was no worse and no better than a load of others I'd dealt with of late, and while I now knew he wasn't responsible for everything that happened, I knew that if he'd been given the chance he would have done it all.

"So…" I said after a few more seconds of blood and screams. "I might have been slightly more upset with him than he deserved."

"Was he responsible?" Sync asked flatly. Did he take our friends from us?"

"Yes and no," I said. "He fucked up, and he took bribes, but the mech? The scavs? All that shit? It wasn't him."

"Fuck."

"It was Major Marcial."

"You're shitting me!" Richie grunted.

"Nope." I sighed. "He's running a black ops APS unit, freelance as near as I can tell, and…"

I explained everything I knew, and I suspected, making sure they knew the difference, and that I could prove only this much. I told them about Luna, Gessh, Todds and Reign.

Weirdly explaining that I was sleeping with Reign, and that we were just setting into the relationship, as well as that she was my second? I felt far more defensive explaining that, than I had justifying torturing Tyrannus, and killing the people I had of late.

Richie, of course, gave me a fist bump and asked if I had any images of the team I'd like to share, waggling his eyebrows.

Then he grunted, and rubbed at his ankle as Sync apparently kicked him under the table.

I set the recording playing again, and showed them the two black ops teams battling it out. That led to me explaining how I'd survived, and led to the recording of my fight with the APS, then specter harvesting and hunting…

An hour later and Richie was laughing his ass off about the 'Errant Mergers' guild job, that they'd kicked the crap outta me, and that I'd then gone back and burned their guild down and pissed on the ashes.

Eventually, after explaining what I thought about the mountain and our possible escape route, I stopped the virtual. I ordered them both to have an hour's sleep while I topped up their nanites, and then cleared the passage at the back of the cave, getting ready for what was to come.

CHAPTER FORTY-SEVEN

I gave them an extra half an hour, resting a little myself, before waking the pair, all three of us triggering stims—they had opened their reservoir and shared some for me, I'd not even considered that they'd not be already loaded in my armor, but they'd not been—and then the three of us gathered up at the entrance to the cave system.

"You're sure about this?" Richie asked me.

"Not even fucking slightly."

"That would have been a great place to lie, you know that, right?" Sync said. "What happened to all that long term NCO training? Lie to your operators, always."

"That's officer training," I pointed out. "Lie to everyone, but especially to yourself."

"Who do NCO's lie to then?" Sync asked, amused.

"Hookers," Richie added quickly. "Things like 'no, it's the first time this has happened' and that old favorite 'I'm over six inches and can go all night', you know, the one that all engineers say."

"Then the next morning they admit it was an estimate." Sync snorted. "Okay, so—"

"SO!" I interrupted, stopping them before they could go any further, despite the smile I couldn't help. "According to the Lidar there's another big cave a few hundred meters down from here, and then more passages beyond that. Hopefully we can make it a fair distance down the mountain and then get outside, we've got six hours before the helo is due, every meter closer to the city we can get gives us a better chance of being picked up."

"Just waiting on the order," Richie pointed out and I growled.

"Sync you're in the lead, Richie, bring up the rear, we take turns hammering the Lidar, see what we can find as we go, some of these rooms have collapsed, forming massive caverns, and they're likely to have multiple exits I'd imagine, while other areas, well. We're not going to want to stand in certain areas. Go." I ordered.

"Moving," Sync said, her rifle ready as she led the way, with the pair of us following.

The passage was a narrow one. I'd cleared enough stone and debris that we could get in, and a little past the collapse just in case, but after a dozen meters it opened wider and then narrowed down intermittently, the constant downwards angle we ran made more difficult by the constant run off of water that ran down one wall and formed a rushing, gurgling river.

Minutes passed as we went deeper, radioactive warnings spiking, temperatures rising, then falling as we passed location after locations.

They were minor, on the whole, but the radiation helped to keep the temperature inside considerably higher than outside, and kept the water running.

But twenty minutes later we reached the first large cavern, and all that changed.

My Lidar had mapped out part of the cavern, including the branching passages that ran off in all directions, but it wasn't a great tool for real pictures. The image I'd had was of a cave system with a load of thin, almost translucent overlapping returns disrupting the result.

When we got there?

Well, we started fucking swearing alright.

"Boss this isn't supposed to be here," Sync told me flatly, while Richie giggled over how cool everything was.

"I know," I agreed, sharing my theory on what the mountain actually was again. Some of it certainly was looking likely as we looked out across the cavern full of fungal blooms, massive mushrooms and lines of growth that dangled from the ceiling.

The various counters and sensors were going nuts as well, telling us that we'd better not linger in this chamber unless we wanted either some new limbs, or a new description for our armor that included 'half-life' as part of it.

I had to guess that it was the radiation that was providing the warmth and the growth medium, and the fungi the bioluminescence, but either way, I was damn well recording, and I ordered the others to do so as well.

Moving forward, it was clear as our clawed feet crunched down on gravel, before being carpeted in moss and growths, that this wasn't a minor detail for the cave as well.

"We need to move here through quickly," I ordered them. "The radiation is too high." The suits could take it, admittedly, but the helo pilot wasn't likely to let us aboard if we were fucking glowing.

Sync led the way, weaving in and out of the cave, doing her best to touch as little as possible, even as Richie stomped straight through, enjoying that in his APS he could mulch the organic growths with ease.

That lasted all of a minute, as we reached the center of the cavern, needless to say.

"Boss." Sync growled, highlighting and sharing an image.

I frowned looking at it, then winced. "Chances it's hostile?" I asked.

"Fucking likely," Richie said suddenly. "I've got two more back here, suit didn't pick them up on scans, but a search and isolate algo brings them up clear as day."

"Share it." I ordered, getting a file a few seconds later and approving it instantly, knowing that while he was mad, he wasn't mad in a bad way. The file that ran integrated a pattern recognition algorithm, using the face of the half hidden creature to scan the area for similar matches.

"Oh shit." I whispered. "Twelve…"

"Look up." Sync whispered.

"Thirteen," I said after a second of staring up into the nest suspended above us.

"I'm betting that's their mother, and we're about to be fed to the kids," Richie said conversationally, eyeing the thing.

It was spider-like, a dozen legs led off a small body, almost comical in the tight clustering, but the massive head was clearly designed for nightmares, five eyes gleamed malevolently, arranged in a half arc around a mouth filled with serrated teeth. The body ended with a tail that it was using as an anchor, clinging to a section of the roof and dangling, watching us.

"No explosives." I ordered. "We can't risk the cavern roof coming down.

"Railguns and rifles?" Sync asked and I grunted an agreement, ordering my own to deploy. Clearly when we'd stopped, that was the wrong thing to do, as before my railguns could even finish sliding out from the locked position in my back, the fucking *thing* above us dropped, and that set them all off.

The spider—I guessed that was what it had started off as anyway—was insanely fast when it moved, and when it landed on Richie, he went apeshit. The thing was perhaps two meters tall, the 'little ones' about a half a meter to a meter and a half in size, as they burst from cover and closed on us.

They almost blurred as they darted here and there, the mother clinging to Richie's back and vomiting a clear, sticky liquid over him as he screamed and spun, trying to get his rifle into play, before abandoning it and grabbing the damn thing by the head.

It screeched, trying to get off him, or to bite him, I guessed, as he panicked and squeezed in return.

While it might be an unholy terror of the cave system, it was still organic, it was bone and chitin and whatever else, and we were titanium and powered more by fusion cores.

The head burst, the body spasming and going crazy, twitching, kicking and trying to crush him as the final signals ran through it. Richie gagged and hurled the body free of himself, before stomping on a smaller one that tried to attack him.

It exploded, literally, bits flying everywhere.

My first instinct was to fire on them, to take them down in a hail of flying bullets, but honestly? It wasn't needed. Sync was the sharpshooter, and even she hesitated, having seen the result of Richie splattering the mother.

Then it was melee range, and it didn't matter anymore.

I punted one that ran at me, crushing the head in, sending it flying backwards, knocking over another of them, and stepped up quickly stomping on that as well.

One leapt onto my railgun, dangling from it and scrabbling for purchase on my chest armor, lunging forwards, maw like a descent into hell and nightmare opening up and…I smacked it.

It crumpled.

In seconds we'd gone from surrounded by freaky, possibly terrible enemies, to pest control detail. Ten seconds later, the last two survivors were running like fuck as Richie screamed and ranted, grabbing a boulder and hurling it after them as they ran.

"Well…" Sync said brightly into the silence. "That got the blood flowing."

"Yeah, not ours as well, which is always good," I admitted.

"What is this shit?" Richie swore, dragging his fingers across the crap covering his carapace, and Sync stepped up, scanning it.

"Acid," she confirmed, then snorted. "Some sort of flesh dissolver, not dangerous to us in the suits, probably lethal if we weren't though."

"Wash it off." I ordered Richie, nodding to the running water on one side of the cave. "You don't need to risk that shit when you come to clean the suit later."

"Ah man, I forgot about that." He groaned. "No maintenance and cleaning crews!"

"Yeah, so unless you want to be scrubbing it off your armor with a toothbrush?" I pointed, and he went.

"Wonder what the hell they fed on?" Sync asked while we waited, searching around and finding piles of mush here and there that we assumed were spider shit, or dissolved remains. "No bodies."

"No clue." I admitted. "But that they're here, and all of this?" I gestured around at the thriving ecosystem, taking the time to look, and seeing bugs and more running here and there. "There's going to be a fuck load of stuff in here."

"Think it might be a better idea to fuck off outside?" Richie asked, and I shook my head.

"We've got more than five hours left before the helo is due, we can continue for an hour, then if we've not found a way out we turn back. I'd much rather climb down a gentle slope like this than try and leap our way down, especially as fucked as my jump jets are, but if that's what we have to do? We will."

With Richie clean—more or less—we set off again, clearing the rest of the cavern with no more attacks, and headed down into the first of the passages.

Worryingly, the one we were following quickly narrowed down, and we were forced to kneel, then crawl, the ceiling coming lower and lower by the second as we moved, the decline growing steeper and steeper as we continued, until we were forced to pause, sending a long, and powerful mapping pulse ahead, making goddamn sure we were heading the right way.

Several of the other passages that we'd checked were wider, but they all ended in sections we couldn't pass, or went nowhere. This was the only one that didn't end, as near as we could tell, and was judged to be high and wide enough we could pass through.

An hour more we continued for, making me more and more uncomfortable, as we pulsed again and again, crawling over piled debris, under sagging sections of roof and occasionally being forced by the angle to slide into the swift running river and submerge ourselves.

We passed things that were clearly once rooms, and occasionally even power systems that flickered and ran, pulsing weird interferences as we emerged from the gloom, then vanished again, wondering at the millennia since living, sapient beings saw these things.

We passed recognizable weapons systems, some of them terrible, bomb-pumped neutron laser banks were VERY identifiable after all, but looking at them, we knew they'd never be salvageable, and even if they were?

They couldn't be fired, not without such an extensive repair and refit that it'd be cheaper to build them from scratch.

Still, it was terrifying to see, regardless.

Another hour came and went, and the sweat that was soaking me over this decision became a river of regret. I was dealing with the sure knowledge that I'd fucked up, and that we were going to be walking to the city, when Sync set off her latest pulse.

"Exit!" she comm'd, and we all paused, looking at the map.

At the very outer edge of the Lidar's reach…was an exit from the passage, and considering we were still passing tracks and more down here? There had to be something up ahead.

"Move it." I ordered, renewed hope rising as we kicked off, crawling with more vigor. Meters flew by as we scrabbled along, minutes passing as we closed on the cavern, and after three hours of travel, we could at last, stand again.

The dropping temperature the last few minutes had made it clear that there was indeed an exit coming up, and when we reached it? We burst out into the storm with a sense of relief I'd rarely ever experienced.

We were over a mile down from where we'd started and nearly two closer to the city than we had been, the decline having done a hell of a lot for the speed we'd travelled, but still, the storm raged.

"Move out!" I ordered, taking the lead, Sync's battery heavily drained by the constant Lidar pulses, as I started running my own.

We ran then, as fast as we safely could, following a valley that ran more or less in the right direction, passing more caves, most covered from above, overhangs that created the impression there was nothing here, but the Lidar?

"You know there's more fucking life here than in the entire wastelands?" Richie commented as we ran. "Seriously boss, if your little kit works? We could harvest this place for months, and I'm betting there's a shit load of nanites here."

I slowed for a few seconds, seeing his point and seriously wondering at it, we'd need to test it after all, and should I not…

"Next time," I said, picking up the pace. "But good point, Richie!"

There was no way I was opening my armor here, the storm was battering us with constantly shifting winds as it was, and we weighed multiple tons each, and that didn't even mention the fucking temperature.

It was still well below freezing, and the winds were vicious. Now that we had the new design though? We'd make some changes and make some kit for each of the APS. Maybe make use of the section on the back that was supposed to hold our termination charges, we'd need a section mounting that would look like that after all, so maybe fill it with the nanites in a storage chamber?

Either way, it was only a few more minutes before Richie managed to pick up the helo, and I set a rendezvous point, two hours from where we were, and a solid run according to the mapping systems.

We made it in ninety-seven minutes.

CHAPTER FORTY-EIGHT

The flight back to the city was almost anti-climactic, the three of us spread out in the interior of the helo and slept for the first four hours. When we woke up, we started sorting the details we needed to get back to the 'real world' again, all while the pilot tried to explain why we owed him so much more credits. There was the increased risk, the flight time, the wear and tear, the jobs he'd lost that day because he'd had to come back for us, all of it.

He knew it was bullshit, we knew it was bullshit, and eventually we tuned the fucker out, Richie and Sync cursing as they found that as they'd been declared legally dead, they'd lost their credit accounts.

Both had been transferred to their 'next of kin'. In Richie's case a cousin, who he hadn't spoken to in ten years and after the death taxes were taken off? It wasn't worth the risk to trace and get the credits back.

Sync, on the other hand, admitted that the credits had gone to her ex-husband, and that fucker would have been laughing all the way to the bank. She spent a long minute looking over everything she and Richie could dig up on him, and quickly realized that there wasn't a cat in fucking hell's chance she was getting anything back.

He'd spent it all on partying, he'd given an emotional speech about her death—laughter and cheers were born of emotion after all--and his new wife had apparently already filed for divorce and half his money.

Sync's only legal method of getting anything back was to come out as alive, she'd be arrested as a deserter and thief of an APS instantly, most likely, unless she was insanely lucky? At best they'd make her return to the army for the next few years to finish her tour.

That left illegal methods, anything that left the ex-husband alive and knowing she was, would result in him trying to blackmail her—the divorce wasn't a good one—and for the little money that would be left once the partying was all done and the new soon-to-be ex-wife's claim?

It wasn't worth it.

We came up with the plan to fuck his life up a little more, possibly either hire some goblins or something, maybe have Bowdoin fuck him over, just because of the speeches he gave over her supposed death, and moved on.

By the time we were coming into a landing at the warehouse? We were all exhausted, emotionally and physically and I'd ignored seven attempts at calls from Julius.

I sent twenty percent on top to the pilot, knowing that would cover any expenses he had, and we clambered out, hurrying into the warehouse and out of prying eyes as quickly as possible.

Luna and Gessh had opened the doors for us as we landed, and quickly closed them again, even as I sent approvals to the various turrets and sensors for Richie and Sync.

The warehouse seemed insanely small with all three of us in our suits and moving, but I had Richie move into position with the storage and maintenance crate, Reign and Todds hurrying down the stairs to join us as he stepped back, the cranes locking into place on his APS.

"Are we clear?" he asked me, and I checked.

"Confirmed, cameras are down, and we're secure," I said, smiling. "Welcome home, both of you."

"Ummm, any chance of some privacy?" Sync asked, and I winced, turning to the others.

"Okay everyone, clear the room please, we need some clean clothes, a fuck load of wipes, and we're all going to need showers before anything else. We've all been in the suits and there's processes that aren't nice to share. A little privacy would be good."

"We'll be upstairs," Reign said, nodding. "Give me a minute and I'll get a selection of clothes."

"Thank you." Sync sighed.

I winced, I should have thought about it after all, there were waste elimination facilities built into the suit, but they were basically glorified catheters, and they needed removal. There was an automated process to do it, and it sucked ass.

Far better to do it yourself, you knew your own body after all, and while we usually had a dedicated room each, we'd done it in front of each other enough times that it wasn't an issue. In front of the others though?

I just should have thought about it.

Julius started calling again and I growled, accepting it finally.

"Julius." I growled the greeting.

"Kabutt, are you back?" He asked grimly, and I nodded.

"We are."

"All three?"

"Yeah."

"And…and they're functional?" he asked, hesitating and clearly preparing himself for the worst.

"We are, although we need a rest and a goddamn shower before we can do anything.

In truth the four hours of sleep on the flight had done wonders for us, but still, that wasn't the point, we'd all been bouncing and jostled in our suits the entire time, so while there was rest, it wasn't 'good' rest.

"Tonight," he said. "We need to have that nest clear by dawn or we fail the contract."

"We'll be there," I assured him. "We'll get the job done."

"Thank fuck." He sighed, sagging, then grinned. "On the upside, though? I had a little good news an hour ago, I called you, wanting to make sure you weren't involved, but I guess you couldn't have been as you were out of the city."

"What happened?" I asked curiously.

"Our friend Trees was apparently mugged, or something anyway. Something certainly happened, because he's been dropped by his team and he's in a hospital clinic."

"What?" I asked, confused by fucking loving it. "What happened to him?"

"Nobody knows, but his team are all like him, purists, so he's fucked either way, if he's in the hospital it's something that a medikit can't fix, and his kind won't permit regrowth or cybernetics..."

"Oh for fuck's sake. He's one of those?" I cursed, it all making sense now. "A fucking 'church of the pure' lunatic. That explains so much."

The church were one of hundreds scattered about the city, everything from the AI being gods to this being the end of days was actively believed in and worshipped by some nutter somewhere, but the purists were fucking idiots as far as I was concerned.

They preached that any and all mods were befoulment of the 'pure' body, and things like regrowth, bio-grafting and so on were just as bad. How that worked with them using nanites and medikits? Nobody knew. It was the usual mind bending, jumping through hoops bullshit that religious fanatics came up with to justify their belief, but that these lunatics had latched onto it?

It made sense for Trees and the rest. They believed that this whole 'breed out the lesser races' plan of the elven leadership was heretical as well, and while I agreed there, it wasn't because they felt it was wrong to do something with that kind of an aim, or to abandon the children.

No it was because they were disgusted by the 'lesser races' and believed they—we—should all be enslaved.

That someone had done him an injury serious enough he was in a hospital? That was his life over. He couldn't allow regrowth or mods, not without losing his moral high ground, and to a scumbag like Trees? That was impossible to countenance.

I didn't know what had happened, but I fucking liked it. That his team had abandoned him was just an extra gold fucking star for me. I really needed to send him a fruit basket or something.

Maybe with a fresh turd at the bottom, one that was nice and squishy.

"Kabutt?" Julius said, and I blinked, having gone off into a fantasy of eating a load of chilies and sending him the result.

"Sorry, Julius, miles away, what did you say?" I apologized.

"You'll be there, tonight?" he asked again, clearly worried. "It's a normal nest, but it's a big one, and its mainly underground, and..."

"And?" I asked, not liking the tone.

"And, well, if you could make a point of a fast, and impressive clearance? Like a real slaughter? An advert for what the APS can do?" He winced. "I'm sorry to ask, I know they're literally just back from the dead, but if you could, it'll make damn sure nobody wants to risk losing us as their clearing team."

"It'll be fine, but I'm going to need a lot of extra ammo if you want us to clear it fast and impressively, no offence, but you want us to do it with a lot of fire and brimstone? That's not cheap. I don't mean on our effort, that's fine, I mean on the sheer ammo expenditure. Our ammo isn't something you can just pick off the shelf, and it's not cheap."

"I'll cover it." Julius said. "This is the kind of advert we get to do once. Nobody knows of any APS that would do this, so when you all march out of the darkness? The client is going to shit themselves, and you better believe they'll be screaming to the various reels about you, wanting to sell the vids."

"We're going to need a fucking respray," I muttered, looking at the APS, and wincing. "We're all in army official decals at the minute."

"Can you do it?" he asked, biting his lip and I nodded.

"We can, but we're going to need some time. Fuck."

"I'll leave you to it then," he said, quickly ending the call before I could add that bill to his tally as well.

I sighed, then triggered the release, forcing a smile as I looked to Richie and Sync. "Hey guys…you ready for some fun news?" I asked, groans rising instantly at my tone.

The next ten minutes were a sheer fucking joy, for all of us. The rear plates that covered Richie's APS' ass were still dented in from the crash and we had no replacements. So we decided to rip them off and check underneath, just so we knew if the suit was usable or not.

Two of us pulling, one pushing and a crowbar inserted into the gap in the release plate finally broke it free, slamming it into my face and nearly knocking me out in the process.

That the unit was fine under the armor was a vast relief, but we had limited time before the mission tonight and using a medikit for my aching face seemed frivolous, so I just put up with it, while Richie put the panel aside, swearing he'd fix it with a hammer later today.

An hour later, we were all showered, dressed and sat around a table, eating and drinking, making plans, when I got a call from that lazy goddamn hacker Bowdoin.

"Hi there, Kabutt. It's so damn good to see you again. Did you miss me? I'm betting you missed me," he said cheerily, as I glared at him. This, this was exactly the wrong time, and I damn well knew he wanted something.

I stared at him grimly, my face throbbing as I reminded myself over and over that it wasn't his fault he was annoying, and he was an asset. I needed to keep him, just in case. No telling him to get fucked on general principles or anything.

I sighed then forced myself, again, to be polite. "Bowdoin. Yeah, sure, like I'd miss the cock rot." Well, *sort of* polite.

"You had the cock rot? You know, that would explain—"

"What the fuck do you want, Bowdoin? This is NOT a good time, alright?" I snapped.

He shrugged. "Well, seeing as how we're buddies and I've helped you quite a few times—I thought that turnabout would be fair play. I've got a job offer for you. Like back when Richie did a job for me."

"Huh. Well, didn't see that coming. So, what's in it for me?" I asked, actually amused, wondering what use a hacker had for a guy like me.

"From what I understand, you're quite a fan of cold Credits? I mean, I can get you all sorts of weird merch too, if that's what you're into. We also have a good bunch of dealers on our turf. I can get you Char, Skiff, any—"

"Drugs made by slum peddlers? Don't think so. As for merch, if you're going to buy it with Oshbob, don't bother. I'm able to visit that green bastard and get ripped off on my own. Credits are fine. You haven't mentioned what the job is, though." I snorted, waving off Reign's curious look.

"Sending it right over."

MISSION OFFER:

Bowdoin Katamari, on behalf of the Snid, offers the following mission to Harry Kabutt:

At a time and place of Bowdoin's choosing, Kabutt will assault the AWF headquarters and then pull back. He will keep any chasing forces occupied and distracted until the Snid give the green light.

The Snid will supply:

- A list of known defensive forces in the AWF headquarters.
- Blueprints of the surrounding area, including a nearby entrance to the Underground
- Any information they can give Kabutt from inside the organization during the mission

Reward: 30000 credits

That was it, no fucking real details, no timescale, and AWF? The Artem Workers Foundation? They were a fucking corporation! For us to hang about for as long as he wants? Fuck no!

"You're trying to get me killed, is that it?" I asked, trying to control my rising irritation.

"What? No. Of course not. Listen, I don't get what you're so damn upset about. You just need to get in there, toss a couple of grenades and then retreat while you take the occasional potshot at the pursuit to keep 'em interested. Meanwhile, I can sneak in the back door and do what I need to do," he protested, seeming confused.

I glared at him, seeing he genuinely had no clue, he'd watched an op through my damn eyes, and still he had no clue, this. This was why civilians and military never mixed well.

"Bowdoin, you're an idiot," I muttered, scrubbing at my face with the heel of one hand, trying not to snarl. "Yeah, sure. I just need to distract them 'until you give the green light'? What's that? Two minutes? Ten? That shit won't work. Especially because these aren't like the poor fuckers Richie messed around with back in the day. AWF are the real deal. That means, *if* I should take the job, it would be for a lot more than thirty K, and we'd need to work on what I need to do. I need intel. Numbers. Everything you have. And we need hard limits. I need to know how many minutes I'm staying. Fuck, Bowdoin, it's like you've never done something like this before!"

"Whoa, whoa, whoa. First off, where the fuck is Kabutt and what have you done with him? I seem to recall somebody thinking I could 'just do my hacking thing' on a corpo tier AI. This is nowhere near as insane. Now, if there's anything that needs adjusting, we'll go over it, man." He agreed. "I'm cool with you doing your thing and then taking a judgement call on when to pull out."

My left eye twitched at his words and I could feel a migraine starting. I swear, just speaking to the lunatic was an effort. "That's a start. We still need to know what we're up against." I explained as patiently as I could.

"Totally fair. I'm working on assembling a full list of the guards at the headquarters. Then, there's a couple of mercs that hang around to protect the place. A group led by somebody called Min. Now. as for price—"

"Wait. Did you just say... Min? Tall fucker, slick as hell. Half orc, half elf?" I interrupted, remembering the comments by Luna and Gessh. He was supposed to be a corpo bodyguard type, heavily armed and skilled, as well as some poster boy type, they'd make sure he had a good team if they were using him for something.

"Yup. That's the guy. He's got a crew of—"

"I've heard of them. If he's in charge of defenses, that makes it a whole lot tougher. The price will—" I broke off, as Luna leant in close, having heard my half of my conversation and I cursed.

"What's this about Min?" she asked. "We got a job with him? Seriously, Kabutt, you don't know, but I'm not doing a—"

"No wait!" Gessh snapped, cutting her sister off and grabbing my arm on the other side. "He said that Min's the TARGET!"

"I'm in," Luna said flatly. "Fuck yeah. Where and when? Wait, are we killing him? I mean, we're friends with Santos…"

"I don't fucking know, do I?" I snapped, shaking my head in disbelief, they could damn well hear we were in the middle of the conversation after all.

"We're doing it," Luna said firmly. "Look, boss, we ask for nothing, alright, we've helped with loads of shit and for you to not be willing to do this for us…"

"GIVE ME A FUCKING MOMENT," I snapped at them, waving them away.

"I'm... not saying anything," Bowdoin complained and I glared at him.

"Not you, damnit! Fucking idiot. I mean these harpies. Give me a minute." I muted the call and looked around the room, seeing that Sync was grinning, she was always happy when I was getting grief, Richie was trying not to laugh, the difference between having a military team and being the sarge, and having an ex-military team where I was just 'the boss' was massive, clearly.

"How bad's the job?" he asked and I sighed.

"Honestly, sounds fifty-fifty, we'd just be a distraction, cause a fight, maybe blow the door up or something and kill…actually better if we use non-lethal, Bowdoin is a bit of a pussy anyway, maybe a load of stuns?"

"That works!" Luna agreed quickly. "I get to kick the shit out of Min and not actually fuck things up with Santos? I mean, Min was a fucking asshole, but, you know, that's not really a killing offence."

"You sure?" I asked, and she grimaced. Clearly a lot had gone on between them that I wasn't party to, but the look on her face at the thought of doing this? "Okay, look. Seriously, is this important to you?"

"It is," Luna said genuinely. "We've got some history and…"

"You don't have to tell me," I said. "We're a team and a family. If you want him fucked up? We'll do it."

"Just like that?" she asked, looking at me, then glancing away as if not believing it.

"Just like that," I confirmed, dead serious. "How much have you all done for me? Running around to help me get these two fuckheads out of their ice apartment? Seriously, if it's that important, we'll do it."

"To be fair, if this is the AWF? They don't really do defenses it's just the guards that are armed, because nobody big league is going to risk fighting over that place. If we were going to hit a corp that makes mods? We'd hit someone with really good shit, not the average gear," Reign said. "We could have some fun with this."

"Fun?" I asked disbelievingly.

"Yeah, you know, use Min for this. We make it clear that the aim of the whole thing was never AWF, that way they don't come looking for us. We make it all about him," Luna said excitedly.

"I don't know…" I muttered, looking from one to the other. "Seriously, this could go badly wrong."

"I could stay in stealth," Todds offered. "Ready to take a hand."

"I'd be ready to snipe…That is, unless you want to…" She broke off looking at Sync, who shook her head.

"You're second, we can share the load, and besides, when is this? We're gonna be really busy for the next few days…"

"Good point." I sighed. "Alright, we'll take the job, he was offering thirty thousand, It's a pathetic payment for the job, but hey, I guess this is more of a laugh anyway."

"Thirty grand's pathetic?" Richie winced. "If you don't want it I'll take it…?"

"We'll have earned a hundred or more by sunup," I assured him. "Don't worry about shit like that, brother. You two sort your fake IDs out and your new accounts, that's more important."

I took one more look around the room at the beaming Luna and Gessh, the happy Reign and the amused others, then I snorted. "I better not act like I'm willing to do this normally, just in case he thinks he can get this shit for favors again." I took a deep breath, then reactivated the link.

"Apparently, my very professional colleagues have wanted to kick the shit out of Min for ages. They've pulled strings, and yeah, we're in. We have three requirements. You provide all the explosives, and believe me, we want a lot. You make sure we have an escape plan, and you make damn sure that if there's a defensive AI or anything it isn't just going to go straight for us and fry our keystones."

He stared at me openmouthed, then shut it with a click and—grinning like an idiot—sent me a new offer with those details in.

I accepted it and got the details…before starting to swear.

I *knew* it was too good to be true!

CHAPTER FORTY-NINE

Six hours.

Six goddamn hours later I was sitting, wrapped in the robes of the Church of the Pure, a handful of the other 'faithful' wandering around and making pests of themselves to the various people entering the AWF building.

It was, like the mods they made there, entirely utilitarian, and even boring; squat, oblong, like almost any office block in existence, and with wage slaves slowly tramping their way in and out, heads bowed in defeat.

You could tell the management types and shareholders though, walking in, head held high, while everyone else shuffled along, ready to get their day over with.

I shook my head, wondering how much of their lives they wasted like this, toiling for someone else? I'd been there for half an hour, and I'd been approached by two other 'faithful' that seemed surprised by my appearance, and that I wasn't joining them.

"Special assignment." I grunted. "Forget you saw me." They moved off, then went to others of their group and muttered questions, watching me.

I wasn't exactly blending in, but I was also concealing a lot of mods, and if one of them saw them? The gig was up.

"Enjoying yourself?" Reign asked, sliding onto the public bench next to me, and staring across at the building before us. "Ugly place isn't it?"

"Guess it doesn't need credits spending on the outside," I said. "It's an R&D, manufactory and warehouse, everything they produce comes from here, so I guess utility over beauty."

"Just like you." She sighed, nudging me with a shoulder. "You know, maybe I should trade you in for a better looking model? I hear this Min character is a good looking guy?"

"I'd shoot him in the face," I assured her, and she laughed.

"So, you're happy with the plan then?" she asked me again and I shrugged. There really wasn't much to it in all honesty.

We were to trash the front of the building, draw the security forces out, and then make it all as confusing as possible. Bowdoin would be doing whatever he was doing at the back, and we were the distraction. Basically we should be as noisy and confusing as possible, then run away.

We were wearing the outfits of the Church of the Pure because they were anti-mod fanatics, they spent all day harassing people here and at other mod production sites, and practically everyone hated them already.

They'd tried shit like sticking themselves to the road out the front of the Nemesis factory a few weeks back, and since then they were a little 'shorthanded' now—the corpos had used construction clearance equipment to remove them, mainly just leaving smears of blood behind—they were back to a mixture of walking around harassing people, and threatening 'significant action'.

Nobody really paid them a lot of attention, but they were well known as a lunatic fringe group. They had hardly any control over their own members, and when we claimed we were acting on their behalf? People would just accept it.

Best of all the upper leadership of the church would never really be sure they didn't do it, so they'd not be convincing in denying any involvement.

The trick was going to be making enough of an impression that it kept everyone's attention, while not being 'big' enough that anyone called in heavy artillery and the army or anti-terrorist units.

That was where Min came in.

He was notorious on his own for essentially 'fucking and chucking' as it was called in the army, seducing women and then moving on. That wasn't a big thing, well, it wasn't nice, admittedly, but it wasn't a 'big' thing.

What Luna and Gessh wouldn't tell me about was clearly a lot more than just that though, and judging from the evil smiles they were wearing?

Today was all about revenge for them.

They wouldn't kill him, but they were making an example of the fucker apparently.

I was fine with it, I'd be setting off the explosives then keeping the rest of their security forces pinned down while they did it.

The fact that two 'priestesses' of the church were going to be seen kicking the shit out of the security force leader? It was basically a classic misdirection.

The AWF wouldn't be sure they were the target, and to add to that impression, they girls were bringing some 'props' with them.

"Kabutt?" Reign asked and I nodded.

"Yeah I'm happy with the plan," I said, shaking my head as I checked the time again. "If we can call it a plan, I mean seriously?"

"It has a start, a middle and an end, and it even has an escape plan in place, it's better than most of our plans," she pointed out and I glared at her from the depths of my hood.

"I could be offended by that," I said eventually. "I'll have you know I spend a lot of time on my plans."

"Kabutt, honey, you run at the enemy screaming and beat the crap out of them, then we all run away. It's fine, you don't have to pretend any more. We know you were never a planner…"

"I make plans!" I snapped, opening my mouth to point out the last few that had gone so well, and flapped my lips uselessly for a few seconds. "Okay, look, we all lived!"

"All?" she asked, and I thought back to our first mission together.

"That was a bit uncalled for."

"I know, but seriously? We always escape by the skin of our teeth, this plan? He's got us escape routes, he's got fall back positions, and even a timestamp to go on."

"We always win."

"That's because we're lucky bastards and we believe in heavy firepower," she pointed out, and I grinned.

"We really do, don't we?"

"Well, we've got five hours after this before Julius wants us at the job, so, Sync and Richie are painting the armor, Luna and Gessh have arranged to meet Dondo to let off some steam, and Todds is going to take his babysitter out to dinner…"

"Uh huh?" I prompted when she fell silent.

"So…?" she suggested, looking at me.

"So…we should do something?"

"That's it," she encouraged. "You can do it."

"We should, uh…go for dinner?" I tried, wincing. "Look, it's not a good idea to relax too much before a mission, after, sure, but…"

"But we might be pulled down and slaughtered tonight." She cut me off, shaking her head. "We're going out for dinner. If we pull this off quickly we'll have about two hours before we need to leave, you and I are going for dinner, and we're going to have a goddamn date!"

"Okay," I agreed quickly, grinning to myself. "All the ammo sorted?"

"That was the delivery before we left to come here," she said. "Three full cases of ammo, and a box of filters, fusion pellets and more. We're ready for tonight, okay? There's even a case of three hundred small medikits, empty and ready to go."

"So there's nothing to do?"

"Nothing?" she growled.

"Nothing to stop us relaxing together, I mean," I corrected.

"Nothing."

I nodded. "Then I'd like that," I said quickly. "Of course I'd like to have dinner with you."

"That's the right answer," she said, just as the alarm went off on the timer I'd set.

"Well, looks like it's the final countdown," I said, switching back to 'work mode' as I shifted on my seat, triggering the tac-net and messaging everyone as Reign stood, moving off quickly.

"Okay people, five minutes," I said, smiling to myself as I felt the cares and worries fall away.

It was always like this, I felt distracted and worried about all the things that could go wrong before a mission started, but once it was on? That was it.

I also liked, admittedly, the fun new toys we'd ordered from both Oshbob and Gunther for this little job. Bowdoin hadn't liked the bill, but fuck it.

I set off strolling towards the building, the pair of guards out the front focusing on me and straightening, knowing that they couldn't let 'one of the nutters' inside.

I smiled, crossing the street, heading towards the front door…then turning right and walking along the front of the building, just before they could take action.

They hesitated, then stood down, watching me, as I in turn watched them, the link from Reign's sniper rifle popping up in my HUD and making my shoulders relax.

This was always the worst bit, if some ACE patrol or security team came past? Or worse yet, some anti-terrorist scanners registered what I had in the backpack over my shoulder? That'd kick all this off far sooner.

Fortunately it was half an hour after shift change, so there were few people wandering about outside, and with the dour glares the church 'real' priests and supporters were giving them? People moved off fast.

I moved along the front, the map Bowdoin had provided keeping me right as I counted my steps to the right spot.

"Here we go," I muttered, grinning to myself as I swung the bag off my shoulder, triggered the sealing charges—sticky panels that sealed something to something else—and triggered the directional explosives.

Not to detonate, not yet, but I slapped the bag against the wall, making it stick with a wet 'splat' before the air between the wall and bag was forced out, sealing it tight.

The explosives beeped in my HUD letting me know they were active, and ready, and I moved quickly, striding back away from the building, before picking up speed as I returned to my seat, a long stone bench that Luna was standing behind now, and Gessh taking up post behind another seat a dozen meters away.

"You ready for this?" I asked her, getting a massive smile, and I shook my head. We were all wearing masks, specialist ones that were intended for parties more than anything, those 'special' parties where people wore very little clothing, and bowls full of room keys were offered round.

They were black and oval, hiding your real face entirely, unless you had the scrambling code. We all had them, letting each of us see the others fine, but to anyone that looked under our hoods?

We looked like a particularly hated corpo leader, 'the evil one that shall not be named' from M-Corp. The title was from a recent skit on a comedy channel, and it was doing the rounds.

She'd predictably had her own version edited up and released, cutting and pasting sections of the conversation until it looked like she was the innocent one, being bullied, instead of the evil creature she was, but nobody was fooled.

As the timer hit the last few seconds, I turned and stared at the building ahead, and sighed.

"Some days I fucking love my job, you know that?" I said philosophically to nobody in particular, before triggering the detonator.

The seismic charges were designed to crack stone in mining, reducing sections of solid stone to sand, and they were packed in at the bottom, flush against the wall.

Atop them were packed a trio of pulse detonators, essentially, where the first level would turn a section of about two meters into sand, the pulse detonators would send out a wave that would crack all the walls nearby into shards, taking that section of the building down.

It'd do minor damage to flesh, pretty major damage to machinery, and coincidentally, absolutely bury the security team's armory under several tons of building.

That left only the quick response team, and the guards at the front.

As soon as the explosion had gone off, Luna and Gessh had lifted up their new toys, and had opened fire.

The guards were stunned by the explosion and had been looking in totally the wrong direction when they did so, and when the first few hits landed?

It was all over for them.

A single hit from a Riot Suppression [Non-Lethal] Electro-Impact Lance, or RSEIL, was fucking painful, the three the girls managed to hit the pair with?

Well, the arse-lance, as it was more affectionately known, was slightly tempered by the armor they were wearing, but as each rubberized, electrified round hit them, they just danced more and more.

Some might say 'dancing' was the wrong word, but they shook and jerked, then fell over, and really, that was close enough for my mind.

I hoped they'd not killed the guards, that was why we'd gone for these weapons, after all, but two was probably not enough to do the job, with their armor, so I'd agreed to three hits as a maximum.

Now we waited.

The real purity priests had run like their arses were on fire, along with most people on the street, and I got a message from Reign a few seconds later, who promised the guest of honor was on his way.

"I'll take that," I said to Luna, taking her toy from her as she hefted the jury rigged party gifts, and started to count.

"And throw on three…" Reign spoke into the comms. "One, two…three!"

As she spoke, five figures, two of them only partially dressed, came running out of the breech in the wall, handguns up and aiming. Luna threw the grenades, and I took aim as well, firing a half second after Gessh did, then the three of us ducked down and hid behind the stone bench.

"You ready for this?" I asked Luna conversationally, as she lifted the final new toy, locking the pistons and charging handle.

"I have never been more ready for anything in my life," she assured me, grinning, ear to ear, as bullets slammed into the stone on the far side, blasting chips free, but doing little real damage. Had they been able to lay hands on their much heavier riot loadout? It'd have been a very different story.

"You know, I'm going to have to get more intel on future raids." I mused. "All the stress for this one, it's just gone…"

The detonation of the two grenade bundles were almost overpowered by the screams from the five that were caught in the blast, and I stood again, turning to look over the bench, rifle raised… and I paused, then relaxed a little.

All five had been caught in the blast radius, the stunners, the stickies and the flashbangs had done their jobs, landing on either side of the charging group and taking them down in screaming, sticky piles.

The slick grenade that Gessh had thrown a few seconds before had helped as well, as it meant that rather than the idiots being stuck to the floor, they were instead stuck to themselves, arms and legs pinned, even as they thrashed and bucked.

Luna took careful aim, then fired her rifle, the harpoon flashing over the distance between us and her target, then punching through his thigh, deploying the barbs, and beginning to retract as she braced herself.

Min was dragged kicking and screaming, his arms glued to his chest, across the slick floor, ending up nearby as I turned to Luna.

"I've got it from here," I assured her. "You go have fun."

"Thanks boss!" she shouted. "You're the best!"

With that she was off, running over to him and punting him hard in the balls, before applying the solvent to counter the glue.

Gessh was there a few seconds later, deploying a hardened glass shield around the chosen point, making damn sure that unless the enemy brought out heavy weaponry, the sisters could finish the job.

Then the pair of them fell on Min.

I ignored them, as they stripped and beat the crap out of him behind the shield, keeping the second wave of guards pinned down with repeated shots from the arse-lance.

I wasn't hitting them, but without access to their main armory, they weren't hitting me either, and all I needed was to keep their attention.

Between my suppression fire, and the beating the girls were giving Min, the minutes ticked away fast, but still, it wasn't until the pair of them flipped him upside down and were busily duct-taping him to their chosen light pole, before starting to write on him, as I threw the omni-directional speaker towards the hunkered down defenders, and triggered it.

"Hold your ground!" I barked. "This is an intervention on both religious grounds, and we are covered by sub section seventeen of the protest bill, if you interfere with us, you will be fined by the religious council, and fired upon by the Enforcers of the Church of the Pure!"

"What?" one of them shouted out after a few seconds. "What the fuck! You blew up our building!"

"It was a religious explosive," I threw back at him. "It was blessed!"

"What are you doing to our captain?" he shouted back.

"Punishment for his sins!"

"For his…just for him?" came the response. "You did all of this, to get at him?"

"Justice knows no limit!" I replied, settling in, making shit up as I went along. "His guilt was established long since, not only for the terrible events of the Summer of Perdition, but for his support of the devil's work!"

I had no idea what the summer of perdition was, but I'd seen it mentioned on some of holograms the lunatics had been projecting and it fit with the whole judgy theme that was going on.

"Are…are you going to kill him?" came the call.

"No, not unless you try to stop us carrying out justice!"

"What's that?"

"Justice?"

"No, what they've got, that…. is that a flag?"

I looked over at the girls, they'd given me a vague idea of their plans, but that was all, and they'd certainly not mentioned a flag until now, but as Luna looked over at me and gave the flag a jaunty little wave I could barely suppress a mixture of the giggles…and a wince.

"It is!" I assured them.

"What are you going to…. Oh! Damn!" I heard a squeal ring out, even through the gag they'd put on him, and I couldn't help but look back over at him.

He was taped—upside down—to the pole, naked, with a dozen slogans scrawled on him, including a print of a dancing cat that was popular on kids shows at the minute in the center of his admittedly muscular chest.

His legs were dangling, as were other bits, and they'd been sprayed silver and pink.

Then a flag, one of the little ones that were meant for mounting to your aircar—if you were a religious nutjob and could still afford one—had been…yup.

The girls had stuck it in his ass.

There was a little breeze that raced around the plaza and that made it stream and dance, as both the girls stood back to admire their handiwork.

"Turn this way!" I called to them, and they did, as I focused, then order the RI to take a selection of recordings, as the girls saluted me.

With that, we had less than a minute to go, and distant sirens could be heard, as I stood, passing the guns to the girls, and we started retreating.

By the time we reached the edge of the plaza, the timer was up, the guards were racing towards their fallen leader, and the sirens were a lot closer.

We darted into the marked building on our map, then into the basement, and sub basements, following the glowing route that we'd been given, and much to my surprise found the door ahead of us into the Undercity unlocked and ready.

We darted through, Reign and Todds joining us, and the five of us sealed the door, dumped the incriminating evidence, set the incendiary grenade off, and ran for it.

An hour later we were in the aircab, flashing through the air to the warehouse, and I was sending the images and recording to Bowdoin, noting that there were already several images circulating online already, and to be out this quickly? They had to have been released by his own people.

Yeah, Min's reputation was toast.

CHAPTER FIFTY

By the time we'd all gotten back, calmed down, separated out the payment and gotten changed and ready, Reign and I ended up enjoying a romantic pizza while I worked on an issue with the transverse mechanism on the left ankle for my suit, and she worked on attaching a new scope to her new toy.

It was a railgun, not a little one either, the full on, must be braced and locked down, *with a tripod* level of rifle, and while I didn't know when she was going to use it, beyond when we went hunting the APS, the sight of her smile as she cleaned and fitted it, and Sync gushed over it, was enough for me.

We might not have made it to dinner, but we'd damn well made it through the day, and we were ready for a wild ride of a night.

"Are you sure you won't need us?" Gessh asked me for the third time, and I gestured to Julius, who stood by the leg of one of the APS, staring upwards, mouth open in stunned awe.

They'd all been repainted in a day, the minor repairs done, the major ones either fixed enough or put off till another day, meaning that we were as ready as we possibly could be.

Admittedly we needed a transport to be able to get there, but once again, Julius had delivered, showing up personally in it, dressed as if ready to go either onto a stage, or into war, everything from his hair to his guns perfect.

"I think we'll need you for the cleanup, but he really wants this to be just the three of us I think," I apologized. "Don't worry, it'll still be shared equally."

"Oh, it's not that." She grinned. "Although I'll not complain, no I just wanted to know if you needed us, or if I could get Dondo round to really finish the day off in style, you know, with you all out for a while?"

"Someone talking about me?" Dondo called from the door, and I turned, annoyed he'd just wandered up—meaning there was still a remaining backdoor in the security software I'd not found, but I would, I resolved silently—only to find that the fucker wasn't alone either.

Clearly he'd shared the exploit with his fucking boss.

"Oshbob," I greeted him, trying my best not to sound defensive or aggressive, as if I expected him.

"Kabutt," the big bastard grunted, barely looking my way. "I heard you'd had some friends move into my warehouse, decided it was time to check the place out."

"Yeah," I muttered. "I think we need to have a conversation about the options here. Either we need to buy this place or we need to be looking for somewhere else."

"Your people told me that you were asking…it's not for sale." He shrugged and I glared at him. "Might be that we can come to an arrangement, but I don't sell my property. Might be that having some operators I can call on for a job now and then would be worth reconsidering your rent though…"

"The rent isn't the issue," I said. "The issue is investment. I'm not leaving our suits here unguarded when we're off the clock, unless I have some serious hardware protecting them."

"Makes sense, don't see the problem though."

"The problem is I'm not investing serious credits in security unless it's our place. What's to stop you deciding that you want the place back as soon as I've invested a few hundred thousand in security?"

"Self-interest," he replied bluntly, stomping over to me and jerking his head to one side, leading me off for a quiet chat in the corner.

"What's all this about?" I asked him warily.

"As I said, Kabutt, self-interest." He leaned against the wall and looked over the suits. "I've heard they're locked to the user, can't be used by anyone else, ever, so why would people try and boost them?"

"They're locked to the user," I agreed. "There's a possible way around that, but it'd cost millions."

"And?"

"And what?"

"And you're worried that others would still steal the suits, so clearly there's those that don't care about the cost, so how does it work?"

"That's classified," I growled. "Look, just because they can't be stolen, unless you've got serious credits behind you, like corpo level credits, doesn't mean that assholes won't try, and in trying they'll trash my place and waste my credits. Also, yeah, corpo scumbags might try for them. I don't need that shit. I need to rebuild the site, make it into a real fortified home for us."

"So do it." He grunted. "Look Kabutt, I don't give a shit if you tear this place down and rebuild it from the ground up, this is still mine…" He paused, eyeing me, and I glared at him, until he shrugged and went on. "That being said, maybe having dangerous neighbors would be worth a little consideration in the deal."

"Such as?"

"Such as this is *mine*…" He squinted at me, making sure I got that, and I nodded, before he went on. "But maybe a set rent for the next five years, regardless of your investment could be agreed. If I need you, you come and help—"

"I'm not owing another gang lord favors."

"Shut the fuck up and listen," he snapped. "If I need you, like I get hit by a competitor? You come help. In return? You get raided? My people view it as my property. They'll defend it, and they fucking know not to mess with my shit. No goblins trying to break in and see what they can scrounge, no gang members trying to fuck with you. You get guards, and I get some security, if the shit hits the fan."

"I…" I broke off, forcing myself to think through the offer.

It wasn't actually that bad. If I moved to another site, as well as having to buy the site? We'd have to start from scratch. We'd be a permanent target for idiots, gangers that think they can just jump in and steal a suit, like that fucknut a few years back that had stolen a training mech.

He'd been ground into the floor for it, but for a short while he'd been a ganger king.

I'd have shit heads like that trying stuff all the time, we'd need guards round the clock, and we'd certainly need to invest hundreds of thousands in security.

We'd also have Dondo hanging around, I had no doubt, and as much as he clearly liked the girls and wanted to be with them, he was Oshbob's through and through. If he ordered him to add security back doors, he'd be sneaking around when we were all in bed doing just that.

That meant that the option was that if we got another place, we'd have to ban him, and that's wouldn't be right, considering that it'd not be 'mine' it'd be 'ours'.

We had the guild of course, and we were to be partial owners there, but, realistically, nothing was going to happen with the guild moving to a bigger site that could accommodate the suits and so on in the short term, and even if Julius offered it tomorrow?

Would we want to live in a guild house? I sure as shit didn't intend living far from my suit either. I wanted it close enough I could reach it when I needed it.

No, we needed a stable home, a safe one, and the simple truth was that I'd have a hell of a job sorting somewhere else out that came with the advantages of this one.

Having Oshbob's people watching over us, instead of regarding us as prey? That was worth a hell of a lot.

"We'd be allies?" I asked after a few seconds.

"We would," he agreed. "I don't like you, but I'm willing to overlook how ugly you are, for Dondo and the girls sake of course."

"I can understand that," I replied. "I don't like that I can smell you even from across the road, but I could put up with it, for the girls sake."

"Then we've got a deal." He grunted. "Oh, and as we'll be allies?"

"Yeah?"

"No need to worry about dealing with others to get your fuel core and ammo supplies. I already had a word with Gunther about selling on my turf. He knows to give you a little discount from now on."

"Downright kind of you," I ground out between gritted teeth.

"Don't mention it." He grinned, a little twinkle in the big bastard's eye. "There's a little gift as well…something to make life a little easier." He tossed me a small box and I caught it automatically, then set it down, not trusting the fucker.

He strolled back to the others, and I forced myself to relax, breathing deeply, as Reign stepped up and laid a hand on my arm.

"You look like you're going to explode." She winced. "Is everything okay?"

"It is." I swallowed my anger, and forced a deep breath down, shaking my head and nodding to her. "No, it's okay, it's just that he always has to get one over on me, you know?"

"He's a crime lord, they don't get to that position without skills," she pointed out. "What's happening?"

"He offered a deal on the site, but it stays 'his'. He'll also have his people beaten into shape and it made clear that we're not prey, we're his allies, and not to fuck with us, as well as have them as security and troops if the shit hits the fan."

"Damn, that's good!" She blinked in surprise. "So what's got you so pissed?"

"In exchange, if he gets raided by another gang or whatever, we help him."

"The girls would have insisted on helping Dondo anyway," she said, and I nodded.

"I know, and if we went somewhere else he'd be setting his boss up to get access to our systems if we didn't ban him."

"Exactly, so…"

"He also agrees with us doing whatever we want with the place, including a full flatten and rebuild if we want."

"That's great…"

"But he owns it."

"Uh huh?"

"And…" I shook my head. "The thing that really pisses me off? Him having control over us. He's gotten to Gunther, he knew we were buying supplies for the suits from him, so he's had a word and we now get a 'discount' on Gunther supplying us."

"That's…" She broke off seeing the point.

It wasn't the discount, it wasn't even that Gunther was only supplying us a few bits and pieces. It was that Oshbob was making it clear he had his fingers in everything and that he was powerful enough to make an old friend—more or less—who'd been giving us a decent deal, not only discount the deal he was giving us further, but that he knew about it. He was making it clear we bought from him, or we didn't buy from another merchant.

"Did he mention the Stingers?" she asked after a few seconds and I shook my head.

"No, and I think they're free of his influence, they're powerful enough that if he fucked with them they'd squash him, and fuck the consequences. Also, if they had him covering for them, they'd not have been hiding where they were. I'm betting Lucky never told him."

"Well, that's something," she said. "Also, what we do is stock up. We run a decent supply of everything here, so that if he does try to turn the screws and fuck with us? We can crush him. Remember that he's seen the vids like everyone else, APS stomping across the battlefield and slaughtering armies. Use tonight, use it as a warning for him as well."

"I like the way you think." I grinned. "We make it into warning, as well as a recruitment and advertising vid for the guild."

"Exactly." She smiled at me and interlinked her arm, squeezing my hand and kissing my cheek. "So, you ready to go play nice for a few minutes before we leave?"

"I am," I agreed, before an evil thought occurred to me. "Actually…he wants us to be allies? Let's use that."

"You've got an evil smile…" She sighed. "This is so going to cost us…"

"No, it's more in the nature of a loan," I assured her.

"From a crime syndicate? Oh that sounds like *such* a good idea…"

CHAPTER FIFTY-ONE

Julius had gone ahead of us, with Dondo flying the rest of the team directly above the transport, ready to give a hand if we need it.

I was also conscious that we were travelling with an absolute fuckload of easily moved wealth, so if Oshbob had any holes in his syndicate, we were likely to get hit.

Then there was the minor risk of the ghost squads as well…and…

The list was endless, but I'd spoken to the rest of the team—once Dondo and Oshbob were gone—and they'd agreed it was the best plan.

We'd also started the ball rolling, by taking advantage of Oshbob's 'services'.

I'd cleaned out our account in paying for this, but he'd sent a load of goblins and gangers on a raid.

'Simpson's Security Services' were apparently a front for another gang's stolen security tech on the far side of the city, and Oshbob had his eye on it as an acquisition anyway.

He was hitting it tonight to clear out all the security gear we wanted, to teach the other gang their place, and was getting paid into the deal, so he was fine with it.

It also meant I owed the fucker a favor, but hey. Might as well test the waters, as we were 'allies' now.

I shifted as we bounced over a pothole in the road, the transport shuddering at the weight of us all, and I couldn't help but feel the absence of Scott and Fergie, as well as yeah, Barnes. He'd been a fucking idiot, and fresh to the team, but he deserved better.

We were crouched, braced, around Oshbob's 'loan' and I couldn't help but stare into the swirling, mesmerizing mass.

He'd had to send his people running in all directions to get this, I had to bet, but a massive container holding three hundred thousand credits worth of pure nanites was going to be a hell of a draw for the specters.

We were too big to go into all the small side tunnels hunting the fuckers after all, we'd have to stay in the center of the nest, and somehow draw them all to us.

Best way to draw Specters? Well, they only wanted two things. Fresh pure nanites, and mods.

We'd be deliberately radiating in the electromagnetic spectrums—the systems we usually employed to hide it, could, and had been flipped to make sure we instead drew attention—and while we didn't have 'mods' they could use in the traditional sense, we should be a target too tempting to turn away from.

"You ready?" I asked on the link between the three suits, getting nods and grins from Richie and Sync.

"Always," Richie said, as Sync just smiled. "So boss, you know how we couldn't make changes to our suits before…"

"You can now," I said. "I know you always wanted to try the drone brigade."

"Fuck yes." He grinned. "You won't regret it," he assured me.

"Can I upgrade as well?" Sync asked, and I nodded, having told the pair everything already. "I'm betting that if the Stinger collective can't get me a better weapon, they can put me in touch with a custom armorer."

She hefted the massive rifle in one hand, and I nodded, knowing that if she went all out on the railgun design she'd been talking about for years? She'd be able to take down anything that fucked with us.

Reign would be able to use the same kit as well, and as much as she kept talking about being worried about being crap compared to Sync, she'd end up with loads of new weapons at this rate.

"We're two minutes out," Reign sent on the Tac-net and I sent her my thanks, before responding to Julius' message that had arrived at the same time practically.

All he got though, was a wink.

We shifted around inside the transport, me mentally adding a secure transport to the list of things we needed, possibly airborne, as it slowed and turned, before backing up.

I got linked into a conversation that was ongoing by Julius and I had to smile to myself.

"…I mean it!" someone was saying. "Look, if you don't have the numbers to take this job on, you should never have signed the contract! You saw the failure clause, you agreed to it, and now you're trying to renegotiate? No, you had your chance. Pay the debt and—"

"Carlton." Julius cut the shorter man off, mid-harangue. "You don't understand, but that's fine. I was offering you the chance to renegotiate our deal, for *your* benefit. Not mine."

"Bullshit, you haven't got the mercs to be able to clear the site. You've only got half your damn squad of 'celebrities' from the cooling towers job," a third man scoffed, and I recognized him as Tree's second in command, presumably the new team lead of the backstabbing elven bastards.

Clearly Reign and the others had just landed, and I could barely contain my grin as I heard the purr in Julius' voice as we finished backing up, the transport stopping.

"What's this?" the elf asked with a sneer. "Some last-minute, desperate ass attempt to save your reputation and guild? You've no chance Julius, accept it, pay the fine and…"

"No," Julius said simply. "This was never the last minute, this was *always* the plan, and you stabbing me in the back and leaving the guild? The only ones that were fucked by yours and Trees' betrayal were you, Atmos."

Julius turned to face the owner of the site we were to hit, and spoke in a louder, and proud voice, clearly knowing exactly the effect this was going to have on the situation.

"Carlton, you hired us to clear out the building nest in your site, you'll remember that I warned you that timing would be tight, but that I'd make sure it was done, you remember?"

"I do," the little man replied, sounding unsure suddenly, presumably at the way that he was being looked at by those around him who knew what was coming.

"Well, you'll also remember that I agreed you could have access to the recording that any of my guild members made as they cleared the site, provided it did not include access to, or demonstrations of guild and government restricted technologies? That anything that showed that, was the property of the guild alone, and we would share only what we chose? That we might decide to share it all, or none, but that we owned it, not you?"

"Yes, yes! Get on with it!" Carlton snapped, waving one hand.

"Very well, I just wanted to make sure our position was clear." Julius smiled toothily. "Well, it gives me great pleasure to introduce The Valiant Heart Dreadnought team."

With that, the roller door on the back of the transport started rising, clattering away as it went, and several of the more trusted of Julius' teams, notably Liolet at the front, shone lights in, and on us, as we stepped out, just as the heavens opened.

I was the first in line, the massive shoulders and head of my APS barely making it out of the transport without damaging it, the concrete under foot crunching as I stepped down, rain spattering across my gleaming armor as I straightened up to my full height with a whirr of servos that hung in the sudden utter silence.

The standard army camo paintjob had been redone in a matter of hours, and it'd need to be redone properly, but for now?

I towered over the stunned and suddenly terrified Carlton and Atmos, fully armored, gleaming in black magnificence, gold highlights reflecting the neon lights. My shoulder mounted railguns unfolded, swinging around, locking into place and extending, cluster-bomb dispensers sliding open as I slid the covers back, then deliberately 'twitched' them.

All the control surfaces that were publicly demonstratable, and imposing, shifted, the suits making small noises as we geared up for war. It was a stupid thing, seriously it was, but the vids of the APS as we bounded into battle always showed us 'powering up' beforehand, just to make us more impressive, and fuck me the effect was noticeable.

I hefted my massive rifle, the feed from my backpack to the bottom of the gun shivering as I loaded the weapon with an ominous clunk, and I hefted a massive cylinder, the same size as one of the cowering figures, full of quicksilver nanites, effortlessly with the other hand.

Richie stepped out behind me, taking up station on the left, and Sync moving to the right, Richie deploying his larger, armed, drone—that had been a goddamn expensive purchase an hour ago, but worth it—and hefted his rifle, and Sync stood ready.

Her sniper variant of the standard rifle was imposing enough, the added length to the barrel, the sheer mass, convincing people that if she wanted to, she could kill a god with it.

That the people before us had seen the vids of the APS at war was made extremely clear as they stared up at us, mouths hanging open in shock and terror.

"Sarge?" Julius called up to me, and I looked down at him.

"Yes, Guild Master?" I grated out, all flat power and distant threat, with just a *hint* of respect.

"Wipe out that nest."

"Yes, Guild Master," I replied flatly, before stepping forwards, the sheer unstoppable bulk of the suit making the remaining members of Trees' squad back up, and then rush to the side out of the way.

The last thing I heard from Carlton was as we were striding past, and he grabbed onto Julius' sleeve, his attitude totally different.

"Ten years!" he begged. "A ten year contract, all our sites! You'll protect them all, as long as we get full rights to…"

"I'm sorry," Julius said, a wide smile on his face. "We already finished negotiations, and you signed the deal, remember? I gave you a chance to change your mind, but…"

That was it, as we strode past and headed to the entrance, Reign and Todds on the left, escorting us, Gessh and Luna on the right, the rest of the guild, the loyal members anyway, moving out to take up position, ready to catch anything that got around us.

Liolet let out a low whistle as we stomped past, before offering a salute, unable to keep from grinning hugely as I nodded to him, with Richie and Sync doing the same.

"Dreadnought?" I sent to Julius, who just sent me an image of a winking face in return, apparently busy fielding calls, as some were already streaming in.

He'd warned us on our way over that in a matter of minutes there'd be a media presence, they were already following the guild after the cooling tower job, but they'd started drifting away to other things.

Now that the 'dreadnought' team had been unveiled? They'd be back, and at a horrific speed.

We'd agreed that if he reached two million credits as a deal—split fifty-fifty, between the guild and my team—then we'd let one of the teams send a drone in to watch.

I didn't want one following us around, but also, I did want a share of a fucking million credits, so, you know.

As it was though, we stomped through the driving rain, the darkness of the night only broken by neon flashes of adverts and sirens in the distance.

The suit picked up and isolated thousands of sounds, locking them into threat zones, identifying distant gunfire, screams and the warbling sirens of the various departments. I dismissed them all, unimportant.

Nothing was closer than half a mile, and while, sure, a sniper could hit me from that range easily with modern mods and weaponry, the sound of the gunshot wouldn't be the first I knew of that. It'd be the fucking bullet plinking off my armor—provided it was a normal sniper—and the boom of Sync returning the favor.

Fortunately nobody was so stupid tonight, and we closed the distance to the entrance, Gessh and Todds hurrying forwards to the main gate, ready for us.

This nest was underground, we knew that, and we'd been warned there would be a mass of tunnels. This was an old sub-level public transport system. Here they'd bring out and send in the carriages for the mag-trains when they needed maintenance.

The doors were massive, designed for heavy machines to enter, and they were in turn set into the side of a massive stone edifice, reinforced over and over to allow more building overhead.

The result was that the place looked like the kind of situation old world leaders liked to believe they could ride out nuclear warfare in.

This had been one of the deeper public transport lines supposedly, and it'd been sealed away when those levels were abandoned. Something had clearly made a hole, and then more, eventually that had led to the specters creating a nest for whatever weird ass logic they followed, and starting to build their forces.

The contract called for minimal structural damage where possible, but the elimination of the specters was the absolute priority. This section was to be cleared out and used for a factory of some kind, and the owner really wanted the fuckers removed.

As we reached the doors, Todds opened them, the massive magnetic locks releasing with a solid clunk that rang through the rain sodden air, before they drew back into the recesses of the wall, exposing the tunnel as it led sharply downwards.

We triggered our floodlights, un-needed really, but damn, it created an impression, as Todds and Gessh stood there calmly, as mere meters away the first of the specters came staggering out.

At the sight of us—and the nanites—they went mad, speeding up, running, stumbling and tripping over themselves, reaching and clawing for us...until we opened fire.

CHAPTER FIFTY-TWO

I was on a closed loop with Richie and Sync as we strode into the darkness, our lights flooding the tunnel and giving no spaces for our targets to hide.

We opened fire in short controlled bursts, the more massive rounds that our guns used passing through sometimes several of the specters before stopping, and Richie and Sync stepped up, striding past me to lead as I carried the nanites deeper.

They both still carried their plasma swords in their left hands, and their rifles in their right, the tunnel lit by heavy gunfire and flames as Gessh and Todds closed the door behind us.

I couldn't help but smile, this had to have looked amazing from the outside, exactly the kind of shit they were used to seeing in the vids, the brave elites of the army stomping into the hellish infested zones of the wasteland and slaughtering everything, in constant horrific danger.

The reality was different, as I changed the orders.

"Okay people, lets clear the area, set up a solid position and bring the fuckers to us."

"Sounds like a plan!" Richie called back, and I could damn well hear the smile in his voice.

"You're enjoying this aren't you?" Sync sighed.

"Loving it," he admitted. "Not only are we making bank with every shot, but we're doing it for us rather than the filthy corpos and their pets. So, yeah, I'm fucking loving this."

"Well, we have to pay for those rounds now," I said, "So, we need to conserve ammo wherever possible, not to mention not bringing the roof down on us all. Sync, I want you to step up and protect the nanites once we've picked a place to stand, I'll swap out with you and stand with Richie."

"Swords?" she asked and I nodded unthinkingly.

"Yeah," I said cursing myself for getting out of the habit of responding and gesturing. "Sorry, yeah, Richie and I will swap out guns and move to melee, kill them as they come, you focus on high concentration areas and any leadership castes."

"Ghouls and Banshees eh?" she approved. "Can't wait to kill a few of those."

"The Banshees are heavily armed," I warned her. "As well as insanely mobile. You remember the Archaeon?"

"The living dead?" she asked, cutting two specters apart with her blade and I grunted.

"Those fuckers make these look like paper soldiers, these are no threat, not to us, and barely to a well-equipped solider, but those? They were our predecessors, the lords of the battlefield, and totally mad."

"And you think these are them?" Richie asked. "Why?"

"I don't know," I said. "They might not be, it might just be that the one that I saw with a similar armor unit found it and added it to its form, or that it's just a logical form to a fucking brain dead psychopath…"

"They *were* created by army intelligence originally…" Sync agreed.

"…but regardless, they're fucking dangerous and they're heavily armed. I looked over records the other day, and the specters weren't really a problem when they made the Archaeons, so it might be they started all of this, or they just weren't in the news yet."

"Why would they come back here though?" Richie asked firing a short burst and shredding a staggering group of specters, before stomping on them as he passed, making damn sure they were dead.

"They came from here," I said. "They were our dead supposedly, so maybe they wanted to come home. Maybe they're something totally different, I don't fucking know. It just seems suspicious as fuck to me that's all."

The next few minutes passed in a blur, with me at the back of our little trio. I spent most of the time stomping on specters that were mostly broken, making sure by crushing their skulls.

Richie and Sync were at the front, and they went full 'rock and roll' for a few seconds, carving their way through the tunnel as it narrowed, more circular than before and funneling our targets in tighter.

Once we reached the bottom of the decline though, the space opened out into what had been a massive complex once. Now, while big, it was clear something had brought a section of the wall down on the far left. leaving a sloping pile of rubble that led up to a smaller chamber.

Machinery and old cranes filled the room, storage areas for carriages and machines to move them into place and out of the tubes were everywhere, as were the specters.

Where in the cooling tower it'd been a clear fucking setup, thousands of them captured and locked into areas, made to fight, and with the ghouls and Banshees somehow caught and locked into place, here the opposite was clear.

This wasn't a set up.

These were specters doing whatever specters did in between feeding and being brain dead.

Thousands of them were waking slowly, even as hundreds were pouring like a slow moving wall of the dead towards us. Further and further back I could see them coming to life, turning from standing aimlessly around a huge central mass, where a few dozen creatures like metal spiders roamed over and over, assembling something.

In the mass were what looked at this distance to be three ghouls, all turned inwards and working on what, if I squinted, looked to be a smaller creature.

"Lock in on that, Sync, I want a recording and an identification," I ordered, knowing that whatever it was, it was important to the specters, so the research geeks would pay for the data.

"Scanning," she agreed, locking down and powering up her Lidar, movement scanners and a dozen others that played hell with the electromagnetic spectrum.

I knew they played hell, because as soon as she triggered them, the pile of swarming, crawling creatures, swung as one, orienting on us, and started racing forwards, claws raised and feral rage filing the air.

But that wasn't the worst of it, because that was when the ghouls suddenly screamed in outrage, disbelief and hatred.

Whatever the smaller creature or creation was, it detonated, an explosion of unstable crap that blanketed the area in radioactives and chemical traces that made utterly no sense, even to my advanced sensor suite.

Of the three ghouls, two survived, more or less, one was badly damaged, the other almost intact, and the pair started moving as soon as they could orient.

The damaged one remained in the middle of the room, while a 'pretorian guard' of Specters gathered up whatever was left of the destroyed creature. They spun on their heels and headed for a far tunnel, the more intact ghoul in their midst carrying most of the remains while others fell in to make sure we couldn't follow.

The other one was making a sacrifice play, guiding the swarm and throwing the entirety at us.

The factory floor before was filled with shattered hulks of long abandoned carriages, mounds of rusted debris were water had seeped in over the years, and rails running here and there, or gantries.

Cranes lay slumped and broken, entire sections had been torn free, and what was most likely once technology broken loose, although if it was by the specters to build whatever that thing had been, or if it was by thieves long since I had no clue.

All I did know was that there were several thousand specters and they were PISSED.

They raced forwards in a great wave, and my carefully laid plans, the nanite bait, the electromagnetic waves we'd plotted to use to draw them close to us, so that we didn't have to follow them down into tighter and tighter tunnels?

All of it was a fucking waste of effort.

There was no need to go hunting them, they were adamant they were coming to us.

"Fall in, three meter separation, full loadout, cut them down!" I barked into the stunned commlink.

They responded as they'd been trained, two steps back to stand on either side of me, I dropped the cylinder of insanely valuable nanites to the floor, drawing my blade as the three of us stood ready.

"I want a line of cluster bombs on my mark," I ordered, picking out a line across the middle of the advancing wave. "Rolling detonation, half a second delay, Richie, me then Sync, three bombs each ten second delay between each of us launching. One barrage to start."

"Oohrah!" Richie approved, getting the green light from me and firing.

The cluster bombs were old tech, built upon and improved for a new era of warfare. Each launcher—of which there were three on either side of the shoulder, just to the side of the swivel mounts for the advanced weapons like my railguns— fired a tiny canister.

That canister flashed across the distance like it'd been fired from an old school mortar launcher.

Once it reached the set target area, a small sail deployed from the rear, a string attached, and attached to that? Tiny sub-munitions.

There were typically a dozen of them, although for specialist encounters there could be more, and as the sail caught the air, it ripped free of the canister, dragging each of the bomblets free as well.

They scattered in predetermined paths depending on loadout, creating anything from a dense cloud of knockout gas, to a shredder pattern of flechettes, to an overlapping explosive pattern that was designed to batter all foes in the area to the ground.

We were loaded with the final option today, and damn they delivered.

The first wave landed in a growling, rabid mass of specters, packed almost shoulder to shoulder, and they literally blasted them apart.

Great holes appeared in the middle of the charging swarm, those that were closer to us staggering and falling, the pressure hitting them from behind, others that were behind the target area being flung this way and that by the explosions.

Those in the middle?

Most of them were rendered down to bone fragments, rotted flesh and fractured mods.

We opened fire, carving overlapping rows of destruction through the charging mass, and I gritted my teeth, remembering that casualties meant nothing to these things.

"Maintain distance, fire at will," I ordered, my own cluster bombs launching in their pattern now, landing on the edge of the area Richie had hit and walking the explosions to the right.

As they detonated, more of the specters that had been racing forwards were picked up and hurled around again, the pressure waves doing as much damage as the explosive detonations. We killed hundreds, Sync opening fire ten seconds after me, and hers taking the edge of my target area, then moving further right to end on the carriage that was funneling them into a narrow squeeze.

The edge of it was shredded, leaving pointed, gleaming metal that still more cut themselves apart on as they were bounced and jounced against it.

The cluster bombs were insanely effective against living foes, taking charging waves out of the fight in a bright flash that left body parts raining over their fellows in splatters of red rain.

Here though? They were effectively useless.

Sure they killed and destroyed a lot of the enemy, but as soon as they fell? More took their place.

"Hold the cluster bombs," I ordered, annoyed at the lack of effect. We'd probably killed a couple of hundred, that was it, and cluster bombs were going to be one of those munitions that we'd have an issue getting our hands on I had no doubt.

"Sustained fire," I ordered. "Cut them down."

All three of us opened fire, carving great lines free of the bodies that raced forwards, and I triggered my railguns, firing a handful of the precious rounds.

Each of them punched through dozens before failing and I barked an order to Sync.

"Get those ghouls!"

"On it," she said, switching from slaughtering the mass, to focusing on individuals.

Three shots rang out in fast succession, and the one that was making its way out of the chamber collapsed, its head and upper body missing.

She shifted, zooming in and spoke up quickly. "The rest of the pack are grabbing whatever it was carrying, do I cut them down?"

I hesitated, then cursed.

"No, take down the other ghoul, that should confuse them all, then you can reorient as we slaughter.

"Aye," she agreed. "Targeting."

Richie fired a drone off his left arm, the small device rocketing upwards to hit the ceiling and lock into place, giving us a bird's eye view of the room, as we continued to fire.

The swarm was closing on us now, hundreds rolling over the fallen, smashing anything that wasn't killed as it fell, into a smear on the floor, and we continued to fire, overlapping fields cutting them down like wheat as the feeds for our rifles chattered like magpies.

Hundreds of rounds filled the air, the hiss and whine of feeder mechanisms rang out and bodies exploded, hit in the crossfire, carved in pieces, they simply ceased to be recognizable, as Julius called me.

"Hey, Kabutt, how…" he said, and I cut him off. I'd added him to the approved list for this job alone, letting him call me, and not get bounced, because I needed to know if there was an outbreak somewhere outside.

"Little busy here," I shot back, flicking my feed to him, and getting a stunned silence for a few seconds as he watched the true devastation that an APS could bring.

"I…can I send in a drone?" he asked after a few seconds.

"You get the two mil?" I asked him, surprised.

"The bidding hit three point seven. A studio wants to use it in a movie."

"Whatever," I snapped, "Slave it to Richie."

"Incoming…" He gulped and a few seconds later something at the outer edge of the rear sensor range something sped down from the levels above.

"Richie, incoming drone, it's slaved ready…"

"Got it," he agreed. "I'll maintain."

"Good man! Sync?" I changed direction on the fly, firing a barrage to the right, cutting down a pincer attempt from that side, and she grunted, then fired, four shots into a carriage on the far side, each round hitting and penetrating, bursting from the far side in a shower of desiccated remains and electrical parts as mods were viciously parted from their former owners.

"Fucker's hiding," she growled. "I know where, but he won't stick his head up…"

"Richie, cluster here," I ordered, marking the exit that the racing group were making for, and he shifted, the 'chunk-chunk-chunk' of the containers leaving their holders solid and felt in your stomach as they rocketed across the room.

"If that doesn't draw the fucker out then we go to him." I growled. Whatever they were carrying was important to them, and the cluster bombs would most likely destroy it all, but it was that or wait for the fuckers to come to us.

Sync switched to local area suppression, her rifle switching to rapid fire as she carved through the incoming mass, punching one that made it too close and splattering him across a nearby wall.

Then as the explosions rolled out, the first few landing a handful of meters from the exit, and each subsequent one closer and closer, the ghoul apparently lifted its head in the carriage.

Sync shifted, clearly having been monitoring it with some sniper split situational sense of kit, and locked it down to a single shot.

It rang out just as the drone came to a halt over the battlefield, and the ghoul was scrubbed from the face of the planet, the shot hitting it in the side of the head and ripping what was left free in a single spray.

The swarming specters sagged, load of them collapsing, still more simply slowing, stumbling and tripping, as I barked out the next orders.

"Sync, overwatch. Richie, with me, rack the rifle!" I barked, slapping my rifle to my back where the magnetic plate shifted and locked it into place.

I lumbered forwards, switching the plasma blade to my right hand, and setting to work, wide sweeping rolls of my wrist burning through multiple figures as they threw themselves at me, and I stomped forwards.

Some of those that had fallen never rose again, crushed by their companions, or by my own multi-ton feet, as I raced into the middle of the mass.

I swept the sword left and right, dozens flaring into flame as the light of a miniature sun carved its way through them, purifying their atoms back to stardust.

Skidding, I turned, folding my right arm across my chest as I shut the blade off, the wash of excited photons and plasma washing over me, as I picked up speed, a little voice inside wanting to scream 'ramming speed' for some reason.

I contented myself with an evil grin as I crushed them, one and two at a time, barely slowing until I came to section where two of the carriages were too close together at one end.

Then I leapt, triggering the jump-jets and soared.

I couldn't stay aloft for long, and the repairs I'd done were minor, I needed a lot more time to get them really working, but damn.

The backblast of the repulsors hurled the few that were closing on me from behind and away. They bounced off carriages and debris, and I scrabbled across the top of the nearest one, the old metal deforming inwards over my much reduced weight, as I cut the power and landed with a deafening crash on the far side, in the middle of a press of the rotting fuckers.

I lashed out right and left, knowing that while they were as ants compared to me, enough of them could still take me down. Instead I made sure none lived long enough, punching, sweeping and crushing, battering them aside, feeling ribs pancake, the brittle snap of old bones crushed as bodies flew here and there.

I closed a massive fist over the head of one, and squeezed, almost no effort required to mush its head, before punting another that got too close. The body shattered as it sailed backwards, and I saw the drone overhead swinging to focus on me as I triggered the plasma blade again, swinging low, carving through ten or more at once, the flash of fresh pyres filling the air as their dry, brittle corpses caught light, tumbling backwards.

The fight dissolved into a blur of melee, of dancing the forms in a suit that was meant to inspire bedwetting fear in enemy armies, as I slipped back into my memories, Scott's voice correcting, berating and guiding as I moved, the overwhelming press of the specters fading to something more manageable as the minutes ticked by.

I used them, and I sent a message to Richie and Sync to do the same.

Our blades flashed and wove fiery trails through the darkness as we used the ready-made practice dummies that we so rarely got access to, to improve our skills.

An hour more we fought, as they kept coming, like flies drawn to shit, hundreds upon hundreds swarmed from holes and tunnels, until eventually, Richie caught the last of them in an outstretched fist, before casually ripping its head free and tossing it aside.

The body collapsed, the strings of puppetry cut, and I realized I was breathing heavily.

The fight had been a long one, nearly three hours, all told, when I checked the clock, but damn.

Seven thousand, two hundred and four kills between the group, with Sync just edging the lead over the two of us.

We finished, we straightened, and I looked up at the drone that had shifted to get all three of us, battle weary titans, in frame.

We all looked up, silence hanging there as we stared at the lens, knowing in a strange way, that millions stared back at us.

"Julius," I said, my voice filled with exhaustion as I connected to him. "Get that thing out of here."

"Sarge…" His voice was awed, and he was clearly at a loss for words. "You just, I mean, we…"

"Whatever," I growled. "We need to start the harvest, before anyone else comes in and we lose this chance. Get them out."

"Shit, of course, sorry." He cursed. "I'm on it!"

The drone twitched and moved back, as if knowing it was about to be sent away, then started flying around the room as fast as possible, capturing everything it could, before finally turning tail and heading from sight.

Reign, Gessh, Luna and Todds joined us a few minutes later, as did Julius, and I climbed from my suit, glad that as I'd known I'd only be in for a few hours I'd not had to suffer the indignity of the special underwear and the pipes and tubes.

I sat on a clear section of the ground, as Sync and Richie settled down to sleep in their suits, their bodies still exhausted. I used the harvester to strip the corpses of their pure nanites, filling container after container, as the others searched for the best of the mods that had survived.

The battle was done, and all that was left now, was the clean-up.

Thank fuck.

CHAPTER FIFTY-THREE

We sat in the back of the transport, the three of us exhausted. We nodded, barely awake, as Reign and the team guarded us from above, with Liolet in a cab ahead and behind, their team split in two, making damn sure we got back alright.

It seemed like no time at all, and yet hours, before I was roused by a solid knocking on my armored carapace, and I blinked, realizing I'd slipped from dozing into full sleep at some point.

I shifted, seeing Reign squinting, looking from camera to camera, the tiny bumps here and there giving me all around vision as she tried to work out which to focus on.

"Just look here," I said, unable to keep a tired smile from my face as I tapped the center of the chest. I'm here, and when you look at the cameras? It's like you're staring at my shoulder."

"You stare at my ass all the time," she countered.

"You do have a nice ass," I said, then sighed. "Honestly, I'm torn between wanting to abuse it right now, and the total hope that you'll let me rest for the night first."

"I'll let you rest I think…though you'll need a shower," she pointed out, and I sighed, standing in the transport and making it rock slightly as I moved to the exit, my rifle still on my back, and two canisters of nanites in my hands.

I clumped down the short few steps from the back, and the transport bounced on its shock absorbers as I stepped free, Sync and Richie ahead of me striding into the warehouse, backing into position to lock the suits in place, and exit.

I saw both Julius and Liolet hurrying over and I forced myself to greet them as I strode inside.

"Julius," I said. "Liolet. Thanks for your backup tonight."

"Anytime." Liolet grinned at me. "I got paid almost as much as I normally do a full mission, and I got to see you fuckers up close…is that really you in there, Kabutt?"

"Come on," I grunted, moving in and triggering the transport crate to open. It shivered, moving as the system unlocked, sliding apart as I set both canisters down on a nearby table. I was about to comm Dondo to come over and get the damn things, when I saw him already moving around at the back of the group. I berated myself for getting so distracted and tired I'd forgotten that the fucker was flying the damn aircar.

"This one's yours," I said to him. "Or your boss' anyway. Tell him thanks for the loan, and that I damn well know how much mine is worth. You can take them both, but I want paying by morning."

"You'll get it," Dondo replied unphased, calling a few other orcs into the building from where they were hanging around outside, sending the nanites with them across the road to the warehouse.

I hesitated, that was hundreds of thousands of credits right there…but in the end, either I trusted him, or I didn't, and I was starting to get the feeling that as much of a dick as the miserable old orc was, Oshbob was actually honest.

For a leader of a crime syndicate, anyway.

Besides, if I needed to, I could always turn him into a greasy smear on the concrete, so there was that.

I backed up into the cradle, feeling the connections automatically mating up with the suit, and approved the linkages, mentally flicking switches and basically telling the suit that there was no need to call for a cleaning cycle—we had no dedicated cleaners for a start—and that I damn well knew about the current suit power and ammunition reserves.

Once all the minor details were done, I reached out and set the suit to open, the seals around the outside of the suit cracking and popping as a rush of cooler air sighed in, mixing with my perfectly regulated atmosphere.

I shivered, flicking the restraining harnesses and straps, then climbed out, nodding tiredly to the others, as Reign was there, taking my hand and helping me as I stepped down from the suit.

"So, how'd we do?" I asked Julius, who snorted.

"Three point nine million the stream reached in the end, and because I'm just that nice a guy? I'll even give you guys the two, and I'll have the one point nine."

"Your generosity warms my heart." I grinned, then nodded to Reign. "Send it to our paymaster here please, she'll split it between the entire team and make it fair."

"Fair?" Liolet asked.

"Everyone gets a share, and we all chip in to pay for the things we need," Luna added proudly.

"Like?" Liolet asked.

"Like ammo," I said, forcing a smile. "Sure, ammo for the APS is a hell of a lot more expensive than ammo for the standard rifles, but then there's missions like tonight. On top of the earning for killing…" I broke off checking the 'kill counter' and added in the team details as Richie and Sync, knowing me for so long sent theirs over unasked. "…seven thousand, two hundred and four specters."

"Holy shit," Liolet grunted. "That's what? Another seven hundred grand between you all?"

"Yeah, so near three million for the night's work," I agreed, sighing and forcing a smile. "We'll only be taking a few jobs a week though, boss, that good with you?"

"Certainly." Julius grinned, knowing that while we'd earned the lions share, we were also sharing that out between us all, he had himself and his partners…I made a mental note to look into that, see how many partners were left now. I'd not shared the full details on the guild deal with the others yet.

Always so much to do.

"So…" Julius said slowly. "You remember the cancellations that were being threatened?"

"Yeah, you said we'd need to work our asses off for a few days, I know, then after that we can drop back to…"

"Most of them decided that they're fine with an extension clause," he interrupted me, grinning. "The four that aren't? They're small and clearly linked to Trees and his traitorous scumbags."

"Did we ever find out what happened to Trees?" I asked.

"Did you ever open your gift from Oshbob?" Dondo interrupted, calling across the room. Everyone went quiet, turning to look at the big handsome half orc. "Maybe you should."

"Fuck." I grunted, checking my pockets automatically—despite not having any in the damn suit—then squinted around the room, trying to remember where I was when he gave it to me.

There, at the back of the room on a small shelf sat the tiny box, the kind of thing that you saw in shop windows offering cheap imitation watches and shit in, and I moved over to it, pulling a ribbon the big bastard had clearly tied around it for a joke, off, tossing it aside.

I popped the lid and froze, looking down at the little bag inside, and caught between revulsion and surprise, as Dondo spoke up.

"He said I was to send you this when you opened it," he said, and I accepted the file, playing it, more than half expecting it to be a grisly threat, when instead…

"Kabutt," the old orc grunted, glaring at me from my Key. "Dondo told me about the little fuckstain that was trying to blackmail you. At first I was tempted to let him squeeze you as well, but this is *my* territory, and I'm intending that we work together in the future, less as we are, and more…" He shrugged, clearly unable to say anything nice like 'as allies' even here.

"Anyway. I decided to make an example of the stupid fuck when Dondo told me who and what he was. It took less than five minutes to find out it was some cock called Trees and I always hated elves anyway."

That was it, the recording cut off there, and I glanced down at the sad little sack on the faux velvet cushion in the box and I started to laugh.

"What is it?" Reign asked, moving over, and I grinned at her.

"It's a peace offering from Oshbob…" I looked over at Dondo, and nodded. "I appreciate it, tell your boss I look forward to working *with* him."

"Is that…?" Reign asked, frowning down at the 'gift' and I nodded.

"We know what happened to Trees," I said, closing the box with a click and underarm throwing it over to Julius who opened the box then winced and closed it with a snap.

"What is it?" Liolet asked, frowning.

"He tried to blackmail me for something," I explained. "I wasn't in the mood for his shit, although I didn't know it was him. His identity was hidden, so I passed it to Dondo here, and he had a word with his boss about it. We've got a relationship with the local syndicate lord, and he took exception to someone trying to blackmail an ally."

"It's his balls," Reign said. "Someone cut his balls off and put them in that little box, probably gave him a good beating as well."

"A very good beating," Dondo assured us. "Within an inch of his life, then cleaned out his credits and gear, I'd have killed him, but we found out that he's one of those nutters like the purists, but for elven superiority reasons, not just the usual level of idiocy."

"So you cut his balls off and left him to basically rot?" Julius asked. "His team abandoned him, you took his gear and he's already been kicked out of the elven territories so…"

"So he'll die a bum, without so much as a credit to his name." Dondo said. "We put a pair of people on him, they'll spend the next month round the clock watching him, making sure nobody gives him much of anything, certainly no work and no weapons. He can't end it all, and he can't reclaim anything he used to own. He's going to spend the next month begging for the food and drink he needs, as an example. After that? We'll let him end it."

"That's…" Julius started, but was cut off by Liolet.

"That's brilliant."

"What?"

"That's brilliant," Liolet said. "Trees was a fucking prick to everyone, the only time he was even polite was when you had something he wanted, and aside from that? I'd have stabbed the fucker daily if I thought I could get away with it. That he had his balls cut off for fucking with people and now he's going to live on the streets, reduced to begging for a fucking crust? I'm going looking for him."

"You can't kill him," Dondo warned.

"I won't," Liolet said quickly. "I'm going to take my whole team, point out that we could kill your guards—no offence—and free him, but because he was such a fucking turd to *everyone*? We won't. Then I'm going to take great pleasure in walking the fuck away."

"Here's his location." Dondo grinned. "We tagged him."

I winced, seeing the feral smile on Liolet's face, and the way the others were acting, then I banished the feeling, reminding myself that the fucker had it coming, and that the punishment matched the crime.

That asshole was guilty all day long.

The atmosphere after that changed, most people moving upstairs to sit around on the few soft furnishings we had. I made a mental note to get more and Richie and Sync moved over to me. I filled them in on Trees and the bullshit he'd been responsible for while Reign, acting as the second for the team, organized food, and more than a few drinks.

I showered, as did Richie and Sync, and by the time we'd gotten back down, the food was here. Richie was shaking his head in disbelief over the setup we'd managed to build in such a short time, and he and Sync were doing their usual dance around each other.

I grabbed their attention, then jerked my head towards the main floor below, leading the way.

"What's up boss?" Richie asked, frowning. "You know the food just arrived, right? We could have a conversation any time, but the food will only be hot for so long…"

"Richie?"

"Yeah?"

"Shut the fuck up." I snorted.

"What do you need?" Sync asked, leaning against the wall nearby, as always positioning herself instinctively to oversee the entire room, while being almost hidden by the nearby shelving units.

"It's not what *I* need," I said softly, looking from one of them to the other. "As your sarge I was always warned about this kinda shit, and officially I agreed with it. Unofficially? I never did. You're both specialists, and while relationships in the same team is generally a bad idea…"

"You're playing hide the sausage with Reign," Richie pointed out.

"Yes, yes thank you for that exceedingly subtle interjection into my heartfelt speech, you dick," I growled at him, not really meaning it. "Seriously though, you two have been looking at each other since you joined the goddamn team. I've seen the way you act, and I've seen the way you keep your distance. It was no fucking surprise that when I found Sync on a goddamn mountainside, she'd already found you first."

I smiled at the way the pair of them glared at me, as I dragged it all out into the light.

"Richie, every relationship you've had since Sync joined the team has been with someone that was a poor imitation of her. Sync? Fuck's sake you watch over him like a mother hen, and reserve all your best abuse for him. If that's not love? I don't know what is. If I have to pay for a goddamn hotel suite for the pair of you for the weekend I will, and I'll even order you to share it. Don't make me give that order."

"Seriously, I don't think you could," Richie babbled, panicking as he tried to get back on 'safe' ground "I mean, there's rules about not having to obey orders like that, right?"

"Richie?" Sync asked.

"Yeah?"

"Shut the fuck up and go grab your things." She sighed. "We're taking the room."

"Uh…" He paused, mouth slightly open, clearly not what he was expecting, before shutting it with a click and grinning widely. "Okay!"

He was off, running up the stairs as she sighed.

"Not exactly the way I'd planned it," she said.

"Maybe I shouldn't have…"

"No you were right, and honestly, I'm nervous as all hell right now, but relieved as well."

"You? Nerv—" I said, only to be cut off when the side of the warehouse exploded inwards.

CHAPTER FIFTY-FOUR

I was picked up and tossed across the room by a section of wall paneling, and it was probably only that, that saved my life, as flechettes peppered the walls, shredding the majority of the softer things.

I hit a table and flipped over it, pain screaming out from my leg as it twisted, before hitting the floor face first, stunned.

It was the scream that tore me out of my shock, the pain that filled Sync's voice as she ripped a section of wall from her stomach, her voice dropping to a furious hiss of pain.

I blinked, clenching my teeth at the pain that flooded my leg, and rolled, every instinct telling me that to stay still was to invite death.

"KABUTT!" a voice boomed, the sheer volume making it clear that it was projected by powerful speakers as I grabbed the edge of the desk, dragging myself around it, and squinting in the powerful lights that illuminated the now smoldering wreckage of what had been our workshop. "SURRENDER NOW, HAND OVER THE STOLEN TECHNOLOGY AND PREPARE TO BE JUDGED."

"Judged...?" I hissed, squinting around the edge of the table, then hissing. "Sync!"

More gunfire rang out, our turrets spinning up and opening fire, distracting at least some of the enemy as they took them down. Fuck I needed better turrets, the ones we had were good, but not APS-one-shot-takedown good.

Clearly that was a fucking mistake.

"Boss..." came a weak response, and my mouth went dry.

"You okay?" I asked, heart pounding as the others up above us ran here and there distantly.

"Not really..." she admitted, clearly in pain "Gut wound."

"How bad?"

"I can fight...maybe?" she replied. "Get me to my suit and few medikits..."

"And you'll kill them all," I finished for her. "Here." I had a single medikit on my belt, and I sent it skittering across the floor towards the little of her I could see. "Stay down, heal up, then shoot those fuckers in the face." I grabbed a random armored glove that was on the floor nearby, and sticking it on a section of wall, then lifting it as if I was surrendering, while laid on my back on the floor.

The barrage of rounds that hit the glove shredded it, and then the table directly below, as I frantically rolled, cursing.

"LAST CHANCE," they boomed, only to be hit by a sudden barrage of fire from above. As the light that had been saturating the area around me swiveled, I got on my feet and hobbled as fast as I could, grabbing the edge of a bench and hauling myself forwards as I mentally reached out, triggering the transport crate.

Why the fuck had I stored my suit!

I heard Sync hissing in pain as she used the medikit, and the boom of fire from above as the rest of the team hammered our attackers clear.

Then another 'whoosh' filled the air and the upper floor of the warehouse exploded, a section of the floor giving way as part of the wall collapsed as well.

I swore, forcing myself to jump, despite the pain that screamed at me from the leg that I was fairly sure was fucking *broken*…but I made it.

The suit was barely opening up as I shimmied around, slipping my legs in and dropping, my chest catching, and for a second I was frozen, half in and half out of the suit…then it was wide enough.

I dropped into the harness, the world around me going white with the pain in my leg, as I reached for the tags by feel, booting everything on an emergency start.

We were taught over and over, you *never* do this, not unless you had to, the power core flaring to full before the systems were ready could cause serious systems damage, but fuck it.

It wasn't like I was getting a deposit back for the suit.

My screens flickered as I triggered the release from the supports, still booting they showed sections of the room as the unexpected energy flare battled with the suits own systems, and I was moving.

The transport crate hadn't fully opened, not yet, and worse yet sections of fallen wall and roof were pinning it in place.

It didn't matter.

All that mattered was my team.

I triggered 'overdrive', flooding the suit with power, forcing everything into maximum power mode, as I grabbed the sides of the container and ripped them free in a shower of sparks and a screech of tortured metal.

As soon as the front was clear, I reached up and grabbed a better handhold, tearing myself out…and into a barrage of gunfire.

The first few shots deflected off, ricochets that made the armor ring, but I knew they were more blind luck than anything else. I did what I had to do…and I ran.

I hurled myself across the benches and ran at the wall furthest from the attackers, covering my chest with my left arm as I smashed through the metal and concrete, bursting into the dim morning, chucks of masonry and metal flying in all directions, as I skidded, then staggered.

The shot that had hit me was a good one, focusing on my left shoulder mount, taking it down, clearlt making sure that if it was an uncharged shield, it wasn't going to stop the next shot.

It wasn't, it'd been an additional armor plate, and it served its purpose as I jinked sideways, then back, a second sniper round tearing through the air an inch to my right.

My RI combined with my suit and locked their location in—an APS suit in active camo atop Oshbob's warehouse. I cursed, jinking right again, and boosted my run with the jump-jets, sending me skidding sideways just fast enough that I dodged the next round.

"Kabutt?" Luna screamed into my ear as the tac-net went live. "What the fu…"

"APS Ghost squad!" I shouted, frantically throwing myself down, bouncing across the floor as three more rounds flashed past overhead.

They were fast and they were accurate. They'd clearly waited until they thought everyone was away from the suits, making us a lot easier to take down, and they'd been ready.

I heard a whine as something powered up, then Dondo shouting in the distance.

"You didn't see that coming did you, you fucker!" he bellowed, and I kicked myself back upright, bracing a foot and starting to run, knowing that as long as that sniper had overwatch we were fucked.

A nice railgun like that though? I could do some serious damage with that, provided I could rip it out of the cold dead hands of its current owner.

I needed to start leaving my rifle on the wall, rather than in the fucking storage rack.

My shoulder mounted railguns finished the power-up cycle and swung around, aiming behind me as a figure burst from the side of my building.

Grey and black armor, not black and gold.

I mentally tagged them as the enemy, my system automatically having frozen when it'd been about to 'sweep' the armor, the original settings identifying any APS as 'friend'.

The change took a milli-second to correct, and they were traversing again, locking in on him as he opened fire, chasing me.

I changed direction, ploughing into the side of the next building along—some 'holistic pet food' place, whatever *that* was—and I spun, dropping to the floor on instinct, reaching out and grabbing at the polished floor tiles.

I carved a short furrow with my fingers, bringing my armored bulk to a dead stop, counted to three, my RI finally finishing meshing with our home's sensor suite to provide me with all around mapping of the nearest few buildings.

Then I grinned and set off, sprinting at the hole in the wall I'd just come through.

The fucker that was chasing me raced inside, his rifle panning…and I smashed it aside, punching him full-force in the center of the armor, directly over the pilot's compartment.

The suit staggered and I knew what was happening inside, a weakness that was refined less than a year ago was that where the suit projected the screens, a master relay had been buried dead center.

It was supposedly one of the safest positions for it, considering it affected all of the suits visual systems, but the APS were insanely powerful, and Fergie had fucked Blue Three's entire day up in a sparring session by doing just this.

The pilot wasn't just knocked back, all his screens would be rebooting, flickering and realigning, and when they came back on? The ones set as 'front right' and 'front left' curving to mesh into a seemingly single huge screen?

Well, they often booted back to front.

When they came back on at all.

I blocked a wildly swung punch with a backhand, dropped to one knee and ripped his plasma sword free, thumbing it to life as he dragged his rifle across directly above my head, firing on full auto.

The tint shop was torn apart, heavy rounds that could have taken out old school battle tanks, shredding support pylons, walls, refrigeration and more…

…Until I rammed the plasma sword through the lower chest of the armor, skewering the fucker.

His suit spasmed as the blade did interesting things to him, but I was already moving. I flicked the blade off instead of dragging it free, the wash of disassociated plasma filling the suit as the containment field failed. What was left of the pilot was rendered to fucking charcoal, as I grabbed his rifle, snapping off the connection to his autoloader, and hitting the 'load' for the attached standard magazine instead.

I hesitated then, realization that he'd seemed almost slow and clunky as I'd fought him, not so much predictable, but slow enough to dodge…and I grinned.

There was a reason I'd been able to dodge the bullets I realized.

I wasn't fast enough to outrun a fucking bullet, nobody was, but I was faster than I should be.

"RI, run comparison on baseline integration, and current integration." I ordered, bringing up the area in my vision, then turning and running…at the wall to my right.

I burst out of it in a shower of concrete and glass, bounding across the street, jinking left and then left again, rounds from the concealed sniper hammering into the ground when he guessed I'd go right instead.

Then I was across the road, and at the foot of Oshbob's warehouse, crouching and leaping, grabbing the roof of a first story attached building and hauling myself up one handed as my jump-jets fired.

The sheer weight of my suit meant that without the jump jets I'd be crashing through the wall and roof here. Neither the grip I had, nor the roof could support my weight, but as I boosted myself up I kept firing them continually, despite the stress warnings I was getting.

I'd make better time without the damn rifle in my hands, but even as my railguns were firing almost continually on auto, targeting the fuckers that were racing after me, I let rip with a full burst of fire at the edge of the next story above.

I knew that if I'd lost sight of me, headed in this direction, I'd not have stayed back where I was, calmly taking pot shots, I'd have moved, ready to take me in the face as I appeared over the edge.

So I didn't do it.

I raced forwards and ploughed into the side of the wall ahead of me, racing from the flat, lower level roof, into the upper level of the warehouse.

The stone shattered around me, and I skidded as I came to stop on an internal walkway that ringed the inside warehouse. Almost instantly I was hit by small arms fire from below, making me curse and trigger my speakers.

"Fuck off! It's me, Kabutt!" I shouted waving one hand at the lower floor, even as I searched the roof over my head, squinting as I tried to spot any tell-tales for the suit overhead.

I could use my Lidar, but that would only show my…

My suit screamed a warning as I was hit by a powerful lidar ping before I could finish dismissing using my own. I jumped to my right, starting to sprint in that direction, even as a high powered round punched through from the floor above, taking out a section of wall.

I returned fire, full auto, shredding the ground around the fucker, and continued to run, this time grabbing a support stanchion and launching myself over the side as the sniper came crashing through the roof ahead.

He tried to trigger his jump-jets, twisting, trying to catch himself, as both my railguns—smaller caliber than his rifle by far, but still goddamn powerful—opened fire on him.

I fired the jets in three fast bursts, catching myself so that I landed in a three point 'hero' pose, rifle up and the mag emptying in seconds hammering the fucker as he crashed into the floor.

The railguns coordinated fire on his right arm as I ran at him, punching into the mechanism and jolting his arm sideways as he tried to force himself back up.

Then I was there, skidding to a halt, slapping the rifle aside as he tried to line it up on me, then ripping it free of his weakened grip.

I flipped it, lining up on the center of his body as he frantically pinged me, trying to communicate.

Fuck no.

"Guilty!" I growled, firing three shots from the high powered railgun into the central torso, killing the pilot instantly.

"Kabutt!" The shout came from my left and I spun, seeing that miserable old fuck Oshbob stomping out of a side room, a gun that looked like it could be used to take down orbiting satellites clutched in his hands. "What the absolute fuck…"

"Ghost squad." I snapped cutting him off. "They're here for me, and my *allies*."

"Then they'll get us," the orc growled, pulling the charging lever and filling the air with a whine of gamma radiation charging.

"Reign!" I called, switching from external to internal and onto the tac-net. "Fuck's sake, are you…is everyone alright?"

"Not…really," came the response from Sync. "I'm pinned in the warehouse. Upstairs is on fire…"

"Fuck!" I screamed in fury, spinning and sprinting at the nearest wall to them, smashing straight through it and ignoring the scream of rage from Oshbob as I further damaged his shit.

CHAPTER FIFTY-FIVE

The others hadn't responded to my frantic call, but some of them were alive still, that much was clear, as I burst into the street again, seeing three more of the ghost squad moving into the warehouse, getting hammered by fire from several points from above.

One of their number was down, what looked to have been an insanely lucky shot that had penetrated the non-baffled front on the cluster bomb launcher at the worst time, causing a chain reaction.

The suit was sprawled on the floor, unmoving, with smoke rising from its back and the armor cratered and torn.

The remaining three were split between trying to squash the annoying gnats that were my team, and retrieving our suits, a heavy transport having landed behind them, with the walkway inside opening as I raced towards them.

Here and there soldiers were scattered around the buildings, torn apart by everything from our concealed turrets to Oshbob's goblins and more, dozens in unmarked black military grade armor, falling back on their transport. They'd not been ready for my new allies that was for sure.

For a brief second I reveled in the 'minor' detail that these fuckers had older suits, no shoulder mountings for additional weaponry, only the cluster bomb launchers. Then I opened fire on the nearest, as he started dragging one of our suits out of the burning building.

He was walking backwards, arms locked around the suit, headed towards a small team of regular soldiers that were readying a recovery sled by the rear of the transport, shielded from shots from the warehouse by a shimmering force shield.

My shots hit him from the side, staggering him, before my stolen railgun fired a much heavier round into the upper arm just below where the shoulder joint met the arm.

It deflected off, barely missing my target, and instead of fucking his arm and sending him staggering, he spun, dropping the suit and ripping his rifle free.

The other two turned as well, all three lining up on me, opening fire at once. I was hit, over and over, my armor ringing like a bell as warnings lit the screens and I 'felt' the damage through the system spinal tap linkages.

Armor integrity: 76%

The warning was barely there before it was gone, a second flashing up in its place.

> **Armor integrity: 65%**

By the time it'd flickered twice more and I was hitting the forties, I'd triggered my jump-jets and strafed sideways, avoiding two of the streams of fire, the third ripping free a shoulder mounted railgun.

They'd been returning fire though, focusing on the weak spots of the older armor variants, upper arm joints, cluster bomb dispenser ports and the very center of the armor.

The railgun impacts on the center wouldn't be enough to fuck their visuals easily, but repeated hits would.

I lifted the rifle and locked in the target, firing just as I was hit again and again, my aim thrown off and the round from the heavier weapon taking the arm out of the leftmost target, rather than the chest.

He staggered, and I cursed, diving, rolling and coming to my feet, firing the second, and final, load of cluster bombs I had onboard.

They weren't the high explosive that could have been fucking useful, oh no, they were the flechette version, and more dangerous for my people than theirs…so I had to be good with targeting.

All three landed right on their transport cockpit, exploding and damaging the hardened structure, then tearing into it with hundreds of tiny darts. The shields were limited use on a transport like this, they drew too much power when the damn thing needed so much to fly anyway, so they powered only those needed, generally.

I was insanely lucky that they'd just kept the ones protecting their crew up.

Then I was moving again, all fire from the suits drawn onto me as they frantically tried to take me down before I could take out their ride, the rear shielding flickering as power was diverted, side projectors glowing as they started to power up.

I didn't give two shits about the craft in general, beyond the fact it was an insanely expensive, heavy transport that was literally perfect for mission deployments. No I cared that *they* needed it.

As I sprinted for it, the suits opened fire again, and a pair of turrets on this side of the transport deployed in a blast of pressurized gasses, swiveling to track me.

My surviving shoulder mounted railgun tracked one of the suits as they locked in on me, unleashing a heavy barrage of fire that took my left leg off at the knee, sending me to the floor in a sliding crash.

I returned fire; three shots, three hits, all center of mass, and I saw him pause, his hands coming up as inside the suit the pilot frantically reached for failing screens, cut off from the world around as he tried to get them back.

I locked the stolen sniper rifle on him, and fired three more shots, this time without him moving I managed to get dead center hits of my own, and they fucking punched right through, taking him down.

I was hit twice, left shoulder, driven a few inches back by the force as my left arm spasmed and shuddered, then I was hit again, a fast hard barrage of a dozen or more hits into that shoulder, losing the arm entirely.

My shoulder railgun twitched as I set three targets as fast as I could, two rounds fired before the turrets tore it free, even as I twisted the rifle around to line up…on the transport.

My shoulder mounted railgun had fired on the rifles of the last two figures, a single shot each, aimed at their rifle barrels. One hit, one miss, leaving only one of the two surviving suits with a usable weapon—beyond the cluster bomb dispensers and built in systems anyway.

At the same time I pulled the trigger on my stolen railgun and emptied the last five shots in the mag, straight through the cockpit.

The turrets went dead, as blood splattered the inside of the cockpit glass, and I collapsed back, done.

The rifle was empty, my cluster bomb dispensers were empty, my left suit leg was amputated at the knee, my left suit arm at the shoulder, making me damn glad I was in the suit, not wearing it like the first generation had, arms and legs sticking out into the greater limbs.

I had two weapons left, and as I tried to push myself upright, a kick caught me in the chest hurling me back. The plasma sword I'd stolen from one of their men was ripped free. I was kicked again, then again, before finally I got a call from Major Marcial, the assholes pausing as he clearly ordered them to wait.

"What do you want fuck face?" I grunted at him conversationally.

"That's no way to talk to the man that's holding your life in his hands," he replied. "You've cost me a hell of a price tonight, Kabutt."

"Oh, too bad, so sad," I shot back. "I was kicking back ready for a fucking beer when you sent your pets after me, this didn't have to happen." I snarled, forcing myself to stay on task and not panic over the others situation right now.

"I warned you this wasn't over."

"You told me to run and hide," I pointed out. "I left you alone, hell we kept quiet about you and your fucking team."

"You did," he agreed, before sighing. "Then you turn up with two more suits. Let me guess, Red Five and Six? They survived that little incident and were hiding all this time in the Fingers?"

"We knew you'd be watching," I said, shifting around, wondering if I overclocked the suit…if I lifted the safety limiters on my spinal tap…

I'd already found I was markedly faster than they were, and I'd only just touched the surface of how much more accurate, how much smoother I was. If I removed the final safety lockouts, and went all out?

Then I saw them.

I couldn't help but smile.

"You find something amusing?" the major asked, and I couldn't help it.

"Fuck yes. You've no idea what you've done, you prick."

"Kabutt…" he growled warningly. "I hold your life in my hand. You really think it's wise to piss me off more?"

"Get on with it," I snapped, forcing myself to a sitting position, braced on one arm. "You wanted to gloat? Fine, get it over with."

"I didn't stop them just to gloat Kabutt, but to make you an offer."

I opened my mouth, then paused, I'd certainly not seen that coming.

"Go on." I encouraged, happy to gain a few more seconds.

"Work for me, for real this time." He suggested. "Come and take the second slot in my black ops team. You've no idea how much those corpo scumbags pay me for these jobs…"

"And I've just killed half your team," I finished for him with a grunt, seeing it all. "You need more than you've got for an op!"

"I do," he admitted. "And so you've got a chance. I knew you were good, but Red never stood out above the other teams, not the way you have since leaving the force. What was it? You just didn't bother to put the effort in before? OR did you need a kick in the ass?"

"You stupid fucks." I snorted. "You, dumb stupid mother fuckers."

"I needed more modern suits Kabutt, mine are older, you've seen the difference between them and the latest generation, there was a ceiling on the upgrades they could take. Your suits would have fixed that, and let me compete with the remaining three black teams."

"Three?" I choked in disbelief. "There are *three* more black ops teams out there?"

"There are, and the motherload, Kabutt! There are *fifth* generation suits, prototypes that are being delivered to the army, so classified that if the right people die tomorrow? No-one will even know that they've gone missing!"

"You wanted my suits, to give you a better chance at getting those," I guessed, getting a nod from him.

"They're five, maybe ten years from deployment, Kabutt, everything your suits have? They've got better. We've got them, or we will have. The step between Assault Mechs and the APS. A new Lord of the battlefield! I can give you one of those…"

"Because you're just so trustworthy," I shook my head. "You think I'd trust you? After all of this?"

"I hoped you were smart enough to see your choices clearly Kabutt." The major sighed. "Well, you had your chance, fuck it. What a waste."

"Yeah, no." I shifted, propping myself up as more and more of my systems failed, and I squinted at the screen. "You know what Major? You made some serious fuckups tonight, hell, you made a lot, but you know what the last one was?"

"Enlighten me," he invited coldly.

"Well, besides monologuing like a fucking children's vid villain I mean, that was fantastic, because yeah, I'm going to find out where those suits are now, and I'm gonna piss on your parade! But no, the biggest mistake?"

"Go on."

"You distracted your fucking idiot operators and had them watch over *me*, when they should have been watching…"

Todds triggered his plasma sword from full stealth, standing right behind the suit that still had its rifle, and drove the sword through the weak spot I'd drilled into all of them that was under the armpit.

"Where…" I said.

Sync fired her massive APS sniper rifle, laid across a bench, held in place by Dondo and Gessh, the round taking the remaining APS in the powercell regulator, triggering a full emergency SCRAM, and shutting down his suit. He collapsed to the floor, screaming and twitching as power surges fried back and forth inside his suit, shocking him over and over.

"My team…"

Richie staggered out of the remains of the warehouse, his suit damaged, filthy and the new paintjob fucked, but he was upright, and he was *pissed.*

"And my new friends were."

The massive figure of Oshbob strode out of the darkness, the gamma cannon held cradled in both hands, as he lined up on the transport, and the half dozen soldiers that were left inside, as he glared at them.

"Time to die," he snarled.

CHAPTER FIFTY-SIX

"No," I called over the external speakers, cutting off the major. "Oshbob, don't do it."

"Fuck off, Kabutt! They—and *you*—trashed my shit! Nobody fucks with what's mine!"

"And you can kill them if you want, *later*!" I forced out, planting my one working arm and forcing myself upright again. "I need information, and I need goddamn parts!"

"There's plenty here in scrap," he shot back.

"They're working for Major Marcial!" I retorted. "You want him to get away with this? You want him to win? We need to find him! He's the one that started all this shit!"

He hesitated and I saw the look in his eyes, saw the rage that was barely constrained, before a scream rose off to the right. I twisted, looking over and saw, amongst a line of dead enemy bodies, a blur of blackness, and the flash of blades.

Fucking assassin! Oshbob's, they had to be!

"Stop him!" I called to the orc. "We need the information!"

He looked at me, sneering, clearly seeing some weakness in my demand, rather than the fact I wanted to make sure I could set fire to that cockroach and piss on the ashes.

"Unara," he snapped after a few seconds, having made his point that he did what he wanted, not what I asked. "Leave two to talk, and make them ready to."

With that, he turned on his heel, and I turned, seeing Richie in his suit, staggering over, then stomp one foot down atop the APS that was being repeatedly shocked, and rest his rifle against the damaged armor.

"Open up, or I'll fucking blast you out," he snarled furiously.

I glanced, seeing Richie's bio readout on my suits interior and wincing. He was badly injured, whatever the hell had happened upstairs…

"Reign…" I whispered, flicking the system up and reaching out to her, and getting no response. My tac-net showed she was alive, the bios from Richie far more informative as he was in a suit that was designed to track such data, but she was definitely not doing well.

"Reign! Gessh? Luna?" I tried. "Sync?" I yanked the emergency releases, what was left of my fucking suit popping and clicking around me.

"Reign and Luna are down," Todds told me, moving over to help as my suit cracked open. "Alive, but…Luna needs new legs, again, or one at least, and was knocked out by a falling beam. Reign was shot three times, she's bad."

"How bad?" I asked, hissing in pain as my leg flared, before seeing my left arm refused to respond properly. I glared at it, seeing the shredded limb, more than half of the lower arm just a mangled mess, while the upper was crushed and warped.

When they'd taken the suit arm off, they'd mangled my own, and I was just fortunate that it was a cybernetic replacement, all things considered.

My left leg in the suit had ended below the knee, and while the suit had faithfully transmitted the information to me, my own leg was just the same as earlier, probably a hairline fracture, but that was it.

"She's bad, boss," he admitted grimly.

"Hospital?"

"Already called for an emergency airlift, they'd not set off until all fighting was confirmed over, they're inbound now."

"Liolet? Julius? Fuck, Liolet's team?"

"The team were all killed, I think." He shook his head. "They were outside, most of them, didn't stand a chance. Liolet is alive, but...he's broken, catatonic."

"Julius?" I asked, hobbling forwards as Richie dragged the pilot out of the suit and threw him through the air at the other prisoners with a scream.

"He was the luckiest, explosion picked him up and threw him through a wall, ended up unconscious on someone's bed, out for the entire fight, I hit him with a medikit when I grabbed my stealthsuit."

"That stealthsuit, the kill, you did well," I said, forcing the words out as he helped me through the hole in the wall and into the remains of our home.

"Not fast enough." He growled. "Fuck that fight! It was over so fast, the explosion, the suits..."

"Where is she?" I asked, before pausing, finally seeing Sync. I'd known she was injured, fuck's sake, I *knew* she was, she was my friend, my squad mate and yet, I'd forgotten her in my demand to see Reign.

"Sync..." I asked, looking over at her, Gessh having left her and returned presumably to her sister's side.

"I'm okay," she said, wincing. "Gonna need some work, some mods probably, but I'm okay..."

"Lion!" I snapped, nodding. "We've got a carver. I'll get him here."

"Best make it quick," Richie grunted, tearing a section of the half slumped wall free and climbing in. "That asshole won't give us long."

"Marcial?" I asked, and growled in agreement. "He's got a job. New suits."

"More?" he asked, looking around his armor popping and hinging open.

"He thought he needed our suits to get them," I explained. "Some new prototypes..."

"And he thought he could just hit us, steal our suits, then go get them?"

"Apparently." I growled. "He tried to recruit me, after all of this." I shook my head in amazed disgust. "I'll get the carver."

"Get him, and tell him I need fixing up as well, fast. How long have we got?"

"Before...?" I asked, still leaning on Todds as he helped me across the floor towards the remains of the stairs to the upper floor.

Or what was left of it, considering the morning sunlight was shining through the smoke and shredded building.

"Before that fucker goes after the protypes!" Richie snapped. "If he had a chance at them tonight he'll still be taking it, just trying to do it with normal troops now, if he's lost his ghosts. He'll not let the chance pass by, so we've still got a chance at him!"

"We just need to find out where and when," I agreed. "You and me."

"Me too," Sync demanded, and we both looked at her, seeing the way she was leaning against the table, clearly unable to stand on her own.

"We'll see," I said.

"No," she ground out. "We finish this the way we started it, the three of us, together."

"Together," I agreed, knowing there was no way it was happening, but unwilling to argue it right now. I was already turning away as Richie clambered free of his armor, hissing in pain as he used a nearby hoist to drag himself free. He swore, and gritted his teeth through the pain, his lower body clearly not responding properly as he fell on his way to Sync to help her.

"Lion…" I breathed thankfully as he answered the call through my key.

"Hey, Kabutt." He yawned, clearly half asleep still. "It's early man, what do you—"

"We got hit." I cut him off. "We won, but we've got badly injured and broken people here, I need you, whatever it costs, I'll pay, but we need you *here*, now."

There was a brief seconds pause, then he nodded.

"I'll bring my gear, send me a list of what you need and—"

"Thank you. Talk to Todds, he'll fill you in," I said, adding Todds to the call, then cutting myself out of it, as the first flashing lights illuminated the upper floor, shining through the damaged walls and roof.

"Reign…" I whispered, dropping to my knees by her side. A spar of a roof support had rammed through her upper chest, by her shoulder and into the wall behind her, a bubble bursting through the blood that foamed and ran.

I could see swarming nanites, the only reason she was still alive at all, and the two used medikits that Todds must have hit her with, but fuck…

"Which is the victim?" came a general question from a voice I didn't know, and I turned, staring dully at the two figures that had jumped across from a floating aircar.

"Who the fuck do you—" I started to question, anger rising, as one of them shook his head.

"We were called for a 'Rain'? She's got a medivac and basic suite paid for, which one is she?"

"This is Reign." I snapped, stepping back so that they could get a clearer look at her.

"Move back," the EMT ordered, moving forward as the second one dragged a suspension stretcher into place.

They were elites, that was clear as I stared at them, caught between panic, resignation, fear and exhaustion.

They were both decked out in full EMT suites. As Emergency Medical Technicians they had access to a level of kit that was almost comparable to my own suit, but where that was an instrument of war and death, theirs…

They were dressed in white with red and blue highlights around armored plates, their helmets hiding their faces even as they projected all the information they needed. Both had back mounted additional arms, one sparking to life as the first guy braced Reign. The articulated arm ending in a laser that carved through the metal pinning her easily.

They picked her up and set her on the stretcher, utterly unconcerned about the condition of Luna where she was laid, broken, with Gessh helping her, nor of Julius who'd just stumbled out of the bedroom he'd apparently been napping in.

"The receipt will be sent to the contracting keystone." the EMT declared, all professionalism. "Any additional charges will be notified and treatment paused until the cost has been addressed. Considering her condition? I recommend not taking time to try and negotiate the rate, but that's your call. Remember, as per sub-section five, if the patient terminates while awaiting approval of additional expenditure, you may still be charged for any procedures that were due, and you will not receive any discount on credit extended."

With that, and before anyone could say anything else, they were gone, lifting her into the back of the transport, and taking off.

"How much?" I croaked, knowing it shouldn't matter, but I couldn't leave it to someone else to pay for her care, not to make decisions that might leave her in limbo while they slept or whatever.

"Two hundred grand," Todds said. "It was her only chance though. I paid for it a few days ago, its an insurance policy for me, to be fair—I've got two kids relying on me, after all—and it covers any on site emergency work, with additional work costing. It seemed like a hell of a price, but to make sure I'm there for them…"

"I'll pay you it back." I promised, starting to reach for my access, only to have Julius speak over me.

"No," he said. "This happened because you came out to help me. The guild will pay."

"Thank you," I croaked, before coughing and clearing my throat. "Thank you all," I tried again, before looking over at Luna." How you doing?"

"Good!" she lied, forcing a smile, one leg a mass of smashed metal, the other looking pretty fucked as well.

"Bullshit." I snorted. "Lion's on his way, can you hold on, or do you want me to medivac…?"

"I'll wait," she said. "He's going to have his hands full, but, it's all cyber." She nodded to her legs, ignoring the blood on her face and the generally shitty way she looked.

"What now?" someone asked, and I stared at the bloody remains of the metal that had nearly killed Reign.

"Now?" I replied flatly. "Now we end this."

CHAPTER FIFTY-SEVEN

The next four hours passed in a blur. We all used medikits, the worst of us triaged by Lion, Luna being sent to a clinic for some work after all, along with Sync. The pair of them were more significantly injured than he was comfortable working with.

"I can replace their kit, but I can't heal them," he'd explained. "For Sync? Half her organs are on the verge of collapse, twelve to eighteen hours in a decent clinic with tissue regen and directed nanites? She'll be doing cartwheels, never felt better, as it is though? All I could do was rip them out and rebuild. That's a full day's job, just on her, that's nobody else I can help."

Luna had half a dozen flechettes driven deep into her, and while the medikits were numbing the pain, the longer they were inside, the more damage they'd do. The regrowth was a hell of a lot cheaper and could be done today.

She already had new legs on order—they came as a pair, even for replacements, the bastards—but that'd be tomorrow before they could be fitted.

Richie was keeping himself going with medikits and stims, as well as coffee, cigars and rage, and I was with him on that last one, he was also seriously fucked thanks to the spinal damage, but being an operator, he refused to give in.

Lion had numbed the entire body below mid-way down his back, and as soon as the rebuild of my suit was done, he was heading back to Lion's chop-shop, ready for a new spinal tap install.

Dondo had survived as well, although he'd been with Oshbob the last few hours, he'd arrived back about twenty minutes ago, and started to work alongside us.

Liolet had shut down. His entire squad, a group as close as any family, had been cut down like animals, and he couldn't deal with it, he'd collapsed and was unresponsive. We'd moved him to a section of the building that was more or less safe, and wrapped him in a blanket, leaving him be.

Todds had returned home, the kids needing him for a little, and needing some rest himself, and I'd sent him on his way with our thanks, as well as apologies, as we'd basically taken over his life since rescuing him.

Julius had come through for us, and in a big way. The armorers, weaponsmiths and anyone that wanted to look good before the Guildmaster had responded to his call 'to help one of our own'.

We had seventeen people here now, and we were making headway with the building.

The first thing we'd done, was register the fight as an attack upon the guild. With the guild being an official entity, and currently a rising star in the vid circuit, that shut down any unofficial attempts from assholes like ACE to grab the suits and wreckage.

As a guild property—it'd taken some seriously fast talking to Oshbob to get him to agree to it being classified publicly as that—it meant that this had been classified as a guild *raid*.

Essentially, while these things were frowned upon, they happened, and while the attackers, if we filed formal complaints, would get a hefty fine and a bill for our repairs, that wasn't the important thing.

That important side was that the suits were classed as equipment used in the raid, and that meant they belonged to the victors. We had all the parts we needed to fix up at least one suit, and several older generation suits for sure.

The transport was also classed as a spoil of war, though due to the level of damage we were probably going to have to sell that for parts and scrap.

We'd also need a dedicated pilot if we tried to fix it, but that was a problem for another day. We hired an air-lift, and had it dragged onto our boundary so we weren't getting fined from the city for blocking the roads, then promptly raided it for parts and intel.

Oshbob and his pet assassin 'discussed' the raid with the survivors of the enemy force as well, and Dondo told me that they'd be wanting a 'chat' later, once they were finished, but that I could leave the details to them.

That just left the suits.

They'd tried to steal Sync's suit, and that was more or less intact, but she wasn't. Richie was much the same, his suit was in good condition, his body, not so much.

I was the only one that was really combat-capable, and my suit was fucked.

That, of course, left us with two options. We could 'blank' one of their suits, so that I could use it, but it'd cost a fortune in nanites, then need to be done again so they got their suit back, or…

"I still can't believe we're doing this," Richie grumbled, disconnecting sections of the left arm, as I worked on releasing the corresponding kit on my own suit.

Seven of us were working on my suit right then, with four more under Richie working on Sync's suit.

"She's going…to fucking kill us…both, you know that, right?" he said, grunting as he shifted, dragging himself forwards to see where a guy was tugging on a stubborn connector. It popped loose on the third heave, sending him staggering as the makeshift crane took the weight of the limb.

"That's on you," I said, shifting around inside my suit, freeing the next section. "Right, can you pull now Santos?"

"Whadda you mean it's on me?" Richie asked, glaring over from where he was sprawled.

"Sync," I said as if it was obvious. "Fuck's sake, Richie, I'd literally just gotten you both to fuck off to a hotel for a few days to screw each other's brains out. I was even paying for it, I think the least you could do was take one for the team and break the news to her."

"You think paying for a hotel—one I didn't even get to use—means I owe you this? My spine's fucked, you think I'm getting my end away any time soon?" He shook his head. "The only way we survive this, is if we kill that fuckhead Marcial."

"Well, yeah, he's been gunning for us…" I responded, only to be cut off.

"I mean Sync!" Richie snapped. "We're stripping her suit for parts, she's gonna fucking murder us both!"

"She really that dangerous?" one of the armorers asked, helping to carry some of the arm away.

"She's an APS elite sniper with over a thousand confirmed kills," Riche said flatly. "What do *you* think?"

"Sucks to be you guys."

"You think you're not in the line of fire?" Richie said. "You're helping us loot and strip her suit. I'm alright, I'm already injured, if I play this right—and believe me, I will—she might forgive me. Him? He's the boss. She *might* forgive him too, more or less. Eventually anyway, if he provides her with the fuckers head on a stick as a bathroom ornament. You?"

Richie shook his head sadly. "You guys just send us a message when they do the whip around for the funerals, okay? We'll chuck a few creds in the pot."

"Oh thanks man, I love giving my day off up to get threatened." one of them grumbled.

"Hey, you're married," another of the team called over, grinning. "It was threats at home or here, at least here there's no kids demanding creds!"

"True that…" the first said, shaking his head as he stuck it into the open chest of the APS trying to trace a cable.

The conversation went on and on, the group working well together as we stripped and rebuilt, frantically working, while Richie got slower and slower, until I finally managed to pack him off for medical as well.

The sun was going back down, and I was slumped in an exhausted half doze, when Dondo came to get me hours later, my suit complete and doing recalibrations and integration workups.

"Oshbob wants to see you," he said. "They've talked."

I winced, forcing myself up and yawning hugely. I'd spent the day roaming between the heights of rage inducing adrenaline—those fuckers had come after me in my home, they'd nearly killed my friends, and he had been responsible for killing Fergie and Scott—and barely being able to focus as I'd still not slept properly after the job last night, or for more than a couple of hours here and there since departing for the Fingers of God days ago.

"Did you lose many people?" I asked Dondo as we walked across the street.

"Not really."

"Really?"

"You soldier-boy types forget what it's like in the slums, you stick your head up and make a noise? You get fucked up." He snorted. "Besides the damage done to the warehouse—I'd make a point of apologizing for that if I was you, by the way—we got off pretty light. Most of them were focused on you, and the ones that weren't? They saw street rats, while looking for soldiers and waved us off."

"How'd that work out for them?"

"Unara slit their throats." He grunted. "That's my second bit of advice for you in all this, don't piss her off. She's the boss's right hand, and he trusts her. If she decided to gut you because she didn't like your haircut he'd be more pissed at the mess on his floor than you being dead. Don't fuck with her."

"The assassin?" I asked, and he nodded.

"Assassin, bodyguard, friend, she's like his sadistic little sister, so while she's beautiful? Seriously watch your step. She'd rather stab your eyes out than kiss you."

"I've got Reign," I said pointedly.

"And I've got Luna and Gessh, which is why I'm telling you this, not letting you fuck up and getting someone to mop up what's left of you." He shrugged. "You can listen or you cannot, that's your choice. I'll tell them that I warned you though, and that's my hands clean."

"I'll do my best," I promised, actually meaning it, and surprising myself as I realized I actually did trust him. Maybe I was more tired than I'd realized.

"Kabutt, you fucking asshole." That was how Oshbob greeted me as I was led into the warehouse as he stared at the damage done to the building, and I avoided the conspicuous blood stains on the floor.

"Oshbob," I greeted him, determined to be respectful, as much as I could, we were allies after all and—

"Give me one fucking reason I shouldn't have you dipped into boiling acid by your dick!" He snarled, and I blinked.

"Because I'd kill all the useless fucks that tried it, then I'd leave you as a greasy fucking smear on the floor?" I snapped back at him.

"You know how much damage your little fight did to my shit?" he asked, his voice a hiss of fury.

"I know how much damage it did to me and my fucking friends when I was trying to grab a pizza and a fucking beer!" I snarled. "We agreed that we'd be allies, that I'd back you up if you got hit, and you'd do the same, now you're fucking complaining that you actually had to do it?"

"That was a handful of hours ago!" He practically screamed at me. "Literally!"

"You didn't set a time." I shrugged. "Listen, as much as I love these little chats—and I really don't, to be clear—I need to know where that asshole's going and when."

"You think you can just stroll in here and—"

"No," I snapped. "I came here because you wanted to see me, alright? I've not slept in fucking *days*! I've spent the entire day rebuilding my suit so I can fucking fight tonight, so I can ruin the plans of the asshole that caused all of this! We get one chance Oshbob, one!"

He was glaring at me and I went on, ignoring the sudden feeling that someone was right behind me, breathing down my neck.

"If we miss this chance? He fucks off back to wherever he's been hiding, probably in the middle of the most secure areas of the fucking army! We've taken down most of his forces, all of his APS, and he's gonna have to do this with just his normal troops, he's going after new suits…"

"APS?" Oshbob grunted.

"Yeah, and no, you can't use them, nor can you sell them, they're fucking prototypes, and you'd need years of training. Me and mine can though, we hit that fucker as he goes for the suits, and we replace our damaged suits, we fuck his plans up, AND we get to kill him, all in one go!"

"Why do you think he'll be there?" he asked and I shook my head.

"I don't think he's got a choice," I said. "We took out his ghost squad, he must have been setting this hit up for ages, he was confident enough to say that he was killing anyone that would even know the suits existed, so they're that top secret."

"And why'd he tell you this?"

"He actually thought he could recruit me."

"And you don't think it's an elaborate trap? What, he just did a full evil villain monologue with all his plans for you?"

I froze, not at the suggestion, it'd occurred to me as well, but that he'd seen it the same way I had, and finally I realized why Oshbob pissed me off so much.

We were far too fucking alike.

"He thought I was at his mercy, and he was about to kill me."

"And you believe him?"

"Flip it around," I said. "I took out most of his elite ghost squad only a few weeks ago, taking down half of the M-Corp ghost squad. Now he's gone from a full team of APS to literally two, and one of those has a fucked weapon. He needs replacements, he can't just transfer them from the army, it probably took him years to recruit and slip them out."

"And you're just so special he'd forget all your past?" Oshbob asked sarcastically.

"He's the winner so far, for him it'd be easy to see, I could have learned my place, bow my head, take a knee, whatever. He clearly has no loyalty to anyone, so why would I? If I'm too stupid to see the chance, he kills me, if I behave? He has a dangerous pet, and he'd have put a bomb on me just in case."

"And what's your plan?"

"Honestly?" I said. "It depends on what and where they're going. They need suits, so they'll have to pull out all the stops tonight, instead of gaining ours in what they expected to be a fast smash and grab, as well as wiping me and my team off the board, they lost their suits and gave us spare parts and damaged suits to work with.

"They have one chance to come out of this ahead still, and then come after us. That's the prototype suits. Grab those, get them turned around, then hit us, and goddamn hard. Wipe us out, recover the damaged suits and kill anyone that knows. That's the only way he comes out of this safe. You got some minor damage here…"

"You fucked my walls, shot up my goddamn roof and fucked off!" Oshbob snarled.

"*Minor* damage," I repeated. "You remember that tactical weapon he used on the M-Corp facility? He wanted the suits, or he'd have used something like that on us. Until now? You weren't even a boil on the ass of his concerns. You just managed to show up, and he's gonna have to squash you. Give me the data, protect my people and my gear, and I'll finish this myself, tonight."

He glared at me for a long series of heartbeats, before pulling out a battered half smoked cigar and jamming it in his mouth, relighting the end and taking a deep drag.

The fucker was toying with me, I *knew* he was toying with me, but still, I forced myself to wait, patiently.

"Outside the city, tonight," he said eventually. "There's already a team protecting the protypes, blues or something, and they're taking the suits out to a remote location that asshole set up as a 'secret route'. Fucking idiots, if they can't see there's something wrong with that then they deserve what's coming."

"What's coming?" I growled.

"Some rock thing, they were going to use it to grab the blues. Soldiers didn't seem to know how though."

"A rock…an AROC?" I asked, gritting my teeth. "They said they have the AROC?"

"Yeah, sounds about right. What is it?"

"It's fucking classified, and its designed to fuck up an APS!" I snarled. "Where are they, who said about the AROC?"

"That one." Oshbob shrugged, pointing at the third nearest of the bloody stains on the floor.

"That…you killed him?"

"He fucked up my shit," the big orc growled. "So did you…so fucking watch yourself! And of course I killed him, what would you have done? Bought him dinner? You need to grow a backbone! They came for you, and fucked with me because you were weak, and you're making me look weak. Keep this up? We'll be breaking this little alliance off, you get that? Tonight's on you, Kabutt. You fucked this, you fix it!" Oshbob ground out, jabbing a meaty finger at me as he spoke, glaring down and filling the air with foul smoke as he puffed on his death stick.

"Give me the time and location," I growled. "Like I said, you keep an eye on this end, I'll finish this."

"You better, you mouthy little fuck," the big orc snapped, before gesturing at someone out of sight. "They're using some underground passages, from the old bastions, they said the transporters were told the tunnels have been cleared." I received a knock a second later.

Accepting it, I saw an abandoned town about fifteen miles out from the walls of Artem, and a timer counting down, as well as a locational marker for the convoy. Close enough that the guards would feel secure, far enough away the locals and wall guards wouldn't be able to help, nor see anything specific.

Fuckers picked a good place, I acknowledged to myself, nodding once in grim thanks to Oshbob as I spun around, marching for the door.

There were four hours left until the intercept, and I needed to make the most of that time, if I was going alone—and I was—then I needed a few tricks to even the fight up, especially if Blue team was going to be the defenders.

CHAPTER FIFTY-EIGHT

It was a close thing, as I crept towards the top of the nearest hill, but I'd made it, finally.

The small valley that spread out before me had once been part of the farming initiatives that the city tried to maintain every so often.

They got smaller and smaller each year, more and more facilities inside the city being used to grow crops in hydroponic factories that required a fraction of the space, and had little to none of the resident monster risks.

Out here, monster and beast—they were very fucking different things, some of the Great Beasts were almost sapient and mainly avoided the city, while monsters were batshit and brainless, as a rule of thumb—attacks were frequent enough that this entire area had been abandoned.

As a result, the town that had sprung up here, nestled in a dip in the valley and built as a central point to maintain the fields, had been abandoned.

There were a few dozen main buildings in the center, with a massive single building built as a secure fallback position. It was like most of its kind, massively reinforced, slope sided like a thick, stubby pyramid, with wide entrances at the bottom that could be sealed by great blocks of titanium coated stone.

The entire edifice was more than habitable still.

Where the other buildings were failing, the harshness of the storms and acidic rains, the monsters and the inexorable onslaught of time doing a number on the fuckers, the bastion stood solid.

On all sides the buildings sagged, roofs collapsing, walls scoured of cheerful and optimistic attempts at paint and technology dying like the crops that were once planted here.

The bastion towered over it all, and I mentally marked that as the ambush point.

There was no way I'd risk hiding troops in the buildings on either side of the damn thing, that was for sure, not unless they were a hell of a lot more reinforced than they looked from here.

I squinted, zooming in and scanning the area as best I could without breaking stealth.

No, the buildings were too damaged, too fucked to risk putting squishy personnel in, and even APS would be at risk of pinning in a collapse. Checking my map I noted the convoy's location, the military transport's transponder having been shared with the major's team, and through them, me.

Twenty minutes out.

There'd been two sweeps of drones already, one had flown straight inside the bastion, so I was guessing that Blue One was doing his usual thorough job.

That meant that either the fuckers that were laid in wait—I had no doubt they were here, I just hadn't spotted them yet—were either better than his tech at hiding, or…

I frowned.

A full on drone sweep, especially a well-equipped one like the ones I'd seen so far wouldn't be easily fooled. I was using modified, spliced together stealth-suits, five of them in fact, across my armor, and they were plugged into my RI, with it running the interface through my suit's normal camo systems.

I had a suite of additional batteries torn from Richie and Sync's suits, as well as two more from the downed suits in my back to make goddamn sure I had enough power to hide from anything, and I was still paranoid I'd be spotted.

Taking that into account, and inside a well understood, standard layout security fallback bastion, how did they expect to hide at all?

The answer came to me quickly enough and I stifled the urge to swear long and loud.

They expected to, because they weren't letting Blue use their drone. I was betting the major had his people running the drone, sending it on the loops to search for me and mine, other scavs or monsters or whatever, and was feeding a sanitized version to Blue.

That's what I'd have done anyway, that or record it a few days ago, and send it all now as if it was real time.

That way they would have access to real time data, and Blue wouldn't be any the wiser, and—

A sound, something that didn't belong here, something that was alien enough it grabbed my attention, but not enough to be identified. I froze, staying perfectly still.

I shifted slowly. I'd literally used this Frankenstein's monster creation of the stealth suits over my own integrated variant for one damn reason. My own concealed most of my emissions, but it couldn't conceal everything.

Anyone familiar with the tech would recognize the emissions as one of us in stealth, but this? Multiple layers of suits literally glued over me?

It was a botch job, but it worked.

Admittedly there were still some leaks escaping, and sure, the loss of five top end stealth suits was horrific, my bank balance was screaming at me over the potential cost of replacing them.

The figure in stealth armor that crept around the side of a nearby boulder though was clearly tracking something, and he had no clue what it was.

"—confirm," he finished in a low whisper. "No contact." That said, he straightened, a blur in the air, before turning away, an arm extended as he apparently tried to track something else.

I stayed where I was, sure that it was something from me he'd picked up, but that whatever it was, the angle I was at currently was doing a better job of hiding it.

Several minutes passed, while I stayed there, crouched in my suit, cursing that a fucking scout was so close…before I decided I didn't have the time to waste any more.

The convoy was getting closer by the minute, the night wouldn't last forever, and the major needed this to be over with before the sun came up.

That meant that whatever happened here, it was going to be over damn soon, especially if they were going to be keeping a lid on it. I started moving, sliding around the boulders, pausing every few seconds, searching for anything, anything at all that might…there!

A distortion in a pattern of a rock up ahead, laid across it and oriented down on the bastion. I slid forward, scarcely daring to breathe, despite the fact I was in a multi-ton mecha.

One step, two, three…by the seventh I was almost in range, so the eighth of course, was when a pair of pebbles clicked together underfoot.

The figure rolled, a stealth covering falling from a rifle as they spun towards me, and I grabbed on instinct.

My fingers closed over his head and squeezed, the helmet granting a half-second's reprieve before it buckled under my grip. Blood, brains and bone burst from the shattered mass under my fingers, and I winced, really hoping they were the major's team, and not a higher up sting patrol, but there was nothing I could do about that now.

They'd not gotten a message off, I was sure of that, but anyone monitoring their bios would know something had happened here.

I moved, running in full stealth, well aware the systems couldn't keep up, not perfectly, but that it was better to be where they weren't looking, rather than trusting to imperfect stealth where they were.

Thirty seconds later and I was slowing, drifting around the bottom of the hill and through a series of old dead trees, their branches long since torn free, and their trunks scoured down to skeletal fingers clutching at an uncaring sky.

I moved slowly now, but steadily, heading at an oblique angle for the bastion.

There were two main entrances, and two secondary, the largest always falling north and south aligned, with the smaller east and west. Those were the official entrances, but nothing hundreds of meters long could be kept that well sealed.

There were four additional smaller doors, set at the left-most edge of each face of the building, meant for emergency access, and used primarily for the workers that maintained and lived in such places to come and go without the powers that be spotting them.

The first that I came to was buried by several tons of collapsed building, and I cursed, heading to the next. I needed one that was recently used, not sealed for the ages.

Two more sides came and went, and of course, when I finally found one, it was the last of the four. The handprint and code lock were dusty and filthy, but the cherry red gleam of a 'locked' symbol gave me hope, letting me know that it was alive at least.

"Okay Richie, do your thing," I whispered into the comm relay, and he grunted in my ear.

"Already working on it boss, and Sync says you're still shit at stealth, by the way," he replied at a normal volume.

"Can it," I ordered, shaking my head. "Keep contact to a minimum, no unnecessary data transfers."

"My comm is buried in the mass of data needed for a remote link," he drawled. "You have any idea how much data back and forth is streaming right now for me to be able to remote into your suit and then into the lock? We're either already boned, or we're fine."

"Fuck's sake can I put you back on ice?" I muttered.

"And…we're in." He grunted as the lock changed from a bright red to a cheerful green. "I still say you should have let me come."

"You were walking in the suit like you'd shit yourself," I pointed out. "You couldn't run, if you tried moving like that out here you'd be shot in seconds. No dice." I reached up and attached one of the relay drones I'd taken from Richie's suit to the door, knowing it'd be able to pass information through it.

"You could have waited, left my suit alone until we knew for sure that…"

"Ah, the truth comes out…" I whispered, sliding inside, glad that the entrance had been made with farming suits in mind, just in case. That meant that there was just enough space for me to get in, in my suit. Provided I was careful and moved slowly. "…you're just pissed I stole your secondary batteries."

"And my shield emitter, and the one from the older suit, and my drones and…!" He broke off and ground out. "You never bothered with them in the past, why start now?"

"Because right now I'm on my fucking own, so hush." I winced as the door sealed with an audible 'clang' of the lock reengaging behind me. "I really hope that's automatic," I muttered.

"Okay, start the integration." I ordered, as Richie nodded to me, the joking banter dropping form his voice.

"Good luck, boss."

Neural Integration Suite: Confirm additional insertions:

Yes/No

'Yes', I hit, *of course*, and I grunted as the second set of nerve induction points, that we'd stolen from one of the suits and plugged into the expandable slot jabbed into the spinal tap's connectors.

There was a moment of pain, then a strange mirroring as I seemed to feel two of the suit around me, then…nothing.

I climbed the stairs slowly, making it to the next floor, then slipped out, moving into a long but narrow corridor, for me in armor, anyway, and ignored the signs on the wall about parking any exterior suits in the suit storage garage before proceeding.

Panic started to rise in me, a fear that the integration linkup, rushed as it'd been, I'd botched, before a new screen unfurled before me.

Spinal Tap Assessed: Minimum congruent processing points are available.
Assessing second tier congruent processing points.

A small progress bar showed in the corner of my vision, and started counting slowly up as gentle ripples of sensations ran up and down my body.

I moved as quietly as possible, passing from dully-lit light to shadows, the emergency lighting providing spotty illumination as I passed doors on the right and left every few meters.

Several minutes passed, and I was nearly at the end of the corridor when a door ahead opened, and two men in battered leather and scruffy armor exited, their guns gleaming and obviously recently provided.

I glared at them, my stealth camo down to just over half, even with all the additional batteries, as I stood frozen in the middle of the passage.

One frowned, glancing down at me, and cocking his head to one side as if unsure, before shaking it and heading off after his companion as the older man called for him to hurry.

I let out a long breath, surprised to find I was sweating in my armor. All I needed was some random scav to shoot a round down this way to check it or something.

"That was a lucky one," I whispered. "Think he saw my shadow or…" I frowned, clicking on the transmit, checking comms and then gritting my teeth.

Nada.

Comms had gone, and considering I was using a secure relay through micro-drones, that meant that either someone had fucked with the drones, possible, but unlikely, or there was a jamming field in place.

That it'd gone live already? That wasn't good.

I set off again, hurrying the last few dozen meters to the end of the corridor…just as the same figure from before came running in, calling over his shoulder that he'd '…get them…'

Freezing in place I watched him as he ran towards me, gun in hand, swearing as he cursed the 'fucking lanton slurping asshole that left the box in…'

I moved.

He was a meter from me, running forwards, gun in hand, other hand lifting as he neared the door he wanted, and he fucking saw the shift. The door was literally to my right, and I'd hoped to step back, to let him reach it, and keep hidden, but the way his eyes widened in sudden alarm?

My left hand ripped the gun from his right, his mouth opening in shock and pain as a finger—the fucker had it in the goddamn trigger guard—was torn free in a sudden snap and jerk. My other hand closed over his head, and I wrenched it to the right, the reverberation of the bone snapping barely felt.

I dragged him close, tossing him over my left arm and fiddled with the door to my right, the fingers of my suit's hands far too big to use the tiny latch easily, before kicking it open.

The room beyond was a mess, clearly being used as a doss-house and barracks for someone, three bunk-beds on the left side attached to the wall, an enclosed shower and toilet presumably behind the closed door on the right and a little table and chairs area.

These were standard layouts, but the piled boxes of ammunition, the circuits, the memory crystals and food? No, they were all army issue, and there was no way the body I under-arm tossed into the room was army.

From his clothes to his walk, everything had screamed scavenger, and the gun? Current army issue, latest models.

I paused, had that been faster than normal? The way the suit had reacted to me, to grabbing him? Was it more agile, more dexterous already, or was it my imagination?

I dragged the door shut again, every instinct telling me I needed to hide my presence as much as possible, and yet? For anyone to get to the door, they needed to pass down the corridor, and the door from here into the main atrium?

It was 'normal' sized. That was going to be a problem.

I banished the thoughts and moved, the slowly cycling wheel in my peripheral vision ticking along happily.

I walked up to the door, moving slowly as I knelt and reached out and gingerly fumbled with the latch, managing it on the third attempt, expecting to slide it only a fraction open to allow me to peer out...

The door slid open smoothly all the way, and I froze, the atrium before me clearly a level up from the entrance, formed into a bridge, with solid sides that looked out over the lower level.

I froze because right in front of me, crouched on either side of the bridge, weapons ready, were at least thirty scavs, and a good dozen army troops in the distinctive 'unofficial' armor that the fuckers this morning had been wearing as well.

And below?

The hum and crunch of a heavily laden transport convoy approaching the nearby entrance into the lower levels.

CHAPTER FIFTY-NINE

A few of the nearest figures glanced over at the door, most of them looking back away, disinterested, but one, frowning and crouch-walking across towards me, peering through me, the stealth suit faithfully projecting the corridor behind, onto the front of my armor.

He moved closer as I cursed internally, then the door slid shut on automatic, cutting off his confused face. I hesitated, heart hammering as the door opened again, this time to his standing in the doorway, frowning.

We were inches apart now, me frozen behind my layers of stealth and armor, and him looking like a fucking idiot staring the empty corridor behind me.

"Frak!" one of the figures crouched nearby hissed. "Go get 'im!"

"There's somfin 'ere!" the one before me muttered, before twisting around, looking at the nearest figure. "'Ere come..."

"Get back in line!" another of the soldiers snarled at him, hurrying over. "Fuck's sake, you idiot!"

"Eejit?" the one before me snarled. "Ah'm no eejit...dere's somfin..."

The soldier went to grab his arm, only to have his hand slapped aside, the pair of them glaring at each other, as the soldier lifted his rifle warningly. "Get back in line...now," he warned the scav.

"Or whut?" The scavenger spat on the floor, shifting his grip on his rifle as well. "Well sojer-boy?"

"Ten seconds!" one of the other soldiers hissed, and the glare was broken as they both looked to the side of the bridge, the sound of the convoy stopped below as something clearly held them up.

"Get ready!" The order was hissed out, and the pair glaring at each other spun and raced back to the sides of the bridge, getting ready.

There were a handful of swarm missile launchers, a few high powered railguns, but mainly it was rifles, and that made no fucking sense.

If Blue was here, and it made sense that they would be, or someone would be, we were regularly ordered to ride shotgun on shipments in dangerous locations, then why were the ambushers geared up like this?

They'd need much heavier weapons to stand a realistic chance, even with the AROC unless...

...unless this was a *diversion*.

Unless this was to keep the fuckers looking in the wrong direction! The bridge was solid, and heavily reinforced, heavies could take it down, but if the convoy was underneath? They'd not risk that, and as strong as it was, it'd protect the fuckers here for a little while at least, certainly long enough to make sure Blue fully engaged at least.

That meant the real attack would come from somewhere much closer to them, I was betting.

The lower floors here, that opened into the old underground routes—now long since sealed away to stop monsters getting into the bastions or Artem—they had a few smaller rooms I vaguely remembered, but the only real thing down there was the entrance to the underground.

If I was planning this? That's where I'd be. Stealthed, ready. I'd make an attack from above start up, open the doors, let blue see that the passage was clear. They'd split their forces, a few to lead the convoy in, the rest to act as rear guard.

Then I'd shut the fucking door in their face, cut the team off from each other, use the AROC, and be ready when they managed to cut through the door. Use the puppeted, controlled suits to lull the team into a false sense of security, then hit the rest as quick as possible with the AROC as well.

Fuck the distraction of the scavs, let them all die.

The major would be low on soldiers he could trust though, so…

I fumbled the catch again, trying to do it subtly…until the whoosh of swarm missiles firing made me curse. I took a step back and booted the door, hard.

It crumpled, the thin metal folding around my boot and flying free of the frame to impact a scav a few feet away. He was hurled from his feet, unconscious as I snarled and grabbed the door frame, tearing my way through and out onto the bridge.

The soldiers were on the far side now, hurrying through a second door there, the scavs being left to fend for themselves.

They'd been firing enthusiastically over the side, the swarm launchers were being discarded and the railguns were pointed roughly in the right direction, even if to aim them properly they'd need to lean out a lot more into harm's way.

They'd not been expecting me though, and where we were? There was no cover.

I dragged my rifle around from the magnetic grapple on my back and levelled it at them.

"Surren-" Was as far as I got before they opened fire, and I shrugged, the 'rat-a-tat-tat' of standard issue assault rifles doing little more damage to my armor than a hard hail.

Then I opened fire on full auto.

The scream of the rifle in the enclosed space was insanely powerful, and with them having nowhere to go? They were shredded, bodies catapulted backwards in sprays of blood as the upper floor was lit to manic brightness.

It was over in seconds, but the fire from below was only just starting to pick up.

I grabbed a drone and dragged it free, no time to use its delicate systems, but I needed a relay link, and I sure as shit wasn't risking popping my head over the side to establish one.

I flung the drone out to the left and out over the side of the bridge, it hit the wall and bounced, clattering to the floor below, and in less than a second a new series of images were filing my HUD as the drone relayed its feed, two trashed and smoking transports, a single smaller heavy vehicle for the APS and a fuck load of bodies, clearly the 'normal' security team. Fuck.

I selected one of the figures, tapped it, and sent a 'knock'. It was refused.

Fucker.

I sent it again, and again, knowing that my proximity *should* have overridden the team's settings, the same ones that filtered for outside contacts in warzones to prevent distractions.

Great, motherfuckers were on lockdown.

Nothing was ever easy!

I moved up the edge and started throwing bodies over the side, just grabbing them and flinging them one after the other.

One or two could be explained by shots hitting and the dead overbalancing, possible, but unlikely, over a dozen in a handful of seconds?

Nope.

That got their attention and they stopped firing, cautiously.

I flung a few more over the side, then banged on the bridge, beating out a standard 'knock' like I was at a door, then tried communications again.

It took three more attempts before Blue One finally twigged, and by then the fucking knucklehead had lost the convoy to the sealed door.

"Kabutt?" he snapped, when the call connected. "What the fuck are you doing! Interfering with an APS unit in the field is—"

"Oh fuck off, Jon!" I snapped. "Did they shut the door on you yet?" I knew they had, but I was making a point.

"They…you're not with the scavs?" he asked cautiously.

"Which part of this…" I pitched another pair of bodies over the side. "You know, slaughtering their fucking ambushers and all, would suggest I'm with them?"

"What the hell are you doing here then?" he asked. "Fuck's sake, we're on a mission, man, what the hell are you here for?"

"The prototypes," I admitted.

"You're trying to boost the cargo?" He grunted. "Shit, Kabutt, you've been gone, what, a month? Already you're betraying us?"

"*I* was fucking betrayed, not the other way around!" I growled. "Either way though, you've just been hit by swarm launchers and separated from your cargo…what's that tell you?"

"That we've got a traitor," he said softly. "Come out where I can see you, Kabutt."

"So Six can fuck me up?" I asked shaking my head on our commlink. "No chance."

"Then open the fucking door!"

"I didn't close it you dickhead!" I snapped back. "Look, I'm in black and gold, alright? My armor is battered to fuck, so when you get through that door, if you see me? Don't fucking fire!"

"Kabutt!" He growled, but I was already moving.

"It's the major, Marcial I mean, he set up that last job we were all on." I raced across the bridge, heading for the now sealed doorway the soldiers had gone through. "He blamed Tyrannus, because the dumb fuck saw a chance to earn extra credits, and sent us as well as you. That's why we had no retrieval bag, why we weren't ready. We weren't supposed to be there, but the little shit could bill the corpos for sending us and cream a little extra off the top."

"Right?"

"One team would have been taken down by the Mech and the AROC, the Major would have gotten your suits, and the jamming field means nobody would have known, then he'd have hit the area with an orbital strike, killed the scavs and the mech and left enough evidence nobody went looking for you."

"—care, get the fucking door open! You can prove this?" he asked, clearly switching between conversations. "Dammit, Kabutt, where are you going!"

"He sent me after Tyrannus for fucking up his plans, then blew up the building, used his pet black ops to take down the team from M-Corp, taking out the competition." I explained, ducking my head and lifting my arm, shouldering straight through the wall without stopping, and cursing as I found a stairwell on the other side, one that led straight down to the lower floors.

I jumped, rather than falling, and landed on the next level down, switching my gun over and dragging another drone free, palming it then tossing it upwards to bond to the wall, giving me a new relay point for the signal.

"I killed Tyrannus on his orders—" More or less. I'd certainly tortured him a bit and he had died, so fuck it, I still hated the dick and was claiming that one. "-then he tried to kill me, to cover his tracks, I got away. Then this morning he sent his team after me."

"And where are they now?" Jon—Blue One—asked, clearly not sure if he believed me.

"Dead," I admitted. "He tried to recruit me again, telling me about his plans for this cargo, and for you and the rest of the Blue Team."

"Us?"

"They ever find that AROC?" I asked him, knowing the damn answer. "What do you think is going on here Blue?"

"The…oh fucking no way! Three! Open that fucking door!"

I leapt down to the next level, and the next, what was left of my suit still blurring as the stealth field tried to keep up, and the soldiers below came back into sight, staring upwards in fear as they opened fire.

Their guns were better, but not good enough to stop me as I jumped again, landing on the level they were clustered on, trying to make it through the door.

Three were killed outright when I landed, crushing them under my suit and against the wall, two more were flung off the edge, missing the stairs to the next level and landing on the one below in a wet, broken heap as the impact of a multi-ton mecha made itself clear.

The others were through the door, and they'd turned, pouring fire into me as I tore the frame apart, forcing myself in…and then I leveled my rifle.

The scream of the heavy rifle unloading around a hundred rounds in less than two seconds filed the air, as did the blood and shredded bodies. Then I was through, dragging myself upright as I spun, checking out an old storage area that had been clearly set ready for something. There were several large crates, all empty, and some bodies, recently executed, judging from the holes in their heads.

That was it though, no convoy, no suits…I cursed, setting off running to the left where there were doors leading into the direction the convoy had been headed, if a few levels above.

The floor inclined sharply, and I raced up it, the jamming signal keeping me from comms with the outside world or Blue.

The passage on the other side of the heavy door—I'd had to trigger the unlock, just a button, but there was no way I was smashing through this door—headed to the left, then banked back to the right all the way climbing, and I grunted as I ran, recognizing it as an access to the parking garage, and escape from the lower levels of the bastion to the main passage to wherever it led, another bastion or Artem itself.

I pounded up the passage, the sounds of echoing distant gunfire making me curse as I followed it…joining the main passage and skidding a few meters as I turned, doubling back…then running straight into a hail of gunfire.

I swore as armor integrity warnings blared like the laughter of dark gods, and triggered the shield on my right shoulder I'd stolen from one of the black ops suits.

Pops and crackles came from it as it tried to form a coherent barrier, rolling out across my frame only to be pierced by impacts passing through before it could form fully, then tearing back out again as they ricocheted off the surface and went off in all directions.

My RI identified the source of the fire, two heavy military grade turrets dumped in the main passage. I opened fire, the shield blunting the damage as it came in, but unable to form enough to stop it all completely.

The armor integrity warning were going crazy now, as my fire tore one of the turrets apart and I jinked left and right, using my jump-jets to add a little extra speed, then realizing that I *was* faster, a thought cut the jets, and I set my feet, twisting and popping with the hips, adding a swing to the body that brought my rifle around onto the second turret before it could lock onto me, and I fired, my rounds shredding it apart.

I paused, scanning the passage, then set off running again, heading back towards the convoy I could just see around a slight bend ahead. I was just in time to see an APS stagger around the side of the massive main transport wagon towards me.

Slowing, I zoomed in, seeing the tell-tale battered appearance of a suit that'd been hit by small arms fire, but…

…but then the fucker lifted its rifle in one smooth motion, and sighted on me, opening fire.

I swore, leaping to the left, jump-jets triggering and sending me flashing out of the way, even as the rifle twisted, tracking me with metronomic precision. Three more shots were fired as I frantically spammed a knock, getting nothing until…

"Hello, Kabutt," Major Marcial gloated, answering the knock, as my system registered it being rerouted. "So nice of you to come to play!"

CHAPTER SIXTY

I cursed, cutting the link. For Marcial to be able to route the knock alone, he had to be in the suit's architecture, and that could only be done one of two ways.

Engineering plug when the suit was undergoing maintenance, or by full access.

The fucker was in full control of the suit, and for that to happen? The operator was almost certainly dead, a meat puppet bouncing around inside a suit that was on full AI guidance.

I jerked as a fresh prompt popped up, overlaying the middle of my goddamn vision.

> **Spinal Tap Assessed**: Second tier congruent processing points are available. Assessing third tier congruent processing points.

I cursed, banishing the fucker then cursed again as a hit slammed into my shield, followed by three more before I could get the momentum going right again.

I glanced at the shield.

> **Shield Strength**: 47%
>
> **Armor Integrity**: 68%

I'd managed to get the armor integrity back up into the eighties before setting off, so that I'd lost a quarter of it, and over half my shield strength already? That wasn't happy-making.

The massive door behind the convoy main vehicle started to slowly open again, and I picked up speed, knowing that if I didn't get into cover in the next few seconds I was fucked.

Blue would shoot the shit out of me, I knew, it just made sense, how likely was it that I was there to help after all? No, he'd see his 'people' firing on me, and…

A second APS with the identifiable line of blue stepped out from behind the transport as well, swiveling and stepping robotically as the AI learned to move his body, the gun rising, locking onto me…

I kept dodging, right, left, jumping up, dropping to a knee and triggering the jets, but the closer I came the less time I had to react to them, and the less time they needed to predict my motion, even as cluster bomb canisters rained down and railgun round shattered off the shield, too fast to dodge reliably.

I started getting hit, over and over, by the rifles now and then Blue Three stepped through into the passage, and opened fire.

The plasma cannon rounds traced my path, hanging in the air longer than any other form of ammunition, and limiting my options horrifically.

The closer I got to the left hand side of the passage as I saw it—right for them—the less they had to adjust their fire, but if I tried to dodge backwards? I was throwing myself into heavy plasma fire.

I was fast, *fuck* I was fast, I'd never moved this fast in a suit before, not even close, it was like a dream of power, a single thought, a twitch and I was doing it, no longer 'controlling' the suit, I *was* the suit, literally a split second out from perfect synchronicity, and still it wasn't enough.

The bullets hit me at almost the same time as the first plasma shot, my shields whiting out, then collapsing as I threw myself forward, bouncing over and over, paint and remnants of the stealth suits bursting alight.

"Cease fire!" Blue One ordered. "Cease fire, that's the last of them!"

I got a fresh knock from him and a split second communication, then he was gone.

"Play dead."

That was all he said, and I forced myself to bounce and roll, coming to a halt in a screech of metal dragging across stone.

I lay there, facedown, wreathed in flames that were eating away at my limited coverings, the suit's shield trying—and failing—to reboot before I killed it.

Then that was it, I laid there, blocked from the world by swirling flames and smoke, smoldering fabrics and next-gen plastics, frantically focusing on my ears, trying to pick up something, *anything*, over the sound of crackling flames.

When I did, finally?

It was gunfire and fucking screaming.

I snarled and popped into a push-up position, then to my knees and I was running before I'd seen what the hell awaited me.

If I'd seen it before, I might have fucking stayed down.

Three of the Blue team were facing their friends, guns raised as they fired. Blue Three, the most dangerous of them as the team 'heavy', was already on the floor, shuddering as the AROC was deployed against him, screaming in agony as he was literally cooked alive, in his own suit.

Blue One was dragging his rifle up, even as he was staggering back under the coordinated fire of his former friends, and Blue Six?

The team sniper, the only other one with a weapon that could take down APS at range?

He was struggling in the hands of a new suit.

It was bigger, four meters to our three, and fuck it was terrifying, an image not helped as it literally tore Six's right arm free and threw the limb aside, the laughter of a familiar voice filling the passage.

"Oh my yes!" Major Marcial barked, before spinning and slamming the broken form of Blue Six into Jon, Blue One.

All the other suits cut off their coordinated barrage instantly, as a handful of soldiers moved into sight, dragging the AROC around to line up on the battered suits, as Blue Three collapsed to the floor and lay still.

They turned as one, the AI controlled suits, But I was inside their guard now.

I dragged my plasma sword around and slashed it downwards, carving through the barrel of the nearest gun—unaware until then that I'd even drawn it, acting on full instinct as I screamed in rage for my fallen brothers, opening fire on the AROC itself.

It was high technology, insanely complex, and surprisingly easy to fuck up. The first round that punched sideways through the unit probably did most of the damage that was needed, the next fifteen?

Maybe overkill.

I didn't care.

I whipped the blade around, and triggered the jump-jets, blurring to the left, from where I'd been about to pass the trio on the right, their guns swiveled, tracking me, as my shoulder mounted railguns powered up.

Until now they'd been folded down, forced by the stealth suit into retraction, laid flat against my back.

Now they fired over and over, their aim gone from a wide area reticule to pin-point accuracy as perfect as any sniper.

Chinks in the three AI controlled suits' armor were identified by my RI and I exploited them. My rifle emptied its store, hammering the right-most of the group back. His gun I'd already cut in two, and now, as the rifle switched to its internal mag, the next ten shots punched through the damaged armor to take out the power core.

The middle suit hit me over and over, before my sword drove through the middle of his chest, the required body inside for the AI to puppet carbonizing under the onslaught of plasma.

The final suit of the three leapt onto me, taking me and staggering me sideways, his armor penetrated in a half dozen places by railgun shots.

I twisted at the hip and flipped the fucker over me, releasing my rifle and dragging the sword free of its most recent victim, before swinging for the one on the ground…

…and being hit in the side by plasma fire.

I staggered, diving to the side, hitting the ground and rolling, coming up before Blue Three, the AI in ascendence, could smooth out full control and lock in on me.

I sprinted forwards, jump-jets flaring, pushing my feet faster and faster, as I crossed the distance between me and him, then throwing myself onto my back, bouncing and clanging as I skidded under the fresh barrage of plasma fire, which instead washed over the already damaged APS I'd just flipped.

He, or it, detonated a second later, as I kicked up, smashing the plasma rifle aside, and flipped to my feet.

I could hear the sound of battle from Blue One and Six, they were down, but they weren't out, and I dragged the second sword I'd brought free, even as I chopped the heavy plasma's feed cable loose, then rammed the newly forming blade through the chest of what had once been Blue Three.

Spinal Tap Assessed: Third tier congruent processing points are available. Assessing fourth tier congruent processing points.

I staggered, pain racing through my body as the final linkages were tested, and for a second the world around me whited out, and I tasted…purple?

I shook my head, blinking away the notice, just in time to be hit in the chest by the top half of Six.

We crashed to the ground, me stunned as he screamed and convulsed, then I forced myself back into action, there was nothing to be done for him, and the guiltiest motherfucker on the planet needed judging. The last of the combat stims I'd looted from the other suits and I'd been saving all injecting at once.

I bounded back to my feet, eyeing the monster suit as it tossed aside the legs and lower body of Blue Six almost negligently.

It was clearly the next gen assault mecha as much as it was an APS. Bipedal, it stood with a wide stance, a massive chest that the pilot or operator presumably sat inside of, heavy shoulders with a single missile launcher—fortunately empty for transport—sitting atop.

The right arm ended in an attached rotary autocannon, the kind of chain firing insane level of firepower that Artem used on the city walls to bring down attacking aircraft, not loaded aboard individual mecha!

The left arm? Four claw like fingers sat spaced equidistantly around a palm that held a more 'normal' sized minigun in the palm.

It had what looked to have heavy cannons on either side of the chest, recessed into the body, and a flamethrower unit retracted on the back, and all in all?

It was fucking terrifying.

It was also chasing Blue One, and the laughter that filled the air, manic and shrill was that of Major Marcial.

"Run, little man! Run!" he bellowed. "You APS! You fools! Always looking down on officers, all your jokes, your snide comments…you think we don't know? You think we don't hear? We were always better than you! We send you to die because you're worthless! But this…? This was too good to waste on the likes of you!"

I was up in seconds, grabbing the released plasma swords and sprinting at the suit from behind, only to throw myself down at the last second, bouncing and rolling, as it spun with terrifying speed, an arm flashing past inches from my head as I passed under it.

I dug my heels in popping to my feet and lashing out with both blades, crisscrossing the right leg and carving lines of glowing steel in the knee joint, glowing liquid metal fountaining out as I dragged the blades free…then dove aside again, this time as a foot flashed past.

I tried to roll to my feet, but the autocannon smashed into me, sending me flying, a dent appearing in the inside of my armor, the fucker had hit that hard.

Shaking myself, I rolled, assuming the front leaning rest position, and then dipped and shoved off hard, both swords lost, but I was still alive.

My railguns targeted the knee, unloading the last dozen rounds they had into it, and causing the suit to stagger, even as Blue One leapt onto its back, driving his own plasma sword down into the chest from behind.

It sank in halfway, before the major twisted and slammed himself back into the nearest wall, crushing Jon between the enormous suit and the wall.

Then the left hand came up, grabbing him by the arm and dragging him forwards, throwing him in one furious motion into the transport, smashing the cab in and leaving the APS pinned in the wreckage as he tried to free himself.

I raced forwards, jinking left and right then dipped as if about to throw myself under him again, before planting a foot and kicking off, my jump-jets activating as I launched into the air, bringing my fist back and slamming it into the middle of the body with all my enhanced APS might.

He staggered back, twisting, as he tried to catch his balance, then the damaged knee, unable to support the weight, buckled, then sheered free.

I landed, then darted forwards, reaching for the fucker only to be caught by a flailing foot and thrown backwards, crashing to the floor. I rolled, my vision filling with a final prompt as I popped back to my feet.

> **Spinal Tap Assessed**: Fourth tier congruent processing points are available. Activating remaining systems.

I hesitated, then screamed as pain, pain unlike anything I'd ever experienced, flooded my body. I felt like I'd been dipped in acid, my skin flayed from my flesh, muscles shredded strip by strip.

In my mind's eye my bones were cracking, marrow boiling. My teeth felt like they exploded, then reformed, a thousand years of agony, in a handful of seconds, before finally, mercifully, it all fell silent, and I refocused my optical sensors, the feeling of the world around me subtly different as I shifted, tiny stone cracking under my armored bulk.

I pushed up, rising to my feet, as the world around me changed. I felt my powercore sustaining me, my armor protecting me, and my senses?

I reached out, sensors twitching and realigning as they adjusted from the mere tools they had been before, granting me unparalleled focus. Information was flooding me, I pulsed my Lidar, radar, sound and gravitational sensors all at once, blending them seamlessly, then stared as I saw the world for the first time.

All around me the world shivered, as data flowed in and out, I felt the packs of nanites stored in my rear storage, and I drew on them, feeling them flood me, augmenting my body as they repaired me.

Tiny machines, tens of thousands of clusters that the suits were always designed to integrate with and yet they'd never been…

They'd never been ready.

Not the suits, not the pilots, not the operators nor the nanites. Not until…

I looked down at my hands, then my body, a curious mirroring sensation as I sensed my flesh-body inside my chest, slumbering as I became, well, *more*.

The Major twisted around, and clearly saw me, standing there, then reached out, expecting to crush me.

I scanned his suit, I scanned him, and I shook my head in disgust.

This wasn't an *advancement*.

His suit was a bastardization of various forms of tech, certainly, the powercore was impressive, and the sheer lethality that they'd managed to pack into a single frame was impressive, but it was crude.

I examined the suit as time seemed to slow, the massive clawed hand reaching for me as though moving through molasses. Then I stepped aside.

The claw snapped shut an inch from my armor, and I watched it, in a daze, before the world seemed to slam back into focus.

The major was inside this piece of shit, tin can, this knockoff that some idiot was trying to peddle as MY successor and replacement? No.

I stepped to the side, then took two quick steps to the right, triggering my jump-jets and darting clear again as I dodged and the major flailed, then I was moving, not dodging, but darting in.

I punched, my powercore flaring, additional power reserves being fed to my servos, as my fist blurred.

I hammered it into the elbow joint of the left arm, the metal denting visibly, before I struck again, then leapt back, he flailed wildly, his autocannon swinging around. I stepped back, literally a meter, watching the tips of the multiple barrels flash past inches from my armor, I was glad all over again that the fucker was unarmed for transport.

I waited, as he crashed down again, having to brace on both arms to support himself, screaming about distantly over what he would do to us, before I struck again, fast, hard strikes each time into the wide ring that protected the elbow joint.

Each blow that landed caused the armored ring to deform, to crush inward, and three it seemed, was the magic number.

I dodged back, jumping to land lightly, jets triggering, my suit and I no longer operator and armor, but a single symbiotic entity, the fourth tier of the spinal tap creating a link that allowed me to mirror the suit entirely as my own body.

I gloried in the power and grace of this new body even as the major tried to swing for me, his elbow crunching, whirring as servos whined, power being fed into them as they tried to overcome bent and damaged connections.

He cursed and I slid to the right dodging the lunge before I'd even seen it consciously, rolling to the right as he tried to grab me again. This time when I came to my feet though, I held a plasma sword in either hand, and I slowly strode forwards, letting him watch me come as I triggered the blades.

The plasma flowed forth, the containment fields carving them into ionized paths of brilliance, as Marcial shifted around, bracing against the wall and forcing himself up on his one good leg.

He hesitated only a minute, letting me come in range, then kicked off, throwing himself forwards, expecting to take advantage of his massive armored bulk and to crush me like a bug, presumably.

Instead I lunged forwards, ducking under his arms and twisting to the left, dragging the blades across his remaining legs, carving great divots in the armor, before spinning behind him, and cutting the fields to their minimum length of half a meter.

I'd never used them this short, always believing that the longer range was the better, but right now? I hammered them into the side of the massive behemoth over and over, each attack sinking deeper, carving more and more of the suit's vitally needed systems out from under the major, before I slid sideways again, roaming around behind his back.

The major twisted, the enormous claw like hand swinging for my head, and rather than duck or dodge? I braced.

I lifted both swords and braced ready, the blades one behind the other.

As plasma, they couldn't be physically locked against each other, but that didn't matter when they sizzled into the massive, dented elbow joint.

The arm dragged to a halt inches from me, before the joint ripped free, the lower arm and hand collapsing to the ground, as the rest flashed past, the suit pivoting and throwing itself forwards to crush me.

I took it, dropping both swords and bracing, my feet sliding back several inches, but I managed to hold the fucker's weight…right up until he smashed the autocannon into my side.

I staggered, my armor crumpled inward, the massive strength of the behemoth enough to bend even my armor, and I snarled, flaring my powercore, demanding more from it than I ever had before.

The response was instant, a full third of my remaining fuel was converted in the core, fusion forcing my servos to flare to their maximum, as I heaved and shoved the fucker back, then smashed my fist into the side of his armored chest, leaving a dent of my own.

Then I darted back, letting him crash to the floor, before I turned and jogged to where Jon lay stunned, watching us fight.

"Are you alight?" I asked him grimly, and he activated his external speakers.

"I…I am. Your suit? Fuck Kabutt, how much did you spend on upgrades?" he asked, and I snorted.

"It's not the suit," I said, striding past him and picking up a discarded rifle, his I think.

Then I strode back to the major, who was apparently discovering that when you activate a jamming beacon, you really should consider that sometimes, just sometimes, you want to be able to turn the fucker off again in a hurry.

"It was never about the suit," I said as I stood over the major, who was frantically keying his speakers, his voice an unintelligible babble of panic and pleading. "It was always about the operator."

"Please…" The major whimpered. "…I have credits! I can help you!"

"Major Marcial," I said in a loud, clear voice. "You are responsible for the deaths of at least a hundred men and women here tonight, and two of my closest friends…how do you plead?"

"I…I…"The major fell silent, the reality of his situation apparently dawning on him at last, as I sneered, before unleashing the full magazine into a fracture point on his chest that my combined scan had identified.

"GUILTY." I declared with finality.

EPILOGUE

It was three weeks before Reign and I finally made it out for our date night, but there was one last job outstanding before we could relax and truly unwind.

I strode along the reinforced balcony of the penthouse, my scanners flickering out and pouring over every inch, searching for threats, as I hefted my rifle.

It was new, hell, half the panels in my armor were these days, hardly a day went by that there wasn't a new prototype to test. After the fight with Marcial—he'd been stripped posthumously of his rank and any army rights, including a decent burial—I'd made sure everyone was okay, then I'd gone looking for the designer of my suit.

I'd found her working in a shitty little factory designing improved sex toys. I'd asked her if she'd rather stay there, or come and work for me, with access to a fabricator as soon as we could manage, and being able to improve all our suits.

She'd jumped at the chance, but included settling a vendetta she'd had against the man that owned the factory as part of her cost. That was fine by me. It meant I stood over her, scaring the shit out of a bunch of rent-a-cops and making sure nobody interrupted, while she beat the crap out of the owner with a twelve inch purple sparkly dildo.

Life can be fun like that.

Since then, things had been running smoothly. I'd accepted a role in the management of the guild, and we were generally seen as a guild to watch now, rising steadily through the ranks.

Occasionally though, I still took a little personal contract, here and there, like this one.

Oshbob was more or less happy. Well, he was slightly less grumpy, and he'd glared at me for at least a whole second less than normal when I saw him last. The renovations to his warehouse, and ours had apparently mollified him slightly.

Possibly because as a 'guild strongpoint and armory' we were permitted legally to install heavy weaponry around the building, and we'd used a bit of a grey area to make sure that if he wanted them on his building? That was fine too.

He'd have managed it himself, I had no doubt, but he didn't complain when I let him know we'd arranged that section of the contract as a thanks for his help.

ACE didn't want the kind of toys we had getting into the wrong hands, mainly because anyone that got them was likely to have a reason to use them on those fuckers first.

I idly tracked an ACE aircar as it passed, my railguns locking on and zooming in as I fantasied about shooting the fucker out of the air, before it diverted hurriedly.

Reign turned the corner ahead of me and strode towards me, smiling. "So, you ready?" she asked.

"Never been more so," I assured her as the pair of us walked back inside.

"Sir, I'm legally making you aware that our employment contract with you ended fifteen seconds ago, and we are no longer responsible for your safety, do you accept this?" I asked of the figure slumped on the plush seating, frantically tapping his foot and glaring at me.

"No, no I fucking don't!" he snarled. "Your contact might be up, but I can't get a replacement! Nobody, and I mean NOBODY is answering…fuck's sake, fine! I'll pay you for another week and…"

"Unfortunately we're unavailable." I cut him off smoothly, staring down at him from my armor.

"What? Well fuck *that*, you don't know the shit bags that are after me!" He snarled.

"Made some bad deals did we?" Reign murmured, shaking her head. "Tsk, tsk."

"Fuck off, whore," he snapped at her, before shaking his head and drawing a deep breath. "Fine, whatever, what's this gonna cost me?"

"We're already hired by another," I said, burying the desire to squash the fucking bug for that comment. "As I said sir, we have made you legally aware that we are no longer responsible for your safety and we are not accepting any further contracts from you. Your ident has been scanned and recorded as being present. This contract is over."

"Yeah? Yeah well fuck you too asshole!" he screamed, getting up and grabbing a drink and throwing it at me. "You'll regret this!" He promised. "You don't know who I am! Not really!"

"Oh, I think we do," Reign purred, moving to the door, and pulling it open, letting two people in.

I nodded a greeting at Doul, who'd taken over the squad from Timur after the cooling tower incident, and his second, Liolet.

"Good to see you again," Reign said, hugging them both, then smiling. "Now, before we leave you fellas to 'talk', let's keep our accounts current shall we?"

"How much was it again?" Doul asked, grinning evilly.

"A credit."

"Worth it ten thousand times over," he assured her, transferring the credit.

"What…what the hell is this?" our previous employer asked, backing away, then grabbing a gun from the table and trying to use it.

It clicked loudly.

"That was the fee for us making sure you were disconnected from Aug-World and the cybersphere in general, and unloading all your weapons," Reign said sweetly. "Now you might not remember *us,* but I assure you, we remember you, as well as the cooling tower job that you hired us for. Your name changed, but you were easy to track down."

"No…no wait…" he mumbled, shaking his head, while pulling the trigger over and over.

"You sent us in there to die in a death match," Doul said as he folded his stealth gear up and dumped it on the couch nearby, before drawing a hammer from a small case he'd carried in. "You tried to kill us, and our friends, and you never even gave a shit, because for people like you? There's never any consequences."

"Until now," Reign said firmly. "Now, Liolet doesn't speak, not anymore, but you're going to find out that he has no issues in making himself understood."

"Have fun, everyone," I said with a smile, before turning my back and striding out of the living room and onto the rooftop of the penthouse, Reign by my side.

I clambered into the back of the heavy transport that was waiting for us, and waved to Dondo to take us home, as Reign settled across from me on one of the smaller jump seats.

The transport lifted into the air as Reign leant back, her rifle resting across her knees, her hair falling loose as she took her helmet off, a kink in it from being constrained for too long, and I couldn't help but smile at her.

"You're watching me again," she said without looking. "I can feel your sensors."

"You'll be feeling a lot more soon," I promised with a laugh, and she grinned at me.

"First we get home and you get out of that armor and shower! Then dinner, some drinks, and maybe, *maybe*, if you're very good, then you'll get some later," she said almost grudgingly.

"What if I'm bad?" I asked.

"Oh, well then you'll definitely get some," she assured me, glancing up and winking at my sensors. "You know, we've got twenty minutes before we get home…how long would it take you get out of that armor and kill the cameras in here?"

"They're already dead," I assured her, triggering the emergency release on my armor.

She burst out laughing and reached for me. "I love you, Kabutt, I really do," she said, saying the words we'd danced around for weeks.

"And I love you, Reign," I said, reaching out to take her in my arms.

THE END

REVIEWS

Hi everyone! Well, I hope you enjoyed that?
If so, please, please do leave a review.

Recently authors across the genre have been hit with a massive upsurge in 'blank' (nothing written) 1* reviews, primarily from bot-farms and then we receive offers to remove them, *IF* we pay the poster a fee.

Frankly it's a killer, as if we did? It'd be classed as manipulating the reviews, and we'd then be banned from amazon.

So, please take the time to leave a review if you enjoy the books, and not just mine. Any of your favorite authors would be thrilled to receive an honest review, or if you don't have time? A star rating or agreeing with other reviews left? Ticking that you do find them helpful really helps us all.

Amazon relies on an algorithm to know which books are popular, and which they should advertise, and that's based on the review numbers so believe me, your reviews really can make, or break, a book.

ARTEM 3: RECLAIMER

By Jez Cajiao

Lost ships. Forgotten lairs. Monsters from the dawn of time.

Steve and the team survived the assault on their new home, and their enemies learned a valuable lesson about trespassing… their bodies now help to form the very walls his people live within.

The Old Ones have agreed to his offer, Steve has a month to get his affairs in order, then he must present himself before the oldest of his kind, and for now? He is to be left alone.

But as much as Steve has gained? He's lost access to the greatest of his advantages. Its only a matter of time before the edict expires, and unless he presents himself as agreed, it's open season on him and his group.

Steve needs to recover the Harvest Blade, to gain access to new and more powerful abilities, and to protect his friends and family.

Only one location is likely to be able to grant him all of those things… its time to take back his birthright.

It's time to reclaim Humanity's place in the stars.

ARTEM

Okay everyone, well, that's it, that's a wrap on the tale of Harry Kabutt! There's a lot more I could tell, and more adventures to be had in the world of Artem, but I wanted to leave it open, so that if anyone wanted to explore the world further, it was all laid out there for you.

As I said before, and as we're sharing in all the promotions and 'lives' etc on social media, the world of Artem is a shared one, and its one that I created with three other authors.

Those authors are Kevin Sinclair, Lars Machmüller, and Dawn Chapman, and these are their stories:

THE RISE OF OSHBOB

By Kevin Sinclair

The thing about Artem, it's a damn hard city to live in if you haven't got creds, and for creds you need opportunities.

The thing about opportunities is that they're thin on the ground for Orcs. One of the most reviled races in the sprawling city. And if you happen to be an Orc, stranded outside of the immense city walls, left for dead on the front lines of Artem's roving monster problem, then you're doubly screwed.

Like Oshbob.

The thing about Oshbob, he's tough and he's pissed! Missing a couple of important appendages, but with a will to survive like few others, if he can make it back to the city, he's determined never to be subject to the whims of the elite ever again.

He's gonna make something of himself, no matter the cost to those around him.

ARTEM: UNDERDOG

By Lars Machmüller

Start from behind? Cheat the system!

Out of credits, with trash-tier mods and no hope, Bowdoin Katamari resides at the bottom of the pile in the city of Artem.

A place where megacorporations, merc guilds and inner city pricks live like royalty while the rest suffer.

In spite of his poor prospects, this self-taught hacker does have a few things left. A seething hatred for the upper castes, a mind bursting with plots, and a like-minded crew determined to get ahead.

Down with the corpos—let the towers burn!

ARTEM: TAILSPIN

By Dawn Chapman

To save his family, Ruslan will risk it all…

Ruslan is determined to get his family out of debt by taking part in a dangerous race. With dreams of being a pilot, he is quickly brought back down to earth when he crashes and almost dies.

Now homeless and close to death, Ruslan's future is in peril. Abandoned by his family and friends, Ruslan agrees to risky cybernetic surgery to save his life. Unaware of the implications, Ruslan soon learns that the procedure is more experimental than he thought, but it could lead him to finally becoming a pilot.

After being enrolled in M-Corps hottest flight school, Ruslan makes some friends and more than a few enemies. Pushing himself to the limits, he knows it is only a matter of time before his new tech fails him completely, but he is determined to fight for as long as possible.

When a mutated abomination attacks the city of Artem, Ruslan and his comrades are deployed to take it down. A fight they must win, or the city will fall.

Does Ruslan have what it takes? Or will his body give out before he gets the chance to be the hero he always dreamed of being?

FACEBOOK AND SOCIAL MEDIA

If you want to reach out, chat or shoot the shit, you can always find me on either my author page here:

www.facebook.com/JezCajiaoAuthor

OR

We've recently set up a new Facebook group to spread the word about cool LitRPG books. It's dedicated to two very simple rules;

1; Lets spread the word about new and old brilliant LitRPG books.
2: Don't be a Dick!

They sound like really simple rules, but you'd be amazed…
Come join us!

https://www.facebook.com/groups/litrpglegion

I'm also on Discord here: **https://discord.gg/u5JYHscCEH**

Or I'm reaching out on other forms of social media atm, I'm just spread a little thin that's all!

You're most likely to find me on Discord, but please, don't be offended when I don't approve friend requests on my personal Facebook pages. I did originally, and several people abused that, sending messages to my family and being generally unpleasant, hence, the author page:

https://www.facebook.com/JezCajiaoAuthor

I hope you understand.

PATREON!

Okay then, now for those of you that don't know about Patreon, its essentially a way to support your favorite nutcases, you can sign up for a day or a month or a year, and you get various benefits for it, ranging from my heartfelt thanks, to advance access to the books, to me sending them books, naming characters and more.

At the time of me writing this, the advanced Patreon readers are finishing up Artem 2: Vengeance, and they're also getting access to Arise: Reclaimer, book 3 in that series. By the time this launches? I *think* they'll have access to Arise 4 as well, so yeah, you get plenty for the support!

There's one of my wonderful supporters out there that I have to thank personally as well; ASeaInStorm, you utter legend you. Thank you for sticking with it mate.

http://www.patreon.com/Jezcajiao

LEGION

Okay everybody, if you've not yet seen or heard, well, the secret is out! My wife Chrissy, and our friend Geneva and I have launched the Legion Publishers! We're taking on new authors, as well as experienced ones, focusing primarily on the LitRPG side of things, but we're open to anything really, with one very clear rule that guides our company:

Don't be a dick.

That's it. Our contracts aren't hidden behind layers of legalese, you can find them here:

https://www.legionpublishers.com/legioncontract

If you want to reach out an ask any questions, get an idea of the support we offer, and possibly become part of the family? We'd love to hear from you, just tap the link and fill in the form:

https://www.legionpublishers.com/contact-and-submissions

Hope you're having a good one!

-Jez, Chrissy and Geneva

RECOMMENDATIONS

I'm often asked for personal recommendations, so if this book has whetted your appetite for more LitRPG, please have a look at the following, these are brilliant series by brilliant authors!

The Ten Realms by Michael Chatfield

The Land by Aleron Kong

Challengers Call by Nathan A. Thompson

Quest Academy by Brian J. Nordon

Wandering Warrior by Michael Head

Endless Online by M H Johnson

The Good Guys/Bad Guys by Eric Ugland

God of the Feast by Kevin Sinclair

The Wayward Bard by Lars Machmüller

LITRPG!

To learn more about LitRPG, talk to other authors including myself, and to just have an awesome time, please join the LitRPG Group

www.facebook.com/groups/LitRPGGroup

FACEBOOK

There's also a few really active Facebook groups I'd recommend you join, as you'll get to hear about great new books, new releases and interact with all your (new) favorite authors! (I may also be there, skulking at the back and enjoying the memes…)

www.facebook.com/groups/LitRPGsociety/

www.facebook.com/groups/LitRPG.books/

www.facebook.com/groups/LitRPGforum/

www.facebook.com/groups/gamelitsociety/